W9-AZA-210

Selbyville Public Library
P.O. Box 739
11 S. Main Street
Selbyville, DE 19975

AT THE EDGE OF SUMMER

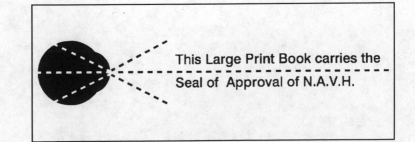

This Large Print Book carries the
Seal of Approval of N.A.V.H.

AT THE EDGE
OF SUMMER

JESSICA BROCKMOLE

THORNDIKE PRESS
A part of Gale, Cengage Learning

GALE
CENGAGE Learning®

Farmington Hills, Mich • San Francisco • New York • Waterville, Maine
Meriden, Conn • Mason, Ohio • Chicago

GALE
CENGAGE Learning®

Copyright © 2016 by Jessica Brockmole.
Thorndike Press, a part of Gale, Cengage Learning.

ALL RIGHTS RESERVED
At the Edge of Summer is a work of historical fiction. Apart from the well-known actual people, events, and locales that figure in the narratives, all names, characters, places, and incidents are the products of the author's imagination or are used fictitiously. Any resemblance to current events or locales, or living persons is entirely coincidental.
Thorndike Press® Large Print Peer Picks.
The text of this Large Print edition is unabridged.
Other aspects of the book may vary from the original edition.
Set in 16 pt. Plantin.

LIBRARY OF CONGRESS CATALOGING-IN-PUBLICATION DATA

Names: Brockmole, Jessica, author.
Title: At the edge of summer / by Jessica Brockmole.
Description: Waterville, Maine : Thorndike Press, 2016. | Series: Thorndike Press large print peer picks
Identifiers: LCCN 2016034036 | ISBN 9781410494726 (hardcover) | ISBN 1410494721 (hardcover)
Subjects: LCSH: World War, 1914–1918—Fiction. | First loves—Fiction. | Large type books. | GSAFD: Love stories. | Historical fiction.
Classification: LCC PS3602.R6324 A95 2016b | DDC 813/.6—dc23
LC record available at https://lccn.loc.gov/2016034036

Published in 2016 by arrangement with Ballantine Books, an imprint of Random House, a division of Penguin Random House LLC

Printed in Mexico
1 2 3 4 5 6 7 20 19 18 17 16

*To my daddy, who taught me to see
the world through the eyes of an artist*

■ ■ ■ ■

PART 1
THE SUMMER

1911

■ ■ ■ ■

Chapter 1
Clare
1911

The colors in France were all wrong.

I was used to the grays of Scotland. The granite blocks of Fairbridge, the leaden sky, the misty rain, the straight stone walls bisecting fields. Even the steel of Father's eyes.

Scotland wasn't all gray, of course. In summer, the hills of Perthshire were muted green, in the spring flecked with the yellow-brown of gorse, and in the autumn, brown. But washed over all of it, gray. It was the color I knew best.

Lately, though, I saw more black than anything. It was draped on our front door-knob, it edged my handkerchiefs, it hung in my wardrobe in a modest row of new dresses. Six weeks of mourning black. Six weeks of sympathetic looks, of waxy pale lilies, of whispered conversations about what was to be done with me. But then Madame Crépet swept into the house, smelling of violets in a dress the color of honeycomb, and set about straightening things. The household was too happy to leave me in her hands. They didn't know what to do with me anyway. As soon as Madame had my new black dresses packed up, we left for France.

Right away, France was too bright. From the blue-green of the Channel lapping the edges of Calais, past orange-roofed houses and yellow rapeseed fields, all the way to a château rising up white in a jewel green lawn. An automobile brought us down a slash of a burnt sienna drive, past golden-blossomed lindens and sprinkles of violets. Madame Crépet leaned over to me and said, "Welcome to Mille Mots, Clare."

The people waiting in front were no different. Two young girls were introduced as maids, though they wore green flowered dresses instead of dark broadcloth. The butler had a great drooping orange mustache. The cook had her hair tied up in a paisley scarf. I heard the whispered buzz of French and was suddenly afraid to step from the car.

But then Madame Crépet took my hand. "It's your home for as long as you need, *ma chère.*" Her words brought a lump to my throat and I swallowed it down. She slid off the lap shawl. "Are you ready?"

Was I? I didn't know. A week ago I'd been back at Fairbridge, in the same square parcel of Scotland I'd spent the past fifteen years. I left with Madame Crépet, thinking I was setting off on an adventure. I forgot that polite, well-bred girls weren't supposed to have adventures.

My head ached with the color and the light and the unfamiliar words my ears strained to catch. The air smelt like roses — heady, drowsy roses. Wasn't it too early for them to be in bloom? A man approached the car, in a waistcoat speckled blue like a raven's egg. He smiled widely and held out both hands.

"Can it be the *petite princesse*? I remember you, only as high as my knee and charming us all with your smile." He spoke English casually, Glaswegian vowels slipping in and out of his French accent. "Do you not remember me?"

It was an unfair question. Knee-high, I hadn't noticed much beyond the nursery. I stepped down from the automobile and regarded the man beneath the brim of my boater. He had a soft brown beard curling over his cravat and eyes dark as currants. Maybe I did remember him.

"Monsieur Crépet, is it?"

11

His grin broadened. *"Oui!"* He took both of my hands in his. "Mademoiselle, welcome to my Picardy." He leaned forward and deposited a tickly kiss on each of my cheeks. Father always smelt of Rowland's Macassar Oil and the faint wood of pencil shavings, but as Monsieur Crépet leaned close, I smelt coffee and garlic, turpentine and tobacco. His cravat was spattered with green and yellow paint.

"Your Picardy?" I asked.

Madame Crépet linked her arm through her husband's. "*Cher* Claude, he'd lay claim to all the most beautiful parts of France if he could."

"Only long enough to paint them," he said with a kiss to the back of her hand, one that sent her blushing like a schoolgirl.

"And you'll meet the last of our family tomorrow," Madame said. "Our *petit* Luc, he'll be home from school. You probably don't remember him either."

Madame came to visit us in Perthshire each spring, staying for two weeks at Fairbridge, in the rose moiré guest suite. Only once do I remember her bringing her family along. I'd forgotten that she had a son.

A mottled cat streaked out from the open front door, followed closely by a dog. The pair darted between legs before tearing off

12

across the lawn. A maid yelped and jumped aside, Madame laughed, and the butler dropped his spectacles with what I was sure was a French curse.

Suddenly I was exhausted. Everything here was too bright, too loud, too different. I pressed my hands against the scratchy crepe of my skirt. In front of this aching white château, I was the only spot of black.

The bedroom was a quiet, faded blue.

The room was perched up at the top of a tower. Round stone walls were hung over with drooping tapestries that looked as though they'd been there since Louis XVI; dusty, pastoral scenes of sheep and boys and overdressed shepherdesses. In the center of the room was an ancient bed, a heavy four-posted affair draped all around with curtains. It sagged in the middle and was piled with azure and lace and far too many pillows, but it was clean. I dropped my valise onto the bed and wished I was alone.

But the Crépets lingered, Madame fussing with the towel on the mismatched washstand and Monsieur adjusting the most crooked of the tapestries.

"I'll send Yvette up to unpack your trunk," she said.

Monsieur Crépet let go of the tapestry.

"Rowena, I'm sure the child wishes to rest."

"Of course, of course." She rubbed her hands together. "And supper . . . should I send up a tray?"

I nodded. "Thank you."

As they left the room, Madame paused in the doorway. "I hope you will regard Mille Mots as your home as long as you need to, my child. Your parents were dear friends and we mourn with you."

"Thank you, but I'll only be staying until you can find my mother."

Madame and Monsieur exchanged glances, the same kind that grown-ups had been exchanging over my head for the past six weeks.

"Father always said she'd return for me." There was that lump again in my throat, one I'd been carrying around since the night he died.

Madame hesitated, so it was Monsieur who finally said, "I'm sure she will."

When the door closed behind them, I fell onto the bed and wept.

Later that night, I woke grainy-eyed. A candle burnt low on the dressing table, next to a supper tray. I rubbed at my eyes with a wrinkled sleeve and pulled myself up from the bed. The tray held some slices of cold roasted duck, flecked with herbs and black pepper, a crusty chunk of bread, and some kind of soft, pungent cheese. Miss May, my governess, always said that pepper excessively aroused the constitution. I ate the bread in small torn bites and left the rest.

As I chewed, I went to the window and pushed it open. I wondered how late it was. Stars sprinkled across a sky as black as the one I'd known in Scotland. Maybe France wasn't so different after all. In the dark, it didn't look as intimidating.

After Mother left, I used to slip from my bedroom onto the roof of Fairbridge, to look off across the night sky and wonder where she was. One night, I found my father while I was out on the roof.

He was in a rumpled cardigan and slippers, his hair uncombed. He leaned out of his own window, eyes fixed on the dark sky, the way mine were every night. I thought to creep back into my room, but without turning his head, he said, "Do you know the constellations?"

I stayed where I was, knees drawn up under my nightgown. "No, sir."

He drew in a breath. "That there, that's Pegasus." He pointed up at a faint collection of stars. "Do you see? Look, there are his forelegs. That rectangle is his body. And straight on that way is his neck and head."

He traced shapes with his finger, shapes that I couldn't see but trusted were there.

I scooted closer. "And what else?"

"There, next to Pegasus is Perseus, with his sword. There, and there."

I didn't want him to go inside and end this quiet conversation, the most I'd had with him in a long while. "I like the constellations."

"I do too." He sighed, a puff of frost in the dark night. "The world may come and go, but the stars always stay the same."

I thought of that now, leaning out of the tower window of Mille Mots. Much of my little world had changed. I'd lost the only person I had left. I'd left Scotland. And yet, here in this strange château in this strange country, the constellations were still spread about above, keeping their stories for always.

Somewhere below my window, someone turned on a gramophone. I didn't recognize the music — something lively and quick on a piano — but a weight lifted in my heart.

"Good night, Father," I whispered up to the stars, and crawled into bed with the gramophone music at the edge of my sleep.

CHAPTER 2
CLARE
1911

The next morning, my growling stomach woke me up. Sunlight pushed against the corners of the bed curtains. France was still as bright as yesterday. I sat up. My dress was wrinkled and spotted with crumbs from last night's almost-meal. My impolite stomach informed me that it hadn't been enough.

I washed up and waited, but no one came to dress me or do my hair. No one brought a fresh tray. Maybe I was meant to dress myself and go down to the dining room. Did the French eat porridge for breakfast? I didn't know. They probably ate strange things like I'd been given last night. My stomach growled again.

Somewhere outside my window there was a rhythmic thumping. I pictured woodsmen with axes, like in fairy tales, I pictured giants with butter churns, I pictured marching soldiers. I leaned out over the windowsill and looked for the sound, but all I could see was green lawn, tangled roses, and the mossy slate of the château's roof.

I took off my crumpled dress and all of my underthings. My trunk had been halfway unpacked at some point while I napped yesterday, maybe by whoever had brought my supper tray. I had to search through the trunk for fresh combinations and petticoats, for new stockings and garters, but those hateful black dresses of mine hung in a row in the crooked wardrobe.

I'd had six weeks of black. I'd had a lifetime of gray. In France, the palette was much bigger than that. The colors I'd seen since arriving, they were ones I'd only ever read on the unused tubes in Mother's paint box. Maybe that's why they overwhelmed me. I'd never even seen them splashed across a canvas. But to see the ultramarines and viridians and carmines painted across a country, across a house, across people, I wondered. Did people feel the same when their lives were as bright as a painting? Could they mourn and wish and hate and dream when their days glowed with color? I thought again of the gramophone music drifting up through my window last night, those exuberant trips and trills of the piano. Here, so far from Scotland, so far from the

18

life I'd always had, could I be different, too? I shut the wardrobe and opened my valise.

The dress in there wasn't black and it wasn't new. It was an old dress of Mother's, a tea dress already five years out of fashion when she left it behind at Fairbridge. It had a pouty bodice, a froth of a skirt, and sleeves ending at my elbows in tiny pearl buttons. It was utterly romantic and as green as the Scottish hills in springtime. I'd cut it down and basted it with my embroidery needles when Miss May wasn't looking. It wasn't stiff crepe, it wasn't mourning black, it wasn't sedate as schoolrooms. It was just the different I needed.

I slipped into the green dress. It felt faintly rebellious, to be putting on a color only six weeks into mourning. Miss May, that old Victorian relic, would faint at the thought. But she wasn't here. Madame Crépet, with her honeycomb yellow dress, Monsieur with his paint-spattered coat, and Mille Mots, so white and green and twined with flowers, they were here, and I meant to be part of them. I sent a quick, guilty prayer up to Father, hoping he'd forgive me.

I finger-combed my hair back and regarded myself in the mirror. I wondered if I looked older. I wondered if I looked like a little girl playing dress-up. I supposed there was only one way to find out.

The rest of Mille Mots was as shabby as my bedroom. The hallways were lined with peeling wallpaper and mismatched furniture. Here and there, on scuffed tables, perched sculptures, some grotesque in their subjects, some heartrendingly beautiful. I found a staircase carpeted in a faded green runner that led down to the front hall I remembered from yesterday, all pale stone and dark wood and a cacophony of paintings. I hadn't been given a proper tour. I wasn't sure which way to the breakfast room.

As I was standing in the hall, contemplating four equally quiet doorways leading to places unknown, the front opened with a bang. A boy entered, whistling and swinging a tennis racket. It barely missed me.

I ducked. "Blast, but France is a dangerous place!"

The boy broke off with his whistling and stared.

He wasn't exactly a boy, I realized upon second glance. He was fully a head taller than me. Fresh from his exercise — his dark hair damp and curling, his shirt spotted with sweat, his face pink from exertion — he looked a man.

"Pardon," I said, and stepped back against

the wall.

He tilted his head. I didn't know who he was to stare. He wasn't dressed like a gentleman at sport. Father always wore a jacket, even when playing croquet. I felt a pang thinking of Father, always respectable. But this man wore neither jacket nor vest. Just a white shirt, open at the neck, tucked into loose trousers. Like a pirate, he'd tied a crimson scarf around his waist.

My face burned under his scrutiny and I looked down at the toes of my boots.

"But you're right, of course. France *is* a dangerous place." I looked up to see his eyes twinkling. He brandished his racket like a fencing sword. "It is a country of the three musketeers, of the guillotine, of opera ghosts. But it's also a place of art and of love."

"We have art in Scotland," I said, a trifle defensively.

"Ah, are you an artist, mademoiselle?"

"I'm only fifteen."

"And I'm nineteen, but what does that matter?"

Maybe he'd understand about the scores of sketchbooks in my valise. "Are *you* then?"

"I sketch Paris for tourists. Amongst other things."

Paris! "And yet you're here, in the country, playing tennis?"

"I have to visit my *maman* occasionally." He gave an elaborate bow. The red scarf at his waist swept the tops of his plimsolls. "Luc René Rieulle Crépet."

He certainly wasn't the "petit Luc" Madame Crépet had promised. "Clare Ross. Just Clare Ross."

"Clare Ross." He tried it. From his tongue, the familiar sounds that made up my name suddenly sounded exotic and magical. I wished he'd say it again. "But surely you weren't wandering Mille Mots in hopes of meeting me."

My traitorous stomach answered for me.

"Ah, but you've missed breakfast, haven't you?" He poked his tennis racket into a nearby umbrella stand. "We should go to the kitchen to find you something."

"To the kitchen?" The kitchen at Fairbridge was presided over by Mrs. Gowrlay, a humorless woman with hairs on her chin. I thought it not impossible that she was an ogress disguised as Scottish cook. "You can meander down to the kitchen whenever you want?"

"I spent most of my time there as a boy. Marthe has five sons and a collection of parakeets. She never minded, as long as I stayed away from the stove." He stepped towards a doorway. "Come on."

I took a step towards him. "If you think she wouldn't mind."

"She takes pity on anyone who comes to the kitchen hungry." He said it with a wink. "There's sure to be a loaf of *ficelle,* some Maroilles cheese, some garlic sausage. Maybe even almond chouquettes."

I didn't know what half of those things were. "Really, a bit of tea and toast is fine."

"Nonsense. You are in France, mademoiselle. In our kitchens, there is so much more." He pushed open a door, leading to a set of hidden stairs. "Unless you are afraid."

An adventure, I told myself. "I'm never afraid."

Marthe was a tall, rangy woman with pink cheeks and a mane of hair caught up under a knotted scarf. She kept a pocketful of seed for the half-dozen parakeets in cages along a kitchen shelf. When she caught sight of me, she clucked her tongue and declared that I needed feeding, as I was as skinny as a ghost. Luc looked halfway embarrassed as he translated that last bit.

"She said the British don't know how to eat properly," Luc translated, looking down to my wrists, thin beneath my pearl-buttoned sleeves. I stuck my hands behind my back. "All boiled meats and overcooked vegetables. You need salt and herbs and rich cheese. She hasn't been to market, but if she had the president's kitchen at this moment, she'd make you something warm and sticking. An *aligot* or a *garbure* with wine."

"Really, just some toast." I was almost desperate for something plain. "Porridge?"

Marthe clucked her tongue again, but Luc waved away her protests. He looked me straight in the eye and said, "Mademoiselle, do you trust me?"

It was a funny question from a boy I'd only just met. "I suppose so. You're not planning to poison me, are you?"

"Well, I *did* say France was dangerous." The steam in the kitchen made his hair curl against the tops of his ears. "But you are safe in Marthe's kitchen." He patted a tall stool. "You are safe with me."

Though the kitchen was full of unfamiliar smells, I was reassured to see loaves of rising bread dough, peeled white onions, potatoes. On the stove, Marthe's pan popped. I inhaled butter and onions and warmth. "I believe you." I smoothed my green dress and sat.

Luc grinned, quick and sudden. He swept a striped towel off Marthe's shoulder, leaving a kiss on her reddened cheek in exchange. "When I'm not sketching pictures of Parisian tourists, I'm a waiter." He draped the towel over one arm and held a finger above his lip as a mustache. "Mademoiselle," he said, with an exaggerated whine, "I am at your service. What will you be dining on today?"

I almost smiled. Almost. "You've said no to toast, but what about bread? I had some on my tray last night."

He snapped his fingers. "But it is not just bread." He brought a loaf, long and thin, and broke off a piece from the end. *Ficelle.*"

The crust was warm and crackled between my teeth. It was marvelous.

"Do you like it?" he asked. "Here, try it with a bit of lavender honey."

"We have lavender growing in the garden at Fairbridge." The honey dripped from the bread onto my palm. It tasted like flowers and summertime.

Luc brought me a checked napkin, thin and soft from many washings. As I wiped my mouth, he lined the edge of the table with small jars and spoons. From her place by the stove, Marthe nodded approvingly.

"You really are an excellent waiter," I said as I accepted a spoonful of translucent gold.

"Pear jelly," he said. "Didn't you believe me when I said I was one?"

The jelly was sweet and smooth. I ran my tongue over my teeth. "Why would anyone go to Paris to be a waiter?"

"And an erstwhile artist, remember." He passed another spoonful, this one sun-yellow slivers suspended in preserve.

"Marmalade?" I guessed.

"Preserved ginger. Bite and then hold it on your tongue for a moment."

It made my mouth tingle. "This is nothing like gingerbread."

"The Romans ate ginger for digestion; the Greeks, for love."

I swallowed. "You know more than serving."

"In my free time, I'm a university student." He took a squat glass from a shelf and filled it with water.

I'd never seen a university, not in person. Mother used to keep a photograph hidden in the drawer of her dressing table, of her with a young and exuberant Madame Cré-pet, posed with sketchbooks in hand in front of a serious-looking building. Inked across the border was, *Eena and Mudge, pens at the ready!* "Are you studying art, like our mothers did?"

"Oh, even better." He spooned out something thick and as brown as winter leaves. "The ancient world. Philosophy. Rhetoric."

I tasted the jam with the tip of my tongue. "Apples?"

"Medlars. They're best picked after the first frost."

"So what will that make you in the end? Aside from Aristotle?"

"A teacher. The École Normale Supérieure, it puts out the best teachers in Europe."

"Teaching?" I put the spoon in my mouth. "That's so . . ."

"Bourgeois?" He raised his eyebrows. "I know." He disappeared into the larder.

"It's not what I expected from the son of artists."

"Maman, she rebelled against her parents by running off to Picardy with a painter twice her age. I rebel by becoming respectable."

"I don't know if you could ever be respectable in that red sash."

He returned to the table with cloth-wrapped bundles and covered plates, a knife between his teeth like a corsair. "Once a bohemian, always a bohemian, I suppose."

"Did you grow up wanting to be a teacher?"

"Of course not. I wanted to be an expert swordsman, naturally. And an ornithologist. And, for one solid summer, a brilliant

27

English detective, like Sherlock Holmes. Mostly, though, I wanted to be a tennis star." He offered a paper-thin slice of ham on the tip of the knife.

It nearly melted on my tongue. "So sweet!"

"Bayonne ham. It's cured in sea salt and air-dried on the ocean shore."

I imagined I was tasting the sea. "Aren't you already a tennis player?" I knew nothing about the sport, but he'd come in swinging his racket like an expert.

"Not just a player. A star. Like Paul Aymé or André Vacherot or Max Decugis." He brushed back a dark curl from his forehead. "Playing in the Championnat de France, the French Covered Courts Championship, the Riviera Championship. They even have tennis in the Olympics now."

I'd never heard of any of those men or any of those tournaments, but the way he said their names, the way his face glowed and his words slipped over one another in excitement, I leaned closer. "And will you? Will you be a star?"

He busied himself unwrapping a wedge of bright orange cheese. "There's nothing all that practical about dreams like that."

"Whoever said dreams had to be practical? If they were, we wouldn't have to hide them in the middle of the night." I didn't wait for him, but broke off a crumbling bite of cheese myself.

He looked up under a fringe of lashes. "So what are yours?"

The cheese was sweet and nutty and utterly delicious. "My dreams?" I brushed crumbs of cheese from my lips. "Well, I've never told anybody. I'm sure you can guess."

"Mimolette."

"I'm sorry?"

"The cheese. It's Papa's favorite." He cut me another piece, but held it just out of reach. "Confess all or the mimolette goes on the fire!"

"Of course it's art." I hopped down from my stool and snatched the slice of cheese. "The Glasgow School of Art, like our mothers. I want to learn to draw, to paint, to sculpt, to carve, to etch, to . . . arrange, to design. To learn anything they'll teach me there." I ate the cheese in a single bite. "And I won't leave school, like my mother did. To give up on all of that, for marriage?"

"My *maman* left the School of Art to marry, too."

"Was your father also a student there?"

"Worse. He was her instructor. It was quite the scandal."

"Mother spoke fondly of your father. She

29

omitted all the good details, it seems."

"They were all friends, I think. Our mothers, our fathers." He wiped the knife on his towel. "I've seen some of Papa's studies from that time. Boisterous dinner parties, cafés, picnics, rowing on the Clyde."

Mother always spoke of art school longingly, but never of her life in Glasgow. Had she once worn Gypsy earrings like Madame Crépet? Drunk black coffee and argued socialism in smoky cafés?

Father had been part of that life. For a brief time he'd stepped outside of his architecture apprenticeship long enough for night classes at the School of Art, long enough to fall for a redheaded art student named Maud. I'd always wondered what had brought them together. I wished I'd asked him about it when I had the chance. I wished I'd asked him about a lot of things.

"And then they married and left all that behind," I said. "The rowing, the parties, the school."

"They stayed friends, though. Even when my parents left Glasgow for France." He uncovered a dish and, with a corner of bread, scooped something pale brown and creamy. "Here, this is garlic pâté."

I took the bread but didn't eat. "They couldn't have been as close. They lived in different countries, they had different lives. They only saw each other once a year." I ran a finger through the pâté and put it in my mouth. It tasted like garlic and herbs, like autumn in the woods.

"I suppose I've never had a friend to grow apart from," he said.

Neither had I. After Mother left, Father kept me close. Maybe he was lonely. Maybe he was worried I'd disappear next. "One must always begin somewhere," I said, the taste of pâté still on my tongue. For the first time in a long while, I let myself smile.

CHAPTER 3
LUC
1911

Clare Ross wasn't the first stray that Maman had brought to Mille Mots. She was forever carrying in some wretched creature, a sore paw or a broken wing tied up with her pocket handkerchief. Apart from Marthe's parakeets, we'd housed numerous dogs, several scrawny cats, a handful of birds, a baby mouse, and, on one occasion, a three-legged squirrel. To me, a teenage girl was as mystifying as a pet squirrel.

It must have been just as mystifying for Maman. She wrote me from Calais to say she was bringing home a visitor, her old friend Maud's daughter. *Will you come home at the weekend, Luc? Your papa is working on that frieze, the one with the serpents and the swans, and is in Reims most days. I'm sure Clare doesn't want to be stuck here with no one but me.*

And though I had lessons and work and tennis games I'd rather be playing, I didn't argue. There was a note of desperation hidden in Maman's note. I pinched the inside of my wrist, the way Maman always had when I was a boy and swung my legs during church. A good Crépet. *I'll be there Saturday night,* I wrote back.

I didn't want to play nursemaid. I expected black crepe and tears, stiff-necked Britishness. I expected dreary hours of being polite. Instead I found a girl, hesitant in the front hall of the château, with a halo of Titian hair and a wispy dress the color of summer leaves. She might have been one of Papa's fairy queens. Her face was shuttered, yet her eyes were intense and curious, flicking from one thing to the next. I wondered how she saw Mille Mots.

Though I tried to study on the train ride back to Paris, my thoughts kept going to Clare Ross and her single, careful smile. I sensed that she didn't offer them often. Though I hadn't planned on it, I knew I'd be back soon.

When I returned the next Saturday, Mademoiselle Ross wasn't in the château. I found her out under the old chestnut tree with a sketchbook resting against her knees. She still wore that leaf-green dress. Two of the dogs stretched out on the grass beside her, one snoring, the other watching my approach with rapt attention and wagging tail.

"There you are." She pushed her straw hat back from her face. "I haven't seen you in days." Despite the hat, the tip of her nose was pink.

I bent to pet Bede the springer, who jumped up, wriggling, and licked my wrist. The other, a pudgy mutt we called Ripper, yawned without opening his eyes. "Paris. Remember?"

She nodded. "Anyway, you're dressed differently. At first I thought you were a country curate coming across the lawn."

I looked down at my black suit, narrow cravat, ink-stained shirt cuffs. "The unofficial uniform of a student."

"I liked your red sash. The one you were wearing while you played tennis?" She poked the end of the pencil in her mouth. "You looked like a pirate."

"Have you met many?"

"Pirates? Not as many as I'd like." She patted the grass and I dropped down next to her, easing my satchel from across my chest. "I used to pretend my grandfather was, though. He was always gone, traveling."

"Sailing the seven seas?"

"Nearly. Africa, India, the Far East. He's a linguist, you see." She said this with an air of confession, as though it were a shameful secret. "I haven't seen him in years. I don't even know where he's at now. His last letter came from Ceylon."

I cleared my throat. "Does he know about . . ."

"Yes." Her hair swung out over her shoulders so that I couldn't see her face. "I wrote to him. I told him about Father."

A bird fluttered up from the tree, sending down a leaf onto Ripper's nose. He sneezed and rolled over. "And your mother?"

She busied herself with her sketchbook. "Oh, I wrote to her, too. I've written to her almost every day for the past four years." Her pencil scraped across the paper so hard the tip broke. "I only wish I had an address."

I didn't know the right thing to say. What to say to a girl whose mother ran off without a backward glance? Maman said that Maud Ross was passionate, vain, impulsive, and stubborn as a she-goat. She loved her friend to the end, but knew Maud would never return.

Cicadas filled the silence. I scooted closer. "So what are you drawing?"

"Nothing." She hunched her shoulders. "A castle."

The hem of Clare's dress brushed my leg.

"You're drawing Mille Mots, aren't you?"

"Are there any other castles around?"

I stretched. "It isn't really, you know. Just the fantasy of a silly vicomte some centuries ago. He had royal aspirations."

Maman fell in love with the château instantly, and Papa had his easel set up outside the tumbled-down old chapel before the first crate was unpacked. The gardens were left wild and overgrown, at her express instructions, and she spent all summer carefully cultivating that wildness. I spent my early years with the outdoors as my classroom. I learned to read amidst the scent of roses and river. Mille Mots was our little heaven.

"If I had such a house," Clare said, "I'd have royal aspirations, too."

"Not if you knew how much it cost to keep it from falling the rest of the way down." I regretted the words right as I said them. This girl, with her fancy green dress, buttoned boots, proper British country house, she wouldn't understand. With all of the money going towards this ragged château, to preserving this precious little bit of paradise, there was nothing left over, even for my tuition. I pushed out a smile, hoping she wouldn't take me seriously. "But you're right, it does look like a castle, lost here in

36

the countryside."

"I half expected a drawbridge to lower when we arrived."

"I was always sure I'd find a sleeping princess hidden behind the roses and thorns."

She glanced up from her sketchbook, a look of amusement in her eyes. "I didn't realize boys read fairy tales."

"They do when their fathers found their fame illustrating an edition of Perrault's *Les Contes de Ma Mère l'Oye.*" I made a face.

"Perrault's fairy tales?" The astringent smell of crushed grass rose as she sat up and brushed at a smear of green on her skirt. "Of course! 'C. Crépet.' It's a pale blue book, isn't it?"

I wasn't surprised she knew it. The book had dogged me through my childhood. In boarding school the boys called me "Prince Charming." "That's the book."

"It's . . . what do they call it . . . art nouveau?"

"Don't say that over the tea table if you want to avoid an argument. It's the Glasgow School style, of course. Can we talk about something else?"

She settled herself back on the grass. "I hate fairy tales anyway."

"That's ridiculous. Who hates fairy tales?"

She tugged on a hair ribbon. "You do. You should've seen the look on your face when I mentioned I'd read the book."

I hated that I was that easy to read. She, on the other hand, wasn't. "You're baffling."

From her seat on the grass, she executed a mock curtsey. "Thank you."

"Was that a compliment?"

"Wasn't it?"

"Boys are so much easier. Nothing we say to each other is a compliment. We just expect everything to be an insult and we all get along fine."

And for that, she smiled. It was only a little smile, but unexpected. It filled her whole face with light. I wondered how I could keep it from slipping away again.

"I know where Papa keeps his extra pencils," I said quickly. "He won't notice if we go to borrow a few."

"Pencils?" She sat up straighter.

"Conté pencils," I said. I stood up. "Freshly sharpened."

She followed without further question, her sketchbook tucked under her arm, walking quickly as though any pause would cause me to reconsider the offer of the pencils. Ripper stayed under the tree, but Bede trotted along with us. I led Clare inside, up the stairs, to the part of the house that always smelled comfortingly like turpentine and linseed oil.

"We're going to Monsieur Crépet's studio?" she asked in a whisper. "Is it allowed?"

"Definitely not." There were few things Papa disapproved of. Academic art. Yellow journalism. Spain. Anti-Dreyfusards. And people rummaging around in his studio. "Why do you think he keeps dueling pistols?"

She stopped stock-still in the hallway.

"Or blades? He'll offer you a choice."

"Stop teasing me," she said, but she didn't move from her spot on the hall rug.

"Don't worry. I'll be your second." I reached out and tugged on her arm. "Don't you remember? You're safe with me."

She looked down at my hand on her arm until I let go. "As long as you're not leading me into trouble."

"I thought ladies were impressed by feats of daring?"

"We're certainly not impressed by assumptions."

I bowed. "And the mademoiselle has won that duel."

The hallway outside of Papa's studio was quiet, but I waited a moment with my fingers on the door. I wasn't as offhand as I pretended. Even Bede took one look at the

39

studio door and bounded back downstairs, toenails clicking. Only when I was sure that there was not a sound from within did I push open the door.

The room was almost blinding after the dim, ruby-papered hallway. Windows stretched from ceiling almost to floor and, with no curtains anywhere, light shot enthusiastically into the studio. Papa was too enamored with shadow and changing light to let the south facing windows worry him. Overhead, cords crisscrossed the ceiling, with sockets for electric bulbs. Only the doorway was darkened, with piles of furniture and hatboxes and stacks of filmy fabrics on either side.

"It's magnificent," Clare exclaimed, stepping in.

Though I'd been in the room dozens of times, I understood. Papa's studio had always filled me with an awe that I'd never admit. Not when I'd brushed aside his hopeful suggestions for the Glasgow School of Art or, as much as it pained him to suggest, "even the Académie des Beaux-Arts, if you must." I couldn't admit that, like a cathedral, Papa's studio exuded a peace that I sometimes wished I had.

Clare traced a finger over the arch of the curved mauve sofa Papa used to pose subjects. "Is this where he painted the fairy-tale illustrations?"

"Some." I went to the cabinet where I knew he kept supplies. "In the mornings he likes to work outside, by the river. Afternoons he's in here."

"The easel is empty." She caught up the end of a diaphanous scarf and swirled it over her shoulders. "Where does he keep his paintings?"

I found new brushes, oil pastels, tubes of pigment, but no pencils. "The walls of the château." I peered into the dark at the back of the shelf but only saw more tubes and a jumble of empty jars. "Or the walls of other châteaux. He does take commissions at times."

"But he also paints for himself?"

"He does, though not as much as he used to. It makes Maman crazy. She thinks he should only paint what he will sell."

She paused in front of a mirror and tried on a greenish top hat. "He paints for art's sake, not money's sake."

For some reason seeing her in that top hat made my neck hot, so I pulled over a stool and resumed my search farther into the cabinet.

"Don't you see?" she continued. "Sometimes art springs unexpected from a deeper

41

place. Your soul, it has a story to tell, and the drawing, the painting, the sculpting, are only the medium for that story."

They were heady words for a fifteen-year-old. But her eyes reflected in the mirror were resolute. She understood this passion, this itch, this frenetic creating that seized Papa. I never had, but this young girl, somehow she did.

She turned. "You've grown up surrounded by *this*." She waved a hand around the studio, at the dust and light and smudges of color. "I'm sure you know. Art can be personal, emotional, spiritual. Glorious and expansive. Restorative, even. It's more than shapes on canvas or brushstrokes or curves in clay. It's . . . well, it's expression."

"And when it's a commission — when Papa is painting fairytale queens or Parisian bankers — where is the expression in that?" I leaned against the cabinet door.

"He paints them as he sees them. It is not a photograph, is it? No. It is a fairy-tale queen or a Parisian banker as viewed by Monsieur Claude Crépet."

I pointed at the tiny clock perched on the windowsill. "If you wish to do more snooping, Madame Je-sais-tout, you are running out of time."

She set down her sketch pad on the mauve

sofa. "Where does he keep the rest? The ones he doesn't hang and he doesn't sell?"

Up on the top shelf of the cabinet, I found a small box of square red Conté crayons. I slid a few from the box and wrapped them in my handkerchief. "Most are unframed. In the next room. Some are unfinished."

"Here?"

I looked up to see the end of the scarf float through the adjoining doorway.

"Mademoiselle, you should come out of there." I abandoned the cabinet and walked across the studio. Halfway, then stopped. "Papa doesn't allow anyone in that room."

"It's only canvases, all stacked up. Does he sell these ever? It's horribly dusty in here." Then, to herself, "Oh, how fascinating!"

"What's fascinating?"

"They're studies, done up in pencil. Nymphs, satyrs, a feast." Frames rattled. "There's a finished one. Dancing women in white dresses, like Botticelli's *Primavera.*"

"Be careful," I called.

She sneezed. "And here are some all covered up. I wonder what —" She broke off with a stifled gasp.

"What is it?"

"It's . . . your mother."

"Maman? In a painting? He always teased

43

that she couldn't sit still." I moved towards the door.

"No, stop!" She sneezed again. "You shouldn't see this one."

"Why not?"

Clare was silent for a space. "Because . . . because she hasn't a stitch on."

I froze. "She hasn't?" I backed away from the doorway.

In a house of artists, there was no shortage of nudes on the walls. They had been, dare I say, instructional to me in my formative years. While other adolescent boys had been speculating about breasts, I had an array — in oil paint, that is — to peruse. But never, *never* my own *maman.* I sank onto the mauve velveteen sofa in dismay.

"It's really quite elegant," she said from the other room. "The painting, I mean. She's holding three roses and lounging on that purple sofa out there."

I sprang to my feet.

"Oh heavens, there are *more.*"

"More?" I repeated in horror.

"Here's one where she's standing in front of a mirror, trying on a top hat. Goodness." The hat Clare had been wearing came bouncing out through the doorway. "One where she's reading *Le Figaro* and eating a slice of melon. And this one she's in a chair

44

with . . . what is that? A butter churn?"

"I think we should leave," I called in to Clare, but she continued flipping through stacked canvases with a rattle.

"Here's one with a horse. Well, that doesn't look comfortable."

"Mademoiselle."

"And here's . . ." But she didn't finish her sentence.

"What?"

She appeared in the doorway, holding a small framed canvas in her hands.

"Please, mademoiselle, I don't wish to see a painting of my *maman*." I crossed fingers, like one might do to ward off bad dreams.

"But it's not. It's not your mother at all." She turned the canvas around to show a redheaded woman wearing nothing but a pair of high black stockings and an enigmatic smile. "It's mine."

CHAPTER 4
LUC
1911

I didn't recognize Madame Ross in the painting, though the one time I'd met her, more than a decade before, she'd worn a hat and considerably more clothing. I could see the resemblance to Clare in the tilt of her chin and the steady gray eyes. Clare's hair was that same deep auburn. And those long fingers, wrapped around the handle of a fan in the painting, they looked like the very ones holding the frame. Which, I noticed, were white-knuckled, indeed.

"Monsieur, are you quite finished?"

I looked up to see her mouth drawn in a tight line. "Finished?"

"Ogling my mother. Are you finished?"

"I wasn't ogling, mademoiselle," I said quickly. "I was comparing the resemblance."

I instantly knew it wasn't the right thing to say. Two spots of color appeared high in her cheeks and I could feel my own following suit.

"In the face." I said it perhaps too loudly. "In the face only. I was looking nowhere else." But of course, saying that made my gaze go right to Madame Ross's *nibards.* She had a small mole on the left one.

"Monsieur!" she exclaimed.

I covered my eyes. "*Mon Dieu,* put it away."

"Why did she . . . why is it . . . here in your father's studio. . . ."

"Well, it's one of his works," I offered helpfully, peeking out from between my fingers. "See? His initials are right there in the middle, painted over her —"

"I know where they're painted," she said, face flaming.

"It's really quite clever, how he's incorporated the two Cs right into her —"

She cleared her throat pointedly. *"Pardon."*

"But why?" she wailed. "Why on earth did he paint my mother in . . . such a state?"

"And why did she pose in . . . such a state?"

Clare refused to answer that.

"Are you so sure it's accurate? That he didn't just paint her face and then, well, imagine the rest?" I uncovered my eyes. "Now right here . . . does your mother really have a —"

"Luc René Rieulle Crépet!" She flipped

the painting around, away from my view.

"You've remembered my full name."

"And you've forgotten your manners." She glared at me over the top of the frame. "It's my mother you're talking about."

"*Pardon,* mademoiselle." I went to close up the supply cabinet, trying very hard not to think of *nibards.*

When we left the studio, Clare kept her eyes fixed on the hallway rug.

"Papa has painted me before." I tried to sound reassuring. "Many times."

"And your mother. Many, many times. Once with a butter churn."

I made another attempt. "They were good friends, our parents."

She sped up, still refusing to look at me. "Better friends than I thought."

I stopped walking. Thankfully, so did she. "I'm not very good at this."

She turned.

"I'm not very good at knowing the right thing to say."

"I'm not either." She pressed her hands to the front of her skirt. I realized that she'd left her sketch pad back in the studio.

"I wouldn't worry too much about it." I took a step closer. "Papa, he paints all sorts of things. Not all of it means something."

"Did you not listen to a word I said in

48

there earlier? About art being honest, meaningful expression?"

"But you're wrong. Not all of it means something," I repeated. "You need to see *Hat Rack, with Cat.*"

"I'm sorry?"

"Follow me."

Hat Rack, with Cat, was Papa's very first painting, at least the very first that he allowed Maman to frame and hang on the wall. It was tucked away down at the end of the west hallway, next to the blue powder room that no one ever used. I took Clare there and waited with crossed arms while she puzzled over it.

It was, literally, what it claimed to be. A striped tabby draped on the top of a nearly empty hat rack. Only a singular top hat, shiny and bent, hung from a peg. The painting bore none of the angularity that marked Papa's later illustrations, but it played with color, like a Matisse. The cat's whiskers were lined in blue, the old top hat shadowed in green. Come to think of it, it might have been the same hat Clare had tried on in the studio.

"It's about the weariness of familiarity," Clare said finally. It sounded like the thing an art student would parrot.

"Isn't it just a cat?"

"Is a cat ever just a cat?" She threaded her fingers behind her back and paced, the way Papa always did before a painting. "Is not a cat sometimes a . . . a . . ." She gave the cat an accusatory stare. "Goodness, what else could it be?"

"Friendship." I straightened the frame. "At least that's what Papa always said."

"Friendship?" She took a step closer. "Well, the cat, he's a Manx cat. See here?"

"So? Papa's never been to the Isle of Man."

"Beneath the cat's paw is a herring."

"Herring?" I bent. "There is?" I'd walked by the painting hundreds of times and never noticed the gray herring between the claws. "Papa's never been to Man, but he had a friend from there. Used to visit in the summers nearby when they were boys. I don't know his real name, because Papa always called him 'Herring.' "

"Ah-ha!" She nodded, satisfied. "And the hat rack?"

"Herring wanted to be a milliner? I don't know."

"He wanted to be great." She snapped her fingers. "He wanted to be on top." I was skeptical, but she was delighted. "You're wrong. It is more than a cat. It's a story of boyhood dreams." She waited a moment before adding, "Told you."

Though I thought she was ridiculous, I brought her to *Eleven Apples,* a still life of eleven apples, carefully arranged in a pyramid atop a gleaming plate. "Surely this speaks to him balancing his career and his family," she said. I showed her *The Ribbon,* a rosy ribbon curled on top of a scarred wooden table, with a tight knot right in the middle. "This must be when he met your mother. Lovely, yet strong right at her core." With *Cheese Pots, Unguarded,* a painting with two open crocks of the soft cheese eaten in Picardy, she said, "He was feeling nostalgic, missing Picardy all the way from Glasgow. And he felt vulnerable because of it."

Those paintings of Papa's lining the walls of the château had always been just that to me. Still lifes, landscapes, illustrations, the occasional portrait. But Clare, she found a story in each.

She'd stand before one, hands locked behind her back or thoughtfully stroking her chin, and weave thoughts, emotions, adventures for poor Papa. "Really, they're like the pages of a diary," she said, "spread all over the house."

His early still lifes, down the west hallway, morphed into his illustrations, framed and

51

hanging in places of prominence in the front of the house. Those defiant, forbidding, arresting paintings in the Glasgow School style, all sharp lines and murky colors. Truth be told, those paintings terrified me as a child. Evil queens, stubborn princesses, unflinching knights. Bluebeard's wife, holding a bloody key aloft. Little Red Cap caught beneath the jaws of the wolf. Sleeping Beauty, twined with roses, but with an ogre's eyes glowing beneath the bed. I used to run down the front hall with hands to the sides of my eyes, like horse blinders. I didn't want to catch a glimpse before bedtime.

As though reading my mind, Clare said, "I used to think they were frightening. Perrault's fairy tales, that is. And your father's illustrations fit them so well."

"He painted other fairy tales too. Not as part of a commission, but just because he liked them. Snow White and Rose Red, battling the wily dwarf. Trusty John, turning to stone. Rapunzel, wandering alone in the wilderness."

"I like this one." Clare touched a frame. A girl, red curls resting on a pumpkin, lay in front of a smoldering fireplace.

"Cinderella. He mixed soot in his paint to get the texture exactly right."

"It's not that." She sighed. "She looks so lonely."

A nearly orphaned girl, sleeping in a borrowed place.

"She wasn't completely alone." I reached past and pointed to the mice and crickets tucked into the corners of the painted kitchen, the starlings peering through the window, the lean dog nestled against Cinderella's bare feet. "There are always friends if you look."

She turned and peeked up through her eyelashes. My face suddenly grew far too warm.

"My favorite," I said, clearing my throat, "is the queen from Rumpelstiltskin, sitting on her throne, her spinning wheel in the background. He borrowed a spinning wheel from Marthe's mother and stood it in the corner of the studio for ages while he painted. I played with it until I accidentally 'pricked my finger.' It was only a splinter, but I didn't know that. Maman found me lying in the rose garden, convinced I was doomed to sleep for a hundred years."

"And when you awoke, did you find true love?"

It was a silly question, tossed off over her shoulder. There had been adolescent kisses in country lanes, infatuations with cabaret

53

dancers, and an earnest crush on my uncle's long-legged mistress, Véronique. But no love. I barely had time enough for tennis.

She noticed I'd stopped. "As for me, I don't think it exists. True love. It's as make-believe as a magical spindle."

"I'm French. We're supposed to believe that one can fall in love once a week."

"Then why haven't you?"

Something in her question was expectant. An expectancy that surprised me, given that this was only our second real conversation. Clare Ross, when she gave her trust and her friendship, gave it completely.

But I evaded. "If you see how my *maman* used to dress me, you'll understand why I've never inspired a great passion in any girl."

I took her to see the few portraits in the east hallway. She followed the string of Lucs down the hall — a fat-cheeked baby cling-ing to the back rail of a chair; a scowling boy in a hated lace-collared blouse and long curls; a boy, prouder and freshly shorn, pos-ing with a tennis racket and a smile. She laughed at each one and I blushed.

"They're not very good," I mumbled. "I didn't really have hair as long as that."

"Pity," she said, with a glint in her eye. "I think the curls are rather fetching."

I refused to answer.

"It's interesting, though, how even the portraits of you contain so much more than your face."

"My tennis racket, of course. And in that one, my rocking horse. He put my favorite things in the paintings."

She stepped closer to the one of me scowling at the painter. I was almost seven in the picture, furious to be sitting in a moth-eaten ruffled blouse rather than off meeting other boys. At seven, I was sure I was missing out on some vital part of manhood, both in the outfit and in the time spent sitting still.

"There's more. Right there, around your wrist. A ribbon? And what are you holding clutched in your fist? I can just see the gleam of something."

"Marbles," I said. I hadn't even noticed Papa painting them in. "That summer, I was mad about marbles. We all were. Marthe's oldest son, Alain, would tag along with her and we'd play in the dirt outside the kitchen door. Our playing was fierce."

"And the ribbon?" She touched the painting, where my wrist stuck out from the end of my jacket. "Or was it a bracelet?"

"A ribbon." I yanked my sleeve down as though she'd really touched me. "That was the summer Maman left us." I shrugged, hoping I looked nonchalant, as though I still didn't think of it now and again. "She and Papa, they'd had a terrific fight and she went to my grandparents' in Perthshire. I snuck into her wardrobe and pulled a ribbon from her dressing gown. Wore it around my wrist under my shirt all summer. I missed her."

I didn't tell Clare how the fight was all my fault.

That spring, Papa had just got his commission for *Les Contes de Ma Mère l'Oye.* He'd spend all day in the tumble-down chapel courtyard, sketching remnants of knights and ladies pressed into the stained glass, while I ran from one corner to the other with a makeshift sword, hunting for trolls and monsters. He'd be so wrapped up in his studies that he wouldn't even come for his midday potage. Maman worried and buzzed around him, bringing coffee and sandwiches, keeping his pencils sharpened, making sure the gardener didn't touch a blade in the courtyard. Even though she was halfway through a marble bust, she put aside her own work — her chisels and mallets and rasps — to concentrate on his.

It was one afternoon, where early violets were pushing up along the edges of the shadows, that Papa became frustrated. He was starting in on the first canvas. There was nothing in the middle but a few faint lines and whorls, measured out with his thumb, but I trusted him. Tomorrow those scattered lines would be something wonderful — a princess or a lion or a castle arching to the sky. But at the moment, Papa slumped in his chair, glaring at the canvas.

"Papa, why have you stopped drawing?" I asked. I was crouched by a hole with my wooden sword, harrying the snake inside. "What's the matter?" In truth, he hadn't been drawing all morning.

He muttered an incomprehensible string of something. When he wanted to swear at a canvas, he did it in English.

I shrugged. In the end, the snake hole was more interesting than grown-up words. "You should ask Maman," I said. After all, it's what I always did when I had a problem. "She can help."

But Papa waved his hand dismissively. "She wouldn't know. This is a question of art. It is not for her to understand."

Later I went to find Maman, to show her a newly wobbly tooth and to tell her about the snake's valiant escape. She sat in her studio, high up in the east tower, which, gradually, was becoming less and less of a studio. The piles of unsold sculptures that usually lined the walls were gone, tucked away somewhere in the château. Her old, scarred worktable had been moved against the wall and covered with a green blotting pad. She sat at the improvised desk with her book of household accounts, adding up columns of figures. A stack of letters sat in the corner, awaiting Papa's signature.

She pressed a kiss to my forehead but shooed me away. "Maman is working, *mon poulet*."

I stepped away, kicking the edge of the rug. It covered up the chips of stone that had always littered the floor before. "I'm sorry you aren't an artist any longer."

"Of course I am." She licked a finger and turned a page in her ledger. "I'm just busy with other things today."

"I don't think so." I wiggled my tooth. "Papa said that you aren't. He said that you don't understand art the way he does."

The row that followed, out in the chapel courtyard, shook down three panes of stained glass. The next morning Maman was gone.

I moped around that summer, hiding in her wardrobe and hoarding marbles. I suppose Papa was moping, too, though he was always at his easel. He painted in nothing but blues and blacks. I learned later that he'd been writing her letter after letter, pleading in English for her to come back to him. She resolutely stayed in Perthshire at her parents' house.

Since the whole mess was exactly my fault, I knew I had to be the one to fix it. It could be a quest, like Sir Gawain, I decided. I was old enough to be a hero. With Maman's sewing scissors, I cut off my long curls and left them on her dressing table as an offering. I found a dented helmet in Papa's costume box and, armed with my wooden sword and an old palette for a shield, I set off through the woods in the general direction of Scotland.

I didn't get far before my feet went right out from under me. Deep in the woods, I'd found a well, dry and forgotten beneath the leaves, and I tumbled down.

I was far enough from Mille Mots that Papa couldn't hear my calls, though I shouted myself hoarse. The stones crumbled back down on top of me when I tried to climb up. The skies darkened and I swore I heard wolves howling. I stayed awake all night, hands crossed over my head, until Alain, checking his snares early in the morning, found me, crying, shivering, and bruised up and down. He brought Papa, who took off his jacket and hauled me up with a rope. I had nothing worse than a broken ankle, but Maman was on the next boat. Papa spent two days filling in that well himself and was once more her *cher Claude.* I never did set off on a quest again.

I didn't tell Clare all of this, as we stood in the hallway in front of Papa's portraits. She'd noticed the faded ribbon around my wrist in the painting and that made me feel vulnerable enough.

I think she knew that. She didn't say anything, didn't touch the painting again, but she moved very close, so close I could hear her breathing.

"Maman came back, though," I said without thinking, then felt awful for saying so. Because for Clare, her mother hadn't.

Her face was closed. "You must have needed her so much, she felt it across the miles." She tipped her chin up at the portrait. "The way you kept that ribbon close, so close that you forgot all about it while you posed."

"I didn't know Papa saw all of that." The ribbon, the marbles, the boy frustrated that his *maman* had disappeared.

"I told you that art is more than circles and lines. More than branches and fruit and piles of stone. It can tell a *story.*"

"Then what is your story?" I asked.

"Maybe not so different than the one your father captured here. Though instead of a ribbon, I have a green dress."

The one she was wearing now, far too elegant for a fifteen-year-old girl. It had been her mother's, I knew now.

She turned serious eyes to me. "Luc," she said, and I realized it was the first time she'd called me by my first name. "Do you think she'll return?"

"What?"

"You wished as hard as you could, and your mother returned for you." Her eyes glistened, but I knew she wouldn't cry. "Do you think mine will? Will she come for me here?"

I knew Maman had been writing to friends, to colleagues, to old classmates from the School of Art, seeing if anyone had an address for Maud Ross. "Not a word from her," I overheard Maman say to Papa. "What are we to think?"

I wished I could tell Clare that everything would be fine, that her mother was safe and near and missing her madly. "Mademoiselle," I said. "Clare." Her eyes flickered, and I knew it was the first time I'd used her name, too. "She left home to draw her story. All you can do is draw your own and hope that she sees it one day."

She swallowed a sigh, but she nodded.

"But don't wait for that. Don't wait for her or for anyone to see what you've created." Papa had always been too expectant of critics, and Maman too shattered by indifference. "Draw it for you. Draw it because it's your Something Important."

"Something Important? I'm not sure I'll ever find that." She rubbed at a smudge of pencil on the side of her hand. "Why do we choose to draw what we draw?" she asked. I wasn't sure she wanted an answer. "Aren't they the things that speak to our heart?"

Once I thought it was nothing but tennis that spoke to my heart. But standing in the east hallway, with Clare standing in front of me, waiting, I wasn't so sure. I pressed my pocket, where I had the Conté crayons wrapped in the handkerchief. My fingers itched to trace her face. "I think they must be."

CHAPTER 5
LUC
1911

The next weekend it rained without cease and I didn't come out to Mille Mots at all.

I had a theme to write on Alexander the Great and not nearly enough time to get it done. Macedonia, Egypt, Persia, Babylon — did he have to conquer so many places? I sent a telegram to Maman and then shut myself in my *turne* with far too many books and maps. When I emerged from the library, blinking, there was an envelope waiting at Uncle Théophile's apartment, addressed in a round girlish slant. *Monsieur Crépet,* she wrote, that one spontaneous "Luc" put aside for the formality of a letter.

I'm sorry that you could not come to Mille Mots this weekend. Your *maman* said that you had much studying to do. Is it more philosophy? Anyway, it's raining here. You aren't missing much of anything. I've been trapped inside the château so that I'm not swept away into the Aisne (your *maman* swears it could happen).

So I thought, if you could not come to Mille Mots, I would send Mille Mots to you. Please accept this little drawing, monsieur. It was done with the utmost expression.

Sincerely,
Miss Clare Ross

Tucked into the envelope, folded into thirds, was the sketch she'd been working on the day I found her out under the chestnut tree. Mille Mots, leaning out over the river, with those wild tangles of roses climbing the walls. I leaned to the paper, convinced I could smell them. It was a hesitant sketch, the lines faint and nervous, but it showed promise. She had a good sense of perspective — that much I could tell — and a sure hand. I wished Papa could see it. Though I'd gone weeks before without coming home, I suddenly wanted to be nowhere but.

I washed and changed into a fresh shirt. I was due at the Café du Champion by half past five, while the tourists were still lingering over their Beaujolais, but before the students and laborers arrived. Between serving, I earned extra tips sketching the patrons tucked in at their tables with carafes and good conversation. Several glasses in, most were willing to buy the commemoration of their holiday.

It was a busy evening, with plates from the kitchen, refilled glasses, and many crossed fingers that I was far enough from École Normale Supérieure to avoid seeing any of my classmates. At the end of the evening, over a dish of *ragoût,* I scribbled a response on a cognac-spattered sheet of drawing paper, my last.

Mademoiselle,

I've never gotten more than a note or two from Maman and the occasional cramped letter from my grand-mère in Aix. As yours doesn't include a treatise on your current health, a reminiscence on how things used to be better a generation ago, or a reminder to wear clean socks, it is already magnitudes more interesting. And to come with such an expressive sketch, I should really feel honored.

I truly do, you know. I remember how reluctant you were to show your sketchbook, how precious your drawings are to you. That you trust me, mademoiselle, it means much.

It's been raining here as well, but I've hardly noticed. I'm only outside when passing from my study *turne* at the university to my job at the café then back to my uncle's apartment to sleep. If I disregard the latter, sometimes there's a spare corner of time for tennis. There's a German student here, who I tutor in English, and he's as mad for tennis as I am. Sometimes we'll have a "lesson" across the net. He can now swear in three languages.

Well, I have a theme due for which I am woefully underprepared. If only I'd spent more time reading Callisthenes and less time accidentally discovering salacious paintings, I might be better prepared. . . .

Forgive me, I've had too much serious reading this week and too little sleep. And yet, once more into the breach!

Thank you, truly, for the sketch.

Luc René Rieulle Crépet

I posted it on my way back to the university, along with a brief note to Papa. *The demoiselle, she has talent in drawing. Papa, can you teach her the way you taught me?* That stack of books on my desk somehow didn't seem so towering the rest of the weekend.

Her response didn't come straight away and then I was too into the weekday routine of classes, study, and work, with the occasional late tennis match, to notice. Then Wednesday I came home, dripping in my tennis flannels, to find a letter waiting.

"It arrived last night," Uncle Théophile said. He pursed his lips. "If you'd come home at a decent hour, I would have told you."

"I'm sorry, Uncle." I reached past him for the envelope on the hall table. "It's been a busy week. I've been studying a lot and I've been working a lot. I must pay my tuition somehow."

He looked pointedly at my racket. "I can see that."

Without changing, I took the letter and racket straight back out the door. Rather than sit across the table from my sour-faced uncle, I'd eat supper at the café after my shift. Again. The other boys in my *turne,* they always teased that I had it easier living in the city rather than boarding at the university, the way they all did. As draconian as the rules were for boarders, they couldn't be any worse than Uncle Théophile's. Home by seven, lights out by eight, no sugar in my coffee, no wine on weekdays. And absolutely no gramophone music.

Gaspard, the owner, rolled his eyes at my tennis flannels, but passed me an apron. "Clear those three tables, and I'll have Hugues make a plate for you."

I tucked Clare's letter into my apron pocket, unread, and went with damp towel to clear the tables for the next customer. Of course, it wasn't until three hours later that I finally had a corner table, a plate of lentils with tomatoes, a glass of cheap wine, and a moment to read her letter.

Dear Monsieur Crépet,

I don't believe that it is as dreary as you say. You're in Paris, after all. Universities, clean socks, unexpected letters. Living on your own rather than with someone telling you what you should or shouldn't do. What can be better than that?

I haven't been reading my Callisthenes either (should I be?). Your mother did give me a copy of *Les Contes de Ma Mère l'Oye* to keep me company. I can't read more than a handful of words (*l'ogre, les roses, la petite princesse*) but it's as marvelous as I remember. It makes me feel that I'm sitting in my nursery with

68

Nanny Proud, my old nurse. She couldn't read any of the French either, but always pulled me onto her lap to trace the pictures and tell me the stories in her own words. I think she made up half of them.

You know, I remember when your mother brought me the book. It must have been right after it was published, now that I think back on it. Of course then I had no idea your papa was the illustrator. Only that the nice lady who spoke with the lovely accent had visited from France and brought me a beautiful present. You were there, too, on that visit, weren't you? You and your papa. You brought a rubber ball, but Nanny Proud told me that laddies were too wild to play with. I always wished that I had tried anyway. I'd never had a friend before.

And here I've rambled on. Hopefully this letter will give you a moment or two between your essays. If you're able, maybe you'll be back at Mille Mots this weekend? At least your mother hopes.

Sincerely,
Miss Clare Ross

The chair across from me squeaked.

"What's this, Crépet?" Stefan Bauer leaned over the back of the chair, fingers laced. "A letter from a girlfriend?"

"No." I folded the letter and stuffed it back in the envelope. "Just a girl. Who is also a friend."

"A girl and a friend." He reached across the table and helped himself to my wine. "Is that not how it is defined?"

"Your English is rusty, Bauer."

He shrugged and drained the glass. "The whole language is rusty. Only German is strong as steel."

I pulled my dish closer, hopefully out of his reach. "What are you doing here anyway? I thought you were going home to restring your racket."

"I am following you. I am . . . I am stacking you like a deer." He waggled his eyebrows.

"Stalking." I retrieved the glass from him and gazed mournfully at the dregs. "And one generally doesn't steal the food of one's prey."

"You forgot your satchel at the club." He swung my battered canvas bag up onto the table, knocking my spoon onto the ground. "You will want your copybooks and texts, yes?"

I swore in French and opened up the

satchel. Nothing was missing. "Thank you."

Bauer shrugged again. "Now that you and the satchel are reunited, a cabaret?"

I never liked the cabarets like Bauer did. Too many loud-faced women and jingling coins. "I have a lot of reading to do tonight." I buckled the satchel closed.

"Because of your girlfriend, eh?" He nudged me. "Tell me about her, Crépet." He swiped my heel of bread and tossed it back and forth between his hands like a tennis ball.

"You're imagining things. It's a letter from my *maman,* that's all." I tucked the envelope into the satchel pocket. "When have you ever seen me talk to a girl? You're delusional."

"I do not know this English word. But I know that you are a liar." He pointed. "Your ears, they are pink right there."

"It's the wine." I brushed my hair over the offending ears. "Gaspard serves it strong."

I couldn't say why I was evading Bauer. What did it matter if he knew that Maman had a ward staying with us for a little while? Clare was at Mille Mots, and besides, she wasn't his type.

"Does she have big . . ." He proved my point with an unmistakable mime.

"I'm not teaching you that word in English, you degenerate." I retrieved my spoon from the floor and wiped it on my apron.

"But you knew what I was talking about, eh?" He nodded. "She does, does she not?"

"Of course not. She's only fifteen." I stuffed a heaping spoonful of lentils into my mouth above Bauer's cries of "Aha!" I'd slipped.

"Why have I not met her? She does not come to the café with you or to the courts at Île de Puteaux. Young girls like to watch men at sport."

I swallowed and wiped my mouth. "She's not in Paris. But I wouldn't introduce her to you anyway."

"You are afraid she would see what a real man looks like?" He winked.

I was more afraid she'd see the questionable company I kept.

"Ah, then she is a country girl?" he persisted. "*Ein Süßling* from home?"

"She's not a sweetheart." I bent my head to my plate and ate faster. "She's my *maman*'s ward. I hardly know her."

He leaned his elbows on the table. "This is why you go so often on the weekends to your château. And also why you do not bring me."

I never invited him to Mille Mots, but it wasn't because of Clare Ross. The urbane

Bauer with his tailored Berlin suits, with his straw hats and his Horsman rackets, with his casual change tossed down on baccarat tables or in the laps of showgirls, he didn't belong at Mille Mots. Maman, in her aesthetic dresses and reform corsets, Papa in his knickerbockers and painting smocks. The château's crumbling walls, leaking roof, moth-eaten curtains, halls lined with terrifying paintings and nude sculptures. The maids in their brightly colored uniforms that Maman had designed, "because happiness is more dignified than black." Marthe in her crowded kitchen, birdcages hanging between the dented pots. Papa's lunchtime potage, Maman's English tea, both of them feeding the dogs under the dining table. Papa's habit of cheerfully coming down to breakfast in absolutely nothing but a dressing gown. Among all of that, Bauer wouldn't belong.

"You're right." I pushed back my chair and picked up my plate. "If I never invite you, I never have to share."

He nodded approvingly. "You are a sly weasel, Crépet."

"See you tomorrow?" I reached across the table for a handshake, but he yanked his hand away and offered an obscene gesture instead. He lit a Murad cigarette and disappeared in the after-supper crowd.

Tucked deep in my satchel, I had to forget about the little letter until after my shift in the café. I simpered and scraped, I balanced trays and poured wine, I washed each table a dozen times over. I did three sketches of a young trio visiting from England and they rattled down far too many francs for the souvenirs. I didn't complain. After the café closed, Gaspard let me sit and study, sharing the light, while he finished hanging up the washed glasses, ready for tomorrow. After he hung the last, he pulled a squat bottle of cognac from a hollow spot behind the bar. He poured a finger out and toasted the thin air. Once I asked him what he celebrated. He tugged at his beard and said, "Another day, conquered. Isn't that something to celebrate?"

I waited until I was back at Uncle Théophile's apartment, shut in my narrow bedroom with the desk lamp on, to take out Mademoiselle Ross's letter again.

I don't believe you that it is as dreary as you say. You're in Paris, after all. Paris it was, but not the city I'd fallen in love with years ago. Between classes, study, tennis, and the evening jobs that helped to pay for all of that, I had no spare time. I didn't have time to sit in the Jardin du Luxembourg. I couldn't roam the museums on rainy days — the Louvre, with its brass air registers and Rembrandts, the Petit Palais, the Musée de l'Armée, the exquisite little Musée d'Ennery. Sometimes on the weekends I stayed in the city I'd trek up to the nineteenth arrondissement, to Parc des Buttes Chaumont, green and rippling with waterfalls. But I usually didn't see much of Paris outside of the gray stone and leaning buildings of the Latin Quarter.

I wrapped myself in a sweater — Uncle Théophile kept the apartment as cold as November — and smoothed a sheet of paper on the desk.

Dear Mademoiselle,

If I were you, I wouldn't envy the life of the university student. Indeed I am in Paris, but I'm not dining at the Ritz. I can't afford more than beans for supper, washed down with the vilest of wine. I don't ride omnibuses when my feet work perfectly well. I don't go to the opera when I have the collective complaining of the three who share my *turne*.

And I don't have much more freedom than I did at Mille Mots. I'm living with my uncle, you see. His name is Théophile, a dour, hairless gent who teaches

Greek at the Lycée Montaigne. He's Papa's second oldest brother, but even Papa can't stand to be in the same room as him for longer than four minutes. He has an overfondness for boiled eggs and for telling me what to do. I'd begged Maman to let me stay instead with Uncle Jules, who keeps an actress as a mistress and two parrots, but she seems to think Uncle Théophile more reliable. This, coming from a parent who used to send me into the woods with the dogs and call it "school."

But I do have my tennis. The Racing Club, the Tennis Club, Stade Français — Stefan Bauer and I borrow time on any court that will let us in. Véronique, Uncle Jules's mistress, calls him my *grand adversaire,* which is dramatic enough to suit her. Stefan is very good, even better than me, though I'll disavow all if you tell him so. We've been keeping a mental tally of our matches (which he always takes seriously, no matter how casual) and our wins. He's currently up on me, 26 wins to my 18.

How goes the reading of *Mère l'Oye*? Have you expanded your French vocabulary beyond talk of princesses and ogres?

Luc René Rieulle Crépet

"Monsieur, extinguish that light!" Uncle Théophile pounded on the bedroom door. "Do you hear me?"

I sighed and folded the letter.

"How can a man get to sleep when it is lit up like a bordello?" he grumbled.

I crossed my eyes at the closed door. "Have you been to a bordello, then, Uncle?"

The pounding resumed. "Go to sleep!"

CHAPTER 6
LUC
1911

Thursdays we had afternoons off from classes. With promises to meet Bauer later at the Tennis Club de Paris, I changed into my brown jacket and blue scarf and set off for a stroll along the Seine.

The *bouquinistes* sat on their stools, smoking, as customers browsed the sagging wooden boxes of secondhand books on the stone quayside. I rarely stopped — I barely had enough left at the end of the week for my train ticket home — but today I did. I had those extra francs from the generous tourists. Across from a café where women in flowered hats ate lemon ices was a stall selling English books. The proprietor was a retired English colonel, or so he always said, and had been there as long as I remembered. He wore a filthy khaki army jacket, smoked Latakia tobacco, and always kept a spyglass in his box for the children to peer out over the river.

Sometimes I picked up something for Ma-man — *Jane Eyre,* a translation of *Madame Bovary,* or whatever new he had by Edith Wharton. Today I idly flipped through the stacks. Some mysteries, a fair copy of *The Ghost Pirates,* a crumbling book about the Welsh education system.

"Je peux vous aider, young *monsieur?"* He took the pipe from his mouth and squinted up at me. "I have a copy now of *The Last Egyptian.* You were looking for it before, *non?"*

"Maybe." I jingled the coins in my pocket and wondered about an ice cream later.

The *bouquiniste* got heavily to his feet. "Your *maman,* she likes *Cassell's Magazine.* And this issue has the newest Father Brown story."

I tugged on my jacket collar. "Do you have any translations of Perrault?"

"His fairy tales? I think so." He dug through stacks, sending up a cloud of dust. Finally he held one up. *"Tales of Passed Times,* yes?" He brushed off the cover before passing it to me.

The volume was small enough to fit in a pocket, but printed with a color frontispiece. The illustrations weren't Papa's, of course, but they were nice enough.

"It's been hiding there for a while. I don't sell many children's books." He wiped off the stem of his pipe. *"C'est la vie."*

It was too cold for ice cream anyway. "How much?"

Clare could read it side by side with the French, learn more than the few words she could pick out on her own. The best things began with fairy tales. I paid and tucked it in my jacket pocket.

The day was golden, with meringues of clouds above Notre Dame. I didn't want to go back to that dark apartment smelling of cabbage and cheap cigarettes. I passed the art students with their pads of paper and their portable easels. One was doing a passable painting of the Louvre buildings across the river. He frowned down at a palette of blues and grays.

I walked past the galleries lining the Quai du Voltaire. Watercolors and ink drawings hung in the windows, above the occasional nude bronze statue. Everyone wanted to be Rodin. I'd never bought anything from the galleries — not on the little I had left at the end of the week — but looking cost nothing. Once, I'd seen one of Papa's paintings in the window of the Galerie Porte d'Or. It was a portrait of his friend Olivier, one that had sat in the room off Papa's studio after

Olivier went bankrupt and fled to Patagonia. I never told Maman he brought it to sell in the Quai du Voltaire, but I did help him pick out a new hat for her with the proceeds.

Today it wasn't the portrait of a penniless poet hanging in a window that caught my attention. It was a painting of a red-haired woman in a bottle-green evening dress. I froze before the window.

There were Clare's gray eyes, her long white fingers, that defiant tilt to her chin. That pile of auburn curls. I pushed open the door. Inside were more paintings of that same woman in other evening dresses. Sapphire blue, purple, rich cabernet red. In some her hair was pinned up in a mass, in others it cascaded over bare shoulders. No painting was the same. They showed different moments of Paris life. She was sometimes on a stage, sometimes on a sofa, sometimes in the center of a glittering party. A dancer, a courtesan, a society lady. In one she stood before a bed with that jewel-colored evening gown in a puddle at her feet.

The gallery owner, Monsieur Santi, came to my side, his nose twitching as he noticed my interest. *"Excusez-moi, je peux vous aider?"*

I left before asking who the artist was.

I forgot the golden afternoon and stopped in a stationer's for a paper and envelope. I crossed the Pont Neuf to the Square du Vert-Galant, that little teardrop of green caught in the Seine. Sitting on a bench, I wrote a letter with the drawing pencil in my pocket.

Dear Maman,

Do you remember the Galerie Porte d'Or, that place on the Quai du Voltaire with the shifty-eyed Neapolitan fellow? I was by there today and, Maman, I saw a painting of Madame Ross. I saw a painting of Clare's mother.

Clare told me she didn't know where her mother was, but she must be in Paris. One painting shows the stage of the Lapin Agile cabaret. And then for all the paintings to be here, for sale on the Quai du Voltaire.

M. Santi would know the artist, who can tell us where his model lives. I know you've been looking for her. Will you write to M. Santi, Maman? All Clare wants, more than anything, is her mother back.

Luc

I stayed in Paris that weekend, too. I walked down again to the Quai du Voltaire and loitered outside of the gallery, but didn't go in again.

Clare sent me a letter, something light and wistful, recounting a story about how her nanny had bought her a Little Folks' Painting Book for her birthday, so she could be a "lady artist" like her mother. *When Mother comes for me,* she wrote, *I can show her all I've learned since then.*

When she comes.

Maman's letter arrived the next day.

My Luc,

Maud was in France, it's true. You were away at school in Switzerland, so you weren't here when she appeared at our front door. She'd only just left Scotland. I was angry that she left, angry that she came here, to Mille Mots. I won't get into the reasons. Clare was scarcely eleven.

I should have talked to her rather than sending her from my door in a fury. Maybe I could have persuaded her to return to Fairbridge. But she didn't and I felt responsible. I wrote to Clare often. John did his best with her, but she was lonely up in that big house. Occasionally

I heard news of Maud, through friends. She was here and there, never staying very long in one place. After a while, I lost track of her. I wish that M. Santi had better news, but he confirmed what I already knew. Maud isn't in France any longer.

Luc, please don't worry about this matter anymore. When Maud wants to be found, she will. Until then, we'll give Clare all of the friendship we can.

Your Maman

I had met Madame Ross once. I was eight and had been dragged on one of Maman's flying trips to Perthshire, the one Clare remembered. Scotland was grayer than France, the flowers were smaller, and the food saltier. There wasn't much for a disgruntled boy to do but wish he was back at home.

Maman adored Madame Ross, that was clear. They called each other "Eena" and "Mudge" when they thought no one was listening. Clare was only four then, with short curls and an enormous hair bow that was forever falling out. She was too little to play with me, but kept trying to escape the nursery to find her mother. She adored her even more than Maman did.

She had that Little Folks' Painting Book, the one she mentioned to me in the letter. I remembered her running into the room with a colored picture, proud that she'd stayed mostly in the lines. "For you, Mother," she'd said. But Madame Ross just frowned and sent her away with the instruction to "do something original."

After Clare had slipped from the room, tears on her cheeks, Madame Ross said, "Really, Eena, maybe that's the best I can expect from her. After all, not everyone is an artist."

Ten years later those dismissive words hadn't left me. I used my tips that week to buy Clare a dozen soft Conté pencils and a wooden box to keep them in. I knew her best was more than anyone could expect.

That weekend, I came home to Mille Mots. I didn't tell Maman I was coming, so no one was waiting for me at the station in Railleuse. It was the kind of summer day where the trees lazily waved as I passed and the air smelled like fresh grass. I'd brought only my school satchel, weighted down with books, a pair of clean socks, and one dusky gold plum. I tried to put from my mind the paintings in Galerie Porte d'Or and Maman's letter. I inhaled and thought of home.

The walk was dusty, winding up the ridge

that bristled through the countryside like the spine of a dragon, then through the village of Enété, where I used to sneak as a boy to buy sugared almonds and poke the glassy-eyed fish in the market. I ate my plum and tipped my hat to a woman sweeping her step. Past the last house in the village, the one with green shutters and a crooked door, the road wound down towards the Aisne. A sandpiper darted past, chirping enthusiastically. I whistled back at him, smiled, and stretched my arms.

A few kilometers past the village, the road narrowed. Against the summer green of the fields, I saw the lindens lining the drive to Mille Mots. And, behind the green, the château itself.

I slipped around to the back. Maman would be at her battered table in the garden, going over accounts. Papa might be at his easel, near the river, unless the horseflies had driven him inside to the studio. And Clare, maybe stretched under the chestnut tree.

But when I rounded the corner, to where the poppy-dotted lawn stretched along the river's edge, I saw them. At the old table in the garden, Clare and Papa sat, facing each other across a trimmed sheet of paper. He'd read my letter, it seemed, my plea to fill

Clare's lonely weeks with lessons. Papa sipped from a small cup of coffee, tapping his pipe against the corner of the table but not lighting it, not yet. Clare bent over the paper, pencil flashing, the tip of her tongue escaping as evidence of her concentration. Papa never touched her drawing, but traced shapes in the air. I knew the voice he was using, that slow, patient voice that always made you feel your efforts were golden, even when riddled with errors. He leaned back and tugged his beard, quite obviously content.

Clare was less so. She frowned. She erased. She gnawed at the pencil when she didn't think Papa was looking. Papa nodded over her sketch, satisfied, but Clare only seemed to grow more and more frustrated. She wanted to be drawing the château, I knew, the landscape around Mille Mots, not the lines and circles Papa was insisting upon.

Finally Yvette came out with the dented coffee pot and Clare took it as an invitation to drop her pencil and push back her chair.

She looked up then and noticed me standing on the lawn. She brought her hand up to the brim of her hat. Scratching her eyebrow? Shading her eyes? Waving, at me? For some reason, my heart beat faster. I waved back.

She jumped to her feet, tipping the chair back. Papa didn't admonish her. He tugged at his beard and watched her skip off towards me, her braid swinging down her back. Her hat fell off.

"You're in your 'students' uniform' again." She bounced to a stop in front of me. "And I have a new dress. See?" It was plain and white, but of a fine fabric. She smoothed the front. "Your mother, she said the queens of France used to wear white for mourning. She saw no reason why a fifteen-year-old girl couldn't do the same." The dress came up high on her neck and down to skim the top of her high, buttoned boots. Around her waist she wore a wide sash.

"It's very nice, mademoiselle."

Something fell, just a fraction, in her face, but she twirled with a pasted-on smile. I swallowed.

The other times I'd seen her, in the front hallways and out beneath the chestnut tree, she'd been wearing the gauzy dress that was her mother's. Its raggedness, its repurpose, its oddness, almost made her seem part of Mille Mots. A young bohemian, dressed in the green of the countryside, dressed in a way that made her happiest. But this new dress was unmistakably a girl's dress — short, flounced, and modest. Reading her letters, I kept forgetting she was exactly that. A girl. I slipped a hand beneath my jacket and pressed it over my heart. It had no business beating the way it was.

"Luc!" Maman came bustling from the kitchen door. "I thought you weren't coming until tomorrow." She set a plate of cakes by Papa and wiped her hands on her skirt.

"I like to surprise you, Maman."

I was sure she didn't believe me, but she walked heavily across the lawn, her gold earrings twinkling. "Even a cat is full of more surprises than you, *mon poussin.*"

"I was eager to be here." I didn't meet the demoiselle's eyes.

I did see the look in Maman's, though, and it drew hard. "I see."

"I was bringing Papa a new package of Conté pencils," I said quickly. "Number threes." I dug into my satchel for the wooden box. "The last time I was here, I saw he was out of them."

Maman frowned at the elegant case, but held out a hand for the pencils.

The copy of *Tales of Passed Times* I left in my satchel, but I touched it once through the canvas.

"I should go to greet Papa," I said, as though I hadn't walked from the Railleuse train station only to see Clare Ross again.

Maman watched me with eyes inscrutable. I bowed, quickly and stiffly, and walked away.

CHAPTER 7
CLARE
1911

I'd waited for two weeks for Luc to come home from Paris. I wanted to hear more about Uncle Jules and his parrots. I wanted to talk about castles and ogres. I wanted to hear that funny, teasing Luc I'd found in the letters.

But the boy who came unexpectedly from the train station, buttoned up tight in his black suit with a school satchel over his shoulders, he was someone altogether different. He looked like a banker, not a pirate. Dark amid the breath and color of Mille Mots. I thought for a moment he looked happy to see me, but something changed in the time it took me to cross the lawn to greet him. He called me "mademoiselle," as though we weren't becoming closer than that. And then he kept himself at a distance.

So when, early the next morning, I looked through my window and saw Luc stealing through the kitchen door with a small rucksack and Bede by his side, I didn't even think. I pulled my hat from the wardrobe and slipped from the house after him.

He'd been heading for the stand of trees that ran along the river, so I picked up my skirts in one hand and ran in that direction. There was no sign of him among the trees, but I jogged along the tree line, peering through the branches to where they thinned out along the bank. When a bevy of larks startled from a tree up ahead, where the staggering tree line met the denser forest, I knew I'd found him. I darted into the woods.

He walked and I followed for what felt like hours. I stayed close enough to see the back of his brown jacket but far enough behind that I could stay out of sight. As he hiked, he stabbed the ground ahead of him with a found walking stick and sang American jazz songs. Even though I didn't know the words, I wanted to sing along with him. I stepped over rocks, edged around trees, and stayed quiet. I didn't want him to turn around and send me home.

I was just wondering if he was ever going to stop when the trees opened up onto a clearing, bordered by a rock face. It was empty. The face was high — maybe as tall as it was up to my tower window in the château — and jagged, as though someone had carved it away with a chisel. I crossed the clearing and put my hand against the rock, but there was no way Luc could have climbed it.

To the right, the rock face curved down to, unbelievably, a railroad track, grown over with weeds. I peered down the track, narrow and straight as a ruler, but didn't see him or his rucksack.

So I followed the rock face to the left, past crumbles of rocks that soon began resolving themselves into old, battered-down walls and doorways. I was seeing the outlines of long-gone rooms butting up against the face, with charred stone and dirt floors grown over with matted grass.

The face sloped down and I passed more rooms and then little pockets, carved clear out of the rock. Shallow little caves, tucked in at regular intervals, with wood violets scattered in front. Overhead, trees spread shade over the entrances. Luc could be in any one of them. And I could be walking home alone.

But then I spotted him, stretched beneath a plane tree. He'd shucked his jacket and his hat and rolled up the sleeves of his shirt. It was white, coarse, tucked into a pair of loose blue pants. On his feet, braided leather sandals. He lay on his stomach, surrounded by curls of orange peels. But he wasn't eating. With a wide pad spread out before him and a red Conté crayon in hand, Luc Crépet was drawing.

He'd once tucked a sketch into a letter, a quick, breathless Paris café scene, yet I'd never seen him with a pencil. I wanted to see more of his world, of the restless city where he lived during the week. It was the City of Light, the city of love, the city where revolutionaries stormed the Bastille and Impressionists stormed the Académie. I had been waiting, with each meeting, with each letter, for another glimpse of Paris. I had to be content with his words; they painted nearly as vibrant a picture.

I stepped closer, breath held. I wanted a peek at his sketch pad. Luc, away from his black suit, away from his studies and tennis, away from his *maman,* away from the château dripping with art, he was drawing. I wanted a peek at this private, stolen moment.

But it wasn't Paris or even Mille Mots, those crumbling stones I always drew. It wasn't the trees or the caves in this solemn little clearing or the carpet of wood violets. It wasn't the orange peels. On his paper, Luc drew me.

This drawing, it wasn't casual, like the inked Paris café, dashed off over, I imagined, glasses of wine and heady conversation. This one was careful, lines overlapped, erased, drawn in again. In sanguine, the drawing glowed. It was me and not me. My hair was pinned up, for one. My neck longer. My shoulders bare above a froth of lace.

I took another step and a branch cracked under my foot. "That's not me," I said.

Luc spun at my voice. An elbow crushed into his sketch pad as he pushed upright, leaving a streak of red on his shirt.

"I said it's not me." My face was hot. "You've made me look much older."

Something about it — whether the upswept hair, the bare shoulders, the challenging expression — made me think of Mother and the painting I'd found in Monsieur Crépet's studio. A forbidden pose, something undoubtedly adult, and it made me furiously embarrassed.

Luc looked every bit as furious. He flushed, then scrambled to his feet, snapping the book closed so quickly the cardboard cover tore. "Who asked you anyway?"

"That's exactly it. Nobody asked me." I rubbed my cheeks. "Did you? Did you ask if you could draw my likeness?"

He didn't look the least bit apologetic. Rather, just discomfited at being caught out. "You're the daughter of an artist, aren't you? You should be used to it."

Maybe the son of Claude Crépet would be used to posing. I'd seen the hallways of portraits. But my own mother, she never let me near while she was at her easel. I asked her more times than I could count if she'd paint me, draw me, trace me in the dust on the piano, but she always refused.

I parroted the response Mother always gave. "Artists do not choose what to paint. They are chosen." It's what she said as she sat in front of blank canvases, waiting for inspiration to strike. She looked so beautiful, so confident, so *artistic,* that what could I do but believe her?

"That's ridiculous," he said. "The world is full of things to capture on the page. To say otherwise is to ignore a world of beauty."

His scornful tone incensed me. As though, as a Crépet, he was the expert. "And how do you know what inspires someone?" I asked. "Are you the keeper of the muse?"

"If you wait for inspiration to strike, you sit before an empty canvas. And then what have you gained?"

"Greatness."

"Wasted time."

I shook my head. He was wrong. Mother knew what she was doing. Her empty canvases, her discarded studies, they were waiting for perfection. "The masters were patient. They created, they perfected, and they achieved."

"Even the masters had to put bread on the table."

"And where is the romance in that?" I protested. "In painting for money rather than painting for art's sake?"

"What is romantic about starving in a Paris garret? About begging rent from friends 'for just one more week'? About waiting for that next big commission that might never come?" He tossed the crayon aside. "In the meantime, you eat soup and lentils, if that's all there is in the kitchen. You stop up the leaks in the roof with old canvases that you'll never sell. You chase your children out into the world to pick up education as they can." He drew in a broken breath. "You tell yourself that it is all in the name of art. You tell yourself that it's worth it."

I looked to the red crayon lying in the leaves. "Clearly we don't agree."

"Mademoiselle," he said, "I wouldn't expect you to understand."

I left, before he could see hot tears in my

eyes. I was upset by his secretive sketch, by his disagreement, by his assertion that, all along, my mother had somehow been failing. I furiously kicked a rock.

As I wound back around the stone face, past the dark openings of the little caves, he called out behind me.

"Wait, mademoiselle." Dry leaves crunched. "Clare."

Back to the "Clare" of that quiet moment in the hallway of paintings, the "Clare" of the letters. I turned.

"I'm sorry." He exhaled. "Being an adult is sometimes exhausting."

"Everything you said about the leaking roof, the children being sent out into the world . . . that's all real, isn't it?"

He rubbed at his eyes and nodded. "I work in a café, as a waiter, after my classes are done for the day, after my studying, after my precious few matches with Bauer. Something has to fund all of that."

"But your parents . . ."

He shook his head. "It's all they can do to keep Mille Mots."

I shifted. No one had ever talked to me about money.

"I do some tutoring. That's where I met Bauer. At the café, sometimes I sketch the customers. Mostly tourists. They buy the sketches as a little remembrance of their trip." He shrugged. "It's not drawing what I want, but it buys my wine, my books, my coffee, new strings for my racket." He touched his inside pocket. I wondered what else money bought.

"You must do what you must do." I tugged at the sides of my skirt. "I didn't mean offense."

"I know."

"You startled me with that sketch. That's all." It sounded inane when said aloud. What was there to be startled about? Being noticed? Being pinned to the page? "I don't look like that, you know."

Softly he said, "To me, you do."

He didn't see me as an insubstantial girl, like the rest of the world, chipping as easily as china, wilting like a hothouse orchid. He wrote to me like an equal, he talked to me like a friend.

"Luc," I said, to remind him we were beyond the "monsieurs" and "mademoiselles." "I didn't know."

"I didn't tell you." Bede darted through the clearing, tongue wagging, and Luc looked away.

"Did you want me to think you someone else?"

"I remember your house in Scotland. It

was filled with real wallpaper, not cobwebs or disrepair. Your father wore smart suits, your mother had silverware that matched. I'm sure you don't want to hear about my woes."

"You said you were exhausted. You said that you were weary with your life." I took a step closer. "Can't matching silverware be exhausting? Starched dresses and governesses? Empty dining tables?" Overhead, a rook screeched and I wrapped my arms around my chest. "Do you think it's not exhausting to be a fifteen-year-old girl who nobody wants?"

"I want you," he said quickly, unthinkingly, and something skipped in my heart. He closed his eyes, just briefly. When he opened them again, they were clear. "I want you around."

I let my arms drop.

"Would you like to come sit down?" he asked, almost shyly. "I'll share my oranges."

"We won't argue again, will we?"

There was a little flash of a smile. "Only if you won't try to run away again. If you do, I might start an argument to give you an opportunity to come back and shout at me."

"Monsieur . . . Luc . . . it is a deal." I held out my hand.

He hesitated for a handful of breaths. But

finally he stepped closer and he took my hand. His was warm, rough, and sticky from the oranges. It was smudged red on the knuckles from his sketching. His bare wrist was sprinkled with freckles. It felt nice.

He noticed me noticing. "Right," he said. "It's a deal." He shook my hand vigorously, then loosened his grip. As he pulled his hand back, he unrolled his cuffs and tugged them back down over his wrists.

"Right," I repeated softly.

He cleared his throat. "Anyway, this isn't a place to fight." He tipped his head up, to the skim of sunlight falling through the trees. "It's a place of refuge."

The clearing was as still as a cathedral. "It is."

"This was always one of my favorite places to come as a boy when Maman and Papa were arguing. I'd steal away with something from the kitchen and a stack of history books and hide out here until things quieted down."

"Did they fight often?"

"As often as anyone, I suppose." He went to where his coat lay spread beneath the tree. "Maman would shout that Papa wasn't paying her enough attention, Papa would shout back that she clung too close, like a vine of ivy — that's exactly what he used to say — then Maman would declare that she'd have to tattoo her breasts like a Samoan islander before he'd notice her."

I wonder if he'd realized he'd used the word "breast." I pushed on my suddenly hot cheeks with one hand. "Astonishing."

"Of course, the rows only lasted as long as that. They'd shout, they'd cry, but then Papa would come to sit next to Maman on the sofa and everything would be forgotten. He always said that she fought as well as any French woman. He was quite admiring."

"So they weren't real arguments, then."

"What is real? The fights came when one of them had something to say to the other." He shrugged. "Sometimes Papa can be too preoccupied and sometimes Maman can be too smothering."

"My parents never fought." It wasn't, I supposed, a Scottish thing to do. I shrugged like he had, hoping I looked as casual. "Really, they just quietly ignored one another."

I followed him back towards the plane tree, in front of a larger cave entrance carved over the top with *143 Carrière* in rough, blocky letters. The clearing around the tree was grassless, covered over with leaves from last autumn. A solemn owl guarded over us from above.

"What is this place?" I asked, this corner of the woods filled with cool air and violets. Along the edges of the stones, poppies and purple-blue cornflowers clustered in the spots of sun. It smelled like rain and snow and summer all run together.

"Le Bois des Fées." He shook the leaves from his coat and spread it down again for me. "At least that's what I always called it."

"What does that mean?"

"The Fairy Woods." He lowered his voice dramatically. "Where little boys are tossed down wells like wishes."

"What?"

"Never mind."

Bede dashed in and out of the clearing, stopping to sniff the orange peels as he passed.

I dropped to my knees onto Luc's brown jacket and sat. "And in 'The Fairy Woods,' are the caves for trollish treasure?"

"Not caves." He tossed a stick for Bede. "Quarries."

"For stone?"

"This area here around Enété village, it was a quarry centuries ago. All of the white stones you see in the houses between here and Soissons, they came from the ground beneath us."

"The stones of Mille Mots?" The château, aching white above the river. "They came from here?"

"I hope so." He dug into his rucksack and pulled out a pair of small Spanish oranges. "Brindeau farm, on the ridge above here, is older than that. It used to be an abbey farm back in the days of Charles the Wise. At some point the monks discovered the granite below and it was a quarry ever since."

I dug a fingernail into the orange peel. "Did they run out of stone?"

"Papa says that they ran out of stonecutters. He blames Napoleon."

"Who doesn't?"

He raised an eyebrow. "Well, if we're talking about those who supported his decision to —"

"We're not." I bit into a section of orange and caught the drip of juice from my chin with a thumb. "One of us isn't at university."

He grinned at that and opened a canteen.

"What's inside, then?" I peeled off another section of orange and rose up on my knees. "Medieval chisels? Skeletons?"

"Oh, I don't know." He dribbled water on his hands.

"You haven't found one yet?"

"No, I mean I don't know." He shook his fingers and then wiped them on his trousers.

"I've never been inside."

"What?" I dropped the rest of my orange. "That's ridiculous."

The quarry was fronted by a wall of carefully squared blocks. Around the edges of each block, though, were neat rows of grooves, evidence of the medieval stone masons and their tools. Sunlight pushed through the doorway, onto a packed dirt floor. Beyond, still darkness.

I scrambled to my feet.

"Clare, no!" He jumped up, too, and caught my hand.

He didn't say anything for a moment, just held my hand. A rabbit darted from the bushes, across the clearing before the quarry entrance. I couldn't hear a thing other than my heart in my ears. His fingers were still damp.

"Is it haunted?" I finally asked.

He ducked his head and let go of my fingers. "No."

"Then why can't I go in?"

"It's dark. The ceiling might fall in." Again he wiped his hands on the sides of his trousers. "It might be full of wolves."

He stood so straight and still, shoulders tight. Either he was terrified of caves or he was terrified to let me go. Not since Nanny

Proud had anyone worried about me like that.

"Don't worry. I refuse to meet a wolf." I straightened my straw hat. "I'll only be a minute."

Inside the cave, it smelled like fresh earth, the way I imagined it would smell if you were buried alive. The very thought made me breathless. "Hallo!" I shouted back into the dark. Not even a flutter of bat wings answered.

I walked back into the cave as far as the light went. It bled into little galleries off the main one, but I couldn't see a thing. I turned into the first and walked with my hands outstretched until I felt cold, damp stone. Counting steps, it didn't seem very big. Maybe the size of the dining room at Mille Mots.

"Clare!" I heard Luc call. "Be careful!"

I was careful. More than he knew. If for a moment I stopped being careful, everyone would see how un-grown-up I was. How, every night, I cried into my pillow. My heart ached with missing my father. It had never stopped aching with missing my mother. If for a moment I stopped being careful, every-one would see that I wasn't as strong as I wished I was.

I leaned against the wall. Limestone

crumbled in my hair. Something about all of this darkness pressing in around me was comforting. It was the gray and the black that I missed in all the color of France. In the cave, the dark embraced me.

A tear dripped out, then another, then I was turning my face to the wall. The limestone caught my tears, but echoed back an errant little sob.

"Clare?" Luc called.

With a fingernail, I scratched C.R. in the soft limestone. Then thought about how he taught me to taste France, how he wrote me letters from Paris, how he stood outside right now, worrying about me when no one else did, and added L.C.

When I emerged back into the bright, Luc hadn't moved from where I'd left him. Terrified of caves, then.

His face grew sober. "It's so dark in there. I shouldn't have let you go in alone."

How could I explain that was exactly what I needed? How that moment alone in the wild dark somehow made me feel less alone? "But it was lovely," I said. "It *is* lovely."

He shifted on his spot on the leaves and violets. "You never said, why did you follow me today?"

His eyes, I noticed, were brown like

almonds. "Because I didn't want to be quietly ignored."

CHAPTER 8
CLARE
1911

He didn't quietly ignore me after that.

As summer stretched, we were outside as often as we could be. Sometimes the light-speckled chapel courtyard, sometimes the bank of the river, sometimes the woods or the caves. But most often it was the chestnut tree on the back lawn, within sight of Mille Mots. I'd sit, drawing, Luc would lie, reading. When the shadows swung to afternoon, he'd sneak into the kitchen past the dozing Marthe and bring me pilfered pastries or bread and jam or bowls of almost-ripe apricots. He gave me my first taste of coffee and, when his mother wasn't looking, my first taste of coffee with brandy. I fell asleep each night full of dreams, and Luc, he didn't miss a weekend home.

I never saw him draw again, though. It was one of the few secrets he had from me. "I'm not very good," he always said. "You should see me play tennis." Though I never did, I begged him to show me. "Come and watch when I play in the Olympics," he'd tease.

But I wondered where his drawing pad was, the one he'd closed so quickly when I caught him at the Brindeau caves. I wondered if he'd ever sketched me again.

"Why should I say?" he asked one Saturday morning as we sat beneath the chestnut tree. "You won't tell me what you sketch."

"Yes, I did. The château."

"But that was weeks ago."

"And it's still the château. Again."

"Surely there is no shortage of other subjects. The Aisne? The chestnut tree? Marthe and her birds?" He winked. "Or are you waiting for the subject to choose you?"

I ignored that. "Your papa, he gave me some lessons."

"Let me guess." He poked his pencil in his book to mark his page. "Fruit?"

"Far too much fruit." I frowned down at the page. Monsieur Crépet's slow, patient lessons were about shapes, lines, shadows, highlights. The little table in the rose garden was always set out with fruit bowls overflowing. "I don't know if I'll ever be able to look an orange in the eye again."

"Well, then." He took an apricot from the fruit dish. "Here." He tossed it. "Draw that."

"Really?" I gave him a flat stare. "More fruit?"

"You must be an expert by now." He leaned back on his elbows, his book forgotten. "Show me."

"This is ridiculous. I already told you, I'm tired of —"

He waved off the rest of my complaint. "Clare, just try."

It was only a circle; it shouldn't have been too hard. If there was one thing Monsieur Crépet was insistent on, it was circles.

Yet Luc was not as patient as his father, not nearly as forgiving. For every one I drew, he found some fault. "Too lopsided." "Too regular." "Too shadowed." "Clare, where is the fuzz? Where is the stem? Look closer." For ages I drew sphere after sphere, shading and stumping. "Try the cross-hatching," he'd say or "Use the flat of your pencil."

Finally I threw my pencil across the grass in disgust. "I don't want to draw an apricot. I want to draw an orchard full of apricots. I want to draw wagons and ladders and girls in striped skirts filling baskets with them."

He retrieved my pencil. "Monsieur Monet didn't wake up one morning to paint Fontainebleau Forest."

I rolled my shoulders. "He might have."

111

Luc recited with the air of someone who had heard it all before. "Monsieur Monet studied for many years to learn how to hold his brush, how to turn his hand to make a leaf, how to blend colors to dapple a forest floor." He sat back down and stretched out his legs. "And he never threw his pencil."

I crossed my eyes at him.

He ignored that. "Papa started me on fruit, too. You learn so much about shape."

"Now I can see why you decided to be a tennis player instead," I grumbled. "There's no passion in shape."

"Then tell me." He held up a finger. "What do you want to draw?"

"I told you, I only know how to —"

"Not 'can.' " He sat up. "Want to." He leaned forward. The sunshine filtering through the leaves sent shards of gold across his face. "If you could draw anything in the world right now, what would it be?"

The cicadas sang.

"You," I said softly.

He froze. I wondered what answer he'd been expecting.

But of course it was him. Though I knew he was older, a man to my mere decade and a half, I couldn't help but think of him when I fell asleep each night and when I woke in the morning. I'd look out my window as the sun exploded over the horizon, just on the chance that he was down there playing tennis. I wanted to begin my day with a glimpse of his face.

I wouldn't be at Mille Mots forever. Soon someone would come to get me, I knew it. Mother, I hoped, or maybe Grandfather. When I left, I wanted a reminder of Luc to take with me.

But here he sat, frozen, almost fearful.

I read once that in some corners of the world, where tribes lived untouched by modern life, it was forbidden to take someone's likeness. Either drawing or photographing, to capture someone's face, you might accidentally capture their soul.

I sharpened my pencil. "I've never done this, you know. You could end up looking like a Martian."

This seemed to make him nervous. He wiped his brow. "When drawing a face, the shapes are the most important." He cleared his throat. "It's like a skeleton. If you have it right underneath, the rest will follow."

I turned to a fresh page in my sketch pad. "You don't always have to be a teacher. Sometimes you can just be a friend." I propped up the pad on my knees.

He dipped his head. "I'm sorry."

"Head up and sit still!"

Silence stretched, though less companionable than our usual quiet. Even the insects were subdued. A green chestnut fell.

"Do you —" I began, as he said, "Have you —"

He nodded. "Go ahead."

I hesitated. "Luc . . . do you think my mother thinks of me?"

He didn't answer directly, but instead asked, "What made you think of that?"

I pulled my braid over my shoulder. "I'm never not thinking of it." I adjusted the sketch pad. "But she used to sit with her paintbrush outside under a tree, like this."

A bee buzzed near his ear, but he didn't flinch. I sketched the bee into my drawing.

"Is that why I always find you out here, under the chestnut tree?"

"That, out here, I'll feel closer to her? That I might capture a little of whatever she always tried to capture?" My pencil traced the curve of his face. "Maybe."

"What would she paint when she was outside?" He smiled. "Buildings?"

If she painted, she never showed me. All I saw were those empty canvases. "I don't know." I'd watch her from the window, all dressed in pink and perched on a stool before her easel. Nanny Proud would let me watch as long as I liked, but Miss May would pull me away by the hair. "But she looked so lovely and so *happy* out there in front of her easel. Inside the house, with Father, she never looked happy."

He stretched, but kept his head still.

"It was almost as though she loved the idea of being an artist as much as she loved creating. She loved to set up her easel just so, to sharpen her pencils, to hold her palette."

He brushed a blade of grass from his shoe. "She missed her days at the School of Art?"

"She missed a lot of things, I think."

His gaze slipped sideways and he was quiet. "I'm sure she still does," he said finally. "Miss things."

I couldn't trust myself to voice my hope. Instead, I let the scratching of my pencil and the coppery buzz of cicadas fill the silence, until Luc cleared his throat.

"Your turn." I remembered. "What were you going to ask earlier?"

"Your grandfather, have you heard from him?"

"No." I kept my gaze on the sketch. "He's off playing with languages somewhere."

"Didn't he raise your mother? Maman said that when they were girls, playing on the banks of the Tummel, it was Monsieur Muir alone up there at the big house."

115

"Exactly. He's already raised one child. Why would he want to raise another?" My pencil dug into the paper. "Mother always said that he wasn't very good at it anyway. That he kept to his work and left her to the nannies and governesses." So much like Father, who hardly ever came out of his study after Mother left, who rarely came to see me recite in the schoolroom. And yet I had the comfort of knowing he was *there,* that he was looking out at the same stars I was. "Anyway, it's been six years since we've seen each other. We're practically strangers."

"So are you and I," he pointed out.

"And yet I'd stay forever, if you asked me."

The impulsive sentence hung between us. A thrush took up singing somewhere above. For half a moment I wondered if he *would* ask me.

I cleared my throat, smudged a line on my drawing. "Would you like to take a look?" Without waiting for his answer, I flipped the sketch pad around.

I waited with fingers tight on the corners of the pad, watching him. Already I could see errors and I knew he could, too, the way his eyes tightened in the corners. He was thinking of polite things to say.

"This is silly." I tried to turn it back, but

116

he caught the edge of the pad, his fingers brushing mine.

"No, it's quite good."

"It's not."

"This is only your first time, after all."

"You're lying and I should stick to buildings and fruit." I moved to tear it from the book, but he stopped my hand.

"Okay, the lines beneath. The shapes." He lifted my hand from the paper and put the pencil back under my fingers. "The circle behind the apricot."

His fingers were warm. "That's all?"

"Start there."

I squinted down at the paper, erased, drew, erased again. It took shape, almost. He watched, patient. Finally I threw down the book. "It's not . . . never mind. Why am I even trying this?"

He picked it up. "Stop being frustrated."

"Stop being nice. I'm not an artist. I'll never be Mother."

"No. But you're Clare." He took my pencil and used the back end to trace the lines of my drawing. "It's the cheek, right there. And see the line of my jaw? It's not that round. You're almost there."

"Lines and circles, lines and circles," I murmured under my breath. The bones underneath. "Let me see."

Eyes closed, I leaned forward and put my hands flat on his face.

I think he stopped breathing.

I know that, for a split second, I did.

I had more important things to worry about right then. Like the fact that my heart was near to pounding out of my chest. That his cheeks were soft and rough, all at once. That he was close enough for me to feel his breath on my face. Close enough that I could kiss him.

I opened my eyes. He watched me. His were brown, ringed with gold. "So that's your face," I said softly. I licked my lips. "I understand now."

I counted three heartbeats, three seconds of wishing, three seconds where I thought that he really would lean forward.

"When you didn't want me to draw you earlier . . ."

"Yes?" he asked.

". . . were you afraid to be captured to paper?"

He exhaled. "I'm already caught."

His eyes looked everywherc on my face. Beneath my fingers, his cheeks were warm. I could see the light catch on his eyelashes. His lips moved.

I was counting breaths, one two three, when I heard her.

118

"Luc!" Madame's voice carried all the way from the house.

He didn't move, didn't even seem to hear her. He closed his eyes.

"Luc René Rieulle Crépet!"

His eyes flew open, wide, guilty. He jerked back, leaving my hands empty in the air. I could still feel the warmth of his face.

Madame strode across the lawn. She wore a tall turban of brilliant blue silk and looked as imposing as a voodoo priestess. As she approached the chestnut tree, I scrambled to my feet.

"I was just drawing his face, Madame." I fumbled in the grass for my pencil. I didn't even remember dropping it.

She didn't even look at me. "Luc, you have a visitor."

It was then that I noticed the man behind her. He was tall, not much older than Luc, with smooth dark blond hair and a khaki suit. Draped over one arm was a motoring jacket and a pair of goggles. He looked rich and relaxed in his sporting duck, like a gentleman about to yacht or take the automobile out to shoot. Luc yanked off his striped scarf and stuffed it in his back pocket as he stood.

"Bauer, what are you doing here?"

"I was in the area," the man said, with a

raise of an eyebrow and a German accent. "I thought I would visit your château."

Luc ducked his head. "We . . . we aren't prepared for visitors."

"Luc, don't be impolite," Madame said. "I'll have Yvette set for tea in the salon."

In Madame Crépet's salon, each wall was a different color, like a riotous fruit bowl. Strawberry red, plum purple, pear yellow, the deep orange of a nectarine. Embroidered pillows piled on every surface, beneath paintings of long-haired women on tropical beaches, as bright as Gauguin. Her salon was like falling into a paint box.

"Mr. Bauer," she said, with a sudden, coy smile, "I'm sure you'll permit me my Earl Gray. I am not wholly French, after all."

He bowed, but Luc shook his head. "The salon, Maman, it's . . . the rugs are being cleaned."

The rugs scattered throughout Mille Mots had been there since the Crusades, I was sure, faded, patterned things that always put me in mind of a Turkish harem.

"Today?" Madame blinked. "I didn't order that."

"Papa did," Luc said, which was a patent lie. Monsieur Crépet scarcely noticed if he was indoors or out. He didn't care a toss for the rugs.

120

"Well, then." She tugged at an earring. "I suppose it will have to be the rose garden."

"Perhaps Bauer doesn't have time for tea."

"Frau Crépet, I am most delighted for tea." Mr. Bauer bowed. "And Crépet, you may not expel me so quickly. My racket is strapped to my motorbike."

"You've come for the afternoon, then?" Luc looked dismayed.

"If it is to be tennis, I will have Marthe send sandwiches and beer," Madame declared.

Mr. Bauer grinned. "Beer? Frau Crépet, you may not be wholly French, but you are, I think, a little bit German."

Madame Crépet actually blushed and set off to give her instructions to the cook and maid.

"Your mother, she is more charming than you, Crépet." Mr. Bauer touched his hat and nodded in my direction. "As is the fräulein here."

Luc ran a hand through his hair. His friend wore a tweed cap; Luc was bareheaded and in need of a haircut. "Mademoiselle Ross, this is Stefan Bauer, my *grand adversaire.*" This last was said with a raise of his eyebrows.

"*Grand adversaire.*" Stefan Bauer laughed at this. "Do we have such a grand rivalry?

121

Of course, I am usually winning." He winked at me.

There was a set to Luc's jaw. "Not always. Sometimes I win."

His friend still watched me, until I looked away. "For now," he said.

I wanted Luc to follow me back to the chestnut tree. I wanted to finish my drawing. I wanted to finish whatever was begun when I took his face in my hands.

Instead he pushed ahead with his introduction. He didn't look at me as he did. "And, Bauer, this is . . ." He faltered.

This is the girl I almost kissed a minute ago, I filled in. *This is the girl I fed honey and cheese, the girl I wrote letters to in Paris, the girl I waited for outside of a cave. This is Clare, my friend.*

But ". . . this is Clare Ross, my mother's ward," is how he finished. He looked away. "She is staying here . . . until . . . until another situation can be found."

I blinked and, through stinging eyes, watched them walk away towards the rose garden. Stefan leaned towards Luc and said, "So that is what you have been hiding?" He looked back over his shoulder at me, a long, appraising glance.

"The demoiselle?" Luc didn't even turn around. "She's nothing."

CHAPTER 9
CLARE
1911

Madame left me at the table in the rose garden while she went to give instructions to Marthe on refreshments. I pulled on my gloves, straightened my hat, sat back-straight on the crooked wooden chair. Not that it mattered. Luc and his friend didn't look my way at all. I could have been crying my eyes out and no one would have noticed.

On a rectangle of lawn, Luc had ranged out a net and pounded it into the ground, amid apologies that the grass wasn't clipped short enough.

"I thought you were joking when you said you did not have a proper court here," Mr. Bauer said, opening a case with a polished racket. "At the weekends, do you not come here to practice?"

"I come . . ." He glanced at me, barely. "I come to help my *maman.*"

To help my maman. I tightened my fingers on the sketchbook on my lap.

"I know why you really come each weekend," his friend said. "Crépet, perhaps we can teach the fräulein to swing a racket, eh?"

"With the tournament next week?" Luc bounced the ball. He'd changed into duck trousers and a white shirt like Mr. Bauer, though Luc's were unpressed. He'd combed back his hair with pomade. He looked far too respectable. "I hardly have time to play schoolteacher."

Though I hadn't the slightest interest in learning tennis, at that moment I wanted nothing more. "I didn't realize I was such an inconvenience." I stood. "I'll try."

Luc glowered but Mr. Bauer grinned. "Fräulein, if you will come and take this racket, I will show you what to do."

"This is really a waste of time," Luc said, but I walked out onto the lawn and took the offered racket.

"Now, two hands, please, like this. Hold tight."

Luc rolled his eyes.

Mr. Bauer was explaining how to keep my back straight, how to extend my elbow, how to keep my arms just like *that,* when Madame came out of the house with her writing case tucked under an arm.

"Mademoiselle!" Her voice was sharp, and I jumped away from where Mr. Bauer held the racket.

"Madame, I was just . . ."

She strode across the lawn to me. "Perhaps you've been in the sun for long enough." Madame, who dug in the rose garden until she was as brown as a Gypsy, didn't worry about the sun. And yet her brow was creased in a worry that I couldn't explain. "Please gather your things."

"Fräulein." Mr. Bauer touched his hat. "I regret your departure."

Luc, concentrating on his shoelaces, didn't say a word.

Madame Crépet escorted me upstairs, leaving both me and my sketch pad in my tower room. She nodded, once, and said, "Perhaps it's best if you stay up here the rest of the afternoon. The day has grown warm." With no other explanation than that, she left.

The windows were open and I threw myself onto the bench beneath one. The breeze cooled my face. I hadn't done a thing, and here both Luc and Madame were acting as though I'd done something awful. Why couldn't they just explain things to me? Why couldn't Luc just look me straight in the eye and tell me what I'd done? I leaned out and saw the stretch of green lawn and the river, but no sign of him or Mr.

Bauer or their tennis match.

I took off my hat and gloves, pushed up my sleeves, and climbed out of my bedroom window.

I could hear the thwap of the tennis ball against rackets, punctuated by the occasional laugh and shout in French. I pressed my back against the wall and inched up the roof towards the ridgepole. The tiles were slick with moss, and my boots were worn on the bottom. I swallowed down any thoughts of how far it was to the ground and edged up, sidestep by sidestep.

But it was worth the climb. I could see clear around the house, from the river to the linden-lined drive in the front. Down the other side of the ridgepole was a window bordered in faded blue drapes. Through the window I could see a burnished tennis racket hanging on the wall. Luc's room.

Over there, down on the wide back lawn, was the impromptu tennis match. Mr. Bauer moved, loose-limbed and nonchalant. He was the one laughing and calling out French insults. Luc played rigid and intense. Even from my perch on the roof, I could tell that he was silent.

I didn't know what it was, why, in a breath, Luc had changed. When Madame and the sophisticated Stefan Bauer crossed the lawn, reminding us that the world was bigger than our quiet moment, Luc pushed me away. He acted the way he had that day he'd come home from the train station and saw me in my new white dress.

I didn't know why I cared so much. He was just a boy, a boy I'd only known for a couple of months. Luc turning away from me wasn't the same as Mother leaving. It wasn't at all the same as Father dying. It wasn't the same as Grandfather never coming home for Christmas. I balanced and let go of the roof. Then why did it feel the same?

I crept back down and into my room. I thought about finding Madame and apologizing for whatever it was that led her to send me there. I wanted to go back outside. I wanted to wait until Luc smiled again.

I hadn't seen Madame's blue turban down on the lawn, so I slipped from my room and down the hall to her morning room. Luc said it used to be her studio, back when she still sculpted. Now it was where she wrote letters, kept the books, and managed the business of Claude Crépet, artist.

The door was ajar, but I didn't knock, not when I heard Monsieur Crépet's voice within. He spoke softly, but Madame, her voice moving in the room as though she were pacing, did not.

"She's not mine to worry over, Claude, yet I do. She doesn't have a mother to do so."

His reply, I didn't understand, but I did understand the edge that came to Madame's voice.

"If you'd seen her with her hands on Luc's face, on his friend's tennis racket. So like Maud."

"*Ma minette,* you were always too hard on Maud. She had too much of her heart to share."

"That wasn't all that she shared."

He made a soothing noise. "Come, sit." He murmured something in French. The sofa creaked. "It was so long ago. You've forgiven me, but you haven't forgiven her?"

"She did it to spite me."

"She did it to best you. There is a difference."

"It wasn't enough that she was one of the most talented in the school. She had to have you, too."

I thought of the painting of Mother, tucked away up in Monsieur's studio. Only one, but he'd never gotten rid of it.

"She doesn't have me now."

Madame must have stood, because I heard her pacing again, quick steps around the edges of the room. "I should have written to John Ross when she showed up on our doorstep. Did you know he hired an investigator?"

"The investigator did not come here."

"And why would he?" Her heel came down sharply. "Would he go to question all of her old *amoureux* to see who else she begged to run away with her?"

"*Ma minette,* I didn't go." This was said almost wearily. "I wouldn't have gone, even if she'd asked me twenty years ago." He sighed. "Maud always spent more time lamenting the past than changing the future. She wore her regrets like a hair shirt."

I clenched my fists at my sides. They talked about Mother like they didn't know her. If she wasn't looking to the future, she wouldn't have left Perthshire, would she have?

"She said she'd paint her way across the world and not care what anyone else thought," Madame said, the words rolled up in scorn. "I don't know why I do."

"Because she was and always will be your friend, despite all the rest. You worry about her like the mademoiselle does." He patted the sofa softly. "Now sit back down."

The springs creaked again as she settled in. "Did I tell you, Luc saw a painting? In the Galerie Porte d'Or right along the Quai du Voltaire."

"Maud?"

I covered my mouth.

"Painted by Arnaud Duguay. Do you remember him from Glasgow?" She made an indelicate noise. "Second rate, even as a student."

"But the painting, it was in Santi's gallery?"

"Luc wrote to me. He thought it meant Maud was in Paris."

I stepped back until I felt the edge of the hall table against my spine. Mother, in Paris? Could she be so near? Luc hadn't said a word to me. All of those weekend afternoons together, all of those letters, and he hadn't said a thing about a painting of Mother in a Paris gallery.

I inched back to the door in time to hear Madame say, "The girl needs a place, Claude. Is this really the best one?"

I ran back up to my room and out to the roof. At the top of the ridgepole, I could see over to the front of the house, at Mr. Bauer wheeling his motorbike down the linden-lined drive. I ducked into Luc's bedroom window.

It was as shabby as the rest of the house, with a sagging bed and cracked leather armchair, but somehow neater. No spider-webs, no jumbles of knickknacks, no riotous confusion of colors. His room was more somber library than bedroom. An old, gilt-edged desk, monstrous and magnificent, stacked with books and drawing pads. That leather armchair tucked near the side, with a curved desk lamp next to it. Deep yellow bed curtains — the color of marigolds, of French mustard. The gray walls were un-painted and mostly bare. A tennis racket, its wood worn bright, hung like a work of art. Two watercolors of the crumbling château, signed *C. Crépet* were as soft and blotted as though viewed through a rainy lens.

One painting was done in haunting oils — a thin woman, all angles and edges. She wore a drapey dress, touched with gold where the light hit, and slouched against the armrest of a square throne with arms carved into dragons' heads, staring chal-lengingly at the painter. She might be a queen, but she was no damsel in distress.

That queen, she wouldn't let anyone put her in a corner. She wouldn't let anyone leave her behind. She wouldn't be over-looked.

And, in the middle of this room, this room of books and art and attempted respect-ability, stood Luc.

For a moment I didn't say a word. He stood without a shirt on. His chest was thin and pale. A smooth brown stone, threaded on a thong, nestled beneath his collarbone. Standing shirtless, with head bowed, he looked so private and almost vulnerable. But I saw tacked above his desk that drawing of me, the drawing where I looked more like Mother than myself.

I stepped over the windowsill. "I thought you were my friend."

His head snapped up and his eyes opened wide.

"I thought you were my friend, but now I can't even trust you. You saw a painting of my mother in Paris, and yet you never told me. Why?"

But he didn't answer my question. "You can't just . . . push in like this," he cried. He picked up his damp white shirt from where he'd dropped it on the floor and yanked it on.

"Push in?"

"That's all you've been doing since you arrived. You've made me miss tennis matches and weekend studying. You made Stefan Bauer come all the way here and now he's met you and I'm hearing about it. And then I had a lecture from Maman, as though it were my fault that you held my face like that."

None of what he said made sense. I'd been the one dismissed earlier, when he introduced me to Stefan Bauer, but now he was acting as though I'd done wrong merely by being there.

"Push in?" I repeated.

"Into my room, into my life, into my mind, into my —"

"I haven't pushed into anything. I was *invited.*" Now I was furious, too.

"I didn't invite you."

"But yet you come almost every weekend. You wrote me letters and brought me fruit under the chestnut tree. You've been always here."

He angrily buttoned his shirt. "When Maman asks me to come to meet her newest stray, what am I to say?"

"I see." I pulled myself back up into the windowsill. "I'm just another of Madame Crépet's dogs or cats. Somebody else's castoff. You're only here to be sure I'm walked and watered, no?"

"Oh, that's not what I meant."

"It's what you said," I shot back. "One more person who doesn't want the burden of having me around."

"Now you're twisting what I'm saying."

"I heard your *maman* say that she didn't think my place was here." I swung my legs out of the window. "Don't worry. I'll find someone who does. I'll find someone who cares."

I slid down the roof to my own window, only realizing after that Luc hadn't answered my question about the painting, the whole reason I'd gone looking for him. But what did I expect him to say? Confess that he'd kept things from me? Confess that, all along, my mother had been a train ride away?

I opened the door to my room. The little brown-eyed maid was in the hallway right outside my door, looking concerned. Clearly, she'd heard the shouting all the way from Luc's room upstairs. "Please tell Madame that I am feeling unwell tonight. I won't take any supper, thank you. Tell her I will be going to bed early."

The maid left and I pulled my small travel valise from the wardrobe. I filled it quickly, watching the door, afraid she would come back in. I buttoned up my new gray jacket and tucked in my little purse of money. From the valise, I took a yellowed envelope. In the corner was an inked fleur-de-lis. I opened it and, in my coat and hat, read the short note inside, though I could recite it by heart.

My Clare, I must go, to see the world, to find the art that I lost long ago. It's no longer in Scotland. I'll wilt away here if I stay. Forgive me.

I folded the note, folded the envelope, and put it in my coat pocket. Maybe she found that art. Maybe I could find her.

I slipped from my room and down the back staircase to the kitchen. Marthe was out cutting herbs, so no one saw me leave the kitchen and Mille Mots.

I only had the faintest idea of how to get to the train station. When Madame had brought me to Mille Mots all those weeks ago, it had been in a borrowed automobile, my first. I retraced my steps as best I could, along the river, through a village, up a ridge, until I saw the gleam of train tracks in the distance.

The waiting room at the station was empty, but there was one more train to Paris due.

"You can wait outside on the platform," the stationmaster said.

I patted my pocket to be sure I had my small purse and stepped outside.

But the station wasn't empty. I saw, in the

135

shadow of the platform, a pale suit.

"Mademoiselle." Luc's friend stepped from the shadow, wheeling a motorbike. "Or, as we say in my country, 'fräulein.' " He touched his chest. "Stefan Bauer."

"Ah, yes." I looked back over my shoulder. "How do you do?"

He followed my glance. "Are you being followed, fräulein?"

"Yes." I shifted the valise in my hands. "I mean, no."

"May I?" He gestured towards my bag.

I hesitated, then handed it to him. "I'm going to Paris, too."

"How exciting for you." His English was so correct, like I imagined the king's to be. "Visiting friends?"

Hands behind my back, I crossed my fingers. "Visiting family."

He leaned forward, almost confidentially. "All alone? You are brave, fräulein."

"I'm not alone right now, sir." I hoped I sounded confident.

"No, you are not." He offered an arm. "You are certainly not."

CHAPTER 10
CLARE
1911

Stefan Bauer was a gentleman. After he loaded his motorbike, he led me onto the train. He found a quiet carriage and spread out a clean handkerchief for me to sit on. I watched as he hung his hat and patted his jacket pockets, finding a little candy tin. Though the car was empty, he sat right next to me and offered a sweet.

"The family you are visiting . . . Luc did not say you had family who lived in Paris."

I pressed my pocket to hear the crinkle of the envelope. "My mother is there." He glanced down at my hand over the pocket. "I just have to find her."

"Fräulein." He took my hand in his. It was cool and dry, like paper. "You have my help."

"I do?"

He inched closer. "I told you before, you are not alone."

His kindness unraveled me. Holding tight

137

to his hand, I began to cry.

They weren't the sort of tears I'd been saving up since Father's death, but tears of frustration and loneliness that had been building since I left Mille Mots. I cried because maybe I could have found my mother weeks ago, if someone had only told me, and I cried because, for a guilty instant, I wondered if I really wanted to.

"Please no tears. I could not bear it." Mr. Bauer cupped my face and wiped an eye with a thumb. "There, please."

His hands smelled clean, like soap. "You're so kind, sir."

"Please, I am Stefan." He smiled. "We are friends now, aren't we?"

I bit my lip.

"I would very much like you to be my friend, fräulein."

I decided. "Then I will tell you the truth. I don't know where my mother is, not exactly." I sniffed. "You see, there's a painting."

The story came tumbling out in bits and pieces. What I'd overheard, what I still didn't know, even what Luc had hurled at me in our last fight. Mr. Bauer listened gravely, shaking his head and exclaiming in all of the right spots.

When I finished, he handed me a spare

handkerchief. "Luc would not help you, this is clear." He nodded. "He is not so much a man."

Luc wasn't, was he? More a boy, as I thought of him. Stealing treats from the kitchen. Hiking through the woods, singing American jazz songs. Drawing when he thought no one was looking.

"Ah, but we are arriving in Paris." He stood to take his hat down. "Come with me. We will find you somewhere to stay for the night."

He had an aunt in the city, he told me. "She is a generous woman. She will have a bed for you for the night."

In the dark outside of the Gare du Nord, I took a step backwards onto the pavement. "You do not live in Paris?" As little as I knew him, he was the only familiar thing in this city of cobbles and streetlamps and fog. "But I thought . . ."

He smiled and his teeth gleamed white in the dim. "I live at the university. There are no accommodations for young ladies there."

"Luc's university?"

He nodded.

Luc. Suddenly I wasn't as angry with him as I'd been on the train ride. I'd always imagined that he'd be the one to first show me Paris. "Maybe I should go back to Mille Mots. For tonight, at least."

He let me go to the window and inquire. He looked contrite when I came back to tell him that there were no more trains to Railleuse that day.

"A hotel?" I had seen a picture in a magazine once, of a hotel lobby, tiled and glittering with chandeliers and electric light. "Perhaps, sir, if I could only borrow some money . . ." I was instantly embarrassed by my request, but he seemed to consider this. With his smart suit and the motorbike he leaned against, surely he had the funds.

He touched his pocket, but then inclined his head regretfully. "I wish, fräulein, that I could help you more."

"You've helped me already, Mr. Bauer. I shouldn't have asked for more." His earnest gaze flustered me. "Already I am in your debt."

Something in his eyes lit. "My debt?"

"Of course all I have to offer in return are a few sketches and some questionable French." I tried for a joke, but it felt stifled. "Sir, if there is a way I could repay you, I will."

"I think you are too kind to me." He paused, suddenly thoughtful. "I mentioned Lili. My aunt. She lives nearby. Yes, that

140

would be best, I think." Again solicitous, he smiled. "She has plenty of rooms and welcomes visitors. It would only be for tonight, yes?"

I nodded. I had no idea.

"Fräulein, I do not wish to leave you friendless on the streets of Paris." He offered his arm. "They can be a very dangerous place."

I hesitated. I took it.

Mr. Bauer left his motorbike at the station and secured a taxi. His aunt didn't live far, he was right. In the time it took me to decide that, yes, I would return to Mille Mots on the earliest train, the taxi slowed in front of a nondescript building.

I waited in the dark taxi, ignoring the stares of the driver, while Mr. Bauer went to a door and spoke with a woman in an ice blue dress. She must have been on her way out for the evening, as she hustled us in and made us wait while she straightened her earrings in the hall mirror. She was a lovely woman, with a rhinestone comb in her hair and masses of chiffon flowers along the dipping neckline of her dress. Mr. Bauer introduced her as "Tante Lili" and kissed her on the cheek.

The front hall showed a house shabby but with a faded elegance. A chandelier in need of a dusting, a mirrored hat stand with a man's derby, and a somewhat bald velveteen sofa. A man in ill-fitting livery came through a swinging door balancing a tray with little glasses full of golden liquid. I'd never been offered an aperitif and certainly not in the front hall. I shook my head no, but Tante Lili took one from the tray and pressed it into my hands. I took a sip. Whatever it was, it was bitter and made my tongue feel warm. Mr. Bauer drank two in quick succession.

As Tante Lili pinched her cheeks, she spoke rapidly to her nephew in French. I wondered why they didn't speak German. It was all so strange and I was beginning to get a headache. I took another sip. Beneath the bitterness I tasted sweet oranges.

Finally Tante Lili broke off talking with a wave of her hand. She bustled away through the swinging door the manservant had used.

Mr. Bauer looked suddenly uncertain. "Would you please like to sit?"

"Here?" Was there to be no supper? No drawing room?

"If you would like." He pulled off his cap. In the gesture he looked younger. "We could talk. We do not know each other well."

I set my glass on the hat stand. "If you please, I would like to be shown to my room, Mr. Bauer. It has been a tiring day."

He set his cap down next to my glass. "I had hoped for more time to become friends."

Tante Lili returned then with a bottle to refill the glasses. I glanced up the dark staircase.

She smiled and called me a dear waif, or so he said. "She does not speak English, but she said you can stay. She asked if you would like to see the bedroom."

"Please." I tightened my grip on the valise. "I would like that very much."

Tante Lili laughed at this and then pinched my cheek.

I stepped backwards, but Mr. Bauer caught my arm and said, "She will show you to your room."

She rolled her eyes at him and he followed up the stairs with my valise. We passed shadowed portraits on the stairway, portraits of couples, of dancers. Not as fine a quality as Monsieur Crépet's, I could tell that much, but when I paused to look, Mr. Bauer put a hand on my shoulder and steered me up. Tante Lili giggled, high like a girl.

The room was plain, with a narrow bed and none-too-clean blanket. A washstand and a stool with a pillow were the only other furnishings. Mr. Bauer put my valise on the bed as Tante Lili bustled out to fill the water pitcher. I was exhausted.

"You must rest, please. Tomorrow we will begin the search for your mother."

Though I felt more alone in this place than I ever had at Mille Mots, I forced a smile. "Sir, I thank you."

He frowned. "Please, Stefan. And I can call you Clare."

I held my coat tight. "Maybe."

He looked back over his shoulder at the open doorway. "Fräulein . . . Clare. You appreciate my help, yes?"

"Yes, very much."

He turned back to me, took a step closer, and I realized how tall he was, taller even than Luc. "And if all I asked for in return was your friendship?"

Tante Lili pushed through the doorway in a slide of satin and a cloud of perfume. She glared at Mr. Bauer — Stefan — and set the pitcher on the washstand. He met her glare and something seemed to pass between them.

"I will leave you to your washing," he said with a stiff bow, following Tante Lili out. I heard whispering behind the closed door, but then the hallway was finally silent.

I let out a breath I didn't know I'd been

holding. It wasn't late, but the night already seemed too long. I slipped from my jacket and looked around for a wardrobe or, at the very least, a peg, but saw nowhere to hang it. There wasn't even, I realized, a chest of drawers in the room. Guests must not stay long at Tante Lili's. I tossed the jacket onto the bed. My hat I unpinned and set on the shelf of the washstand.

I filled the washbasin. I didn't see any soap, but there was a towel that looked clean and I washed my face and neck. My face in the mirror was pale. I unbuttoned my dress, one of the new ones Madame had ordered for me, with carved buttons that ran all the way down the front.

The dress, I smoothed out and draped on the bed next to my coat. I slipped from my petticoats and shook them out. I unsnapped the valise and found my folded nightgown. It was the only thing I'd packed apart from a clean pair of socks, my comb, and Mother's letter in the pocket of my coat. In only my combinations and elastic corset, I stood in front of the mirrored washstand. I untied my ribbon and ran hands through my hair. It was damp at the temples. My head ached.

In the mirror, with the door ajar, I saw Stefan Bauer watching me.

I whirled around and wrapped my arms

145

around myself. "Stefan."

He actually smiled at that and pushed the door open farther. "It is Stefan now?" He stepped into the room. "Ah, it is nice when you say that."

"Don't come in here." I backed up into the washstand. Water sloshed out of the basin against my back. "Please."

"I am sure you don't think I would hurt you, fräulein." He set an empty glass on the wooden stool. I wondered how many times it had been refilled. "I want only to say good night."

My arms broke out in goose bumps. "Why were you watching me?"

"Clare." He licked his lips. "You are nice to watch."

I felt behind me until the hat pin scratched across my hand. I grabbed it and swung it out in front of me.

"Please!" he cried, but took a step back.

"I'll stab out your eye." Holding the long pin in front of me, I circled back towards the bed. "I will." He moved farther into the room.

"Please, I do not wish to hurt you." He held up his hands, palms out. "You will see I have no weapons."

The backs of my knees hit the bed.

"Clare." He looked at my hat pin, then

looked at my face. "We are friends."

With my other hand, I felt behind me for the linen of my jacket and the cracked leather of the small valise.

"I wish only to become better friends." He took two steps across the room. "Rotkäppchen, I am not a wolf. You are safe with me."

I hooked fingers into the handle of the valise and swung it up towards him.

It wasn't a big swing, but I was near enough that it hit him in the face. Even almost empty, it made a thud. He cried out and stumbled back against the stool. The glass fell and shattered. My stockings slithered out of the bag. I swung it again, this time letting go. I heard a thump and a crack, but didn't stay to see where I had hit. Snatching up my jacket and dress in a bundle of cloth, I fled the room.

Downstairs, Tante Lili sat on the velveteen sofa with a man, her dress unfastened to the waist. She winked at me as I passed. Upstairs, I heard a string of German curses.

I ran out into the night.

CHAPTER 11
LUC
1911

The next morning, Clare didn't come down to breakfast. Yvette told Maman that she wasn't in her room. Her bed was unslept in and her valise gone.

Maman was frantic. She dispatched the maids, the butler, even Marthe and Papa, to comb the house and the grounds. Clare couldn't have gone far, could she?

I checked the chapel courtyard, the chestnut tree, and the fairy woods beyond. I brought Bede, who bounded off to bring me sticks, but no Clare. I walked as far as Brindeau farm. Though I had no candle, I clenched my fists and walked four steps into the big cave. "Clare?" I called out. "Clare?" There was no reply but my echo.

When I broke through the tree line to the lawn of Mille Mots, I saw Papa and Alain down by the river in a crooked little barge. They must have rowed from upstream, where the bluffs where lower. I wondered, until I saw Alain probing the bottom with a long pole. I went icy all over.

"Maman!" I ran straight across the lawn, as far from the river as I could.

She came from the house, hands twisting her shawl. She was red-eyed and exhausted.

"I'll find Clare, Maman." I kissed her cheek. "I promise."

It had been my fault, I was sure. After our fight, when she shouted that she'd find someone who wanted her. Had she gone to the village? Had she gone all the way back to Scotland?

I jogged the few miles to the train station, but she wasn't there waiting for the early train. I saw nobody but a man in a blue hat, sweeping. "Please, have you seen a young lady?"

He stopped and pushed back his hat, showing a shock of white hair. "I've seen many ladies."

I resisted the urge to hit the door frame. "Monsieur, here at the station."

He scratched his head. "This morning, no." He leaned on his broom. "But last night we had two passengers from this station. A young lady and a young man."

Bauer. He'd brought his motorbike on the Paris train, I knew. Maybe he'd seen Clare on his trip home. I needed to get to the Rue d'Ulm. I needed to see what he knew.

I paced the platform and then, once the train arrived and I boarded, I walked from one end to the other all the way to the Gare du Nord — as though I could make it go faster through sheer force of my restlessness. If Clare had left last night, when Bauer did, she'd been in Paris since then. She'd been all alone.

After the train arrived, I hurried to the university dormitories. Bauer was half awake and sporting a black eye.

"Please tell me you saw Clare at the station last night," I said without preamble.

He scowled. "She is not very polite, is she?"

"She can be outspoken. Is that a yes?"

Bauer hesitated. "She was on the train, yes."

"Where did she go from the station?"

"How do you think I know? She left. She did not give me her itinerary." He put a hand to his head and winced. Apparently his evening had involved too much wine.

"You look like hell. Where were you last night?"

He hesitated again. "Lili's," he said, cradling his head. "The night did not go as I planned."

"That's what you get when you spend

150

evenings at *les maisons closes.*"

"Whores are nicer than fifteen-year-old girls. No wonder you did not help her."

I stopped. "Help her with what?"

He buttoned up his sweater tighter. "She talked again and again, always about her mama and a secret that you would not share."

The paintings in the gallery. She'd come to Paris not to escape me, but to find her mother.

"You should find some coffee." I clapped Bauer on the shoulder and he winced again. His evening must've been rougher than I thought. "I'm going to go find her."

"Crépet."

I turned in the doorway.

"You should be careful near her."

"What, so I avoid a black eye?"

"She seems to like older boys." He rubbed his shoulder. "Watch that she does not throw herself at you."

"Clare is only a child."

"Not as much as you think."

I thought of her following me through the woods, insisting on drawing me when I'd tried to keep my distance.

"Don't underestimate Clare Ross," I said.

She was at Galerie Porte d'Or, of course.

151

She hunched in a doorway across the street, wrapped tight in a light gray linen jacket. Somewhere along the way, she'd lost her hat. It was summer, but she shivered.

"You don't hide very well, mouse."

She didn't even look up, just slumped lower.

"Hi." I took her arm.

At my touch, she flinched. She looked up then.

"Clare," I said softly, "are you okay?"

She stared at me, shaking, but didn't say a word. I slipped off my coat and held it out to her, but she shook her head. Her hands clutching at the neck of her jacket were white. Along the back of one was a long, thin scratch, bright red.

"What happened to you?"

"It was my hat pin." She brought her hand up to her lips. "It was an accident."

"But you don't even have a hat on."

She blinked and put a hand to her head. Her hair was loose over her shoulders. "Imagine that," she murmured.

"Have you been out here all night?"

"I had a place to stay." She pressed her lips closed. "At least I thought I did." Her breath caught and she pushed a thumb against her mouth. "Oh, Luc, I was all alone and I didn't know who to trust and I can't even trust that painting. I've been staring at it all morning through the glass, and I don't know if it's her or not."

"Did you go inside?"

She swallowed. "No."

"I'll take you in there." I reached for her arm again. "If you'd like me to."

Hesitant, she lowered her thumb. "I would."

I took her in the shop, waving away Monsieur Santi's solicitations. She stood before the five other paintings and slowly lifted her chin.

Looking at them again, there was no doubt in my mind. Maman's enigmatic directive to leave well enough alone seemed to confirm it. But Clare's face, so near, was mirrored in the paintings.

"It can't be her, Luc, can it?" She stepped closer, touched the frame. "She couldn't have *really* been in Paris all this time. Been so close and not come to Mille Mots to find me? It can't be her."

Through her jacket, her back was straight.

In the center painting, the model reclined on a curve-backed sofa in a dress the color of rubies. The neckline of the dress was edged with puffs of lace and it fell unabashedly off one shoulder. There, right by a pink nipple, was that same mole.

Two artists and seven intimate paintings of Maud Ross. How many others were there? Clare hadn't wanted to see the first one.

Her gaze roved from one to the next to the next. The model danced with flashing calves. She sipped absinthe with a heavy-lidded expression. She leaned towards the painter with her dress dipping forward. She stretched, languid, disheveled, on a sofa. Clare's breath caught.

"Is it her, Luc?" She asked the question hesitantly, almost fearfully, as though she didn't want an answer.

When I didn't reply, she turned her head away.

She wanted her mother. But she wanted the refined Scottish mother who raised her, the elegant woman who had elegant dinner parties, the lady artist who sat so beautifully tortured at her easel. Not this woman who ran off to be painted like a courtesan. The mother Clare talked about and wished for was an icy ideal. I couldn't give her the one here in the painting, not when she held her breath, willing me not to. "You know, I was wrong," I said, moving forward. Near to her, but not touching her. "It's not her. Clearly it's not."

"Really?" She turned to me, hopeful.

"Actually, now that I look at the paintings again, I think it's Sarah Bernhardt."

Her face cleared. She exhaled. "It does look like Sarah Bernhardt, doesn't it?"

"Absolutely."

Monsieur Santi approached again, a disapproving look on his face. "Young man, this is not a museum. You come in here all of the time and never buy."

"I'm sorry, monsieur." I put a hand against Clare's back, just barely brushing the linen of her jacket. "Please, let's go."

To my surprise, she leaned into my hand. "Luc, please take me home," she whispered. "Take me back to Mille Mots."

I used the money Maman had pressed on me for an omnibus to the Gare du Nord. Clare looked as though she'd blow away across the Seine.

On the train we sat next to each other, knees touching. She kept herself tightly wrapped in her jacket, wrapped in her thoughts. I whistled a little Scott Joplin, to make her smile, but she stared at her hands in her lap.

There was nothing waiting at Railleuse station to give us a ride back to Mille Mots. "Can you walk?" I asked her.

"Unless you have another omnibus tucked

155

in your pocket." A ghost of a joke, but it gave me hope.

We walked along the ridge that led to Enété village. I asked if she wanted to stop, to rest for a while, but she didn't say a word. In the village, I led her to a bench in the shade outside the smithy and sat her down, brought her a *cidre* to drink, but she hardly touched it. From within one of the houses someone played an accordion.

"Do you like the music?" I wanted a conversation. She just sighed, so slight it was nothing more than a flutter of her shoulders.

Her silence unnerved me, so, as we walked on, I narrated. I told her how I'd roll down the ridge as a boy, for the grass stains as much as for the spinning feeling. I told her how I'd tag along with Marthe when she came to market in Enété. She'd buy me sugared beans that I'd eat out of a paper twist and then I'd help her carry home the sack of parsnips or fish or summer plums. I pointed out to Clare all of the trees and fence posts I'd once insisted on stopping at to rest, not because I was weary, but because I always knew Marthe was. I told her how Papa bought me my first tennis racket and how I spent all summer marching up and down the Enété road, hoping to show it off to passing farm wagons. I showed her the rock where I'd been bitten by a spider and the poplar tree where I'd had my first kiss.

She stopped at that, and I broke off my nervous rambling. She went under the tree, back against the trunk, and looked up into the branches. A mourning dove cooed. I couldn't read her face. "Luc," she said suddenly, "if I ask you a question, will you tell me the whole and complete truth?"

Could a girl ask a more terrifying question? I followed her under the tree. "That depends."

Her body went rigid. "It shouldn't. Aren't we friends?"

"Is that the question?"

"*A* question."

"Yes."

"Then you should have no trouble being honest with me."

I felt like saying that she hadn't been honest all the time. I was learning to recognize that little tightening around the corners of her eyes, the way she bit her lip and avoided my gaze when I'd found her outside the Galerie Porte d'Or. Over the summer, I'd learned, in bits and pieces, how to read Clare Ross.

"Fine. I'll be honest. Ask your question."

She swallowed, cleared her throat, swallowed again. "I just wondered . . ." She inhaled. "Yesterday, while I was drawing your face, did you want to kiss me?" Her words came in a jumbled rush. "Do you want to kiss me now?"

"That's two questions."

"Will you?"

"Answer?"

"Kiss me."

The blue sky pressed down on us. I licked my lips. "Clare, I can't do that."

"Because I'm too young?" Her voice grew tight. "Because you're too old?"

"Because I did and I do."

Her face was tipped up to me, pale, drawn, surrounded by a cloud of hair. She looked as though she might shatter. "Please," she whispered, and closed her eyes. "I want to forget."

Though I didn't understand, I stepped closer. I put my hands against the tree trunk, on either side of her face, and I leaned in and kissed her.

It was just a little kiss, light as rain. I was afraid of breaking her into a million pieces. But when I pulled back, she smiled, the first I'd seen all day.

"So that's what it's like," she breathed. "It's sunshine." She reached with one hand to touch the side of my face, the way she had yesterday afternoon. As though my heart weren't already racing like a steam train. I turned towards her hand and kissed her again, on the palm. "Beautiful."

I wanted to tell her that she was the beautiful one. That this moment was a poem. That I wanted to kiss her again, right now, and maybe not stop until the morning.

She must've seen that all in my eyes. She covered her mouth with an open hand and ducked under my outstretched arm. Without looking back, she ran down the road towards Mille Mots.

Clare Ross, she was an orchid in a gale. She bent under the rain but always straightened in the sun. I only wished I could keep her from the storms.

I caught up with her at the front door. It was open and Maman stood with her. Not comforting or examining or anything else I might have expected, given that I'd brought Clare back from the streets of Paris. Just watching, almost warily. Next to her, Clare stood still, with back straight.

Maman said to me, "Clare, she has a visitor," and, like that, the summer was over. I didn't know who it was but I knew she'd be leaving, I'd be staying, and the poplar tree would be one more memory.

"Go ahead, Maman." I moved into the doorway beside Clare. "We'll be right there."

Maman exhaled, but she nodded and went down the hall to the salon.

"Luc." Clare drew in a breath. Even in profile she was lovely — the scoop of her nose, the feather of her lashes. "Do you think?"

It felt traitorous to hope it wasn't true, that her mother hadn't come to take her away, not when that's all Clare had been wishing for. But I didn't want her to leave. So when she asked, all I could do was nod.

She took that as a promise and reached for my hand. Hers was warm and soft. I never wanted to let it go.

"I went to Paris to look for her, and maybe all along she was looking for me."

We went down the hall to Maman's color-splashed salon. But Clare paused outside the closed door.

Finally she turned to me. "But what if it's not? What if it's . . ." She hesitated. "What if it's more bad news?"

I squeezed her hand and then let go. "You're not going in alone."

She nodded and opened the door.

There was a frozen moment, breath held beneath all that gray linen. And then a "Grandfather!" said with swallowed shock.

Across the room, a man leaned against the fireplace, tall and lanky like a heron. He was mustached, with untidy white hair and a face the color of an English penny. In his eyes I saw something of Clare. He stood stiffly, in a pale, rumpled coat, a straw hat in his hands. When Clare stepped in the room, he straightened and dropped the hat.

"Grandfather!" She stopped halfway across the room and stood, uncertainly. "Sir."

The man brushed at his mustache with a thumb. Marked right onto the skin on the backs of his hands, in faded blue-black, were crosses and dots. Tattoos, like a pirate. I could see why she thought him that. In the center of his right hand was a five-rayed sun. Clare glanced back over her shoulder at me, then lowered into a graceful curtsey.

"Patricia Clare," he said.

"Clare." Head bowed, she wobbled. "I'm called Clare."

I stepped into the room. I wanted to take her arm, to steady her to her feet. Behind me, Maman caught my hand and shook her head.

"Clare." The man cleared his throat and looked away. His heavy mustache twitched. "Of course."

"Ma chère . . ." Maman moved into the

room, her shawl held tight. "Monsieur Muir has come to take you home."

"Home?" All I could see of Clare was her back, that narrow bit of gray. I saw as she sucked in a breath and held it.

"To Fairbridge." Maman forced a smile. "It will be nice for you to return to all of your things, won't it?"

He shifted his feet. His boots were streaked with reddish mud. Maman noticed, too, as her mouth tightened in disapproval.

"But can't I stay here?" Clare ignored her grandfather and went to Maman. "I won't be much trouble. I haven't been, have I?"

Maman's face softened and she reached to Clare's cheek. "No, no trouble at all, *chère.* But your place is with your family."

She took a step back. "Family? I don't have any family." Her face twisted. "My father is dead."

It was the first time she'd said the word aloud, and it hung in the air. She still stood straight, but quivering like a poplar.

"My father is dead and my mother, she's never coming back, is she?"

Her back to her grandfather, she didn't see when he bent to pick up his hat, didn't see the quick wash of anguish on his face. As Maman took Clare's shoulders, murmuring soothings and endearments, I alone watched the lanky old man blink and worry the edges of his straw hat.

"I needed my mother there with me at the funeral. I needed her to come for me afterwards." Clare's voice broke. "I needed someone to want me and stay with me and not disappear."

"Patricia Clare," her grandfather said. "I won't disappear again."

Clare turned to him, flushing, as though she'd forgotten he was right there listening to every frustrated word. "Grandfather, I didn't mean —"

"You did and I can't fault you." He sighed. "I should have been there and I'm sorry I wasn't. But I'm here now."

She hesitated, then nodded. "I know."

"And I won't disappear again." He met her eyes. "You have my word."

She wrapped her arms across her chest. "Everyone leaves me in the end." Eyes glistening, she hurried from the room.

He blinked, once, twice, and then held his eyes shut for a moment too long.

"Really, monsieur," Maman said. "We could keep Clare for you. She's no trouble at all and I know your studies take you away from home."

A wild hope leapt in my chest.

"She'd have many opportunities here and

you can visit as often as you'd like."

"Madame." He spoke French, gliding his vowels in an odd way. "I made the mistake of staying in one place once before, all in the name of 'opportunity.' Both Maud and I regretted it." He sighed and passed a hand over his face. "But leaving Patricia Clare behind, that's another regret entirely. She'll come with me." He twisted the straw brim of his hat. "I want the chance to know her."

Maman didn't argue any further. "I'll call for Yvette to begin packing her things."

"Tonight, if you will. I've left my bags at the station."

"Tonight? But surely the lass needs time to get used to the idea."

"We have years, don't we?" He clapped his battered hat on his head. "I'll call back for her after I've arranged our tickets."

"Sir." I stepped forward. "She doesn't show much, you know. All this summer, she's kept her grief hidden."

He stopped and regarded me with eyes as gray as Clare's.

"You should know, too, she's stubborn as anything, and can't resist a challenge. She'll wear herself down to the marrow to succeed." I didn't know what I was saying, but knew it needed to be said. "She'll spend all day drawing, even if she has nothing more than a stick and a flat patch of dirt. She detests bananas, but loves oranges and apricots, especially when they're underripe. You know when they're tart like that? She can eat a bowlful without making a face." I spoke all in a rush, before Maman could interrupt me, before Monsieur Muir could dismiss me and take Clare away forever. "But, she doesn't want anyone to know when she's frightened. Ever. One of her biggest fears is being seen, even for an instant, as vulnerable."

"I see." He folded his hands, reminding me of those tattoos.

I was terrified of him, with his marked skin and new-penny face. But Clare, she was worth being bold for. "Sir, she may seem strong and impervious and wholly self-reliant, but she's not. Inside, she breaks, and she never tells a soul." I took a deep breath. "Please don't let her fall to pieces."

He held out his hand, like a gentleman. "Young man, you have my word."

■ ■ ■ ■ ■

PART 2
THE LETTERS

1911–1913

■ ■ ■ ■

Perthshire
4 September 1911

Dear Luc,

I don't know if you'll welcome a letter from me, but you did once and, besides, I have no one else to talk to. I don't know how to talk to my grandfather. I haven't had a proper conversation with him since we left Mille Mots. He spent the journey up to Scotland talking to me as though I were nine, which I suppose is the last time he saw me. He kept asking if I still read *Father Goose* and collected china dolls. Conversation faded after that and he seems unsure of what to ask me next.

I miss all of our easy conversations beneath the chestnut tree. I miss the walks through the woods, the songs you would teach me, the dogs weaving between us. Back here at Fairbridge, I miss all of that more. I'm remembering the muteness of regular life. The days that could go by without me talking to a soul. The emptiness. The way everyone seems to forget me in the silence of the house. It's almost as if the past few months never happened.

I hope that you write back, if for no other reason than to remind me that there was a summer in Picardy, where I made the best friend I've ever had.

Clare

Rue de la Montagne Sainte-Geneviève,
  Paris
Mardi, le 19 septembre 1911

Dear Clare,

I've never received a letter from across the Channel, apart from the time I was twelve and Maman sent a letter from Perthshire lecturing me on that term's marks. That letter was accepted red-faced; know that yours was received with a smile.

I've probably told you how, from the age of eight, I was at a Swiss boarding school. I'd come home summers, but, along with most of the boys, would spend my other holidays at the school. Every July I'd arrive in Railleuse, a year older and (I'm sure) a year wiser, yet Maman and Papa acted as though no time had passed. Maman would have last summer's clothes aired in my wardrobe, last summer's favorite dishes prepared, last summer's conversations ready to revive. But, of course, I wasn't the same boy each July. I'd had a year to grow, to learn, to like and to hate, to have my heart broken and then caught up again by the next passion. Though I may not understand the silence and emptiness you wrote about, I do understand the rest. I understand that mute frustration. I understand the feeling that, for a time, the rest of the world stayed still while you alone kept moving towards the future.

Luc

Perthshire
11 October 1911

Dear Luc,

There is a room at Fairbridge that has always been my favorite. Since I was small, I'd go hide in there whenever I was angry. It's full of curiosities from around the world — shells, fossils, baskets, bowls, feathers, and bones. On all of the walls hang masks — carved, painted, and generally terrifying. I'd sit in the middle of the room with my knees drawn up and wonder what faces those masks used to hide, what tales of exotic lands they told.

I told you that I used to pretend my grandfather was a pirate. I needed an explanation for him to be gone all of the time. But he wasn't always a pirate in my mind, you know. I used to imagine he was a sea captain, kept far from us by the whims of Neptune. Sometimes I'd imagine that he was a missionary, bringing holy words and warm blankets to the world's down-trodden pagans. An opera singer like Caruso, an explorer like Scott, a showman like Houdini — anything where celebrity and dedication kept him, regrettably, from his family back in Perthshire.

As a child, I only saw him occasionally. He'd appear at Fairbridge, without warning, and spend an uncomfortable handful of weeks pacing the gardens and generally avoiding any and all conversation. Mother kept up all pretenses of politeness and studied affection, but when he finally left, she complained bitterly. I realize now that she was envious. She had to stay back at home with me, but Grandfather, he had the world to explore. He was the adventurer she couldn't be.

It's funny, though, how sometimes our guesses can be closer to the truth. Grandfather may not be a sea captain, but he's traveled nearly as far. India, Africa, the South Seas. "Chasing languages," he says. To each place he went, he sent something back to me. All those hints of the world — each mask hanging on the wall, each shell and woven basket, each dream I had about the lands they showed — were from my grandfather. It was his way of staying close to me, even when he was so far away. So much of the world in one room and, Luc, he promises he'll take me there.

Clare

Lagos, Portugal
1 November 1911

Dear Luc,

As you can see from the heading, we're in Portugal now. Portugal! And to think, less than a year ago, I'd never been out of Scotland. Now I've been to both France and Portugal. I feel so continental.

Grandfather is happy as a lion, jumping here and there across the city after "smatterings of Berber." That's what he's doing, you know, researching a book that he swears will change linguistic scholarship. I don't know much about "linguistic scholarship," but it involves him following lost little bits of a Berber dialect, remnants of the Moorish conquest, through the Portuguese. He's given me a dreadfully dull tome tracing the paths of the Moors. I don't understand how he can find this at all interesting. Or, indeed, worth anyone's time. He tried to excite me about our travels, by saying "Us explorers, we have to stay together!" I don't know why he thinks of me as an explorer. I'm not, at least not yet.

But I don't have to pay him much mind. I keep to myself and he lets me. He gives me pocket money and, as long as I don't stray too far from our lodging, I can explore. I eat fish stew and olives. I ride in donkey carts. I wander in and out of churches laid with painted tiles.

This freedom, it's nervous. I've never had so much space to roam. The first few days, I could only see the shadows between the buildings, the stares, the footsteps behind me. So like Paris. But then I learned to navigate the streets. I caught up a few words in Portuguese. And I began to see the spots of sunshine.

Everything is so different here, at least from Scotland. I'm writing this on a stretch of beach, a beach that doesn't have rocks or icy water or pale-legged men in striped swimming costumes. The sand is all warm and golden and the water is blue-green. The colors remind me of those landscapes you keep hanging in your room, from that one week your father pretended to be an Impressionist. Has your father ever painted here?

Grandfather says that the sun is putting a little color on my cheeks. I say it's sunburn. He bought me a straw hat, the kind that Portuguese women plait in the shade of the boats. Of course I won't wear it. Can you imagine a French woman wearing such a thing?

Clare

Mille Mots
Vendredi, le 22 décembre 1911

Dear Clare,

I am at Mille Mots for Christmas and I wish that you were here. It feels like quite the party. Maman has two new kittens and they are in the punch bowl almost as much as Papa is. Both have new things to wear — Maman a glossy dress the color of mistletoe and Papa a peasant shirt embroidered all around with holly berries. The household is so used to their bohemian wear that no one raised an eyebrow when Papa added to his costume a little round cap like they wear in Bethmale. He bought one for each of the staff, women included. They are completely ridiculous, but, at Christmas, everyone will forgive him.

They even relented to invite Uncle Théophile, the only time of year he will spend the money on a train ticket out to Railleuse. He's always goggle-eyed at the wine and meat being served, but that doesn't stop him from eating himself into indigestion. Alain and I hiked out into the woods today for the perfect Yule log and greenery for the *réveillon* table. Marthe is busy making nougat and candied citron and the sweet orange-water cake she only makes this time of year. She has the fattest goose hanging in the pantry, a behemoth with a black feather in his tail. She stuffs him with chestnuts and sausage, and we are driven mad as he roasts all day for our Christmas Eve feast. Marthe's midnight supper, it makes up for all those months of eating lentils in the café.

You'd adore the *réveillon* feast (I know your weakness for Marthe's nougat) and also the family *crèche.* With Papa's help, I built the manger with stones and sticks and bits of straw from the Bois de Fee, and the little figures inside, the *santons,* Maman sculpted those with clay from the riverbank. She used the faces of those in the household, so Joseph has Papa's beard and there is an angel, a drummer, and a water-carrier, all bearing an uncanny resemblance to me. She's put her own face on one of the Wise Men. You've seen Papa's work in the hallways and in *Mère l'Oyle,* but I think you would be quite impressed to see what Maman used to do.

How are you celebrating Christmas in Lagos?

Luc

Lagos, Portugal
18 January 1912

Dear Luc,

You've made me ravenous! We always had goose with chestnut stuffing for Christmas, and black bun for Hogmanay. Here it seems to be salt cod and boiled potatoes. I've never eaten so much fish in my life as I have since coming to Portugal. But they have at least a dozen kinds of custard, so I will forgive them the fish.

We are staying in a skinny house painted bright green, one that I worry might lean over in the sea wind. Grandfather borrows the landlord's bicycle and wobbles around the town with a phonograph strapped to the handlebars. He makes recordings on wax cylinders of the bakers, the fishmongers, the little girls with their baskets of clams. Anyone who will talk to him is duly recorded, both on the cylinder and in one of his ubiquitous black notebooks. His notes are mystifying. Though he says they're marking down not the words but the way they're said, I can't make heads or tails of it. Visible Speech indeed.

I meant to ask, has your papa had

another book? I passed a bookseller in the market the other day and there was one propped up that looked so like your papa's style that I was sure it must be his. No illustrator named and I'm not quite sure what it was about, as it was all in Portuguese, but there was a nymph on the front all covered over with seaweed and rainbows and two bear cubs. Do you recognize it? The trees behind looked almost like the lindens at Mille Mots and there was something of your mother in the nymph's face.

Clare

Rue de la Montagne Sainte-Geneviève, Paris
Jeudi, le 8 février 1912

Dear Clare,
Papa has had no commissions for Portuguese books, no. Perhaps it was someone else from the School of Art? He had students who went on to illustrate.

To be perfectly honest, he hasn't been painting much at all lately. Not even drawing. I was at Mille Mots last weekend and Maman was out of sorts. Really, it's not my fault that the roof is leaking (again) and Papa hasn't taken a new commission in months. He's been tutoring a pair of sisters who have their eyes fixed on L'École des Beaux-Arts, now that women are admitted. Maman is scandalized that a proper artist like Claude Crépet has stooped to tutoring.

And you, Clare, are you drawing? You've talked about the beach with the nets stretched over boats, the market with the fishmongers, and the green house, but nothing of the sketches I am sure you must be making of all this. None for me? I've never been to Portugal, but I've never before wanted to see it more than I do from your eyes.

Luc

Seville, Spain
14 March 1912

Dear Luc,

They say that the streets of Seville smell like oranges. They do. I almost feel like I'm back in the Fairy Woods with you, eating oranges until we had stomachaches. Remember how all you'd have to do is hold one under my nose to make me smile?

They have a museum here, a museum

of fine arts. Grandfather brought me, thinking I'd like it. The paintings, they're so unlike what your father does. Dark, raw, Spanish. Haunting paintings, centuries old. With all of the sunshine and music out on the street, I didn't expect the museum to be filled with so much murky sorrow. They made me sad like I hadn't been in years. When we left, I had to run off for a moment to be alone. I found a narrow street that reminded me of the caves at Brindeau and I pressed my face against the stone of the wall until the waves of sadness passed. When I returned, Grandfather didn't scold me. But he gave me a box of paints, real paints, and a palette to mix them. "I know you can see more color than they could," he said. He's a funny man, isn't he?

So here's a painting, just a small one, and not on proper paper either. Of what else? An orange.

Clare

Rue de la Montagne Sainte-Geneviève,
  Paris
Samedi, le 13 avril 1912

Dear Clare,

Don't be cross, but I sent on your little painting of the orange to Papa. It was too dear a painting and he promised to only look quickly and send it right back to me. He does ask about you, you know. Well, he sent it back, and also a letter for you, which I include here. Not a letter; a treatise. All about your technique with paint and your mixing of colors and "mademoiselle, your form." He seems quite put out with you for forging ahead into a new medium without instruction. "All shades of yellow and reds. So fiery a palette!" On a more cheerful note, he does say that your practice with fruit shows. I told him about the apricots and the thrown pencil. "Like your first lesson, Luc," he said. "No?" So, you see? Everyone begins with fruit in Monsieur Crépet's classroom.

I do think your grandfather is right in fixing his sights on Spain next, after leaving Portugal. He's tracing the path of the Moors in reverse, isn't he? Following that dialect back to its source? You mock, but I think it all sounds fascinating. This delving into the depths of a language, plumbing its origins, is new to me. I didn't know there were historians who did more than look at facts and dates and dusty old manuscripts. Words and sounds? I see what draws your grandfather.

As for me, not much draws me these days. We are on to Charlemagne, and I wish him as little as I wished Alexander. I'd much rather be studying about kings and emperors who didn't do too much, at least nothing beyond a page or two in the history books. Clovis the Lazy? John the Posthumous? Perhaps next term.

Until then I am playing as much tennis as I can. I'm currently ahead of Bauer, 89-62. He avoided me all autumn and then moped through the winter. He clearly does not have a friend in Spain sending him cheering paintings. Did you take his good humor away with you?

So, if you can forgive me for showing Papa your orange, know that it's tacked inside my desk drawer here at school. Know that it's brought me a bit of sunshine in the middle of a gray French spring. Know that it's made me think of you.

Luc

Mercredi, le 1 mai 1912

Dear Clare,

I wanted to tell you, Papa has taken on another illustrating commission. It's for an edition of la Fontaine's *Fables*. Of course Maman is ecstatic; it'll be a return to the sort of stuff he painted with *Mère l'Oye* all those years ago. Poor Papa, though, has tried to separate himself from that style for too long. But he'll do it. He'll do it for her. I've been watching him work on the preliminary studies. Never fear, *le Monsieur* Crépet still has the golden brush.

Since Papa is quite occupied, Maman took it upon herself to write to you, and has instructed me to include her letter (really, almost a novel) with mine. Papa told her that she must write to you about color and brushstrokes, that someone must, so that you can capture the sands of Iberia or Africa (or wherever else you venture next) without resorting to nothing but Indian yellow.

Enclosed (also from Maman) is a

packet of brushes, as they are both quite certain that you can't find a decent brush outside of Paris. Do you even have badgers there? Papa's guess is no. He's added a postscript onto her letter (if you can call a whole page of cross-writing a "postscript") with instructions as to the proper care of said brushes.

Since a parcel was already coming to you, I added my own bit of inspiration to the bundle. It's not much of a pebble, but it's from the caves below Brindeau. I even took a step and a half inside to fetch it for you. Perhaps it will lead you to a fairy or two.

This will be my last carefree, unhurried summer, did you realize? I'm already planning weekends at Mille Mots: lying beneath the chestnut tree reading Dumas and Hugo and Nodier, eating all of the mushroom potages coming from Marthe's kitchen, wearing out a bagful of tennis balls against the wall of the chapel, pleading with Maman yet again to install a clay court.

Because come next autumn, I'll be in army camp, for my two-year compulsory military service. Can you think of a greater misuse of youth than that? When I'm done, there will be a couple more years to finish my course at École Normale Supérieure and then hopefully a steady job at a school somewhere. In the meantime, Bauer and I are planning for one last hurrah (he's also bound for military service, in Germany). In only a few months, the Olympics are in Stockholm. We're doing what we can to get there. He has a cousin with a yacht (but of course) and a Swedish dictionary. I have nothing but crossed fingers. Will it be enough? Cross yours for me, Clare.

Luc

Seville, Spain
3 June 1912

Dear Luc,
  You talk of plans for a steady job. But no plans for taking the tennis world by storm? Of sketching Paris? Of taking sail in search of pirate treasure?
  I've seen your face glowing as you talked of the Championship of France and of all those tennis players. You speak almost with reverence. Your mentions of your games and the practices you sneak in when you really should be studying or working. I've watched your face as you played at Mille Mots, so focused, so

devoted, so *good*. I never feel the same passion when you write to me about your studies, about the history and rhetoric and philosophy. I never see the same excitement underlining your words.

Of course your future is your future. But is it the one you want it to be? Would you be content, sitting in the stands at the Stockholm Olympics, already resolved to never standing on the courts?

Clare

Stockholm, Sweden
Mercredi, le 10 juillet 1912

Dear Clare,

Eight days of tennis. Can you believe it, Clare? I shook hands with Otto Kreuzer and fetched balls for Albert Canet during a practice. He gave me advice and a ball he had used. I even saw the King of Sweden, who sat straight down the row from me. One day when the competitions were interrupted because of a downpour, Bauer and I snuck onto the outdoor courts for a stolen game (because what is a little rain to the pair of us?). Halfway through, a man in a dripping overcoat approached us and I was sure we were caught and would be deported straight away. Bauer, rule-following German that he is, was terrified. But it wasn't the Swedish police. Our audience of one was none other than Monsieur Thibauld, the writer and coach. He said that if he didn't see us on the courts at the Berlin Olympics, he would eat his left shoe. Bauer and I shook on it right there.

You're right, Clare. The way I feel when I'm on the court, it's nothing like how I feel in the classroom. Out here, the sun in my eyes, arms burning, feet aching, I feel alive. The way Papa feels with his paintbrush, you with your pencil, even Uncle Théophile with his *Iliad.* Like this is what I was put on earth to do. Like this is *my* Something Important.

The games are over, the prizes have been given, and the boat sails tomorrow, but my head is still in the clouds. Clare, do I ever have to come down?

Luc

Marrakesh, Morocco
14 August 1912

Dear Luc,

We've moved again. That Berber dialect. You were right in your guess of Africa, as now we are in Marrakesh.

Oh, Luc, all of the languages swirling in the marketplace, the stacks of warm clay jars, the smell of spices in the air! Rugs woven in reds and oranges and deep nighttime blues. Women swathed in white, edging through the streets with baskets on their head. Melons as big as fairy tales. Rows of pointed leather shoes, every color on the palette. Streets tented by billowing sheets of cotton, freshly dyed and drying in the hot breeze. I try to paint the way your father explained, to capture all the quickness and light of the souks, but my colors run together. There's too much here to take in. Grandfather had an easel made for me by a man in the Carpenter's Souk. It's flimsy, but it stands straight and folds when I want it to and smells wonderfully of cedar.

I read your letter from Sweden, knowing that you understood. I'm in the clouds and, Luc, I can't feel the ground

189

beneath me. I feel the way I did that time in the steam of Marthe's kitchen when we confessed our passions. You doubted yours then, but now, hearing you claim it, hearing you *want* it, I feel we can conquer the world. I won't let anything weigh me down. I can't imagine stagnating away in that house in Scotland the way my mother did for so many years, rather than being here, where everything is warm with life and possibility. I can't imagine trading all of this for a quiet domestic life. At this moment, I'm standing at the path to my own Something Important. I just have to trust myself to take the first step.

Clare

Rue de la Montagne Sainte-Geneviève,
  Paris
Lundi, le 9 septembre 1912

Dear Clare,

He's gone and done it. Poor Uncle Jules has gone to the great dueling ground in the sky.

The other night he was as drunk as a marquis and, at intermission, challenged a playgoer who made some uncomplimentary remarks about Véronique's legs.

Uncle Jules's secret shame was that he'd grown nearsighted and so his shot missed by a kilometer. The other gentleman was just as nearsighted and, unfortunately, hit my uncle square in the chest. He'd planned to delope, as he was Uncle Jules's next-door neighbor and oldest friend, but didn't miss the shot as he intended. We are sad, of course, but Jules always said that it was the way he wanted to go. Either that, or on the field in glorious battle. He'll have to settle for a somewhat blind and botched duel.

Véronique has draped the apartment in meters of black crepe, even down to the birds' cages. She goes around dabbing at her eyes and murmuring about what a "good run" they had. She's vowed to not drink Champagne until after the funeral. Uncle Théophile is measuring how long before he can evict her and sell the apartment to cover Jules's latest round of debts. In the week before his death, he bought seven new pairs of shoes. Jules, that is; Théophile has worn the same pair for a decade. The apartment, though, is in Véronique's name, and she won't budge a centimeter. Papa spends his time sniffling around the black-draped salon and leaving all the arrangements to his older brother.

The amazing thing is that I was in Uncle Jules's will, too. He left me a sizable amount, to be held in trust until I turn twenty-one, only a year off. It will come in handy when I'm in the army, I'm sure. I've heard that recruits are willing to be bribed in wine. He also left me Demetrius and Lysander, though two foul-mouthed parrots are less of an asset in the army. Véronique has said she'll care for them when I leave next fall and has invited me to come visit the parrots, and her, whenever I happen to be in Paris.

Life moves on in its grand march. Though some companions only walk along with us for part of the journey, we'll always hear the echo of their footsteps.

Luc

Marrakesh, Morocco
1 October 1912

Dear Luc,

Things are as usual here. Grandfather's widow friend brought over a tagine again. It's disgusting, how he'll smile and simper and eat around the pieces of mutton so that he doesn't have to admit that he follows a Pythagorean diet. With as often as she comes around, I don't imagine she'll stop if she finds out that he doesn't eat meat.

When she started making camel eyes at him (and she always does), I escaped to the Djemma el Fna. Grandfather thinks it's too crowded and no place for a girl, but I wear a robe and scarf and, anyway, I have a bicycle now. I'm faster than I used to be. And besides, I can't resist going. All of the snake charmers and storytellers and dancers in their horned hats. The square is so full of life.

With that heavy paper you sent, I've taken to sketching the water sellers. They're usually young boys in tattered robes, bent under the water skins on their backs and the strings of tin bowls around their necks. If I keep buying bowls of water, they'll patiently ignore me while I draw. There's one, a boy with a limp, who reminds me of you. He's always on the edges of the group, looking like he's waiting to begin life. But his eyes watch me. Though he's afraid to say a word to me — a girl, and a Western girl at that — he looks as though, more than anything, he needs someone to listen. It still amazes me that, after so many years, you let me listen to you. As long as I can, I'll walk with you on your "grand march."

I love it here, the swirl and commotion of the markets, the color-drenched scarves and robes, the aching warmth of the clay walls. I speak Moroccan French now, and a spattering of Arabic, and I can bargain like a camel trader. Everything is so alive. And yet, all someone has to do is mention the word "Scotland," and I'm suddenly hungry for it. I can smell gorse in the air, hear the Tummel rippling past, feel the breath from the Highlands. In those moments, I want to be there, too.

Grandfather doesn't understand. Whenever I mention Perthshire to him, he just laughs and waves a hand and says, "Isn't it better to be away from there?" I know Grandfather and why he's been away so long. It was my grandmother's death and all of the things that remind him of her. For him, memories haunt the halls of Fairbridge, though they are memories softened by distance. It has been too long since he's known the word "home." These days, the whole world is his home.

Distance has softened my memories, too. Instead of a cold, echoing, lonely place, I can't help but think of Fairbridge with a warmth not warranted. I remember my old nursery, with my collection of china dolls tucked high on a shelf. Father used to buy those for me, you know, every time he finished a commission. The curiosity room, packed full of things Grandfather sent from his travels. Even when I felt alone and adrift, there was someone in the world who loved me. Even the way Mother's room used to always smell like lilacs. I miss her, Luc. I know now that she's never coming back, but I miss her still the same.

Maybe it's because, out here, I understand her a little more. I know why she couldn't wait quietly in one place when the world is so full of possibility. I wouldn't trade my travels for anything. But, even so, I don't understand why she left. I don't know if I'll ever be able to forgive her that. She chose the world over me. She couldn't have both.

I know you're like me. Adventure is adventure, but there's something about home. Maybe it's because it makes us feel like children. Maybe it's because it reminds us of summer. When I talk about the river, the grass, the flowers on the air, you understand. Because you're thinking about Mille Mots.

I do, too. Think of Mille Mots, that is. It's not my home, but sometimes, during that one summer, I'd pretend it was. Before my grandfather came, I'd pretend that your home was mine. I wanted to have a place to belong. That's why I was always outside drawing the château, you know. I wanted to be able to capture Mille Mots down to every blade of grass, every ripple in the Aisne, every crumble of white stone, so that if I were ever to leave one day, I could bring the château away with me. I didn't know that once you fall in love with something, it never really leaves you. Does it? I've even found a sweet chestnut tree here that reminds me of ours, though it's lonely beneath it all by myself. I've sent you a leaf, pressed flat. Remember?

Yearning for home, yearning for those warm, safe days of childhood, that doesn't halt our steps forward. It doesn't mean we regret or fear. It means that we're built of so much more than our future. We have the past to stand on. And we're stronger for it.

Clare

Rue de la Montagne Sainte-Geneviève,
   Paris
Mardi, le 29 octobre 1912

Dear Clare,

This time of year is so melancholy.
Rainy and gray, as the world slips into
winter. I read your letter and it made
me wonder, what does "home" mean to
me?

Autumn at Mille Mots is just as gray,
of course, but warmed by the fireplace
in the drawing room and by stands of
goldenrod around the edges of the garden. Stacks of books read on the sofa in
my room, fresh honey for my bread, all
of the apples, grapes, and medlars I can
eat. In Paris, I can still find all of the
fruit, if I'm willing to go to the market
at Les Halles. But everyone rushes past
me. Unless you are Uncle Jules (rest in
peace) or an English tourist, you are not
in Paris to savor it. You're here to work
or to study, like I am. You're living in a
borrowed space, like I am. In a year I'll
be gone.

Perhaps it's disillusionment, what with
this time of year and with my military
days looming. I wish I felt settled enough
to savor. But I can't help but think of

months ahead and wonder where I'll be.

Do you know my favorite spot in Paris? The Île de la Cité is a little island in the middle of the Seine, the same island that the great Notre Dame de Paris sits on. At the other end is a tiny triangle of land called the Square du Vert-Galant. I'll go stand on the edge, point my feet to match the angle of the land, and close my eyes. When the wind from the Seine, smelling of fish and of stone and of history, blows across my face, I have a moment where I feel that I'm at home.

Those days, I remember why I first fell in love with the city. I remember my first puppet show at the little Guignol Theatre on the Champs-Élysées, my first ride on an omnibus down the Avenue de la Grande Armée, the first time I caught the brass ring on the carousel at the Luxembourg Garden, my first taste of Maman's rum baba, my first boat on the Grand Basin, my first run across the teetering bridge in the Parc des Buttes Chaumont. Writing this, pinning each of those memories to the page, makes me content. For all its gray, that golden Paris still lurks beneath. Maybe when all this is over, maybe Paris will be the place I call home.

Lately I've felt like drawing more often. I'll go and sit by the Seine, in the Square du Vert-Galant, and sketch until I can't feel my fingers. I draw the river and the barges, yes, but my pencil also turns to the things I can't see. I draw Papa's queens and knights and fairy-tale ogres. I draw the château and the gargoyles above the courtyard chapel. I draw the Aisne, Enété, and the caves around Brindeau. Would you be angry if I told you I also drew you?

Luc

Marrakesh, Morocco
27 November 1912

Dear Luc,

I've drawn Mille Mots more times than I can count. I've drawn the caves and the chestnut tree and the light falling on the courtyard. I've drawn the row of copper pots in Marthe's kitchen, the vases along the mantel of your *maman*'s salon, the mauve sofa in the studio upstairs. And I've drawn you. Would I be angry at anything you've sketched? Would I be angry that you are thinking of me?

I wish I had seen Paris while I was in

France — really seen — that golden Paris you love so much. I wish I'd had a chance to capture it on my sketch pad, the way you are now. The museums. The puppet shows and omnibuses. The rum babas, the carousel, the trees in the park. Will you send me something of it? Because the only Paris I remember, from those few hours there, is not as bright.

Grandfather has spent longer here in Marrakesh than any of the other places. It has become less about scholarship and more about the brown-eyed widow. His passion always used to belong to linguistics, but now I don't know. Can love ignite the same way?

I've become so accustomed to wandering that I'm beginning to feel restless. I think he is, too, though he ignores it. He's run out of things to transcribe and has talked to everyone in the market three times over. If he is to ever find the source of his dialect, if he is ever to finish his book, he must move on. As we grow, we all must.

Clare

Rue de la Montagne Sainte-Geneviève,
  Paris
Jeudi, le 18 décembre 1912

Dear Clare,

You really should consider coming here when you're done wandering. I'll show you the Paris I love, the Paris that you never had a chance to see. And you could be accepted into one of the fine art schools, I'm sure. Remember those dreams you told me through a mouthful of mimolette? I worry that you've forgotten those in your wanderings. Where's your portfolio? Your letter of application? Where are those plans you once had?

Clare, you should, you must go. Find someplace where you can surround yourself with art. Someplace where you can breathe it in, smell the paint and freshly sharpened pencils, feel the wet of a brush on your fingertips. It's all well and good to be sitting in the marketplace with your sketchbook, drawing the world, but you need to be with other artists. You need to be appreciated. You will be.

Luc

Constantine, Algeria
25 January 1913

Dear Luc,

I can't think about that. About abandoning Grandfather? Now that we've left Marrakesh, now that he's left his widow friend, all he has is me. If I leave, who will pour his tea the way he likes it, with a lump of sugar unmixed at the bottom? Who will make sure he has a fresh supply of the Alizarine ink he prefers? Who will be here to crank the phonograph while he scribbles away in his notebooks, then help him later decipher that hen scratch he calls an alphabet? I can't go off on my own. He's the only family I have left.

Dreams can change. People can grow up. These days I sell my drawings off the back of my bicycle when Grandfather's funds for the month have dried up yet again. I keep us in beans and couscous. Do you understand? I know you must, with all of your old talk about "steady work." I know you can see why, sometimes, we have to choose the earth beneath our feet rather than the clouds above.

Algeria feels quieter than Morocco. Or

202

perhaps that's me. Tomorrow's my birthday. At seventeen, maybe the world doesn't dance as much. Even Grandfather is melancholy, at having to leave his widow behind. He sits in our rooms, drinking strong tea. I can't stand to be in there. With the walls all hung over with dark rugs and cushions piled along the floor, it's stifling. I go out into the baking air, and I walk.

There are more women on the streets here, women wrapped in pale robes and veils, women in colored skirts and head scarves, draped in long shawls. I even see the occasional European woman, sweating in a tailored suit. Before, I would've noticed the patterns on their scarves, the colors of their stitched leather shoes. But now, all I can see is the way they drag their feet in the dust, the way their shoulders bend under their baskets, the way they tug on their veils, just for a second, to catch a mouthful of fresh air. With age, you no longer see the trappings on the surface. You start to see the people beneath.

Luc, do we have to grow older? Does the world have to change for us? Can we return to that one summer, when everything was beautiful? Can't we hold

onto our childish dreams for a little longer?

Clare

Rue de la Montagne Sainte-Geneviève,
  Paris
Samedi, le 22 février 1913

Dear Clare,
You mean to be an artist, so you
shouldn't fear growing older. Experience
brings depth, no? At least that's what
Papa always says. Ask him, and there's
more thoughtfulness in his later paintings, more nuance, more symbolism,
more *expression.* "No art done with
youthful naivety was ever worth discuss-
ing," he says. "You must first *live* it." We
must all suffer to gain experience, to create things capable of emotion.
It's nothing creative compared to art,
but sport can be the same. Between
classes and studying, I have so little
time, but what I have, I give to tennis.
Stretched, exhausted days swinging a
racket, leaning up against evenings of
loneliness, quiet cups of *café.* My goal is
no longer a gold medal tacked to the
wall. It's no longer to have my name in
the record books alongside the greats.

It's to do the best I can. It's to be a better me.

Bauer is in it for the competition, I know it, but he helps me to push myself. We'll play wherever we can. Clay, grass, parquet. Solid ice, if someone propped a net over it. We're stronger, faster, trickier. Bauer has developed this drop shot that gets me every time. He'll lob balls deeper and deeper into my court until they become almost a yawn. He'll wait until I move exactly where he wants me, until I stop thinking so hard about every stroke, then he'll drop a shot just over the net, well out of my reach. I should have learned to expect those shots by now. But I don't. It's so easy to trust Bauer. He lulls me with the easy shots, then blindsides me with the unexpected drop shots. He knows how to set me up to lose. He's up right now on games won, 257 to 228. Once I remember to be wary, I'll turn that around.

Luc

Laghouat, Algeria
31 March 1913

Luc,

We've only just arrived in Laghouat, but we may be moving yet again. The dialect Grandfather has been chasing, sniffing out scraps here and there, he thinks he's found it. But we have to trek to the Senegal River. He was ready to set off with nothing but the phonograph strapped to his back, but I've told him we can't leave right away. We need to be sure we have a stock of ink, paper, rice, dried beans, tea, chlorine, quinine tablets. We need to set up for our mail to be collected. We'll be out of contact for however long it takes to track down a dialect. This is more than packing up to move to yet another city. This is an expedition. But we can manage.

But you, Luc, can you? You let Stefan Bauer trick you again and again. And you still think he is to be trusted? I could have told you two years ago that he wasn't. If I didn't think you'd have figured it out by now, if I didn't want to let the past be the past, I would have.

I won't let anyone trick me, not anymore. Not the fruit sellers, not the paper merchants, not the beggars in front of the Parish House. And not Stefan Bauer. I've spent these past years wandering Iberia and Africa, learning to navigate foreign streets, learning to manage our odd little household, learning to think for myself. Learning not to be as starry-eyed and unquestioning as I once was. I direct my own life and I can do it alone. I've grown too much to let someone else, for even a moment, feel they can outsmart me.

But it's part of growing older, this deciding for ourselves. This deciding who we can trust and who we cannot. The day you led me to that stool in the kitchen and asked if I could trust you, I knew I could. You didn't push, you didn't intrude, you didn't offer yourself uninvited. But what you gave, in those spoonfuls and bites of friendship, was perfect. They told me that, in my grief and loneliness, here was someone I needed. Here, surprisingly, was something I wanted.

But when you continue to put your trust in people like Stefan Bauer, it makes me wonder if I was wrong. I thought you knew more of the world than that. I thought you were clever enough to see when someone wasn't really a friend.

Clare

Rue de la Montagne Sainte-Geneviève,
  Paris
Dimanche, le 4 mai 1913

Dear Clare,

I don't know what I've said wrong.

Bauer, he's always been tricky on the court. He's always taken this game far more seriously than I have. It's friendly competition. Fierce across the net, yet amiable across the café table afterwards. I don't know if I'd count him a friend, but a friendly acquaintance? Someone I can trust? He's given no reason for me to think otherwise.

But you, Clare, I'd trust you to the Amazon and back. I'd trust you across the Sahara, through the Himalayas, from here to Algeria. I've spent all these years writing to you, confessing to you, sharing with you pieces of myself that I'd never before shared. And now to have you write to me like none of that matters? I don't know what to think.

And with you leaving, maybe I won't ever know. Maybe you won't write back.

Of course I'll still be here, worrying, waiting, wishing that I hadn't shaken your trust like that. What else can I do?

I don't know what I'll do without you waiting at the other end of my letters. Is that too sentimental of me? Before I met you, the world was an uncertain, daunting place. But now, a letter from you brings me back to that summer. I read your words and I can hear the Aisne and the cicadas in each one. Like neither of us ever left Mille Mots. I don't understand it, but seeing a sand-dusted envelope from you, and I suddenly feel as invincible as we did then.

So, if you don't mind, I'll keep writing to you. When you return from the depths of Africa, my letters will be waiting for you. And, as always, Clare, my thoughts.

Luc

■ ■ ■ ■

PART 3
THE WAR

1913–1918

■ ■ ■ ■

CHAPTER 12
LUC
1913

I should have guessed that the army would be like boarding school all over again. The rows of narrow beds. The tall boys swaggering around the courtyard, looking for someone else to do their dirty work. The uniforms. The pranks. The occasional opportunities to stand in a line, shivering, in only your underwear and socks. The "Yes, sirs" and "No, sirs" and "Thank you for setting me straight, sirs." It was as though those university years in Paris, pretending to be a grown-up, had never happened.

I had high hopes when I arrived. Watching all of the other conscripts milling around outside the barracks, looking so serious with their jackets and suitcases, I told myself times had changed. We weren't twelve years old anymore. We were soldiers. Well nearly, anyhow.

Soldiers we may have looked after being given our uniforms — as ill-fitting as the getups might have been — soldiers we may have looked after all lining up along the foot of our beds for evening call — exhausted, bewildered, but upright — yet there was still a touch of twelve-year-old boy there. The second-years, seasoned and nudging, had warned us that in order to make it between the tightly tucked sheets of our beds, we had to do it in one smooth motion of a dive over the headboard. I gamely tried, to find that my bed had been apple-pied. My optimistically impressive dive turned into an ungraceful tumble to the floor with my whole person tangled in my bedclothes. The rest watched me carefully and dismantled their beds before climbing in. Me, I had to remake the bed to army standards, in the dark, and went to sleep in a glower.

The next day wasn't any better. From six-thirty in the morning until eight at night, we were busy with drills and marches and gymnastic exercises in the courtyard, but mostly with lectures. In rows of desks, like unruly schoolboys, we were treated to what was promised to be the first of many lectures on the history of the French army, from Charles VII onward. We had lectures on "The Moral Duty of a Citizen" and on "The Evils of Disobedience." Only two hours within all of that to eat — soup at midday; Papa would be pleased — and then two hours between the last drill and "Lights out." I fell asleep with my boots on, only to be awoken with a crash, upside down, pinned between my bed frame and the center partition of the room. A long rope wrapped around the frame, mattress, and my poor feet, then tossed up over the partition, was to thank for this. "Sending you heavenward, recruit," they told me between laughs. By the end of the day I didn't feel any more soldierly, but I did feel more inclined to bayonet someone.

I found solace in the camp canteen, where for a few sous I could get a glass of passable brandy. The canteen was packed shoulder-to-shoulder and reeked of burnt garlic, spilled wine, and cut-rate tobacco, but the drinks were cheap and plentiful. I found a corner to wedge myself in and think about Paris and the countryside. About Clare and the months that had gone by without a letter. About anything but the roomful of men and coarse jokes and whatever it was that I was stepping in on the canteen floor. I already knew the next few years were going to crawl.

The quiet in my little corner, however, was short-lived. Very short-lived. A sip in, a bright-eyed fellow in a too-big tunic squeezed himself onto the bench next to me. His hair was the color of butter and in sore need of a trim. He waved over a glass of brandy for himself and, raising the grimy glass, said, *"Merci."*

I looked around, but he was grinning at me. "For what?"

He slipped his kepi off and pushed hair from his eyes. "For buying me a drink."

He nodded to the waiter, who was waiting with hand outstretched.

"It's the height of bad manners to drink alone. *Faire Suisse,* they say. You buy me a drink in punishment." He took a slurping gulp. "Shall I order another?"

Grumbling, I dug for a few more coins. "Nice to meet you."

He reached around his glass to extend a hand. "Michel Chaffre. I have the bed next to yours, remember?"

I couldn't tell him what color my blanket was, much less who slept next to me.

Chaffre took another noisy slurp of the brandy. He wasn't one to talk about manners. "You look like a fellow who likes to be left to himself."

"Yes, please." I pointedly took a book out from where it was tucked in my jacket.

He laughed. "You don't think anyone will let you read that here. Are you trying to get a pounding?"

"Who said I was reading?" I extracted a square of stationery and smoothed it on top.

"Writing in a café? How very Proust."

"This is hardly a café."

Chaffre wrinkled his nose. "Smells like one."

"What sort of cafés do you eat in?"

"Ones that make this place look like Fouquet's."

I fished around my pocket for my gold pen. Chaffre whistled when he saw it.

"Looks like I picked the right chap. With a pen like that, you can afford better cafés. I hear the officers' canteen has brandy that costs *three* sous."

"And yet here I am."

He hitched up the sleeves of his jacket. "You're really going to write a letter in this slophole?"

"Some of us like to remind our mothers we're still alive."

" 'Dear Clare'? What an odd way to address one's *maman.*"

I covered the greeting with my thumb. "Don't you have some brandy that needs your attention?"

A boot came hurtling past, narrowly missing me but taking out both of our glasses.

"Not anymore," Chaffre said cheerfully.

"Listen, if we stick together, maybe no one will notice that we're really just trying to be alone. No *faire Suisse* to worry about."

I couldn't tell if he was in earnest or hoping to get another drink out of me. He didn't look nearly old enough to be there.

"We could watch out for each other. For boots and all that. I don't know a soul here."

A damp balled sock followed, landing in a heap on our table. "I don't either."

A recruit with shoulders like sawhorses stalked over. "That doesn't belong to you," he growled, and snatched the sock up from the table, spitting within a centimeter of my foot. "I don't like thieves."

Chaffre exhaled as the soldier left in search of his boot. "It would be good to have someone in this place to depend on." He sat straight and easy, but his hands curled protectively around his now empty glass. "What do you say?"

I gestured for two more brandies. "Deal."

Chaffre was true to his word. He was as persistent as a burr. With him sitting on my bed, polishing boots and keeping watch, I could read or write letters without fears that my mattress would be tipped or my head doused with water from over the center partition.

Though I hadn't heard from Clare since

that last letter in the spring, the one where she talked about the expedition to Mauritania, I still wrote, as often as I could. Not knowing where else to send them, I addressed them to the general post office in Laghouat, the last address I had. She'd make her way out of wilderness at some point. She'd find my letters waiting.

Lundi, de 20 octobre 1913

Dear Clare,

And to think I found school a slog. It has nothing on the army. I know by now you must be tired of hearing my epistolary complaints, but egads!

Despite the drills twice a day, our bunch is still trying to master "right" and "left." Instead of a corporal, they need a dancing master. We might make more progress. But marching may be all that we can do. The rest of our soldiering, we've thus far learned from a series of books and pamphlets, which I think half of the recruits can't read a word of. And those are the practical books. Did you know, yesterday we had a lecture on civic duty and, tomorrow, we're to have one on *mushroom farming*? France had better hope that no one challenges us to battle. We may only be able to respond with a volley of morals and morels.

Must go . . . they are tossing Chaffre in a blanket again.

Yours,
Luc

I was always retrieving Chaffre. After those first few pranks, the others left me largely alone. But poor Chaffre, they waited for him when he stepped out to use the latrine. They lurked right inside the barracks with a wool blanket outstretched, and caught up my hapless friend when he came in. It was usually only after my shouted promises to buy jugs of wine for all the next day that they'd unfurl him. That may have been their intent to begin with. Uncle Jules's inheritance was coming in handy.

Chaffre always shrugged it off with a smile and a "no hard feelings." He was a funny kid.

Dimanche, le 23 novembre 1913

Dear Clare,

After a month, I think I've finally broken in my uniform. It's really a ridiculous getup. The jacket comes down nearly to my calves and, underneath, the trousers are pulled up to my armpits (excuse the indelicacy). But just imagine, those trousers are as bright red as a cherry. The jacket and cap are dark blue. Is the plan to make us look too patriotic to shoot? Yet another reason why I could never be a real soldier. I'd never be able to attack. I'd be laughing too hard at myself to aim.

I do admit, though, that there is something comforting in all of the wool this time of year. It's been icy. However, our uniforms would be far more comforting if the other seventy-nine men in my barrack would, on occasion, launder them.

Speaking of, the others have hidden Chaffre's trousers again. I must go help him. *Au revoir!*

Luc

Chaffre sat on a bed next to me, mending his rescued trousers. "Thanks so much for helping me, old man." His cheeks were pink. "Pass over yours and I'll fix that rip you have in the seat."

"You really don't need to," I said, folding the letter to Clare.

"You don't want to be pulled out of line during roll call over a hole that will take me a few minutes to stitch." He grinned. "I'll keep you out of trouble. You'd do the same for me."

Apart from finding his trousers and keeping him from the blanket tossing, I'm not sure I was as useful as all that. I didn't want to turn their attention to me instead. But I passed over my trousers with a "Thank you." I was all thumbs with a needle and thread.

He poked a finger through the hole, then smoothed it down with a finger. "Who is it that you're always writing?"

"Clare. A friend." I stretched out on my bed. "She'll never be in the army. I have to keep her informed."

"Of course you do." He looked up and smiled. A balled-up pair of socks hit him in the side of the head.

"Mend these too, mam'selle!" followed.

Chaffre's smile tightened, but he bent and retrieved the socks from under my bed. "No problem."

Jeudi, le 15 janvier 1914

Dear Clare,

We're beginning to learn topography, and to that I say, at long last, something useful. Now, when the French army is out foraging for mushrooms, we'll be

222

able to find our way back to the battle.

We have our first set of examinations coming up, though what they'll be testing us on, I'm not sure. We've had recent lectures on mutual associations and beekeeping. Perhaps that? Poor Chaffre has been flipping through all of our books, worried that he'll get some crucial question wrong and disgrace his family forever and ever. I keep having to reassure him that as long as we can walk in a straight line and can spout off the tenets of the Republic, we'll be fine.

I tell you, Clare, I'm glad that this is all rather ridiculous. I'm not made to be a soldier. As a boy I was nervous just standing in front of the class to give a recitation. To stand and face someone across from a field of battle, to know that it's kill or be killed, I can't even imagine that. It's much easier to relegate worries like that to the dustbin now that I'm training to be a very patriotic mushroom farmer instead.

Luc

I found Chaffre out by the stables, sitting with his back against the wall. Blood trickled from his nose and an ugly bruise was already starting to spread up into his yellow hair.

"What happened, man?" I broke an icicle from the overhang of the roof and wrapped it in my handkerchief. "Who did this?"

He took the icy handkerchief with a grateful smile and pressed it to his head. "It's nothing. Honest. You should see the other guy."

"I will. Just tell me his name." I'd never thrown a punch in my life, but I would.

He straightened from his slouch and sighed. "I'm supposed to keep you from getting in trouble. I'm not going to send you into a fight."

"Oh, you're not sending me anywhere." I hoped I sounded confident. I was furious. "Look, you tell either me or the sergeant-of-the-week." I got an arm under him and pulled him to his feet.

He lurched against me.

I tightened my grip on his arm. "Steady there."

"Thank you," he said quietly. He exhaled. "It was Martel."

I left him on the bench outside and went up to our quarters, taking the stairs two at a time.

Martel was a mean, wiry fellow from the streets of Paris. He was probably also a full head taller than me. When I flew across the barracks at him, though, I didn't even think of that.

I managed a lucky punch before he realized what was going on, a punch that split his lip and made him yelp. Startled, I had no idea what to do next. I didn't expect to actually land a blow. He leapt up from his bed and I went the other direction. I wouldn't get another lucky shot.

The others, though, blocked my exit. They bunched in front of the doorway, cheering. Behind me I could hear the hobnails from Martel's shoes. I closed my eyes.

"What's all this?" someone bellowed. The sergeant-of-the-week pushed his way through the crowd at the door. "Line up!"

The shouts cut off as seventy-eight boys raced to stand at the foot of their beds, me included. Martel still stood in the middle of the room, blood dripping off his chin.

The sergeant sent a glare around the room before fixing on Martel. "What happened to you?"

Martel, the rat, lifted his face. "I was attacked, sir."

"By who?"

I bit the inside of my cheek but Martel stayed quiet.

The sergeant set his feet more firmly on

the ground and crossed his arms.

Martel shifted.

"I asked you a question, private."

From behind came, "It was me." Chaffre stepped into the room, holding his side. "Sir."

"You?" The sergeant looked little Chaffre up and down. The boy tossed in blankets, the one they couldn't lay off pranking. "You hit him?"

"What can I say?" Chaffre cracked a smile. "Clearly it was a lucky shot."

We all had to stand and listen to a lecture about respect and discipline and our moral duty to our fellow soldier. Chaffre didn't seem to mind; he wore that sly little smile. Martel looked like he swallowed a lemon. In the end, Chaffre was hauled off for a week in the camp's Salle de Prison, but not before he threw me a wink.

CHAPTER 13
LUC
1914

It had been a year since I'd been back to Paris and my old haunts, a year since I entered the army, but it felt like a decade. Back then my biggest worry had been whether I had enough sous left at the end of the week for a bottle of wine. Now, after July, the month of assassinations, the streets of Paris buzzed with uneasiness.

In the spring, Gaston Calmette, the fierce editor of *Le Figaro,* was shot six times in his office by the Minister of Finance's irate wife. Was that what France had come to, where the written word could drive someone to murder? And then, in June, the Austrian Archduke was assassinated in Sarajevo. Whispers were going through the barracks even before Austria declared war on Serbia. We polished our boots and wrote to our *mamans.*

Paris ran with emotion. All leaves had been canceled, but I wasn't the only one who bribed the adjutant sergeant and bought an overnight train ticket. I went by Uncle Jules's apartment to visit Véronique and the parrots. I needed to escape the whispers on the street.

No one dared breathe the word "war," but everyone thought it. Russia mobilized, the newspapers said. Would we? Walking down the Rue de la Montagne Sainte-Geneviève, I could feel eyes on me, on my uniform still crisp and officious. I kept my chin to my chest and wished I didn't have it on.

Then Jean Jaurès, the antimilitarist who was France's hope for staying out of the war, was shot over his dinner at the Café du Croissant.

Suddenly, the streets weren't as quiet. No matter what you thought of Jaurès, his death meant something. Some wrung their hands in relief. With Jaurès out of the way, we could push forward to war. And those who opposed it right alongside Jaurès, they mourned and they feared. All of Paris held its breath.

Maman, come to see me? I'd telegraphed. *I only have today.* Though she hated the city, she came with Papa. She brought me a rose from Mille Mots, a little reminder that somewhere in France it was the same summer it had always been.

As Paris waited, we sat in Café du Champion, waiting, too. Gaspard let us have the table in the back, the one I used to hunch over between shifts with my hurried suppers. Three untouched cups of coffee cooled. They'd pulled their chairs close, on either side of me, and held hands across the table. Maman blinked a lot, Papa cleared his throat and tugged at his beard, and I watched the door. When it happened, we'd know.

"Will you write to me, Maman?" I asked, not knowing what else to say to fill the silence.

Blinking away tears, she shook her head. "You're not going anywhere." She wore a little hat, tied through with pale blue ribbons. In it, she looked years younger. "You won't need me to write you."

Papa squeezed her hand. "She'll write to you. I promise."

"And if you happen to get any letters from . . ." I pulled the rose closer. "Well, if you do, will you send her my address?"

It had been too long since I'd heard from Clare. A year and a half and I still wrote her, but nothing came in return.

Maman caught tears on her cuff. "She'll write, *mon poussin.*" She straightened. "She'll write and tell you all about her

229

journey."

I didn't want to think about all of the reasons Clare might not return, all of the tropical diseases and ailments that could befall her. Malaria, trypanosomiasis, river blindness, dengue fever. Snake bites. Lions. Rushing rivers. Something could've happened years ago and I wouldn't know. Who would think to contact me? Who in the Laghouat general post office would do anything with the stack of waiting letters but throw them away?

A boy leaned around the doorway, panting. "Gaspard!" His hair hung sweaty on his forehead. "It's time."

Gaspard swung his towel up over his shoulder and came out from behind the bar. He looked grim. He had a son my age. He had every reason to look grim.

"Luc." Maman caught my hand as I stood. "Don't go," she said in English.

I kissed her forehead in reply.

Papa and I followed Gaspard out onto the street, to a freshly pasted poster. Above a pair of crossed tricolor flags, stark black letters announced: ARMÉE DE TERRE ET ARMÉE DE MER: ORDRE DE MOBILISATION GÉNÉRALE. Paste dripped down, smudging the handwritten date. Tomorrow we were to report to our units.

Crowds were starting to gather around the poster, men bleak-faced, women quietly clutching up the fronts of their coats. I swallowed and tried to pretend that I wasn't completely terrified.

Papa stood behind me, still tugging at his beard. It's what he always did when he was thinking far too hard about something. At forty-nine, he was still in the territorial reserves. I could see his fingers already tracing against the side of his leg. He would have to learn to paint war now.

"Papa . . ." I started. "I don't know . . ." But I couldn't say it. I couldn't confess, not to my papa who was French to his core, that I felt more fear than patriotism. That I was confused and exhausted and wanted nothing more than to lie in Maman's rose garden and sleep for a hundred years.

He clapped a hand on my shoulder. He didn't need me to say it. "Trust in France." He straightened his hat. "It's all we can do."

I wanted to believe him. I wanted to not be afraid of what came next. The past months of marching and studying and falling asleep in lectures, and we were no closer to being soldiers. And yet, with that paste-smeared poster on the wall, suddenly we were. Just like that.

With another long look at the poster, Papa

231

returned into the café, his fingers still tracing the side of his leg.

Around me I could hear sobs between the murmured chatter. Mothers held onto young boys' arms. Fathers stood stoically, looking everywhere but at the dripping poster. Sweethearts clung together, touching cheeks, faces, mouths. Straight down the street, a boy, much too young for the army, marched with a tattered flag above his head. "Viva la France!" he shouted.

Suddenly cold, I went back into the café.

Maman was gone. She must have slipped away while we were outside. Papa sat alone at our table, drinking the now ice-cold coffee. In front of him were two glasses of dark cognac and a bottle.

"She wanted to leave before you said goodbye."

I wouldn't have been able to turn and walk away from Maman's tears. "I understand."

"We must make a pact," he said, pushing one glass to me. "If we go, go quickly. For your *maman.*"

It was absurd. We both knew it. What was war if not messy? But we silently shook hands and picked up the cognacs. It was the sort of oath that men took when they didn't know what else to do. Words that masked helplessness. We drained the glasses in one swallow.

I looked to Gaspard, standing at the bar slicing cheese. He shrugged. "He bought the bottle. Have as much as you like."

I poured out two more and offered Papa a silent *santé.* "She'll be fine, won't she? Maman?"

He tugged at his beard. "She'd do better than you or I would if we were alone. Iron, she is."

"Even iron rusts."

He swirled his cognac and drank. "And it becomes more beautiful for the transformation."

I caught a drop on the side of my glass with my thumb.

"Luc, she left this for you." From his pocket, he took a ribbon, pale blue, from Maman's hat.

I remembered a boy with a faded ribbon, missing his *maman* terribly. I tied it around my wrist.

I finished my cognac and took the rest of the bottle to the counter at the front. "Gaspard," I said to the owner, "put the rest of this behind the bar. I know you have that hollow post, where you keep the good stuff hidden. Put this there." I dug all of my money out and put a handful of bills on the counter. "Please, Gaspard. When this is all over, we'll drink together. We'll toast to another day, conquered."

Gaspard sighed, but he took the bottle from me. "Keep your money. Just come back, you hear?"

Papa patted my shoulder and left without another word.

All of those letters I dutifully wrote to Clare, those letters piling up in Laghouat, waiting for a return that might never happen. All of those letters, waiting for an ending to our story.

I tore a blank page from the copy of *Germinal* in my jacket pocket. With the stub of a pencil, the words came out in furious scribbles, a place to direct all of my fear and confusion and anger.

Paris
Samedi, le 1 août 1914
The First Day

Clare,

I don't know where you are or if you'll ever read any of my letters. You're off on a quest, but now, so am I. Here, this day, I'm being called to take up my sword.

The princesses my father painted were always strong enough to take the scissors to their own hair. They waited for no one. Even before you came to Mille Mots, Papa was painting you. I don't have their courage. I don't know how my tale will end.

I once dreamed that my ending would include tennis championships. Paris or Scotland or somewhere farther. Teaching. Maybe you. But then I've had nothing from you these past months and I hate it. I hate not knowing if I'll ever hear from you again. If I'll ever again hike with you through Le Bois des Fées or hear you laugh or just watch you sketch, so serious and intense. But maybe remembering all of that, remembering our summer, is enough. I can think of no better standard to carry into war than the memory of your face.

Luc

CHAPTER 14
LUC
1914

I had Chaffre in my section, and thank God
for that. Because, when we ended up at
Ferme de Brindeau, four months after the
war began, I needed someone by my side.

We'd been moving closer to Enété for
weeks, I knew that, but when we went into
the woods and down the rise to the entrance
of the caves, I almost didn't recognize it as
the place I used to know. The ground where
I stood with eyes squeezed shut while Clare
lost herself inside, it was churned up into
mud from boots and hooves. The little spot
where I'd spread leaves to sit and draw,
horses were tied. It looked like any other
army camp, any other place for a few
thousand men to unshoulder their packs
and wring out their socks. It didn't look like
a fairy woods. It didn't look like the spot
I'd once thought ours.

And, on the ground above, where I was
used to seeing the backs of the farm build-

ings, white in the green of the woods, was rubble. Surely this wasn't the right spot. The constantly gray sky, the shell smoke obscuring the sun, a guy could get turned around. I must only think I was so near to Mille Mots.

But then I saw the crooked tree over the cave entrance, the tree Clare leaned against when she begged me not to ignore her. I knew I was in the right spot.

"You holding up there, old man?" Chaffre nudged me on. I hadn't realized that I'd stopped. "You look like you swallowed a cat."

"You made that up, didn't you?" I convinced my feet to start moving again. "Who swallows cats?"

He shrugged. "I think it works."

I briefly wondered where the farmer had gone, the farmer I'd never actually met, but after all of Maman's admonitions to stay off his property, imagined as stern Mr. McGregor from *Peter Rabbit*. I didn't know if he'd been Brindeau or if the name had been around longer than us all.

"Keep moving, you bastard." Chaffre poked me with the butt of his Lebel. "Or we'll all be sleeping out here."

But it wasn't just the memories suddenly flooding back that slowed my steps. Of course, it was that goddamned cave.

We didn't go in the front entrance that Clare would use when she wanted to be alone in the dark for a moment. We went around to the other side, through a narrow doorway, and down a set of chipped, uneven steps that led farther down into the gloom. I froze. On the stairs, my hand on the damp wall, I wouldn't go another step. It was only Chaffre's hand on my back that nudged me down.

I ducked under a low-hanging lintel. "Did it have to be caves? Did it have to be *these* caves?"

"Medieval quarries. Not caves. Stones were cut out of here by hand for the cathedrals." Chaffre lifted his hand, but he stayed close. "Have you always been this tall?"

"Have you always been this talkative?"

"Yes."

"I must've been desperate that night in the canteen."

"Stop closing your eyes. You're going to walk into a wall and the whole cave will collapse."

"Quarry." My eyes flew open. "It will?"

He grinned. "Joking. Really, though. Look around. You, of all people, should appreciate this." My gaze flicked up to the ceiling, wondering if it really would fall in on me.

"Not there," Chaffre said. "The walls."

I caught a hint of color and my breathing slowed. Tucked in the shadows was a carving. An altar hewed straight from the limestone and tinted red and yellow. *Dieu, guardez-nous* arched over the top in careful, blackened letters. *God keep us safe.* Beneath, a crucifix in relief.

"Down here?" I asked Chaffre in a whisper. Around me, soldiers' chatter had turned hushed. "What are they from?"

"Those who were here before, it seems." He reached out and ran a finger along the bottom of the altar, at the regimental number and the *1914.* "So they can forget for a while."

"Forget what?" I asked, but the line was already moving.

"What do you think?"

Chaffre and I had had our baptism of fire on the Marne. We stuck together and tried not to look too wild-eyed, for the other's sake. Stumbling forward, with bayonets fixed, we listened to the different shells, timing how long until they hit the ground. Chaffre was as nervous as a clam out there, ducking every time he heard a squeal tearing across the sky, no matter how far away. When a shell finally did come down nearby, it didn't make a sound. Or, if it did, my ears were deadened to the noise, to the whines and the screams and the raps. There was a streak of smoke and then the ground in front of us sprayed up. My insides turned to ice-cold liquid. It took a few seconds to realize that Chaffre'd been hit. Just a clod of dirt, but the size of an onion, and he went down.

I was terrified of the next shell, so I bent to get an arm under each of his. My pack, half as heavy as I was, threatened to tip me straight over on him, so I shed it. Murmuring, "Here now, you bastard," I hoisted him up and we stumbled back the way we'd come. I was fined for leaving my pack out there, and when I finally retrieved it, found nothing left in it but my can opener and a dry washcloth. All of my socks and tinned meat and old letters from Clare that I couldn't leave behind were gone. At least I still had that copy of *Tales of Passed Times,* the one I bought for Clare all those years ago. I carried it in my pocket the way others carried Bibles. With Maman's rose pressed dry between the pages, it was all the comfort I needed.

Chaffre was fine, apart from a blinding headache for a few days. I squatted by his hospital cot and whispered thanks that his rescue had kept me from thinking too hard about our baptism. We could both count ourselves through with it. With that initial clutch of fear over, we could count ourselves real soldiers.

Both sides settled into trenches, first shallow temporary affairs, then dug deeper, shored up, reinforced with duckboard and dugouts. If I'd been a lesser man, I'd have felt like crying. These were all the signs of a siege. I'd studied history for too many years to think that anyone ever came out of a siege a winner.

By the time we got to the Aisne, our uniforms were stiff with dried mud, that pale, chalky Picardy mud that clings to everything and refuses to wash off. That mud was in everything we ate, everything we drank, everything we touched. We no longer jumped at barrages or flinched at the light from a star shell. Chaffre carried a pocket shrine, a little case with a lead statue of the Virgin Mary. These days he kept her right in his pocket, rubbing in each prayer until her face was worn smooth. I touched the ribbon at my wrist and said my prayers to Maman.

Chaffre's face had lost some of its roundness, his cheeks some of their pinkness. All of us were weathered like the walls of the trenches, beaten by wind and rain and countless sleepless nights. Our uniforms were patched, stained, soaked through with the smell of war. We were tougher, too. Fear was replaced by weariness. It left Chaffre hard-eyed, me numb.

He took to watching my face more carefully, and I wondered if I'd aged more than he had. "What is it?" I finally asked one morning, as we slouched after a night raid. "Have I grown horns? Because I bayoneted a man who looked like my papa. I wouldn't be surprised if I had horns."

He quickly passed a hand over his face, wiped away whatever expression he'd let slip, and pushed out a grin. "Horns would be an improvement on that god-awful mug of yours."

I ignored him and pillowed my pack beneath my head. Sitting up against a trench wall, I'd sleep if given a half-quiet ninety seconds.

Chaffre spoke once more, softly. "You just look all done with this, Crépet."

Of course I was. I'd been done with this the moment the mobilization orders went up all over Paris. Without opening my eyes, I said, "Aren't we all?"

Now we were here, for a few days' rest in these caves beneath the battlefields. Poilus crouched around smoky fires along the ledges, warming tins of clumpy stew. The fires were more smoke than flame, but they bit the chill. The caves were dry and far enough beneath the ground that the sounds of war were muted. Instead we heard hushed voices, the snorts and nickers of the horses, the occasional echoed snatches of song. And, of course, the clank of hammer upon chisel and chisel upon stone. The cave was more than a barrack or a stable or a church. It was a refuge.

"Will you make one?" Chaffre asked as I stopped to run a hand over a picture of Marianne, Goddess of Liberty. It was carved straight into a stone pillar, tendrils of her hair wrapping around the plinth.

"Do you see how beautiful all this is?" I traced the edges of the carving with the side of my palm. "Not me."

"You always talk about how you come from a long line of artists."

And one of them a sculptor. Though Maman hadn't carved in years, I still remembered the shards of stone beneath my feet, the magic of watching a face appear in solid stone beneath her chisel.

I wrote to Maman, dutifully. I reminisced, I complained about the food, I quoted bits from her favorite poems. The sort of letters we all sent home. She wrote back cheery

243

notes of her own. This year her roses had lasted long into the fall. Marthe had a new recipe for galette that used very little butter. Oh, and did she tell me about the poor Belgian family she'd taken in?

But to Clare, I couldn't dissemble like that. The last letter I sent, the day the war began, fear and uncertainty made me write things I'd only ever thought. I didn't write to her again after that. I didn't know what to say. These battles, they were changing me from the boy under the chestnut tree to a grim-faced soldier. What was there to write? How could I tell her that the world we thought was so beautiful was rotten to the core?

And so when I sat back in the caves during that week of rest, reading, watching the artists at work, trying not to look at the ceiling, and Chaffre asked, "Will you make one?" all I could say was no. The soldiers who spent one day killing and the next carving altars and figures and spreading trees, they were sorted. They could separate the human and the machine within all of us. I wasn't there yet.

"Crépet, you think too much." Chaffre passed me a pair of sardines on the tip of his knife. "It's much simpler than that."

I swallowed the oily little fish and washed

them down with a swig of sour wine.

"You've heard of that Austrian fellow, right?"

"Was he that sniper?"

"Not here, in Vienna." He waved his hand and narrowly missed impaling me. "The doctor who asks people about their dreams and their childhood and then discovers that the root of all their problems is that they're in love with their own mothers."

"I seem to have missed that at school."

"These poor saps here, we don't need to ask them their dreams. The chap who carved the regimental insignia, he's hoping to be remembered a hero. The one who carved *la belle* Marianne, so noble and stately, well, he's missing his mother. Note that the one over there" — he pointed to a soldier drawing the curves of a nude woman with lamp black — "misses an altogether different sort of woman."

"And those who carved the altar?" That altar chipped out at the foot of the stairs, that crucifix carved above and a low kneeler beneath. On rainy days, when the stones of the caves seeped, Jesus wept.

"Those who've lost their faith," Chaffre said softly. "And those who are trying to find it again."

"Chaffre, what would you carve?" I finally asked.

"Hand me a chisel, and I'm as likely to gouge out my left eye as the stone wall." He tapped his chin. "My dog, Macquart. Most loyal bastard you'll ever meet. My mother said he's been sleeping at the foot of my bed since I left." He untied the canteen at his waist that held his daily ratio of *pinard.* "Or maybe a decent glass of wine."

"You wouldn't know a decent glass of wine if it crawled in bed with you."

His eyes twinkled above the rim of the canteen as he emptied it.

A lanky soldier, cap pulled low over his eyes, reached over and smacked the canteen from Chaffre's hands as he walked past. I flinched. It rattled off down the tunnel.

He grit his teeth until the other poilu passed. "Or maybe *Joyeuse.*" Charlemagne's legendary sword. "Would I be stronger?"

With bent head, I went to retrieve his canteen. *You are,* I wanted to say to him. *Sometimes I think you're stronger than me.* But I passed it to him with a nudge to the shoulder. "The strongest person I ever knew was a girl. I don't doubt that she could attack any man who looked at her sideways."

He looked wistful. "Clare?"

246

My smile slipped.

"And you?" Candlelight flickered on his face. "What would you carve?"

"Summer," I simply said. The one summer when the world was perfect. When I seemed right on the edge of the future. The one summer before things began slowly crumbling beneath my feet. "I'd carve summer."

CHAPTER 15
CLARE
1914

At first the post office told me that there were no letters. We'd been gone from Laghouat for almost two years. Surely something came in that time. Surely Luc had written. Oily black clouds were rolling in across the city and I begged Grandfather to ask again. To plead.

Finally the postal clerk, an elderly Algerian who probably wanted nothing more than to go home early and take a nap, sighed and shuffled back to wherever they stored years' worth of uncollected mail. Grandfather patted me on the shoulder. "They'll be there." I watched the minutes tick by on my watch, a splendid man's pocket watch bought from the junk market in Constantine that I wore on a chain around my neck. He patted me on the shoulder again. Outside, the sky rumbled. Grandfather began tapping his acacia walking stick. He didn't like to be wet. I shook my watch to be sure it was working.

Finally he shouldered his walking stick. *"Excusez moi!"* he called towards the back. "My good fellow! *Allô?*"

Date palms shuddered in the lift of wind.

The man finally came back, slowly, a small packet of letters in his hand. Not even enough for a canvas sack. "This is all we have. I spent much time looking." My watch would agree, but the crumbs of sugar littering his drooping mustache gave him away.

He handed them to Grandfather, but I pounced and thumbed through the meager stack. A few from the University of Glasgow, where he used to lecture, two from Mrs. Pimms, our ancient housekeeper in Perthshire, a half-dozen from friends of his ("Ah, young Toshie wrote?" he cried, seizing on one), and, at the bottom of the stack, one for me from Luc. One. Nearly two years, and only one letter.

The rain started as we left the post office. I held my one letter against my chest and ducked my head against the weather. Was it a dismissal? A disappointment? A hopeful finger-crossing? As we slipped in through our door and shook off our hats, I looked at the postmark. It had been sent four months ago, the day the war began. Spattered with rain, the envelope had transferred its ink onto my blouse.

I waved a hand at my ink-stained chest. "I should go see about . . ."

"Go." Too impatient to find a towel, Grandfather was drying his hair with a tablecloth. "I know you want to read your letter without an old man staring at you."

I fetched him a cotton towel from my little improvised washstand and then shut myself in my room.

The letter inside wasn't long, scrawled on one side of a thin yellowed page numbered xii in the corner. Luc, the rule-follower, had defaced a book for me. I slid off my stained blouse and sat on the bed in my camisole to read it.

The script was smeared from the rain. It couldn't be from tears, not with solid, dependable Luc Crépet behind the pen, but his words trembled. He must have written it the very moment war was declared. *I don't have their courage,* he wrote. *I don't know how my tale will end.* I wanted to reach through the paper, through the four missing months, and take hold of him. I wanted to tell him that I would be fine, that he would be fine, that someday we'd both return to Mille Mots and sit beneath the chestnut tree. Even if it was a lie. *I can think of no better standard to carry into war than the memory of your face.*

As if I could forget his. A day didn't go by in those two years that I didn't think of Luc, of the way he watched me with those owl-brown eyes, the way he always stood near me, close enough to touch, not close enough that I'd have to worry he would. He'd held my hand on four occasions; I could still remember the way my fingers felt in his.

I wrote to him. Of course I wrote to him. Piles of letters with our precious store of Alizarine ink and paper. I wrote about the seemingly endless camel rides, until my backside ached and my arms itched. The oxen with their curved horns that carried our boxes strapped to their humped backs. The pith helmet Grandfather bought me, like an inverted soup bowl. In it, I felt like a true adventurer. The round, grass-roofed huts where we stayed in each village. The dugout canoe we took down the Senegal River. The donkeys and goats and the one tame lion weaving in and out of the scattered buildings. The naked children standing in the mud at the river's edge. The carved wooden skull mask, traded from an old man along the river for a little sketch of France. The insects. Oh, God, the insects. The sudden fever, where, sweating on a bullock hide on the floor of a hut, I lost track of days. The letters that I planned to mail in one great stack when we reached Saint-Louis at the end of the river. The letters, all lost when one of our canoes overturned. I could only cling to Grandfather, soaked and still weak, watching them float away, one by one, in a trail of white squares.

When we reached Saint-Louis, we finally saw a newspaper. We heard what we hadn't in our meandering year and a half on the river, swatting away mosquitoes, sleeping in huts, and transcribing Berber. We heard that while we were gone, the world had gone to war. In a café, as French as any in Paris, we spread out newspapers and read while our bitter coffee grew cold. The newspapers were in French and out-of-date, so we read through weeks of news at once. Things growing tense in Paris, war declared, young boys marching from train stations in their uniforms of blue and red. Those first battles, in a rushed and bloody autumn — Tannenberg, the Marne, Arras, Ypres, the Aisne. So many other names, scattered across France and Belgium, that I cut a map from a newspaper and marked each and every one with a blot of ink.

Grandfather hung his head over the newspapers at that little café table in Saint-Louis. "Thanks to God that your father wasn't sent to this. Maud, she never could have borne keeping house by herself."

The first he'd spoken of my parents in years. "Mother has borne being alone for enough years, hasn't she?"

He curled his tattooed hands around the coffee cup. "Not the being alone, but the managing. Though Maud would never admit it, your father, he was a steadying influence. Without him, the household would have crumbled."

"But, without her, it did." I leaned back in my chair and spread my fingers wide on the café table. "When she left, Father did, too. He retreated into himself."

"Sometimes we need people without ever realizing it," he said, with a bowed head.

I ran my finger over my map and sent up a quiet prayer.

So many blots were near to the unassuming peacefulness of Mille Mots that I wrote to Madame immediately, asking for news. I didn't ask after Luc, but I hoped she'd read it through my words. I didn't know where to write to him.

Though I wished it was more, to find even that one letter from Luc waiting in Laghouat was more than I expected. Only one to let me know that, at the start of the war, he was still safe. Only one to let me know that he hadn't forgotten me.

I tucked it in my camisole, close to my heart, and buttoned on a fresh blouse. Out in the lounge, Grandfather, draped in a loose cotton robe, sat on one of the low sofas, his own letters spread out.

"This is a blessed mess. All of it." He ran a hand through his damp hair. He needed a trim. "Glandale says the classes are nearly empty. The school has sent all the boarders home. The German master — do you remember Grausch? — he was sacked. His replacement is teaching Flemish. Flemish!" He tossed aside a sheet of paper. "And Johns, his sons are joined up, all six of them. One lost already at Arras."

I pushed aside pillows and dropped onto the squashy sofa. A mug of tea steamed quietly by the brass pot. "Luc wrote."

He nodded. "And?"

I swallowed. "He's gone to war." I shrugged. "What did I expect?"

"A chance to realize what was happening. A chance to know there was a war on before he said goodbye."

I let my fingers trail over the scattered envelopes, strewn on the cushion between us. "You receive nothing but bad news, I receive a goodbye. All reminders of how the world changed while we were gone."

"Ah, it's not all bad news." He picked up an envelope. "I heard from Charles Rennie Mackintosh. You remember Toshie? Was a draftsman with your father at Honeyman and Keppie when they were apprentices."

Mr. Mackintosh was an architect of note and a familiar visitor at our house, all of those times he wanted to escape Glasgow to bemoan the lack of appreciation for bold architecture. "You knew him, too?"

"Not well." He traced the edge of the stamp. "I met him at your parents' wedding."

I poured myself out a mug of tea. Mint. "Kind of him to write."

"He's in Suffolk right now, but is putting together a little exhibit. With so many men gone, he thought to highlight the work of some of the women at the Glasgow School of Art."

I brought the mug up to my face and inhaled the sharp steam. "Mother loved it there, didn't she?"

"Maud was a whirlwind when she was feeling creative. Yes, she loved it."

"Then why did she leave school?"

"You know the answer to that. She met your father. She had you."

"She was only there for a handful of years. Less than that. How much could she have learned?"

"How much could *you* learn from one summer and a few missives?" He slid Mr. Mackintosh's letter back into the envelope. "She produced plenty. And that's why young Mackintosh wrote. He asked for permission to exhibit a few of Maud's pieces."

All of those times I'd watch Mother through the window, sitting in front of an empty easel. "Do any still exist?"

"They do." He crushed the envelope in his fist. "Ah, but they're at Fairbridge."

I pulled a pillow closer and tucked it up on my lap. "Grandfather, we've been away for a long time. At some point we need to stop wandering and return home."

"Home?" He tossed the letter next to the teapot. "The world —"

"Is our home. I know." I pressed my lips to the hot mug, took a scalding sip. "I don't want to return to Fairbridge any more than you do."

He exhaled. "I know." He stared out the window, at the rain falling straight down. "Staying away, it doesn't help. We can't avoid sorrow."

"Have the past three and a half years been sorrowful?"

He reached out and touched my hand. His

fingers were cold against mine. "Of course not. But things will change, whether we're there to see them or not. Look at what we missed while we were wandering in the wilderness."

"Not everything has changed. Some things are constant. Today is Christmas Eve."

"Ah, so it is."

"Merry Christmas, Grandfather," I said, and in my mind I sent out another. *Merry Christmas, Luc, wherever you are.*

CHAPTER 16
LUC
1915

Maman wrote to me of Christmas at Mille Mots. Her household had swelled to include three families of refugees — two Belgian and one French from near Saint-Quentin. Five children among them, so the hearth again had a row of shoes lined up, waiting for Père Noël to fill with nuts and candy. *Not like Christmas used to be,* she wrote. *We didn't have much of a* réveillon *feast. A goose couldn't be found in all the valley, but we had a pair of chickens stuffed with prunes. Oysters, chestnuts, a fine Bayonne ham I've been saving.*

My mouth, rusty with the taste of stale water and dried bread, watered.

The five little ones were worried they would be without Christmas this year, so far from their homes. The oldest amongst them is only eight and still has nightmares of his house burning. I hope to distract them. I gathered up the children and they helped me arrange the crèche. *They implored me, and so I brought in some clay from the garden and sculpted five new* santons *to tuck around the manger. Do you remember when we used to do that? How many shepherds in the* crèche *have the face of my Luc?*

She tried to sound dismissive, as though Christmas just wasn't what it used to be, and maybe it wasn't. But to me, reading her letter in between trudges through knee-high snow, through the half-frozen mud beneath, eating cold turnip and barley soup, my only carols the shells overhead, it sounded perfect.

Christmas passed by and, in the damp thaw of spring, I got leave, at last.

I arrived at a château edged in daffodils, ringing with the sound of laughter. Gray icicles melted from the roof. Overhead a swallow arched across the aching blue sky. Like a cool wash of water, the laughter, the yellow and blue, the soft dripping of the icicles, sluiced away the past ten months. In front of Mille Mots, I was cleansed.

As I stood on the front walk, breathing in tranquility, the front door pushed open. A boy in short trousers, followed closely by two curly-headed girls, tumbled out onto the lawn. He had one of my old footballs tucked under one arm, and the girls were in

259

hot pursuit. I watched as the children, pink-cheeked and laughing, disappeared around the side of the house.

"They remind me of you and Clare." Maman stood in the open doorway. "Younger, yes. But always off looking for adventure." There were new lines on her face, and had she always been so small? But she was Maman.

I stepped forward, uncertain.

"Mon poussin." Her voice broke with a little ripple. "Oh, my Luc."

I let myself be drawn into the peace of the château.

"Your papa is happy," she said later, as we walked arm-in-arm through the tangled hopefulness of the rose garden. The two Belgian women sang as they spread damp shirts on the lawn to dry. "Is that strange, to find satisfaction in war?" Children's shouts drifted from the riverbank.

"He's doing what he loves. And, besides, they all say that La Section Camouflage is a cushy job."

She frowned. "Cushy?"

"One of those colonial words that the Tommies use." I shrugged. "It means easy, soft, comfortable."

"Easy?" She bristled. "Claude's work isn't

easy. It's important."

"Of course." I stepped carefully around a fallen bird's nest. "On the battlefields, men are right out there in the open, for God and the Germans to see straight and clear. There needs to be a way to camouflage that."

"It's the perfect job for him." She tipped her face up to the sun. "Art, innovation, and the discipline of the army."

It was perfect. So perfect that, at times, I was envious. While I crawled through barbed wire and slept on dirt and loaded my rifle with cold-numbed fingers, Papa was in a well-lit room behind the lines, painting and drawing and designing, all in the name of patriotism.

"Both of you are staying safe, that's all that matters." She gave my arm a squeeze. "You're not so near to the front lines, are you?"

Carefully worded letters gave that impression, I knew. I didn't intend to be deceptive, at least not at first. But I didn't want Maman to worry. So I wrote about the food ("not nearly as good as Marthe's"), the conditions ("rainy, but hoping for a break in the weather"), the uniforms ("finally, they've replaced the *garance* red!"), and the future ("when this is all over, Cairo? You've always wanted to see the pyramids"). I

261

didn't tell her anything that was really happening.

"Not so near," I lied, glad she wasn't looking at me. "Really, it's almost . . . cushy."

She nodded with satisfaction. "And have you seen your papa often?"

There were soldiers stretched across half of France. Had she not read a newspaper in eight months? Not once looked at a map? "Maman, no. He's in a different unit. He's posted near Nouvons and I'm . . ." I couldn't tell her how near to Mille Mots I was. "I'm somewhere else."

A furrow appeared at the edge of her brow.

"But I hear much about the *camoufleurs,*" I said in a rush. "And once I even saw a group of them. They'd built a tree stump, all out of metal, but painted to look like bark and smoke and battlefield ruin. They brought it out to our line."

"A tree stump? I thought they were painting barricades or designing uniforms." She frowned. "Why would they need a tree stump?"

"A listening post? A sniper perch?" I shrugged. "Nobody tells me. But I saw them with that make-believe stump. They came in the dead of night to spirit it out into No-Man's-Land."

"No-Man's-Land . . ."

"That's the space between the trenches. That's where the fighting is. It's where the camouflage is needed most."

She ground to a halt. "*Cher* Claude, he goes so close to the battles?" Her face had gone gray as smoke. "But isn't it dangerous?"

Dangerous would be more than tiptoeing out to place a fake tree stump. Dangerous would be going full into the zone between the trenches, weapon drawn, waiting for the shots directed at you. It would be creeping with half an ear on the shells in the sky, half an eye on the guy next to you, half a heart on your mission ahead. It would be leaving behind anything personal, any letters or photos or incriminating addresses, on the chance that you were captured and put everything you loved at risk. Dangerous would be what I did every day out there. "Not at all."

She suddenly threw her arms around me, an uncharacteristically desperate gesture. I hadn't told her about the splinters up and down my back, the ones left after a tree had shattered next to me. The nurses didn't have time to get them all. As Maman's fingers clutched my neck, I winced. She felt the tension and pulled back.

"Luc?" she asked, searching my face.

Her hand was still on my back, and I bit my tongue. "It's nothing," I said. "Just a little sore, I suppose. A soldier's life."

She twisted me around and peeled back the top of my collar. I didn't know what it looked like but I knew what she was seeing when she gasped. Against my shirt, my back felt like a porcupine.

"It's nothing, really," I said. "Only splinters. I used to get them all the time, remember?"

She took off her glove and felt underneath my collar. Her fingers were cool, like when I was a little boy and came to her, ill, scared, heartbroken. Sitting near, smelling like La Rose Jacqueminot and comfort, those cool fingers stroking my face and arms and back were better than any medicine. There was a lump in my throat and I didn't know how it got there.

"My boy," she said. And, at that moment, that's all I needed.

Maman had the copper bathtub brought up to Papa's studio, where the afternoon light stretched yawning across the room. I couldn't lay in it, not enough to soak my whole back, so I sat on the floor in front of her chair. She dipped a washcloth into the warm saltwater and held it against my skin

264

until some of the splinters, soft, worked their way to the surface.

"I saw something in your face, you know." She squeezed the cloth in the basin and brought it again warm against my back. "I've always known when you were lying to me."

"Maman, I'm not. I just —"

"Shhh."

Water dripped down the curve of my spine. "It's really not as bad as it seems."

"Is that what you think?" Her voice was tight. The heat of the washcloth disappeared. "That this seems somehow worse than it is? I'm picking wood out from my baby."

I'd seen men leave pieces of themselves on the battlefield. All of themselves. I didn't answer her.

Around me were the shapes of my childhood. The skeletons of easels. Neat stacks of canvases. Moth-eaten armchairs and scroll-armed sofas. A tarnished cauldron. The head of a papier-mâché dragon. The trunks of costumes, the garishly painted swords and helmets, the swirls of silk scarves tied here and there. The props of a theater, in the studio of an artist. I'd grown up within it.

"I come up here more often these days."

265

Maman dropped the washcloth into the basin with a soft splash and picked up a pair of curved tweezers. "I know that things are dreadful out there. It's a war, after all." I bent my head closer to my crossed legs. "But here, safe in the château, surrounded by the beauty of Claude's art . . . I can forget."

For a quiet space of an afternoon, so had I.

"I try," I finally said. I felt her tweezers against my back. "There's art, even where I am."

She paused. "Truly?"

"When we're *en repos,* we stay —" I caught myself before I revealed troop movements. "We stay in a rocky area. Some of the men, they carve straight into the rock. The sound of the chisels against the stone, the smell of broken limestone, it all makes me . . . it makes me feel like I'm home again. Like I'm a boy again sitting beneath the worktable in your studio."

Behind me, Maman had quieted.

I cleared my throat, embarrassed at my little admission. "There's some real talent there. Men carving things that could find a place in Monsieur Santi's gallery or one of the others on the Quai du Voltaire."

She tapped the tweezers against the side

of the basin.

"Insignia, rolls of honor, tapestries in stone. Memories of the things they left behind." I rubbed at the damp hair at the nape of my neck. "One solider has been working on a wall with an allegory that would impress even Papa. Dancing peasants, toppled towers, swans, laurels, falling moons, Death crowned in crows' feathers. Every time we are *en repos,* he adds a little more to the wall."

"What have you carved?" she asked.

"Nothing." I tensed as her tweezers found a deep-seated splinter. "I don't know how to do that. I'm not the sculptor in the family."

"You've watched me enough. You know the technique. And you've always been able to see beyond the two-dimensional."

I didn't tell her how my fingers traced the grooves in the stone walls, how they twitched to pick up a chisel, how they once drew Mille Mots in the dust on the floor of the caves. "I can't." A soldier who was never really an artist to begin with, he had no business taking up space on the walls of the cave. He wasn't the person to leave a memorial behind. "But you could sculpt. You should. You used to be magnificent."

I thought she'd bristle at the instantly

regretted "used to," but she was pensive today. "I've thought about it. After I made those little clay *santons* for the children at Christmastime, it was like something had been reawakened. I hadn't sculpted in years, you know."

"I know." I looked around Papa's studio, where she'd moved her tools all those years ago, where there'd always been a block of granite, half roughed out. It was all still there, the block covered over by a dust-choked cloth. "Then why haven't you?"

She didn't say anything for a moment. "It was so long ago. My art was a piece of my past, a piece that I had to put away as I grew up."

"Papa never asked you to."

"He didn't have to." Her words were steady, but her tweezing became more fierce. "He needed me at the desk, managing things. I knew that. The household needed someone not always lost in a fairy-tale world."

I turned. "Do you know why I never wanted to enter art school? Why I never sought that future?"

The sunlight touched her graying hair with gold.

"It was because you stepped out of that future and into another. You put art aside in

268

favor of practicality. I grew up watching you make do with Papa's art rather than make your own. And be happy with it."

"I was happy."

"Did Papa and the household need you all that much?"

She stopped and put the flat of her hand against my back. "You needed me."

"Not anymore." I caught her hand. "I'm grown. I'm gone. Why not now?"

"You come to me with a back full of splinters, and then you tell me you're grown and gone." She took my shoulders and turned me around. "You still need me."

I'd spent all these months protecting her, hiding from her the dangers I faced every day. Dodging shells and death, and then writing to her about last night's cabbage soup.

She searched my eyes. "Luc, stay." Her grip on my shoulders tightened. "I'll watch you, I'll hide you, I'll keep you safe." Her voice cracked. "Please."

Instead of answering, I stood and went to the shelf where her old tools waited, shrouded. I took down the bundle, wrapped in soft cloth, and unrolled it on the floor in front of her. A dozen narrow chisels, a mallet, rasps and rifflers. Tools that hadn't been touched in a decade and a half. She watched

269

them warily.

"Take them up again." I picked up the slender point chisel and opened up her hand. "In all of this ugliness, you need a weapon. You need to find beauty."

She closed my fingers around the chisel. "I think perhaps you need it more than I." Her hand wrapped around mine, around the faded ribbon still tied, and she pinched the inside of my wrist. A silent entreaty to stay safe and do my best. To be a good Crépet.

"I promise, Maman."

CHAPTER 17
CLARE
1915

I hadn't been to Fairbridge since Grandfather fetched me from Mille Mots and brought me to Scotland, those four years ago. We hadn't stayed long — enough for Grandfather to settle some of Father's business affairs, to buy an ecstatic supply of Horlicks, and to set me packing up my childhood into a single trunk. By the time I'd set aside my full mourning, we were on our way to Portugal.

Not that I had much of a say in it, but I'd told Luc it was because there was nothing left for me in Perthshire. Really, though, it was another lie. I hadn't been back home in all that time because I was afraid. Afraid I wouldn't be able to walk through the house without remembering.

And I did. How could I help it? Every chair I sat in had once held my mother or father. Every rug bore the ghost of their footprints. I drew a finger over the edges of the straight-backed sofas, the inlaid tables, the high, airy bookcases. All modern furniture that Mother brought into the house "to breathe life into things." The only things Father brought were his heavy desk, burnished black at the edges where he'd rest his elbows while he drew, and the armchair in the corner of his study that he kept just for me, for those moments when I wanted to be near him and his quiet.

But memory can be a fickle thing. Life at Fairbridge wasn't as warm as my nostalgia. The hallways looked darker than I remembered, the curtains more stifling, the air lethargic. Everything, from the rugs to the furniture to the damask wallpaper, was so neat and solid, things meant to last longer than fashion. All of Mother's airy modern furniture looked as out of place as she had been. On Father's desk there was a ring from his ever-present whisky glass. I walked the hallways, past walnut tables and plush stools, wondering how I once found it all beautiful. How had I ever breathed here?

The curiosity room had been left to grow dusty. I pulled back the curtains and blew on the shelves until the air shimmered with motes. Now that I'd traveled so much, I saw many of the items for what they really were. Some were inauthentic, tourists' fare, the sort of claptrap things sold at train stations and bazaars for people to send home to their granddaughters. Others I now recognized as commonplace — curved acacia seed pods, flamingo feathers, the tiny snail shells that littered the banks of the Senegal River. This room that awed me and comforted me as a child was now little more than a collection of junk. Years ago it had given me a peek of faraway places; now I'd actually been there and seen so much more.

Grandfather felt it, too. I found him in the hallway, fingers laced behind his back, staring at the wall of paintings. "It feels different." He sighed. "I suppose enough time had passed."

Though the house was his, he'd spent so little time in it during my childhood. I remembered occasional visits from a near stranger. I was prodded and instructed to call him "Grandfather Muir," but I scarcely recognized him. On those visits, he spent more time pacing the grounds and sleeping than he did sitting next to me and talking. I knew him now, knew that shyness kept him tongue-tied and that those solitary rambles were where he worked through theories in his head.

"It has been four years, after all."

Eyes still on the wall, he said, "Forty-seven."

"Forty-seven?"

The painting he stared at was of a man at a desk, young but wrapped in a jewel-red paisley shawl as he read. Curls of pencil shavings caught in his cuffs and ink stained his fingertips. In the window behind him was a dusty, treeless street.

"Your grandmother painted that. We were in Tangier, newly married."

"My grandmother?"

He smiled, sadly. "You come by it honestly. She amazed me."

"She painted others?"

"Many. She sold four of them, you know." He touched the signature, tucked against the leg of the desk. "She always signed her paintings 'Alasdair' instead of 'Alice,' so that no one would know she was a woman."

I looked down the hallway, at paintings I'd grown up seeing yet not really *seeing*. In each, the little "Alasdair M." hidden somewhere within the picture. Desert-swept landscapes, crowded marketplaces, doe-eyed women in scarves and veils. All of the things that I'd tried to paint and draw myself. She'd captured Africa.

"You were traveling, even then."

"A little. Not as much as we wished. She

274

liked Tangier best."

"That's what she painted here?"

He traced the curved window in the painting, over the shoulder of his younger self. "We stayed in an old monastery. Alice loved the quiet, the lingering smell of candles, the rusting bell high in the chapel tower. She used to say she could still hear the hymns caught in the stone."

Some of that mysticism, that hazy overlay of history, infused her paintings. I smiled.

"But when Alice found that she was expecting, she asked to come back to Fairbridge. She teased that she wanted her baby born under a Scottish rain, but I knew she was scared. Almost as if she knew. I lost her when Maud was born. She didn't have the chance to hold her baby."

"But you did." I took his arm and led him backwards to a stool.

"I didn't know what I was doing." He ran fingers through his thin hair. "I filled the house with nurses and nannies, tutors and governesses, dancing and drawing masters." He sighed, as if it wasn't enough. "Maud saw more of them than of me."

"She knew you cared." It seemed to be the right thing to say.

He shrugged. "She was willful and stubborn. She hated that I spent more time with my books than with anything else."

I'd followed him down the Senegal River. I knew how focused he could be on his books and notes, as focused as Mother always was on her regrets and lost dreams. I also knew that he loved me. Mother had left me behind; Grandfather always kept me by his side.

I had wasted so many years wishing Mother would come back and that Father would step out from his study. So many years wishing I had a real family. And here, in this thoughtful, slightly absentminded old man, I'd found it. I no longer scanned passing faces, hoping to see hers. I had his.

"I always worried that I didn't do right by Maud." He rubbed the sun on the back of his hand with a thumb. "I thought to teach her the comforts of home. But she left anyway."

"She wasn't happy," I said. I knew that. All of her dismissals when Miss May brought me down to recite my lessons. All of her sighing over empty easels she'd never fill. Her icy disregard of Father, the house, our "dreary convention." "She chose one life and then wanted another."

I refused to do the same. When I chose, I wanted it to be for good. I didn't want to live a life tinged with regret.

"I just want you to know that I did my best." He turned from the painting then. "I never loved her as much as she wanted to be loved. I failed her and, because of that, failed you."

I thought of countless little affections, things he probably did without thinking. Leaving me the underripe apricots, my favorites. Sitting in the shadows to give me the best view from the window. Bringing back any English novel that turned up in the booksellers' stands. Never asking about the sudden floods of tears that came on rare occasions, but always having a cup of tea waiting at the end. Knowing, at any moment, when I needed him most.

"Grandfather," I said, "you didn't fail."

He shrugged. "I was given two little girls. Both needed a mother, not a restless scholar. Maud, I kept here in Perthshire, where we both stagnated in this house, where we both spent far too long resenting one another. You, I uprooted and dragged off across the deserts."

"And gave me the world." I dropped a kiss on top of his head. Again, he needed a haircut. "Look at how I've grown, Grandfather. I can speak three languages. I can barter just as well for a mule or a handful of olives. I can row and hike and argue with any phonologist." I tightened my hands on the back of his chair. "Once I was vulnerable; I'll never let anyone be stronger than me again."

"No, my girl." He reached over his shoulder and caught my hand. "I don't believe you will."

"We're not done with the world yet. Grandfather, we're only here for the time being."

He leaned back in his chair and sighed. "Forty-seven years," he said again, his face creased with anguish.

I could see the hallway as he did, hung with paintings showing a brief, ecstatic marriage, framed around with a love that had never died.

"Art," I said, "is a chance to capture a fleeting heart's impression onto paper and canvas." I rested my fingertips on his shoulders. "It's a memory, caught up with charcoal, an emotion, caught up with paint. In a gallery like this, we're not surrounded by ghosts. We're surrounded by the chronicle of a life."

"Then let me show you your mother's."

Mother's pictures were so unlike anything that my grandmother or I did.

"Maud was a designer." Charles Rennie

Mackintosh set his glass of port carefully to the side of the table. "She designed furniture, mantelpieces, the most elegant end tables. She was brilliant."

The sketches were all pen-and-ink, with clean, deliberate, yet fanciful lines, washed in with pale watercolors. A straight-armed dining chair with a back like a soaring castle. An end table crouched like a troll. A headboard curving across like a basilisk's serpentine neck. Her designs, they were fairy tales brought to life in everyday objects.

"I never saw her create anything," I said. "I thought she left that all behind in Glasgow."

"She was prolific at the School of Art," said Mr. Mackintosh. "Saw the world through a wistful glass. Everything that came from her pen was beautiful." He nodded towards the drawings in my hands.

I handed him the stack, somewhat reluctantly. I'd only just found them, these drawings of my mother's, these traces of her. She'd never shared them with me, no matter how often I had asked.

And yet Grandfather knew where to look for them. Up on top of Mother's wardrobe, hidden by the crown molding, was a flat wooden box marked with my grandmother's initials. "Where Maudie always hid things as a girl," Grandfather told me. With the dust on top, the box might have been there since her wedding day.

They were old, but the colors still vibrant. "Ah, but she did good work." Gently, Mr. Mackintosh turned through the pages. "But when her favorite instructor left, Maud lost something." He paused at a sketch of a chair I swore I'd seen before. "It was as though she lost her confidence along with her mentor."

I reached for the sketch. The chair was heavy, square, with carved dragons' heads on the arms. I'd seen it before in a painting. A chair fit for a queen. "It was more than that," I said softly. "She lost a friend."

From his seat on the sofa, Grandfather watched.

"I introduced her to your father," Mr. Mackintosh said. "I thought she'd begin drawing again. Designs to complement his buildings."

"It was a good idea, lad," Grandfather said, though the "lad" was as gray as he was.

"Did she ever build her designs?" I asked.

Grandfather shook his head. "Maud always said they were nothing but a lark."

"Ah, but if she was still at the School of Art when I was working on Kate Cranston's tea rooms!" Mr. Mackintosh was wistful. "If she was willing to see it as more than a lark!"

"As good as she was, she never took design seriously," Grandfather said. "She always said it wasn't 'real art.' She wanted to illustrate like Claude, sculpt like Rowena."

Mr. Mackintosh harrumphed and picked up his port.

"This is as real as I've ever seen her." I pulled over one of Mother's sketches, a dining table with legs twining out from the floor like vines of roses. "This one, I think. It shows a piece that belongs so much that it grows from the house." I handed it to Mr. Mackintosh.

He nodded. "I was going to suggest the same. Young Clare has an eye."

Grandfather settled back onto the sofa with his pipe. "She does. You should see her work."

Mr. Mackintosh lifted an eyebrow. "I shouldn't be surprised. Maud's daughter, of course you'd be drawing."

"She draws, she paints. She's even sculpted with clay from the banks of the Senegal River. Clare, run and get your portfolio."

I wanted to tell my grandfather that I was too old to run, that we'd long since passed the stage where he could instruct me, that I didn't even have a portfolio. But the small hopeful part of me that sent Luc the occasional drawing, just to see what his father had to say about it, that part of me went up to my room for the cracked leather case that had traveled Iberia and northern Africa clutched to my chest. That part of me held my breath while waiting for Mr. Mackintosh's pronouncements.

He looked through the stack — charcoal sketches, oil paintings, soft watercolors of the sunrise over the desert — and then spoke directly to Grandfather. "Do you need help with her application?"

"It's a good fit for her."

"I can see the potential."

"She's had a little instruction."

"I can see, but it's raw and fumbling."

"Still, it's a good fit."

"Please," I broke in. "Are they really that bad? What's a good fit?"

Mr. Mackintosh blinked. "The Glasgow School of Art. Your grandfather wishes to enroll you."

I looked to Grandfather, whose eyes were already evasive. "You mean to be rid of me so that you can leave again." I reached over the table, gathering up my drawings. "Well,

I won't go. Someone needs to take care of you."

"Clare," he protested, clapping his hands down on the painting nearest him, a fantasy piece I'd painted of Luc sitting in the curve of a Marrakesh doorway. "I'm not trying to rid myself of you. I'm trying to do what's best for you."

I tried to tug the paper from under his splayed palms, but it began to tear in the corner.

"Of all the women in my life, given the opportunity of art school, you'll make the most of it. Clare, you're already a traveler. You won't be satisfied until you've seen how far you can go."

"But Grandfather, I know you, too. I know you'll be back on the trail of one dialect or another the moment I'm in Glasgow. You won't be able to stay alone in this empty house."

"I'll stay." He said it, surprised with himself. "Do you hear? I will. As long as you come back to visit, as often as you're able, I'll stay." He shrugged. "I have to start writing the book eventually, don't I?" He lifted his hand from the painting and let me take it. "The two of us, we've been through French West Africa and back. We've braved crocodiles and malaria and eating nothing but goat for weeks. And now . . . now it's time for the next adventure."

"Us explorers, we have to stay together," I said, taking up my painting of Luc.

CHAPTER 18
LUC
1917

On Bastille Day a unit of German gunners was taken prisoner. They'd been harrying our line for weeks and were escorted back to Brindeau amid hurled insults. They were lined up on the parade ground — a P.G., for *prisonnier de guerre,* chalked onto their jackets — and then shoved into a crumbling cellar, our makeshift camp prison, until they could be moved. We all hoped the ceiling would come down on them.

They were kept without water or food for the rest of the day. It began raining mid-morning, but only mud seeped through the stones of their prison. The Germans bore it in stoic silence. When I came to the cellar with a petrol can of the same oily-tasting water we all drank, all I was greeted with were sullen stares.

I stood in the doorway, waiting for them to come forward. Better that then stepping down into the cramped, low cellar full of

Boche. But they stayed hunched around the edges of the room. No one stood. No one even looked up. Muddy rain dripped from the ceiling.

"Yeah, they don't deserve it." The guard nudged me with the butt of his Lebel. "Just get down there and then get out."

I took a deep breath and stepped down the stairs.

I'd been given a can, but no tins for drinking. The prisoners had been stripped of anything apart from the clothes on their backs. I summoned up my long-disused German. *"Wölben Ihren Händen,"* I instructed, sloshing through the mud. A rat skittered out of my way. One of the Boche cupped his palms for a handful of water, but the rest ignored me. They sat with knees up, battered and bruised from the capture, indifferent.

Except one, hatless, filthy, bleeding, who grabbed my ankle as I shuffled past. "Wait," he croaked in French. He tipped his head up and, through the black eye, the swollen jaw, the mud-gray hair, I knew him. "Crépet," he said. "Sorry I missed the Olympics."

I stumbled. "Stefan Bauer?"

He licked chapped lips and nodded.

"Stefan Bauer?" I asked again, unwilling. This hollow-eyed man couldn't be Bauer, couldn't be the glowing, arrogant boy I used to face across the net. Bauer, always so sophisticated and sure. The boy I'd known would never look so defeated. He'd sooner . . . well, he'd sooner die.

Then I remembered what they'd said when they brought the prisoners in, that the tall one had fought furiously rather than surrender, swearing in French all along. Gaunt as he was, his back was straight. He could be that same boy.

"It's really you?" My mind moved like marmalade. "Here? Now?"

"Aren't we all?" He sank back and rested elbows on his knees. It was a sigh of a movement. "These days, nowhere else to be."

"You're talkative tonight, *le Flemmard,*" the guard said from outside the cellar.

Bauer stiffened, so I said, "It's me he's calling 'lazybones.' " I switched to German. "We said we'd meet in Berlin in 1916. Instead, here we are." I held up my can of water.

He cupped his hands. "A Frenchman wouldn't have exactly been welcome in Berlin." Most of the water splashed through his fingers.

I tipped the can back up. "I was busy last year."

He opened his hands and let the rest of

the water soak into his lap. I'd been busy, yes, killing his countrymen. A faded black and white striped ribbon, from an absent Iron Cross, was sewn to the front of his tunic. From his side of the line, he'd been doing the same.

One of the other Boche scowled and said, "Who's this frog-eater you talk to like a friend?"

I started, spilling water down my leg. I hoped the guard outside hadn't heard.

Bauer, though, growled out something that the German master at school hadn't taught us, something that earned him a glare and a muttered oath in return.

I backed up, towards the doorway. The water can banged at my shins.

"Wait." Bauer scrambled to his feet. "A familiar face I never thought I'd see. Crépet, will you come back?" This time he spoke in English, the third language we shared, the one that neither the guard outside or the prisoners inside knew. "We can talk about old times." His English was better than I remembered.

I shifted the can to my other hand. "I shouldn't. I can't." Out in the sunset, the rain slowed. "I . . . I don't have a reason to come back."

"A letter." His eyes were earnest, bright.

"You can bring me paper and ink." He nodded, suddenly looking as boyish as he did when I last saw him, five years before. "I want to write a letter to my mama. Do you remember how often I'd write to her?"

I did. "Every week."

"I always told her what our score was. What was it at that last match?"

"I don't remember," I lied.

"I was winning, wasn't I?"

It was 299-299. "We were tied."

"Crépet, won't you say you'll come back?"

I couldn't. Without a goodbye, I left into the drizzly sunset.

Chaffre was in the caves, sleeping. I tiptoed around him, but he woke, the way he always did when I was near. "Is it mess time already?" he asked with a yawn.

"No." I realized I was still holding the water can, and set it down with a slosh. "I don't know."

"I wouldn't want to miss a mouthful of cold soup." He stretched out first one arm, then the other.

"Stop complaining." I took off my cap and tossed it in the direction of my pack. "Some don't have anything to eat tonight."

"I know that." Chaffre nudged me. "Has it been too long of a week for a joke?"

"I'm sorry." I ran a hand through my hair.

"Don't mind me. Yes."

"Now you're getting this all dirty." He yawned again and picked up my dropped cap. As though it could get any dirtier. "I'll shake it out. It's wet." He was fussing again. He did that when he was worried.

"Stop that. Everything's wet and dirty."

"You should've worn your helmet anyway."

"I forgot."

"They look like brutes, didn't they?" He brushed at the hat. "Remember the helmet next time."

I took the damp cap back. "You worry more than my mother." I pulled a punch on his arm. "I'm fine."

He ducked his head. "I know."

I wrung the cap out. I knew it wouldn't dry. "Can I ask you about something?"

He nodded, but bent to fiddle with his bootlaces.

Just as steadfastly, I refused to meet his eyes. "Someone you haven't talked to for a long time should sound different, right? Even when you haven't heard from them in years?" I set the cap on top of my pack, smoothed it out. "But when they don't, even though they should, and when you want to listen to them, even though your very insides shout out that things have changed

290

and you've drifted too far apart . . . Chaffre, what then? Do you move on? Or do you remember your years of friendship?"

He stood. "Is that it?" The edges of his eyes relaxed. "And here I thought there was something really worrying you."

I shifted. "And this isn't?"

"For years I've been hearing nothing but 'Clare in the deepest reaches of Africa.' " He said it almost wistfully. "She writes, finally, and you're upset?"

"No, it's . . ."

"You knew Clare so long ago, back when things were . . . quiet. Does it remind you of then?"

Though he had the wrong person, he had the right idea. Yes. This Stefan Bauer — battered and beaten, yet not defeated — I recognized. We'd meet on the courts, playing through rain and exhaustion, ignoring our books for just one more match. Refusing to give up. So like Clare, focusing on her art. She set off to capture the world with her pencil, to soak in as much life as she could. Seeing Bauer again, hearing Clare's name, I was reminded of a time when everything was easier. I was reminded of a time when I didn't think I could stumble. "You're right," I said.

"Ah," he sighed. "Those happier days."

They weren't all happy. I thought of the months between commissions, when Marthe tried to make the soup stretch and the wind blew through the cracked window in my bedroom. Clare, arriving at Mille Mots alone, hiding her mourning. Searching for a mother who didn't want to be found. That one night she spent in Paris, the night she refused to talk about. Maybe not all happy, but they had to be better than this.

For a brief instant I felt alive. A surge — furious, frustrated, futile — ran through me. "We can't go back, can we?"

He shook his head, a distant look in his eyes. I wondered what he was remembering. "What did you once call it? Summer." He gave an almost wistful smile. "But we can do our best not to forget it." It was his turn to chuck me in the arm before he left.

For the first time, I borrowed a piece of charcoal and began sketching on the wall. I had to stop a dozen times and smudge out errant lines, but I drew. In those curves and whorls on the limestone, I found my way back to myself.

Summer, Chaffre said. For me, it was Clare who I thought of when I heard the word. That summer, our summer, the last time the world had felt completely and perfectly right. Though it was July now, it felt a thousand miles and a thousand years from then.

For a little while I was able to forget the noise aboveground. The ruin and the cries and the death on the distant lines. The slumped exhaustion down here in the caves. I didn't want to think about my friend, who I never thought I'd see again, up in that cramped husk of a prison just because he'd been on the opposite side of the battlefield. I didn't want to think about my comrades — who I'd bedded down next to, eaten cold soup with, marched, weary, alongside — who had fallen beneath that friend's gun. I drew furiously and forgot.

Chaffre returned with a tin of soup, gray and oily, but I wiped charcoal-black fingers on my trousers and kept my eyes fixed on the wall.

Behind me he quietly watched. His spoon scraped in his tin. "This is something," he finally said. "I didn't know you could draw like that."

I wiped my forehead with the back of my hand. "Neither did I."

He was silent for another space. "What's really eating you, then?" He moved around to my side, close to the charcoal-streaked square of wall. "What's bad enough to get you to draw, after all this time?"

All of this, I wanted to say. All of this destruction, this suspicion, this fighting for nothing we could see and even understand. But, "I'll tell you tomorrow," was what I said.

He clapped a hand on my shoulder. "I hate it, too."

When he left, I dug deep within my pack for Maman's roll of chisels and rasps. The metal was as cold as the bayonet hanging at my side, but each nick along its length was familiar. I remembered afternoons of watching Maman at her stone, singing as she hammered. The tools were battered, but lovingly so, from everything that took shape beneath her fingertips. The bayonet destroyed, but the chisel in my hands, it created.

And so I stood in the caves that echoed with song and laughter and restless horses, eyes stinging with the smoke from oil lamps, and took a chisel to my sketch. I carved the limestone walls and tried to pretend that I hadn't changed like Bauer had. I wanted to still be the boy who'd sketched in Maman's rose garden, the same boy who'd been afraid of caves and dragons and kisses under poplar trees. I swung the hammer harder, drove the chisel deeper, knowing that I wasn't that boy. I knew I'd become the same thing that Bauer had. I couldn't turn back.

I tucked the chisel into my belt, right next to my bayonet. From my pack, I took a stub of a pencil and the copy of *Tales of Passed Times* that I had bought for Clare all those years ago. Inside were my few sheets of paper, the ones I used to write falsely cheerful notes to Maman. I put on my wool cap, still damp, and left the caves.

The drizzle from earlier had settled into a sweating downpour. I couldn't tell how late it was; I'd lost hours in front of that wall of limestone. I tucked the book into my greatcoat and wound my way through the oily dark.

The soldiers guarding the little cellar were hunched over by the door, rain dripping off the brim of their round helmets. One straightened at my approach. The other lit a cigarette.

"What do you want?" he said, tossing his match.

"I'm bringing writing materials to the prisoners."

The first one tipped back his helmet. "I thought you were busy making great art."

"Chaffre, what are you doing here?" I asked.

"Guess." He looked unhappy. He'd pulled guard duty with Martel, the brute who'd hated him since our training days. "Did you eat that soup?"

"I forgot."

"You also forgot your helmet again."

I shrugged. "I could use a bath."

Martel snorted. "Is he your *maman,* Crépet? Or maybe your girlfriend?"

"Fuck off," I said, but my face burned. Chaffre never did his fussing in front of others.

"I dunno. You've always jumped to defend him." He took his cigarette out and spit. "Like some damsel-in-distress."

I started for him, but Chaffre stepped between us. "It's nothing." In the moonlight his eyes were pleading.

I stopped, but Martel chuckled and strolled away for a piss.

Chaffre lifted his helmet and wiped his brow. "He's a bastard."

"He is. But, hey, don't rag on me all the time." I regretted it the moment I said it.

His eyes flickered. "I'm looking out for you. Isn't that what we're supposed to be doing out here?"

I forced a smile. "Sure."

Something clattered onto the ground and I bent to pick it up. Chaffre's little lead Madonna, the one he carried everywhere. For him to be holding it, out here in the rain, to be worrying and praying, something must still be nagging at him.

"It'll feel like summer again someday," I said, and held it out.

He pushed the little figure into his pocket. "Someday." He shifted his rifle. "So what are you doing here? If I were you, I would be sleeping instead."

"Delivering writing materials to the prisoners." I kept my book covered with my hand. "I have orders."

I didn't tell him that the orders were nothing more than a plea from an old friend. I couldn't explain, not even to Chaffre.

"Your own paper? You're wasting it on them?"

I hated lying to him. "Yeah," I said, glad it was dark.

He hesitated. Rain pinged off his helmet. "Okay, but make it quick. I think they're asleep."

They were, but it was a wary doze that ended when I opened the door and let in a sweep of windy rain down the cellar steps. I couldn't see more than the splash of moonlight let me, but one of the figures got heavily to his feet. "Crépet, you came back."

I picked my way down the steps. "For a minute. I brought what you asked." I fumbled for the book inside my greatcoat. "I can't stay. I shouldn't even be here."

His reply was in English, low and guarded, almost private. "Thank you for helping me."

Gratitude, I didn't expect. Not from Bauer. Not now. He'd never thanked anyone in all the years I knew him. I dropped the pencil. "It's nothing."

He moved closer, just a little bit. I couldn't see more than a shadow of his face. "It's more than you know." His eyes glittered in the dark.

I bent and felt along the floor. Rain beat against the stairs from the open door. Outside, Chaffre paced, sending his shadow across the floor. Bauer stepped nearer. I wished I hadn't come.

"Do you remember some of the tricks we'd pull on the court?" he asked, squatting by me.

I edged back. This sudden nearness, this gratitude, this nostalgic remember-when. "You were always much more serious about the game than I was." From outside, Chaffre cleared his throat loudly. "You always wanted to win." My fingers connected with the pencil and I straightened.

Bauer stood, and as he did, the others did, too. I took a step back, my heels against the stairs, realizing that I'd dropped the pencil again.

"It's really not so different these days, is it?" he said. "We all want to win." He clapped a hand on my left shoulder.

"The game ended long ago." I twisted my body away from his hand.

But I'd forgotten about Bauer's drop shot. I'd forgotten that he always knew how to set me up to lose.

Clare had told me not to trust him. I wished I had listened.

When he put his hand on my shoulder and I twisted away, I didn't see it coming. I didn't realize I'd left my hip open. Bauer lunged and metal grated. He swung up with my bayonet in his fist.

I swerved, I tried. I didn't move as fast as he did. That same forehand that won him 299 games caught me full across the left side of my face.

The bayonet was long, edged to the hilt, with a curved quillon. He held it thrust-down when he swung, the way he'd pulled it from the scabbard. The quillon slammed into my nose, snapping my head to the side. The blade hissed cold through my cheek.

I caught myself against the wall, against slime-slick rocks.

"You've never understood 'enemy,' Cré-pet," Bauer said, leaning in close. "You have always trusted too much."

Behind me the others had moved in to block my exit. My head spun but I pushed myself off the wall.

"The little fräulein, she trusted me, too." His eyes gleamed in the dim. "Someone had to show her Paris."

I could still see Clare hunched in that doorway without her hat. "You . . ." Dizzy, I pulled the chisel from my belt and lunged at him. He ducked easily. With the bayonet still in hand, he backhanded. Like a wire through clay, the blade sliced through my shoulder until it jarred against bone. The chisel clattered away.

"Three hundred," he whispered. He shoved me off the bayonet, against the wall. My head cracked against the wet stones as I fell, and I saw stars. He leaned down close. "I win."

I tried to push myself up, to call out a warning to Chaffre, but Bauer squared an almost offhand kick at my mouth. Hobnails tore into my already-cut cheek and I swallowed the cry.

The others waiting by the door parted and let him up the stairs. Someone bent for the chisel, someone else for the pencil. Moonlight skittered across the floor as they followed him up.

I pushed myself up with my left arm,

300

coughing blood. Outside, shadows jerked.

"Luc!" I thought I heard, but the sound was pulled away into the wind.

Something fell through the doorway and down the stairs, something heavy with a round helmet that clattered away. The door slammed shut, throwing the cellar into a thick darkness, but I was already pulling myself up the rocks to my knees, already crawling over.

"Who is it?" I whispered, but got no response. I felt shoes, legs, a long French greatcoat soaked with a night's guard duty in the rain. Buttons straight and neat. Wool sticky and warm, but beneath, faintly, the rise and fall of a chest. "Oh, please. Chaffre."

I pushed down, feeling ribs, hot blood, and a jagged tear. It was nothing, was it? Such a small hole. I could hold all the blood in. I stretched my hands over the wound and tried to swallow down any doubts. All he'd wanted was to be strong enough for all of this. I'd hold him together if I had to.

But his hands scrabbled at mine, pulled my fingers up and away. He brought them to his lips. Against the back of my hand, I felt rasping breaths and an exhaled, "Go."

"I'm not leaving," I said, though my jaw ached to move. From his pocket, I took the

301

little lead Madonna. "Here." I tucked the figure into the hand that held mine.

"Luc." He inhaled raggedly, then gave a cough. Like a breath, his lips brushed my knuckles. His grip loosened. When I pulled my hand away, it held the lead statue.

I don't know how long it took to crawl up the stairs, how much strength it took to push that door open, how far I staggered before I found Martel, coming out of the woods buttoning his fly.

"Jesus, Crépet." He caught me as I stumbled.

"Chaffre," I tried to say. "In the cellar." But the words were as shattered as my jaw.

He stared. "Is all that blood yours?"

"They got away," I managed to say before sliding into blackness.

CHAPTER 19
CLARE
1917

As far as Glasgow was from the war, I saw both ends of it every day. Buchanan Street and Queen Street stations teemed with raw soldiers from all corners of Scotland, scrubbed and hopeful. Glasgow Central brought them back, worn, weary, wary. There were whispers that some of the trains unloaded their cargo far from the center of the city, where no one would be disturbed by the sight of gurneys and bandages. Scotland's brave soldiers could appear nothing less.

Mostly, though, the streets were full of women. Brisk, serious nurses, ruddy shipbuilders and munitions workers, black-draped widows, the occasional Belgian or French refugee. Every day I passed by St. Aloysius' Church, full of women and their quiet contemplation. Though I wasn't Catholic, sometimes I joined them.

I was so far from the war, yet I felt so near

to it with each person I passed in the street, with each troop train waiting at the station, with each pasted newspaper headline, with each kilted soldier, desperate couple, handkerchief pressed to eyes. The breathless, headlong rush of war, brought straight to Scotland.

I kept that smudged map in my pocket, the one I'd torn from the newspaper in Saint-Louis. I kept it to remind myself that the war was just as close for me. Somewhere in France was a soldier I still thought of.

I never knew independence could feel so lonely.

In Glasgow, I didn't have sand or sunshine or the smells of coffee and spices. I didn't have blue skies stretching upwards forever. I didn't have companionable quiet at the supper table. I didn't have Grandfather.

I did have a narrow bed in a rooming house, a crooked desk too far away from the window, a gas ring that never completely warmed my kettle. The other female students, those fresh from under their fathers' thumbs, rejoiced. "A tiny flat?" they'd exclaim to one another. "But it's *my* tiny flat." The only thing that made it mine was the wooden mask hanging on the wall, the one I'd brought back from Mauritania. I'd been to Africa and back. The other women had only made it as far as Glasgow. Listening at the edges of these conversations, I felt lonelier for not understanding.

My first day at the School of Art, I was bewildered. The clean, echoing halls, the well-ordered studios, the big, bright rooms and their high ceilings. I'd been used to painting in the souks of North Africa, strapping an easel onto the back of my bicycle and mixing pigments in the jostle of the crowd as the colors presented themselves. I'd brushed sand from my canvas and picked blown grass from the paint on my makeshift palette. I'd crouched on the banks of the Senegal River, sculpting brown clay. Now, I held my leather case to my chest as I made my way through the pillared front hall of the school, wondering how art could be created in such a sterile place. I wondered how I'd ever find the warmth and color and *life* that I had on my travels.

I thought I could find it in the students. Young women flocked the halls in excited, chattering bunches, exhilarated at being on their own, at being here, at walking the halls of artists. Some were so young. Their dresses high-necked, their hair braided down their backs, they couldn't have been long out of the schoolroom. I could scarcely keep up with their nattering. I followed them, soaking in their radiance, wishing I'd had even one girlfriend in my life to know how it was done. Once in the basement corridor, a girl turned to me, mistaking me for someone in her group, and asked whether I agreed that the Artists Football Club was smashing. By the time I accidentally responded in French, she had already moved on down the hallway.

I was no better with the male students. All I'd had for comparison was Luc. Well, Luc and my grandfather. Both quiet, introspective, absorbed. I didn't find that here. The few male students left in Glasgow were boys — restless, impatient boys. They always kept half a watch out for the news, waiting to see if they'd be called for their turn. I couldn't blame them, I suppose. With nearly everyone else over the age of eighteen in the army, they wanted to be next. The older students were those turned down at the recruitment bureau, and they kept their heads down, hiding a weak heart or spirit. I couldn't talk to them, any of them, not when they made me think of someone else, someone who hadn't escaped the army.

I wrote to Madame when I arrived in Glasgow. I knew she'd be proud, and of course I wanted news of Luc. I tried to sound casual, as though I'd simply misplaced Luc like an errant glove, not that I was so wracked with worry every night that I fell asleep praying for him. I asked where I could write to him, as I had so much to tell.

But she never wrote back, though I tried and tried. I kept watching that map I'd cut out of that newspaper in Saint-Louis, watching the blots of ink march across the landscape, far too near to Mille Mots. Was she even receiving my letters? Was I receiving hers?

While I sat in the still life studio one day, early for class and tracing the lines on my crumpled map, a girl came up behind. "Have a sweetheart over there?" she asked.

I could hardly remember how his voice sounded and, while I had no trouble sketching out the boyish face I knew — all angles and dark curls — I didn't know how the older Luc looked, hardened by war. "A sweetheart?" I folded the newspaper clipping. "No, a friend. A friend I miss very much."

I wanted him to be there. I wanted him to be on the other end of an envelope to share this with me, the way he had been. This, art school, was something he'd always wanted for me, harder than he ever wanted something for himself. This was ours, and I wanted, more than anything, to write to him all about it.

I'd tell Luc how hard it was. Not just the loneliness — that, I knew he'd understand — but the lessons.

I thought it would be easy. Really, I did. I had training, right there at the table of Monsieur Claude Crépet. I'd had further lectures via letter, once every few months, on my technique. I'd sketched and painted across continents. I'd spent years feeling my way through the learning. I'd had a mother who could turn tables into fairy tales, a father who could make buildings rise with pencils and measurements, and a grandmother who had captured a marriage on canvas. Art was in my blood and in my fingertips.

Half of the young women here were like me, experienced, taught at art academies or under private drawing masters. They also carried well-worn cases. The others, hopeful and untutored, their pencils freshly sharpened, their brushes new, I was sure would be the ones fumbling. Little did I know that I'd fumble, too.

Miss Ross, you cannot hold the pencil as though you were writing, or, *When you insist on keeping your paper at that angle, you smudge with your palm, every time,* or, *While arranging your palette, you mustn't put raw sienna beside raw umber. There is an* order *to these things, Miss Ross.* The well-trained students never made these errors. The untrained were taught from the start how not to. But I'd had one summer of proper lessons and then years of filling in the rest by myself. I had to be corrected and instructed all over again. I hated it.

If I'd had an address, I could've written to Luc about all of that. The embarrassment of being told that, yet again, I was doing it wrong. The frustration of learning a second time what I'd already learned once. The isolation of being the only one so singled out.

Or I could have written to him about the parts that weren't all that bad. Of sketching a live model for the first time, and then a live nude model. Of learning modeling in the dusty, clay-streaked sculpture studio. Of putting on that crisp white artists' smock the very first time and seeing it satisfyingly spotted with paint at the end of the lesson. Of being, every single day, surrounded by art. Luc was right; that, I loved.

Until I could find him, until I could write to him, I'd keep all of that tight against my chest. I didn't want anyone else to see these little joys before Luc did. If he did. So I tucked away my disappointments and I

309

tucked away each scrap of happiness as I found it. I focused on my hard-earned place at the School of Art, a place I knew Luc would've envied. Every picture I drew, every sculpture I smoothed, I did it for him. Even without being there, Luc was always my muse.

CHAPTER 20
LUC
1917

I couldn't much smile anymore. Not that I had a reason to. Months from that night in the rain-dripped cellar, and my torn face still ached. Months from that night when Bauer turned my own bayonet on Chaffre, and my torn soul was still numb.

After Martel dragged me, bleeding, to the *poste de secours,* I didn't remember much. I was bandaged and loaded into an ambulance and jolted farther and farther back along the line, from dressing station to dressing station, hospital to hospital. It passed in a fog of morphine and needles and cold bandages. Something stinging was poured into my wounds. I was stitched. I slept wrapped in agony. I remember throwing a bedpan late one night. Someone in the ward was screaming. I didn't know if it was me.

I knew I was slipping towards the edge. Out on the battlefield, I was determined.

But here, in these crowded, desperate hospital wards, in this haze of pain and regret, I was willing to go. It certainly was better than remembering.

When I arrived at Royaumont, I was scorched with a fever. They carried me on a stretcher and I felt every bump. Sticky rain fell on my face. Inside, it was bright lights, soft hands, murmurs. I swore I heard the sound of singing, like angels. They gave me something bitter in a cup, something that made me shudder and retch. And then I slept.

I woke to the sound of Scottish voices. Women teasing, scolding, reassuring. Before I opened my eyes, I was weeping.

One of those voices bent near and a cool hand cupped the side of my forehead. *"Monsieur, tu as de la douleur? Pouvez-vous me dire où se faire mal?"* Her fingers trailed my left cheek. "Ah, his fever is down."

"Please, I speak English." I opened my eyes. Not Clare, of course not, but her lilt made me feel a sudden peace. The nurse was young, dressed all in gray. "You look like a dove."

She smiled ruefully. "A partridge. Little gray partridges are what they call us."

"No, a dove."

"You won't think as kindly of me in a moment." She carefully lifted bandages from my cheek. "You had an infection in your wounds. I'm sorry, but we had to cut your stitches open to drain them. We may have to remove more tissue." She touched my ruined faced gently, from my nose down to my jaw. "Both your shoulder and your nose are coming along nicely, but I think there is still debris in your cheek, right here." I winced. "Will you mind if I clean it?"

"As long as you keep talking, you can do whatever you like to me."

Her name was Mabel and she was my savior. She brought me back from the edge and kept me from slipping too close again. She held my hand while they restitched me, like a worn pair of trousers, and sponged off the mud of the trenches. She spooned broth into my aching jaw. She helped me with my buttons, with my socks, with all of the little things I couldn't do with my shoulder the way it was. She told me about a lazy childhood in Kirkcaldy, until her words washed me clean.

But then I was patched up and was left with the waiting and the healing.

The hospital at Royaumont was built in a medieval abbey. The Scottish hospital unit that had moved onto the grounds had added electric lights and running water, had assembled rows of beds, dragged in grass-stuffed mattresses, scrubbed up operating theaters, yet traces of the old abbey remained. Vaulted ceilings, wide windows overlooking a courtyard, the ghosts of hymns in the stones. The doctors and gray-uniformed nurses and orderlies — all Scottish, all women — moved between the beds, quietly checking dressings, administering medicine, smoothing red blankets. In that peace, we recovered.

But the peace only lasted so long. Eventually, in the quiet, my thoughts returned. I was restless, yet had no energy to move. I didn't eat, at least not often. Some broth, soft eggs, bread soaked in milk. I slept, far too many hours, because it was easier than lying awake, thinking. That last conversation with Bauer, the narrowing of his eyes as he pushed the bayonet in, the final kick as they all left me there on the floor, played in my head again and again. His comment about Clare and Paris echoed. The glint of his eyes as I realized what he'd probably done and what she'd kept from me all those years. How he'd hurt two people I cared about. One night, I dreamed about Chaffre, about the press of his lips to my knuckles, about the smell of blood and wet wool in that little cellar. The nightmares came more often after that.

Mabel knew. She'd bring me a warm draught and sit by me until I fell back asleep. Once she said, "You were betrayed by a friend, weren't you?" I must've looked startled, as she laid a hand on my arm. "You talk in your sleep."

"I was." I automatically put a hand to my front pocket, though my uniform was in the Vêtement Department and I was in red pajamas. That copy of *Tales of Passed Times* was gone. "I was just bringing him paper to write to his *maman.*"

"You should do the same." She smoothed her apron. "It might help if you had your own mam here."

"Not now." I touched my bandaged face. "When I look like a man again."

Mabel bit her lower lip. Once, while she was changing my dressings, I'd caught an unexpected glimpse of myself reflected in the side of her tin basin. Only half a face left. The rest was all stitches and swells.

"I've heard you say that before," she said. "Is that why you don't write to her?"

"I have written. I dictated a letter to you, right after I arrived." I'd been as blithe as always in letters to Maman. "But I didn't tell her I was writing from a hospital. She doesn't want to worry." I remembered that

315

spring afternoon up in Papa's studio, where she pretended not to cringe over the splinters up and down my back. I remembered her desperate, false front of cheerfulness.

The days stretched. My stitches were removed, leaving behind raw pink scars. My shoulder had mended enough for me to see a masseuse and learn exercises to gain strength. As much as I tried, though, I still couldn't wield a spoon with that arm, much less a rifle. I was declared unfit for duty.

The pronouncement left me surprisingly adrift. Yesterday I'd been a soldier recovering, yet now I was just a broken man taking up space in an abbey.

Mabel assured me that wasn't true, but soon she started encouraging me to get up out of bed more often, and dress, and walk. "This will all be good for you, Luc," she promised. She walked with me to the refectory, where the women ate at long tables. She led me to the courtyard and to the gardens, covered over with the first snowfall. I carried Chaffre's little Madonna in the pocket of my dressing gown. Around my wrist, I still wore that tattered ribbon. More and more, Mabel left me to struggle alone with my buttons and socks. "Ah, but you can't stay here forever."

And I didn't. There came a day when I

316

put on my uniform again, hating every centimeter of wool. Where I tightened a scarf around my chin to cover as much as I could. Where I left behind all of those Scottish voices and boarded a train to Paris.

Not knowing where else to go, I went to Uncle Jules's apartment. Véronique had a new paramour, a poet with delicate hands and an unpredictable temper, but she had me wait down across the street while she sent him away for the night.

"You can't stay, *mon petit,*" she kept saying as she fluttered around me. "My life is different now. Edgar, I think he will marry me." But she made me a bath and warmed a bowl of spicy cassoulet.

I ate by the fire in a brocade dressing gown. The heat on my bare toes, the silk sliding on my arms, the curve of the painted bowl, all was almost too comfortable.

Véronique sat by me with a bottle of Château Margaux from Uncle Jules's secret store. "You look as though you could use a rest." She poured me wine, which warmed me down to my fingers. I hadn't had a drink in months. "I wasn't sure if I'd see you again, Luc."

The last time I'd seen her had been early in the war, on a rare leave to Paris. I'd been in my uniform and had stopped to bring her a bag of medlars from the trees at Mille Mots. She'd brushed aside the bag of fruit and exclaimed over me instead. Her *petit* Luc, all grown. She called me "strong" and "brave," then shut the apartment door tight. For one night she taught me all the things she said a man needed to know.

My skin ached beneath the silk of the borrowed dressing gown and I wondered if she'd do the same again tonight. But she said, "How Jules would fret over you. Does it hurt much?" and I knew she only saw my torn face. While she kept my wineglass refilled, she stayed on the sofa and didn't invite me up.

I finished eating and dressed. I would rather walk the streets than spend the night on her rug, feeling pitied.

"When you've settled, you can come for Demetrius and Lysander. Feathers make Edgar sneeze." She pressed on me one of Edgar's old suits, a bottle of wine, and Uncle Jules's wristwatch. It was a Santos-Dumont, something she'd bought him for his fiftieth birthday in a flurry of making him a "man of the age." My wrists had grown thin, but I tightened the band as best I could and thanked her with a kiss on the cheek. She pushed a handful of change into my pocket. "It isn't much, but if you come in the morning, after Edgar has left for the café, I can give you more." For all her shallowness, Véronique was generous.

That night I moved from park to park, from doorway to doorway, drinking straight from my bottle of too-expensive wine. Bleary, cold, I realized halfway through the night that it was my birthday.

The next morning, with head aching, I stood again in front of Véronique's building, unsure whether her poet friend was still in, unsure whether I wanted her pity. As I paced the distance between pavement and door, Maman found me.

"Véronique said you would be here."

Maman was a smudge of color in the gray of wartime Paris. She wore pale green. She was the fresh of a meadow. I swallowed down the sudden lump in my throat. "Maman."

She looked suddenly uncertain standing there on the pavement. "You didn't tell me you were in Paris. If Véronique hadn't sent me a telegram last night . . ." She eyed me up and down, at my civilian clothes, and took a step forward. "You're not fine, are you? She said you . . ."

I took a deep breath and unwound the scarf from my face.

At my raw skin, exposed, she flinched.

Inside, so did I.

"Oh." She turned her head away.

"This is why I didn't tell you." Choking back a ragged breath, I wrapped the scarf around again. "I knew it would upset you." I tied it in a knot, right under my chin.

"Oh no, *mon poisson.*" She straightened. "I didn't mean . . . I'm not upset."

I didn't know whether I appreciated the lie or not. I kept the scarf tight across my face; she didn't ask me to take it off.

"I was attacked," I said.

She swallowed deeply.

"It was Bastille Day and we had prisoners, German prisoners, that we were guarding." The rain against the doorway, the narrowing eyes, the blade across my cheek and through my shoulder. "They fought their way out. It was fierce, it was messy, and there wasn't anything we could do."

Her face flickered through emotion like a moving picture. Sorrow, fear, anger, finally settling into pity. "At least you are alive, my Luc."

That dark cellar, that cry lost in the wind. "Not everyone was so lucky." I closed my eyes.

She reached out and touched my arm.

That touch dissolved me. Standing there on that doorstep, months of tears and memories and regret threatened. I pressed a hand to my mouth.

"Luc." Her hand tightened on my good arm. "It's over. It's past. I'm here to bring you home."

"To Mille Mots?" I asked, as if there was any other home.

"I have Yvette airing out your bedspread and mattress. We can take tea in the rose garden, the way we always did. Marthe, she's using the last of the sugar to make you chouquettes. You'll like that, won't you?"

I didn't answer.

"The refugee families staying with me, you'll hardly notice they are there. They stay in the east wing. The west — your bedroom, the old schoolroom, Claude's studio, I've left that just the way it was. Your tennis racket is restrung, your bookshelf is dusted. You'll see, it's as if no time has passed." She clasped my hand.

It was like when I'd come home from boarding school or from my weeks of study in Paris. Maman never noticed how the years had changed me. She didn't acknowledge it now. "I'll never swing a tennis racket again."

"Don't say that." She squeezed my hand. "You might. We'll try." I tried to ignore the

321

shining in her eyes. "With you home again, it will be as though nothing has changed."

No one could go back and erase the past months. No one could undo the deaths I'd seen or the pain I felt or the regret I'd carry with me the rest of my days.

Her fingers brushed the inside of my wrist, where the ribbon was tied. A good Crépet. I pulled from her grasp.

"I love you, but I'm no longer your little Luc." I leaned forward and kissed her forehead. She smelled, as always, like La Rose Jacqueminot. "I need to find out who I am now."

Chapter 21
Clare
1917

It was cold for November as I hurried along Hutcheson Street, so cold the heels of my boots slid on the cobbles. Already it was getting dark, but that was Scotland for you. Never giving you enough day to do what you needed to do, at least in the winter anyway.

As I sped around the corner onto Trongate, the ice proved too much and I went down. My good pair of stockings ruined. And a tear along the side seam of my blue skirt to boot. It was one of two I'd bought new since arriving in Glasgow, the sorts of solid, serviceable affairs that Scottish women seemed to wear. Within the Mackintosh Building, I could wear my loose striped skirts, my red vests, my bright head scarves, the way I did in Africa. Among the art students, style was a matter of personal taste. But I kept my serviceable skirts and my green coat for venturing out into the city.

323

I stood and brushed dust and shards of ice from my skirt. It really was silly, all this rushing. In the end I'd return to an empty flat and a supper by myself. Likely toast and lukewarm tea again. The flat was always cold, but wrapped in layers of shawls, I'd trace pictures in the frost on my window. Nanny Proud always told me that a cold window could freeze away tears. All of these years, and I still believed her.

But it was in vain, all the rushing. Robert Miller's was shut tight. I leaned against the shop window, shielded my eyes, and peered in, but it was already dark inside. Surely I wasn't that late. Mockingly, the clock on the Tron church tolled out the hour. I was.

"Zut!" I hammered my fists against the window. "Not again!" Of course, the window didn't answer, and so I turned and slumped against it.

"Please, miss, you've been injured," someone said softly. I looked up to see a roughly dressed man with a walking stick politely averting his gaze from my legs. A spot of blood had soaked through the bottom of my skirt, darkening the hem.

Turning from the man, I flicked up the hem far enough to see a scrape on my calf. "Oh for goodness' sake! Torn *and* spotted?" I pulled a folded handkerchief from my sleeve and pressed it against the wound.

"Do you need assistance?"

The poor man couldn't even look directly at my leg without turning red. Little help he'd be. "I'm quite well, thank you." I glared at the darkened window. "I would be better, however, if the shop stayed open long enough for me to buy cadmium yellow. One cannot paint France without it."

He looked up at that. "You paint?"

"I'm a student, you see, at the art school." I tucked the edges of the handkerchief in the hole left in my stocking and drew myself up.

"If you don't mind me saying, you look too young for such study."

Now it was my turn to be embarrassed. I was hardly young compared to the beribboned girls in my classes. "Too young? Or too female?"

"Oh, not at all! Rather, I sometimes think lasses may have surer fingers for art." His accent was thickly northern, words curling in the air. "They're not afraid to let their imaginations spill from their fingertips." Rather wistfully he said, "My sister was an artist. I always thought she had the clearest eyes of anyone."

I'd been hearing "was" more often these days. "I'm so sorry," I said quickly.

He blinked at my automatic response, then shook his head. "She's not . . . she's still alive. We just . . . haven't spoken in some time."

I regarded this man, standing there in front of Robert Miller's. He wore a fir-green sweater, like a fisherman, beneath a home-spun jacket. Though he stood straight and still, he leaned on a carved dark walking stick. Nothing spotted with paint or streaked with clay. No reason for him to be standing here in front of an art supply store.

"Sir, are you an artist?"

He smiled then, either at the "sir" or the question. He didn't look much older than me, except for in the eyes. "Sometimes I come to look through the windows of the shop and wish I was. But, no." He tapped the walking stick. "Though I do carve."

I bent to it. What I'd thought were merely gnarls and whorls were the scales of a serpent, twining around the shaft of the stick until his chin rested on the top. The beast gazed out at Trongate with wooden eyes almost benevolent. "Oh, but it's beautiful!" I exclaimed. "I have a friend who would like that very much."

Had, I should remember to say. Had a friend. If you'd had no word of someone for years, could you use the present tense?

"Thank you," he said, bashful, startled.

"You *are* an artist." I nodded down to the walking stick. "You just have to convince the rest of the world." It was what Luc always said to me. "Trust yourself."

The next day when I stepped out of the school building on Renfrew Street, clay still under my fingernails from a day smoothing the neck of a bust over and over until my fingers ached, my new friend with the walking stick waited.

"Why hello!" I said and rubbed my eyes. "Fancy meeting you again so soon."

"I was waiting," he said, and held out a small tube of brilliant cadmium yellow. "Thank you."

I took the tube, turned it over in my hands. Cadmium yellow was not inexpensive. "For what? We only exchanged a handful of words."

"You said to trust myself. You were right. I've enrolled in the School of Art."

"So suddenly?"

"Evening classes. I can start next week."

"Are you always so impulsive?"

"Not usually," he said softly. "But war can do that." He leaned heavily on his stick. "Life moves on when a man walks away from it. I suppose I'm only trying to stay a step ahead."

His eyes grew red and damp. Though I was tired, I touched his arm. "Oh, not here," I said. "Please, come inside."

I took him into the sculpture studio, cluttered with tables and boxes and canvas-draped figures. He walked slowly, stiffly. The walking stick wasn't an affectation. Inside, I pulled two scarred chairs together, facing one another.

His name was MacDonald, like half of the people at the School of Art. Finlay Mac-Donald. Tucked away off the street, he quietly cried in that way men do, with red eyes, lots of swallowing, but no tears. He talked, in that northern accent that sounded like bens and lochs, like rolling mists, like the sea. He'd left home; they didn't want him there. They didn't want him in the army either, at least not anymore. And so he was here, in Glasgow, without any clear idea of what to do, but knowing that he loved walking the streets, seeing the solid buildings, the windows full of art. He felt at home here. We sat face-to-face, knees nearly touching, me hiding accidental yawns. He had such a gentle face, looking so desperate and heartsore that I finally stopped his tale of woe the only way I could think of. I kissed him.

It was nothing like that tentative summertime kiss under the poplar tree on the road to Mille Mots. In the sculpture studio, warm and smelling like dry clay, Finlay put his hands on my shoulders and kissed me like a rainstorm.

Suddenly everything — the way I'd left my only family behind when I set off for Glasgow, the way I'd been so achingly lonely since coming, the way I knew I shouldn't worry about Luc but I did, Christ help me I did. Everything washed over me like a wave and I knew I wasn't the only one drowning.

In that frantic, sudden kiss I felt a year older. I felt a year beyond Mother, Father, Grandfather, Luc, all of the little things that held me tethered to the past. Finlay tasted sweet, like berries unexpected in wintertime. He leaned towards me. I reached forward and put my hands on his knees.

But he stopped and pulled back. Looking down, he tugged at the fabric stretched across his knees. "You shouldn't," he said, but didn't finish the sentence. Then, "I forgot."

I brought a knuckle up to my lips. "You forgot what?" My eyes slid to his left hand, but he didn't wear a ring.

"I shouldn't have done that. I'm too broken down for you."

329

I thought of a lonely girl clutching a sketchbook on the beach of Lagos and hiding tears in the rain of Seville. I'd spent so many years missing people — my parents, Luc, now my grandfather. I thought of that girl, who dreamt of letters left on breakfast tables. I thought of a woman who dreamt of letters left on fields of battle. "I understand."

He drew in a breath and took my hand. "See." He moved it to his leg, below the knee. Through the fabric I felt wood and metal joints.

I nodded. "See," I said, and moved his hand to the hollow of my chest. "I understand broken."

Something had to change, I knew it. I couldn't be alone the way I'd tried to be, pretending such self-sufficiency, pretending that there was a prosthetic for my heart. Finlay's hand uncurled against my chest.

I went with him that night, to the rough room he rented, bare and impersonal apart from a pencil drawing of a Highland cottage tacked above the bed.

"It's okay," he whispered once, mostly to himself, and then pulled me close and didn't speak again. We didn't have to open our eyes, we didn't have to give excuses or explanations, we just had to be there. We fumbled nervously, until he lay back on the bed with me on top, until my hands at his waistband found instead the leather strap holding on his prosthesis. He stopped and pushed me away.

"It's fine. You can leave." He rolled away. "I shouldn't have expected . . ."

I rested a hand on his back. My lips still tingled. "You didn't." And he didn't. He didn't ask me up to his room. Neither did he stop me when I followed him up.

But he said, "I can't help but think of tomorrow." Beneath my fingers, his back tensed. "You called me 'impulsive,' but nothing done on impulse is without consequences."

Consequences.

My hand fell away.

Consequences, like the ones Mother and Madame fell with. One chose her child over her art, the other, art over her child. If I learned anything from them — from the years abandoned by my mother and from the summer watching her friend stagnate behind a desk — it was that a woman couldn't have both family and passion.

"I wasn't thinking." I pushed my skirt down over my knees.

"Tomorrow you will. You'll wake up then and you'll wish that you were never here with me tonight."

I realized then that he wasn't talking about the same consequences. I worried that one night could change my fate; he worried that one night wasn't enough to change his.

I reached across and took his hand. "Sometimes tonight is more important than all the tomorrows that come after. It lets us face the morning."

He turned back, his eyes black pools. "Stay?"

Half undressed, we lay in the dark and talked as the shadows lengthened. How his girl turned away from him and towards his brother. How his sister just turned away. Impulsive moments that had changed his course. I told him I knew. I'd lost my mother to her restless dreams, I'd lost my father to his heartbreak, and, now, I'd lost Luc, the only person who truly knew me. And, though I knew that life was full of loss, the little girl in me couldn't help but feel left behind.

When the moonlight came through the window, across my bare legs, across his unbuttoned shirt, he sighed. "I shouldn't have brought you here. It isn't right, is it, for me to take advantage of you and your kindness. I'm sorry."

"I'm not." I rested my head on his chest.

"Sometimes we just don't want to feel alone."

He exhaled and my hair stirred. "I never used to feel so alone." He shifted on the bed and I could hear the fabric of his trousers catch on the prosthesis. "But then your best pal dies, and then what?"

I squeezed my eyes shut. "And if you don't know whether he's dead, is that worse? Or have you saved yourself knowing?"

"Oh, lass." He drew a hand through my hair. "I don't know which the blessing is."

"That's why I draw." I caught his hand. "It's me reaching out to the world. Behind all of this — the lies, the loss, the loves lost along the way — there's still beauty. Color, lines, perfect shapes. When I draw, it's me telling them I understand."

"You told me you paint France."

"The most beautiful place in the world."

And, as we fell asleep, he sighed, and said, "Not anymore."

That one desperate, fumbling night was our introduction, and the days after were the belated getting to know each other. He let me draw him with his trouser legs pushed up, over his wooden leg lashed to the smooth stump, and somehow that felt more intimate than any lovemaking could.

333

Of course, wrote Grandfather, when I told him of my new friend. *He recognizes what art means to you. He sees how you light up with it. Those who love us don't ask us to mask our true selves.*

Finlay became my anchor, the one mooring me to real life. At the School of Art, all was imagination. A woman wasn't just a woman under our brushes; she was a queen, a goddess, a sylph. Of course we learned the basic techniques, those shapes and lines that always made me think of shadows beneath the old chestnut tree, but, after our first years, we were meant to aspire to more. Everyone innovated. They took those lines and curved them, shaded them, twisted them, until they were anything but basic.

In class, I'd use a bold brush. I could take the still lifes, the models, the ordinary things before us, and turn them into a fairy tale. After all, wasn't that how I lived my life? Bright skirts and scarves hiding a core of plain, ordinary loneliness. With slashes and strokes, with words on a page, I'd paint the world beneath the skin of a dream.

But, outside of class, with only Finlay, me, and my pencil, I could draw the world as it really was. Finlay, after hearing that his limb had shrunk further and that he'd need a new prosthesis. Sitting on the bed, head in

334

his cupped hands, exhausted. His trousers rolled up over his knee. The leg all wood rubbed shiny, screws, hinges, leather straps. I didn't leave anything out, not the weary hunch of his shoulders, the fingernails bitten down to nothing. In the dusty sunlight, he slumped, defeated.

Then furious, the prosthesis thrown across the room, scattered on the ground in pieces. His eyes flashed, angry at having to start over again, angry at having to relearn those wobbly steps, at having to go back to being a man stared at.

Then remorse, as he crouched on the floor, dust streaking the trouser knee of his good leg. He felt around, gathered up every last screw and splinter of wood. He sat, his stump splayed out, piecing that wooden leg back together. No matter how much it had betrayed him, he still needed it.

I drew all of that — the weariness, the frustration, the desperation — without any of the artifice or gilt I saw in class. I drew Finlay as he was, finding more beauty in that curve in his stump, in the stark strength on his face, than in a thousand queens.

"Clare, you *are* an artist," he said, echoing me that first day. "You just have to convince the rest of the world."

"You can't throw my own words back at

me like that," I teased, but he wasn't having any of it.

"With your pencil, you reveal me. And, in those drawings, you reveal yourself. This is what you were born to do, Clare."

"My Something Important," I whispered. Luc said that, the day we stood in the hallway of Mille Mots, tiptoed on the edge of our future. Two words that made me feel more than hopeful; they made me feel invincible.

I went with Finlay to Renfrewshire to be fitted for his new leg. Sitting in the recreation hall of the Princess Louise Hospital, I realized Finlay had it easier than most. Other soldiers, missing too much to be useful, waited, too. Some without a leg, some without two, some without an arm along with the rest. Not all had their prostheses yet. I watched those soldiers slouched in wheelchairs, propped with crutches against gaming tables, or leaning back against the walls, eyes closed, quiet resignation on their faces, and I memorized it all. On the train back to Glasgow, I let myself sketch.

I sketched a lanky soldier, still straight and proud in his uniform despite the folded trouser leg. I sketched a young man in an overlarge suit, his feet tapping out a One-Step, half the beats done with a stockinged foot, the other half with a wooden sole. I sketched a soldier, head bent, stub of an arm curled protectively around a small boy. Not all in the recreation hall were soldiers. I sketched a nurse, a refugee from Belgium, quietly knitting with three leather fingers.

Your Something Important. All of those soldiers, who'd given so much of themselves on the battlefield that they'd left a piece behind, they'd been out there doing good. Their work was more important than mine. Just a pencil, a few lines of charcoal . . . how could that compare?

One soldier at Princess Louise had lost a nose. It had been replaced by a clumsy rubber prosthesis, thickly painted. It filled the space, but not much more. What he'd lost, he could never fully recover. Me drawing them, it wasn't enough. To keep those sketches in my book and pity. I needed to share them, to show the world that the dead are not the only ones to be mourned.

Finlay, he understood. "When you picked up that pencil, you gave me dignity on the page." He stilled my sketching hands as the train rumbled into Queen Street Station. "Clare, other people should see this. You should send these out."

So I did. With the last of my coal money for the week, I bought heavy sheets of paper and, wrapped in two scarves and an extra sweater against the cold, I copied over my sketches. I packed them carefully between sheets of cardboard and brought them to Fairbridge when I went to visit for Christmas.

Grandfather straightened his glasses on his nose and spread them all out on the empty dining table, scrutinizing until my nerves flickered like electric lights. When he finally slipped off the glasses, his eyes were wet.

"You have something your mother and grandmother never had." He straightened up the pages. "The courage to capture the world as you really see it." He packaged them up and sent them to Charles Rennie Mackintosh in London.

Clare, you're in the right place now, Mr. Mackintosh wrote. *Will you exhibit?*

Are they good enough? I asked. My works were far from what the others at the school were producing. They weren't the sorts of things one hung alongside the bold colors and allegories. All in pencil and soft lines, they faded.

They're haunting, wrenching, honest, he replied. *I'm reminded of Käthe Kollwitz. Those poor unfortunates in the pictures, they are the ones from whom society looks away. You look straight at them and their souls.*

I was unused to praise. *Who wants haunting, wrenching, and honest in the middle of a war?*

Those who know it.

But I didn't. I didn't know any of it beyond what I saw in the corridors of the hospital. Those soldiers brought a memory of the trenches home with them, to carry around always.

Clare, I know a gallery, in Paris. The owner is an old friend. May I send one to him?

I thought and, with a hesitant pen, wrote, *Yes.*

The first one we sent, it sold right away. "A soldier, recently returned from the Front," said Monsieur Santi, the gallery owner. The next two sold just as quickly. "You have an admirer," he said, and asked me to send more.

Checks came to me in Glasgow, checks I held in disbelieving fists, then tucked away in the bottom of my washstand drawer. *Share them with the world,* Finlay had said. I hadn't expected compensation for that.

I wrote to my grandfather at Fairbridge. *I've done it. Like Grandmother, I'm an artist now.*

When a letter came for me, it wasn't from Perthshire. This envelope came from Paris.

The stationery bore the insignia of the American Red Cross.

Studio for Portrait Masks
70 bis Rue Notre-Dame-des-Champs
Paris
January 1918

Dear Miss Ross,

My name is Anna Coleman Ladd and, under the auspices of the American Red Cross, I am attempting to set up a studio in Paris modeled after Lieutenant Francis Derwent Wood's Masks for Facial Disfigurement Department at the Third London General Hospital, Wandsworth. I am not sure if you've read about Lt. Wood's work with mutilated English soldiers, though you may have heard of his department, popularly called the "Tin Noses Shop." Like yourself, Lt. Wood is an artist, and he has lectured at the Glasgow School of Art, so you may be familiar with him. He has pioneered a new and quite astonishing technique of casting thin metal masks that are light, comfortable, and quite lifelike. Not medicine, but rather art.

These masks can cover the whole face, depending on the degree of injury, or can cover only part of the face. Glass eyes can be added with durable lashes made of thin strips of painted metal. For masks that cover one's mouth, an opening can be left for a cigarette. These masks are seamless. It is quite an impressive feat, to make masks delicate and thinner than a lady's visiting card, yet conveying so much humanity in those few ounces of metal.

I have learned his technique and, with the Red Cross, am setting up a studio here in Paris to help French soldiers in similar circumstances (called here *mutilés*). I've made some adjustments to the process — enamel paint offers more lifelike tones of color — but follow Lt. Wood's general method in sketching, casting, sculpting, hammering, and finally electroplating the copper mask.

I have been looking for artists who pay great attention to life detail and who have the compassion to work amongst disfigured soldiers. I have seen your pencil drawings in La Galerie Porte d'Or and, Miss Ross, I believe you have both qualities.

I will be in London next Tuesday. Would you do me the honor of meeting with me? I would like to speak to you more about the opportunity to assist me in my work. Helping these soldiers is such a small thing for us to do, but for them, it is anything but small.

Sincerely, etc.

These days it was hard to feel like art mattered. When men were giving themselves, giving their youth, giving their life, when women were waiting and praying, I was painting. I was sculpting and drawing and creating, as though there wasn't a war, as though my creation could counter all of that destruction. None of what I was doing signified outside of the art school. Anna Coleman Ladd was doing something that did.

I remembered the soldier I used to see waiting in the hospital, self-conscious with his ill-fitting rubber nose. If he'd had the chance to instead wear a work of art, would it change things for him? Would his world seem a fraction less dim?

"You're meant to do this, Clare," Finlay said. "You're more than an artist. You're a warrior."

"You're the one who's been to battle," I pointed out.

"And you're the one who's saved me." He kissed me on the forehead. "Now, go. Go bring another man back to himself."

342

■ ■ ■ ■

PART 4
THE STUDIO

1919

■ ■ ■ ■

Chapter 22
Clare
1919

The soldier stood in the threshold of the Studio for Portrait Masks. The room was bright, but he kept to the shadows.

Mrs. Ladd tried to keep the soldiers at ease and the studio cheerful. The phonograph in the corner, the sun-streaked windows and skylights, the little vases of peonies tucked here and there, warmed the room. Posters and flags were tacked between the windows — a large American flag, for her, and smaller British and French flags, for the rest of us working in the studio. It was a bright spot in an otherwise somber city. Three months after the war ended, Paris was still recovering.

Usually, the soldiers sat in little groups, laughing, smoking, playing checkers and drinking wine. Some were waiting for appointments. Others had nowhere else to go. Since being demobilized, too many lived on the streets. They begged for food, drink, a place to warm up. Here, at least for part of the day, they had all three. But, more than that, here they found people who understood. They found other soldiers just as broken.

This new one, though, he came alone, lurking in the shadows of the hall, not quite stepping into the room. They all did on their first visit. Once fearless in the face of a trench wall, they were now afraid to even step in the light. Light revealed what had become of their dreams of glory.

"May I help you?" I asked in French. Not Parisian French, but the French I'd learned in Africa, tinged with the warm, open sounds of Arabic.

He didn't answer. The way he kept tugging on the brim of his *calot,* keeping a hand near his face, the way he kept his head down — he was a man used to shadows.

I couldn't see his face, but it had to be shattered. Here, they all were. These soldiers who came to the studio, they were missing ears, eyes, parts of their faces. More than that, they were missing parts of their souls.

"Are you here for a mask?" Behind me, sculptors bustled about with plasticine and brushes and tins of enamel paint. A soldier lay back with his head resting on a table as Mrs. Ladd carefully coated his face with white plaster. Another stood in front of the mirror, looking, for the first time, at the copper mask covering the ruined half of his face. "Let me show you our work." The phonograph played "La Madelon."

He shook his head. One hand still hovered near his face, but the other, pressed against his leg, had relaxed. In the room behind me, someone had begun singing.

Through the shadows, nothing but horizon blue and the pale oval of a face. So many of the soldiers who came in had worn their injuries for so long they had the old uniforms, those dark blue tunics and bright *garance* red trousers. France was still trying to live down that mistake. After losing hundreds of thousands of troops in the first months of the war, they thankfully replaced the *garance* with horizon blue. This soldier, though, he wasn't in red. He'd been in the war longer than many.

On his left arm, three chevrons bore that up, indicating three years' service, and on his right, another for each occasion he was wounded. Only one on that arm. Three years faithfully served and then, in return, one injury for him to carry the rest of his days.

"You don't have to stay, but won't you please come in? At least for a few moments?" I tightened my shawl, dark and swirling like smoke. I'd traded it for a still-damp watercolor in Algiers. "Warm up with a cup of tea. I can show you my sketches of the other guests we've had."

He cleared his throat. "You sketch?" His eyes shone in the dimness. "Ah, there's charcoal on your fingertips."

Something in his voice washed over me, warm like summer. "Spoken like an artist."

His hand lowered from his face and went behind his back. I wished I could see his fingertips.

"I have an extra drawing pad." I took a step back. "Stay, please. Stay and sit with me awhile."

He hesitated for just a moment more. Then he stepped out of the shadows.

He was in a bad way, that was clear. A fragmented shell, maybe. They tore like bread knives. Or a bayonet, swung too near. I was learning to identify what caused each injury. Long scars ran from the side of his jaw upwards. More than scars, though; they sank deep, like the trenches running across the Western Front. The right side of his face was unmarred, but the left, that whole side was a battlefield. I kept my gaze firmly on it, forced myself to look at every ridge, every crater, every shell hole. The map a soldier

348

brought home.

He stood tall, shoulders back, as though daring me to recoil.

But I didn't. I knew his face was a private hell for him, but I had seen worse cases in the studio. Men missing noses, men without chins, men whose faces sank in on themselves like deflated balloons. One of those poor men sat over at the checkers table right now, waiting for a few final dabs of enamel paint on his false nose. Then he was planning to go home to see his mother for the first time since he was wounded. Though the soldier standing so defiantly in the doorway had it bad, I had seen plenty worse.

So I made sure to look him square in the eye. I made sure to modulate my breathing so he wouldn't hear an extra hitch in my throat. I made sure he knew that no matter what reactions he met walking down the streets of Paris, he would not find them here. Instead I asked, "How do you take your tea?"

I settled him in at a table and filled a chipped cup. Mrs. Ladd was American and assumed the French thought as much of tea as she did. The few British artists in the studio certainly didn't mind. While I busied myself with unwrapping my charcoals, sharpening my pencils, squaring up my sketch pad, he took a polite sip. I passed him a pad of his own and then the tea grew cold.

At first he didn't do much, just stared down at the paper as though he didn't know what to do with it. I wondered if I was wrong. But then he picked up a pencil and rolled it between his fingers. "These are the pencils my father always used to prefer."

"They've always been my favorites." I took one of my own.

He started drawing.

I began with the outline of his face. "How long have you been in Paris?" In my few months here, I'd learned how to ask questions carefully. A direct "How long ago were you wounded?" would cause that familiar look of anguish to flash through their eyes.

He still flinched at the words. He saw straight through it. "Nineteen seventeen. Bastille Day."

A year and a half, though, to him, it probably felt like more. "Have you been in Paris all this time?"

He pulled a cigarette case from his jacket pocket but didn't open it. "Wouldn't you be?"

I worked on sketching in the good side of his face. A narrow eye, brown like an almond, with long lashes. My pencil loved

350

drawing those in. Thick curved eyebrows. A high, smooth forehead ending in short curls. A sharply angled cheek with a nick of a scar on top. "A work of art," I murmured.

"I'm sorry?" He looked up from his drawing.

"Works of art." I stared down at the lines beneath my pencil. "In Paris."

He watched me.

As though a mirror were down the center of his face, I began copying the features from one side to the other. "What's your favorite museum in the city?" I drew the curve of his chin in an unbroken line. "And you're a liar if you say the Louvre."

He blinked and leaned back in the chair. "Musée Jacquemart-André," he said without hesitation.

"So intimate, yet so elegant."

"You've been there?"

"Where else could I see *Venus Asleep*?"

That lip twitch was definitely an attempt at a smile. "I shouldn't be surprised to find an art lover in a studio."

"And I shouldn't be surprised to find one in a soldier." My pencil smoothed in the lines of his missing cheek. "As a girl, I visited France. It only takes once to fall in love."

"That it does," he said with a touch of

wistfulness. His pencil scratched softly.

"What are you sketching?" I finally asked.

"Just that."

"France?"

"Love."

I didn't ask to see what was on his page. "There," I said. I turned the sheet of paper around to him. "Where should I make adjustments?"

He stared for a moment, then quietly offered a few suggestions — eyes a little wider, nose narrower, a tiny divot in his chin.

"Fine," I said, my pencil already flashing. He waited, watching. And I drew. But something wasn't right. Everything felt shifted to the left, off-kilter. The angles didn't match up.

I set down my pencil and wiped my fingers on the sides of my skirt. "I need an accurate portrait of your face before . . . before now." His eyes flashed understanding. "Would you allow me?"

Without waiting for his assent, I closed my eyes and reached forward.

My fingers found his face, the one side smooth, the other rough beneath my fingertips. Gently, I traced up along the edges of his face, along his cheekbones and the curves of his eye sockets, down the bridge of his nose. I ignored the scars and the jagged edges for what was beneath. With light fingertips, I felt the lines of his face. I opened my eyes.

He sat motionless, breathless, eyes wide-open and on me.

I flushed. "I'm sorry. It's the way I learned to create a face."

His only reply was a deep, ragged inhale.

Mrs. Ladd always said I was too familiar, that I should keep my fingers on the sketchbook. That these soldiers, voluntarily cut off from their families for years, weren't used to touch. But I wasn't sure how one could remain true and accurate without feeling the bones of what they were drawing.

"I didn't mean to startle you."

He breathed a sigh, then said, "You didn't. At least not in the way you think."

Confused, I looked back down to my drawing.

"Please," he whispered, "what is your name?" He'd spoken in English.

"Ross. Clare Ross."

He leaned back and swallowed. "Clare Ross," he repeated. Then straightened. "Mademoiselle Ross, you feel your art."

"I had an excellent teacher," I said softly.

Something tensed in his face. "And where is your teacher now?"

"I'd give everything to find out."

"Please excuse me." He stood abruptly.

As he walked away, my pencil hurried, filling in adjustments, adding what I'd felt beneath his skin. Wondering if the answer would appear on my paper.

When it did, I froze. Those eyes, they were always so serious. That mouth used to smile when I least expected it. And that little scar on the top of his right cheek, the souvenir of a long-ago tennis match. I traced the lines on the page, smudging them beneath my fingertips until it was as hazy as a dream. These days, that's all he felt like.

"Mrs. Ladd," I said, eyes still on the page. "The soldier I was drawing, did he have an appointment? Did he leave a name?"

As she wiped her hands on her smock and went to the book she kept in her desk, I flipped over the sketch that the soldier had left behind. I no longer needed her reply.

On the page he'd left behind was my face. Not the face of the woman I saw each morning in the mirror, but of a fifteen-year-old girl, lonely, scared, leaning out of a tower window wondering if she'd ever be strong enough to fly away.

I didn't need Mrs. Ladd to tell me his name, because it was on my tongue, tasting like oranges and rain and the scent of roses.

Years of memories, tasting like summertime.
  Luc.

CHAPTER 23
LUC
1919

There was a time I thought about Clare every morning. There was a time I mentally catalogued everything beautiful so that I could write to her about it at the end of the day. But as the years passed, it faded. She never wrote back, and soon her tiptoes through my dreams were only occasional. Those mornings I'd wake up not remembering a thing, but blushing. She'd been there.

And then Chaffre died and I dragged myself, bleeding, from that cellar. I never dreamt about Clare after that day. All I had now were nightmares.

But she was here, in Paris. Grown up, but with those same clear eyes, that corkscrew of hair on her forehead, those insistent, gentle fingers. How could I not recognize her?

But Clare didn't look like Clare. Not anymore. It wasn't so surprising that I didn't recognize her. She wore a dress as bright as a Moroccan rug. Apart from that errant curl, the rest of her red-brown hair was tucked tight beneath a scarf. She spoke French, confidently, with a trace of an accent running through her words. But the biggest difference, she stood so still, so calm, waiting for me to step into the studio. Not the Clare I remembered, always coiled as tight as a spring. That Clare didn't know the meaning of the word "patience."

Back in my apartment, in the crooked little garret high above Paris, I paced. There had been days I couldn't even pull myself from bed. Days where it was an effort to prop myself up by the window, button up my shirt, go to buy bread. And here I was pacing.

Something had woken in me the day I'd received a letter from Mabel. She was still at Royaumont but had heard of a new studio in Paris, making masks for French soldiers. She'd write to Madame Anna Ladd to set an appointment for me, if I'd like. For all of these months I was drowning, it felt like a rope. So, with the appointment set, I took my uniform from under the bed, brushed out the wrinkles, and made coffee. Though each step to the Rue Notre-Dame-des-Champs that morning was an effort, I went. And, in that bright, busy little studio,

I found Clare.

She'd been right across from me, smelling like sunshine and summer. She'd looked at me like I was a man, not a monster or an object of pity. I kicked the wall, setting up a volley of knocking from the room next door. It didn't matter, it *shouldn't* matter, that I found Clare again. That the moment she touched my face, my heart beat and I felt nineteen again.

Across the small apartment room in four steps, turn at the desk and back towards the window. The floor creaked and sent up dust with each step. Demetrius and Lysander watched from their gilt cage, uncharacteristically silent.

I couldn't go back to being nineteen. The boy who played tennis, sketched in cafés, studied until he couldn't see straight, that boy who thought he could do it all, he was long gone. Sometime, in the middle of a war, I'd grown up. As I told Maman the day she found me in Paris, I needed to find out who I was.

I crumpled onto my narrow bed and pressed my face into the pillow. My ruined face, that she'd seen, that she'd *touched*. I flinched at the memory. The last time those fingers had traced my face, they felt boyish cheeks, unkissed lips, eyes waiting for wonder. Now those eyes had seen too much. This face — I buried it further in the pillow, hid it, erased it — had felt too much.

I fell asleep like that, half-formed sobs lost in the cotton and horsehair, as Paris quieted. For the first time in years I didn't dream in nightmares. I didn't dream at all. I woke in the sickly gray of dawn, my blanket tangled around my feet. February, but I was bathed in sweat.

My early bedtime, my dreamless sleep, the way the dawn had snuck up on me, I woke renewed and restless. My window was edged in frost. It was cold and overcast, but there was a strange hopefulness around the edges of the day. I stood for a moment at the window, my little finger trailing through the frost.

Part of me wished I hadn't left the studio when I did. That I'd sat and listened to her talk about Paris with that satisfied little glow. I wanted to ask her about her art, her job, her grandfather, her life. I wanted to catch the eight years I'd missed.

But that other, the part that refused mirrors, refused friendship, refused anything that used to make me happy, that part hesitated. I was older and warier, but so was Clare. I'd watched through her words as she changed over the years. I watched her grow strong and self-sure, not one to forgive. Knowing what I knew about that one night in Paris, the night when Stefan Bauer took her off the train, I understood why. I drew my fingernail down the frosted glass with a scratch.

But, in the window's reflection, I swore my eyes were a little less dead today. The only thing that had changed, the only thing new, was her.

The parrots were rattling the sides of their cage. I'd forgotten to cover them last night. "I shouldn't go back," I said to them, leaning close. "I won't." Lysander turned his head and fixed me with a round eye, but Demetrius cackled. I fed them and moved the cage closer to the sunlight coming through the window.

I peeled off my hated uniform, damp and again wrinkled. I splashed my face with ice-cold water from my basin and bent to pour a trickle through my hair. Dripping, I shaved by touch. The last time the concierge had brought me a mirror, I'd hurled it down the incinerator with the rest.

The concierge, she was my mirror. Madame Girard, as round as a *boule* and just as crusty. She'd poke her head out from her *loge* on the ground floor when I left the building, always ready with a suspicious look, as though disreputable characters traipsed in and out of her building every day. No, I was the only one. The way her gaze flit away, the way those hard eyes grew harder. I frightened her.

Today, though, she leaned on her doorway a moment longer than usual. "Monsieur." The word she always managed to infuse with sarcasm. "You're going out, for a second day in a row?"

Despite herself, the sentence was tinged with surprise. Maybe curiosity.

"And you've washed your hair."

I drew my jacket tighter. "Even Quasimodo took a moment to bathe."

She grunted. "I'll take up more water."

The day was unnaturally bright. Frost glittered between the cobbles. I walked against the edge of the pavement, close to the fences and the garden wall, the collar of my jacket turned up. Without my uniform on, no one paid me much mind. At least it was easier to tell myself that. I could go along, eyes fixed on the pavement, and pretend that no one was staring.

And maybe they weren't. These days, only months into peace, Parisians had other things to worry about.

The streets ran black and blue, like a fresh bruise. Black for the mourning clothes, blue for the uniforms. Some were the indigo of factory workers, hoping to earn enough to buy an evening's worth of coal. Some were the tattered horizon blue of soldiers — broken and wretched — begging for coins on the corners. Few children. Though refugees still crowded the city, the children who'd been sent to safety when the Big Bertha started targeting Paris hadn't returned.

Though I was no better than the vagrant soldiers and refugees, I had the trust left to me by Uncle Jules. It was the thin thread that kept me off the streets. I didn't use much. Enough to keep me in a miserable apartment where I wouldn't encounter too many questions, enough to keep the parrots and me fed. Bread and milk and sugar were dear, but I'd never needed much to eat. The most I spent was on art to brighten my walls. To remind me that, somewhere in the world, there was still honest beauty.

I passed through Les Halles, smelling of fresh herbs and meat. The market was nearly deserted. Red-nosed women stood behind overladen tables of cheese or parsnips, while farmers with carts of mushrooms and turnips stamped their feet and burrowed further into their mufflers. At the edge of the market, in wooden sabots and a

362

faded spotted head scarf, the old flower seller caught the sleeve of my jacket. "Flowers for your sweetheart?"

I don't know what was in her basket in the middle of February — something limp and colorless — but her lips were blue. She was the only person in the city who looked straight at me. I pressed a handful of coins into her hand. "Mademoiselle, you're my only sweetheart."

Paris didn't feel like Paris, not anymore. The city I'd fallen in love with all those years ago, with its flat, green gardens, bright-awninged cafés, galleries, bookstalls, rainbow-windowed churches, was gray and still. The Jardin des Tuileries wasn't a place to sit by the basin, watching girls in white dresses stroll arm-in-arm. The statues were still sandbagged, the trees bare, and the gardens pockmarked with small shell craters. At the end of the garden, lining the Place de la Concorde, were captured German guns. Even Notre Dame shone sickly yellow through the temporary windows standing in for its great stained glass. Walking through Paris, you couldn't forget how close war had come to it.

I crossed the Seine, high and green. On the bridge, a woman sang "Auprès de Ma Blonde" and listlessly tapped a tambourine.

I gave her the two coins I had left.

The peace conference had begun only weeks ago. Paris had rushed to sweep the dust under the rug before the presidents and prime ministers and ambassadors arrived. I had gone out the day the American president, Wilson, and his wife came. Parisians thronged the streets, waving, shouting, singing. The city put on a cheerful smile for the arriving delegates, with parades and buntings, flags and flowers, but now that the great men were all tucked into their meetings at the Quai d'Orsay, the petals fell and the festoons had begun to droop.

Of their own accord, my feet traced the path to the Café du Champion, my old haunt. Gaspard had long since sold the shop, and the windows of the building were shuttered. On an impulse, I crossed the street and rapped at the door.

After a minute it creaked open. The doughy woman inside startled at me and hastily crossed herself. "Yes?"

"There was a café here once . . ."

"Yes, but I've bought the space now." She leaned a broom against the open door. "It will be a rag shop."

"A rag shop? No, no. You see, it was a café."

"And they've closed. The owner has

moved away."

"The owner promised to leave a bottle of cognac behind the counter. The good stuff."

"There is nothing there. I would've noticed a bottle of cognac."

"Please, it's behind the bar, in a hollow post. I watched Gaspard hide it."

"I'm sorry, but it is no longer a café."

"We were going to toast the end of the war. Gaspard, my father, and I." I tried to peer over her shoulder. "Another day conquered."

"You've missed the end, monsieur." She stepped back and reached for the door. *"Bonne journée."*

"Wait!" I wedged a shoulder in the door. Her eyes widened. "He hid it for me. We were going to toast to victory. Please let me go look for it. I know exactly where it is."

But she wasn't listening. She held the broom across her body, a trembling quarter-staff.

I let go of the door. *"Bonne journée."*

I stumbled away. I didn't belong out here, on the streets of the city, among the decent citizens. I needed to get back to the apartment, to my sanctuary, and lock myself away. I hurried past all of the open stares and whispered comments, losing myself in the maze of narrow streets. The literature of

Paris was full of monsters. Hugo's Quasimodo. Leroux's Phantom of the Opera. I read all of the stories; I just never thought I would be numbered among them.

When I stopped to take a breath, I was on the Rue Notre-Dame-des-Champs. My feet had made a decision for me. Across the street there was a building set back, fronted by a courtyard and high black fence. I recognized it. I had stepped through that gate only yesterday.

Rue Notre-Dame-des-Champs was quiet and I crossed it, ice crunching beneath my feet. The fence surrounding the house was set into stone ledges. Bare rosebushes spilled over the top of the fence. One of the two gates, iron and almost twice as tall as me, was ajar. Beyond, down a narrow corridor, I could see the airy little courtyard, a crooked tree holding up the center. The scent of tobacco lingered in the air, as though someone had put out a cigarette seconds ago. I leaned against the fence until the cold metal pressed against my cheek. I couldn't see anyone.

"Monsieur?" a voice asked, quite close.

It was a woman, older, dressed neatly in a deep blue coat and hat. She stood behind me on the street. Over an arm she carried a shopping basket filled with paper-wrapped parcels and little brown pears. "Can I help you?" She straightened a pair of spectacles but didn't look away. "Are you here to see Madame Ladd?"

I took a step back, and caught my foot on a stone. "No."

"Are you sure? I can walk you in, if you'd like." She nodded down at her basket. "Or if you'd just like to come in and warm up? I have fresh coffee, real coffee."

"My apologies." I straightened my collar, tucked my face down towards it. "This was a mistake."

She touched my arm. "Monsieur, I don't believe you are one to make mistakes."

I pulled away. "Then you do not know me, Madame."

And I hurried away.

CHAPTER 24
CLARE
1919

I couldn't keep still all the next morning, watching the door, wondering if he'd walk back through. For years I thought I'd never see him again, and now, I hopefully counted seconds.

"You can't keep your mind on anything today." Pascalle, one of the other artists, reached across me for the tin of white enamel. "I've never seen you so restless."

"There's just a lot to do," I said.

"Then why have you been spending so much time on that one drawing?"

Beneath my fingertips, Luc's face took shape again and again. I drew, smudged, erased, and tried again. Trying to convince myself that I'd made a mistake, that the man who'd been in here, broken and tense, wasn't the same boy who sang jazz songs as he hiked through the Fairy Woods. Even when Mrs. Ladd showed me the letter, the handwriting familiar, the *Luc René Rieulle*

Crépet written as plain as anything, I was still sure I had it wrong. My Luc, the Luc who sent me pictures, who told me fairy tales, who sketched in the woods when he thought no one was looking, he wasn't here, he *couldn't* be here.

All of these years, as I tried to ignore the news articles about each fresh battle, to ignore the too-long casualty lists, to ignore the stories the men on leave told in whispers, I had to think that Luc was somewhere else. Walking the grounds of Mille Mots on his mother's arm. Eating mushroom soup with his father in the rose garden. Leaning beneath the old chestnut tree with sketchbook in hand and a smile on his face. I had to tell myself he was there, safe and whole. Because, oh God, I couldn't picture him anywhere else.

Pascalle leaned over my shoulder. "He was a looker, wasn't he?"

Unexpected tears filled my eyes.

"Clare?"

"It's all a mistake."

"Oh, no." She hauled me to my feet. "Out with you." Holding tight to my arm, she steered me out of the studio, down the stairs, and into the courtyard.

It was icy cold out there. Pascalle made sure the door was closed tight and pulled me across the yard near the fence.

"Okay, go," she directed.

I swallowed back the tears. I'd had so many years to practice. "No, I'm fine."

"You are not. And the one thing you can't do in there is cry. Not in front of those soldiers. You know that." She pulled a blue package of Gauloises from the pocket of her smock.

I glanced around, but the brown branches of wild rose twined around the fence and kept us from view. I took an offered cigarette. "No, really, I'm fine. I wasn't going to cry."

"What did you mean, it was all a mistake?" She tucked a strand of her bobbed hair behind her ear and lit one for herself. "You said that in there."

"I . . ." I exhaled. "The soldier in the picture. I know him."

She leaned forward. "Really? The looker?"

"That's the mistake. It can't be him, *must not* be him."

Smoke curled around Pascalle's face. "But you have proof, no?"

"The letter he sent to Mrs. Ladd. It's his handwriting, his name. His face looking up from my sketchbook." The cigarette burned, but I didn't bring it to my lips. "Pascalle, I know it's him."

"Then there is no mistake."

"I wish there was." I leaned back against the fence, ignoring the thorns and the icy metal bars. "It's been years since we've written and even longer since we've seen each other." I pulled my sweater tighter. "He grew up surrounded by so much beauty. A romantic château, roses, art, parents who loved him to overflowing. For one summer, he shared all of that with me. He doesn't know how to deal with all of this ugliness. Not his face — you know I don't mean that — but the war, the death, the mud, the grief. He's not made for any of that." My eyes stupidly filled again. "He won't come back!"

With a cluck of her tongue, Pascalle took the cigarette from me. "You're going to burn your fingers. Off for a walk with you." One-handed, she draped her scarf around my neck. "If he remembers you like you remember him, he'll come back." And she gently pushed me through the gate onto the Rue Notre-Dame-des-Champs.

I did remember him. But how did he remember me? That summer, I was fifteen and naive, unwilling to accept that my mother was never returning, unwilling to acknowledge that my father had loved me. What had Luc seen? A girl hiding tears, hid-

371

ing everything. A girl who crept at the edges of friendship. A girl who didn't even know herself.

I wasn't the same, of that I was sure. All morning, looking down at my sketch, I saw the boy in him, but the girl in me — she'd grown up. I'd been across the world. I'd lost family and found family. I'd redefined "home" a dozen times. I wanted to be an artist so badly that, in Glasgow, I played it like an expected role. I wore my bright skirts and paisley head scarves like some bohemian uniform, I lived alone in a chilly garret, I lived on tea and wine. In Paris, though, I truly *became* an artist.

Grandfather had come with me to Paris. He was compiling all those years of research into a book, a book that surely wouldn't be read by more than a handful of enthusiastic old linguists in the world. "I can write in France as well as Scotland," he said hopefully. "And the coffee is significantly better." So he came along with crates of books and notebooks filled with his Alizarine scrawl. We rented a first-floor flat with big windows and an easy walk to Café Aleppo, where he could get cups of thick, bitter coffee to fuel his early morning frenzies of writing.

And I, I had a purpose. Every day, I walked to the Rue Notre-Dame-des-

Champs and had a sliver of a role in changing a man's life. After years of following Grandfather around, of filling his pens and overseeing his recordings, I was the one with something to do. Something that mattered. In the Studio for Portrait Masks, I felt like I belonged, more than I ever did at the School of Art.

Seeing Luc sent my heart spinning and wrenching, all at the same time. Once, I dreamt of fairy-tale endings, of castles and white horses. But I'd grown up since then. Whether in Iberia, Africa, Scotland, or France, I built my own castles. I never again waited in tower windows. There was too much of the world to see.

But I saw Luc and suddenly I thought of towers and sunsets. The blush and flutter that came with that kiss under the poplar, they returned. Again, I felt a starry-eyed fifteen. I wondered at Madame and Monsieur and the way she used to touch his face and call him *"cher."* I wondered if what she gave up was worth it.

"No," I said aloud, squaring my shoulders. I'd come too far to stop now, to give up all this. For what? To run a household? To take care of one person when I could work to help dozens?

When Pascalle pushed me and her scarf

through the gate, I walked home. I would wash my face and eat lunch with Grandfather. He was already home from his morning coffee, engrossed in a book as he attempted to unlock the door.

"Oh, dear." I hurried over. "Wrong door again, Grandfather."

The door in front of him swung open to reveal a portly bearded man with a string of expletives. Grandfather looked up from his book and blinked.

I took his elbow and steered him to our apartment down the hall.

"Is it already half past six?" he asked. "I've misplaced my watch."

"It's only noon and you misplaced your watch three weeks ago when you gave it to an old soldier in the Gare du Nord." I unlocked the door.

"He was worried he might miss his train." Grandfather set his book and his hat down on the sofa. "Then why are you home so early?"

"Making you lunch."

He held up a finger. "Ah!" From the briefcase tucked under his arm, he extracted a paper sack with five *bichon au citron,* not squashed too flat. "Lunch!"

"Is that real sugar on top?" I asked as I put the teakettle on.

"Marie puts them aside for me."

"Marie?"

"I've mentioned her." He wiped lemon cream off the books in the briefcase. "Owns the bakery next to Café Aleppo?"

There always seemed to be generous widows and sweets despite food shortages. I didn't remember this one. "Of course."

"You've been distracted," he said, stacking the cleaned books on the kitchen table. "I've noticed."

This, coming from a man who had, on more than one occasion, worn his pajama shirt beneath his jacket. "It's nothing." I measured tea leaves. "I've been thoughtful at work."

"It is difficult, I'm sure, to work with these men." He folded up the towel. "But you've never been distracted before over them. Last night it sounded like you didn't sleep a wink."

All I'd wanted to do was help the men who came into the studio. When each soldier was brought in, that first time they looked us in the eye and realized that we weren't going to glance away, in that moment it became personal.

But that wasn't what he meant. That wasn't what kept me sleepless last night. It was those blushing dreams I hadn't had in years, the ones where I woke with my arms wrapped tight around my pillow.

"A soldier came in yesterday," I finally said. I weighed how much to tell him. "But he left before I could finish my sketch." I inhaled. "I don't know if he'll return."

Grandfather sat and pulled a pastry from the bag. "Is that all? You've had *mutilés* leave before. Some aren't ready for masks, you said."

"It's true." I brought the pot to the table. "Some haven't yet accepted the face they wear already. They aren't prepared to accept a new one."

He shrugged. "I'm sure this soldier is no different. He'll return when he's ready."

Without telling him, I didn't know how to explain. I knew Luc, knew how stubborn he was. I knew he might risk much to avoid me. "Not this one." If he stayed away, it would be my fault. "I can't let him go." I poured out his tea and missed the glass. I swore in Arabic.

"I was going to ask what made this soldier different from the rest, but you've answered that." Grandfather handed me the towel he'd used to wipe his books. "When I last saw you this furiously impatient, you were in the Laghouat post office, waiting to see if that Crépet boy had written you."

376

I shouldn't have been surprised that Grandfather knew. Though he often lost track of time, he never lost track of me.

He leaned forward in his chair and rested his elbows on the table, eyes bright. "You found him again, didn't you?"

I bit my lip, then nodded. "I almost didn't recognize him." I pushed away the wet glass and sank into the seat across the table.

The last time I'd seen Luc's face, the face that appeared under my fingertips on the sketch pad, was the day Grandfather came to Mille Mots and told me that he was taking me away. I'd fled to my room and sat on my bed, ignoring the knocking on my door and the pleas to just come out. The window was pushed open and it was Luc. He came over to the bed and said, "You're strong enough for this," and I finally let myself cry. I'd left Paris and Stefan Bauer for the safety of Mille Mots, only to find a grandfather I hardly knew, ready to take me away from that safety. The ground beneath me kept shifting, but this boy came to find me, to hold me up, and to tell me I was strong enough to do it on my own. He didn't shush my tears or murmur "It will be okay," because it wouldn't. He held me until I stopped crying, until my shoulders stopped shaking, until I was as drained as a raisin, and he lay me down on the bed.

I fell asleep, but I knew he was still there. Through my hot, flushed sleep, I heard him talking with his mother at the door and I heard him moving around the room, packing up my trunk for me. He fumbled with my wardrobe, dropping boots and rattling drawers, though I'd never seen him anything less than completely sure about everything. When I woke, in a velvety black night, he was curled up on the floor next to my bed.

The door opened and Madame came in to take me down. Grandfather was waiting; he wanted to leave before dawn if we were to catch the boat at Le Havre. From the light coming in the open doorway, Luc stirred. "Luc, she's leaving," Madame said, then stepped from the room. He sat up on his knees, suddenly alert, his eyes on me. The light from the hall cast one half of his face orange, the other left in angles and shadows.

I'd wanted then to tell him thank-you. I'd wanted to tell him that, yes, sometimes I wasn't as strong as I thought. I'd wanted, with some small part of me, to cling to him and never leave. At Mille Mots, the rest of the world could be forgotten.

But I didn't. I nodded, only once, hoping I could put all of that into my eyes.

Luc, I think he understood. He reached out, took my hand and kissed it. "Always at your service," he whispered. Then he was out through the bedroom window, across the roof. I went to the window and watched him disappear into the dark. Overhead, Perseus and Andromeda shone. It was the last time I saw him.

Sitting across from Grandfather over a table of pastries and spilled tea, I shook my head. "If nothing else, I owe him my help."

Back then, all of those years ago, he'd been at my service. Now it was my turn. I could help him get his face back. I could help him reclaim himself.

CHAPTER 25
CLARE
1919

The casualties of war I saw every day were the men who came into the studio. But they weren't the only ones. As I sped from Paris, I saw from the train window the ruin that the war had spread across the countryside. The colors of that first trip to France, those brilliant greens and yellows and oranges and reds, they faded to memory. All I saw around me now were fields burnt brown, blackened stumps of trees, gray piles of rubble.

I got off at Railleuse, my handbag held tight. The station was deserted but still standing. It had been hastily shored up with new lengths of wood at some point, crooked planks that smelled of sap. I called up a mental map and stepped onto the road to Mille Mots.

The dirt was dusted with new snow. Deep tracks cut through the mud, old tracks. I wondered if they were from armies advancing or armies retreating. Maybe both. Littered along the sides of the road were discarded wheels, torn shoes, scraps of cloth fluttering colorlessly against the rocks. I hurried on. Up ahead was Enété — the little cluster of white houses on the road to Mille Mots, the village where Luc and I had stopped on the way home from Paris.

Enété was no more.

Low piles of white stone marked where the buildings had been. The high street was a slick of churned mud. Here, that outline marked the shop where he'd bought me a cool drink. There, those were the walls of the smithy. I could still see the outlines of the blacksmith's anvil, though the rest of the tools were gone. And, here, the charred remains of the bench where I'd sat while the accordion played. Enété had no music anymore. Holding my handbag tight against my chest, I walked from one end of the village to the other. The skeletons of houses and stores and stables, the crumbled mounds of stone, all were still.

The war had been closer than I thought. It had reached across the river to touch the village, to hurl shells and reduce my memories to rubble. The war had ended, but what was left?

I walked on, faster and faster. I passed

more scarred landscape, more fields twisted brown and barren, more empty orchards, more ruins of houses and barns, more scraps of lives discarded. This, this here, was what Luc brought home with him, worn across his cheek. The wreckage of the life he used to know. This landscape of loss. Even the poplar tree was nothing but a splintered stump. I walked quickly past so I wouldn't cry. After four years of war, I wouldn't cry anymore.

Night was painting the sky violet around the edges when I turned down the long road between the trees. I held my breath until I passed the last tree. Château de Mille Mots still stood.

But it was dark, so dark inside. No light, not even candlelight, shone behind the windows lining the front. Maybe all of this was a fool's errand. The long train ride, the even longer hike. I should have written first. I should have just sent a telegram.

I set my handbag on the porch step and slipped from my shoes. Stretching my toes, I leaned against the door, to summon up an ounce of energy. The wind sang through the few dry leaves left on the trees, and, below, the Aisne burbled. With my eyes closed, I caught the scent of roses on the air. February, and yet I swore I could smell them.

Despite myself, I smiled. Even here, even in the middle of all this, it was summer.

I straightened and rang the bell.

I counted out a minute, then counted out a minute more, before I tried the bell again. *Please oh please.* It echoed in an empty hallway. I waited. Then I slumped against the door.

But, from inside, faintly, movement. And the rattle of bolts being thrown and locks being undone. *"Oui?"* a rich voice asked.

I spun around. "It's me!" I said, lips close to the wood of the door. "It's Clare Ross, returned. Do you remember me?"

Those unlocking hands stopped at my words. Inside, it was silent. My heart pounded.

The door swung open.

Madame stood in the doorway, a sputtering oil lamp in her hand. Behind her, the house was dark and shrouded.

As though she hadn't heard me, she said, "Maud." The lamp in her hand began to tremble. "How have you returned?"

I reached up to touch my own face. Over the years, without me having any kind of a say in it, it had grown into my mother's. "Clare, Madame Crépet. It's your mademoiselle, your guest, Clare Ross."

She inhaled. "You're the very image of Maud."

Suddenly, standing in the doorway of Mille Mots, hearing my mother's name, I was brought back to that day all of those years ago, when I'd arrived, sad and scared and wishing for a friend.

Madame nodded. She must have seen that all slip across my face. "*Chère* Clare. I'm . . . oh, I'm so sorry."

It was then that I noticed her plain black dress.

"Oh!" My hand covered my mouth. I knew it couldn't be Luc. "Monsieur . . ."

She waved her hand, suddenly looking like the brisk Madame I remember. "He's back in the kitchen, cooking me an omelette. My dear child, he's quite all right."

"Then . . ."

"Child, I mourn for France."

The Crépets had been living in a corner of the west wing of the château, just the library, a converted bedroom next to it, and the kitchen.

"There's been no electricity for years and, these days, not enough coal to heat the whole château."

Monsieur Crépet looked up from the pan on the stove. "And that wall in the east hallway. We do not have that either."

"Ah, yes." Madame filled a cracked mug with *vin chaud.* "I'm sorry, there's no sugar. But I can grate some cinnamon."

"It's fine, thank you." I settled onto a stool at the table.

"And in two minutes, mademoiselle, an omelette." Monsieur tossed on a handful of crumbled cheese, looking as sure as he ever did with color and canvas. "I can work with pan as well as palette, eh?"

Madame touched his cheek.

The kitchen was dim and cluttered. It had none of the haphazard order it once had. Also, the line of birdcages was missing. "Marthe?"

"She's well. She's gone to stay with her sister in Brittany." Madame dipped her head to the pan and inhaled the egg and garlic and tang of cheese. "Ah, but even without her, we eat like kings!"

Monsieur quickly kissed her cheek, earning a blush. "*Ma minette,* I will take care of you."

I cradled the mug of hot wine. "Madame, Monsieur, I came here today to talk about Luc."

The air in the room turned brittle. "Luc?" she repeated in a thin voice. "Oh, he's fine. He was lucky, really." She busied herself wiping out two more mugs. "Did you know he's living in Paris, the way he always wanted?"

Monsieur silently slid a plate with a wedge of omelette in front of me.

"I do know." I inhaled. "I saw him."

She froze. "You did?" She set the mugs on the table, suddenly animated. "Please, where is he? Where is my boy?"

"He doesn't write to you?" I asked. He always had before, every day he was in Paris as a student. *Maman, I ate ratatouille. Maman, I read Tacitus. I thought of you, Maman, at the pink sunrise.* She'd read them aloud to me at the breakfast table.

She shook her head. Monsieur Crépet came up behind with a handkerchief, which she took. He sat across from me. "Every once in a while a package will arrive with bread or salt or tinned oysters — something we can't get here," he said. "Once it had a bottle of *La Rose Jacqueminot* wrapped in sheets of *Le Figaro.*" He reached behind for his wife's wrist. It was always her scent.

"And once in the package?" Madame said. "My old sculpting tools that he carried with him into war." She leaned against her husband's chair. "We know he's alive and in Paris. Anything beyond that, he doesn't want us to know."

386

I took a swallow of my wine. No sugar, but there was a swirl of honey. "He was wounded. Did you know?"

Madame hesitated. "Yes."

From his seat, Monsieur closed his eyes.

"I told him it doesn't matter," she said. "I saw him after he was discharged a few years ago. I told him none of it mattered. I just wanted him to come home."

"Madame, I want that too. I came to ask for your help."

Monsieur stood and took her arm. "Rowena." He pulled her into his chair. "Clare, please eat."

They watched while I took a sip of wine, while I cut my omelette. Monsieur nodded encouragingly as he served up the rest. Madame bit her lip. After I'd eaten half — the cheese cooling, the edges going limp — he finally said, "Tell us."

"I work in a studio on the Rue Notre-Dame-des-Champs," I said. "We make masks for *mutilés.*" At the word, Madame flinched. "He needs help, please. I want him to come in, for a mask, for our other resources." I took a deep breath. "I want to help him the way he once helped me."

"And you want us to convince Luc that he should come to your studio," Monsieur said, setting down his own fork.

Madame had a forefinger pressed to her mouth. Eyes distant, she shook her head. "No."

"Madame?" I sat up.

"We can't. We don't know where he is, and even if we did, we couldn't go and plead. He'd never come home then." She turned to her husband. "Don't you see, Claude? He said he needed time to know himself. If we go to push him towards a mask rather than —"

"Don't you want him here, *ma minette*?" He pushed aside the plates and mugs to sit right on the table in front of her.

"Of course. I want you both here, the way things were before. But I scared him off once. I don't want to do it again."

He put his hands on either side of her face. She brought hers up to his shoulders. They made their own little circle.

"He won't be content with any absolution we give him. With any face," she said. "He has to find both on his own."

Monsieur looked searchingly into her eyes. She nodded and, finally, so did he. "Mademoiselle," he said, dropping his hands. "I am sorry, but we cannot help you."

"You must," I pleaded. "This is what he needs." I slid a scrap of paper across the table. "I copied it from our registry book.

His address. And, below that, mine. Please, we've helped many *mutilés.*"

Madame flinched again at the word. "No more." She pushed the address back towards me. "We've always taught Luc by just leaving him be. He learns through his own mistakes and successes."

It was no different than the way Grandfather had raised me, letting me get lost in the maze of Seville's streets, cheated in the Djemma el Fna, heartbroken thinking of Luc on a beach along the Mediterranean. "When I was here," I said, "broken in two after my father died, Luc didn't leave me be. I won't abandon him either."

CHAPTER 26
LUC
1919

I stood before the gate of 70 bis Rue Notre-Dame-des-Champs, a package in my hand. It had arrived Monday, wrapped in brown paper, addressed to my apartment. The only person who had ever written me there before was Mabel.

It was a *santon,* made from red Picardy clay. He was shaped and painted with loving care. But he wasn't a shepherd or a water bearer or one of the usual *santons* Maman put in the Christmas *crèche.* This one, with palette and brush, was a painter. A painter wearing my old face.

On the back, written in gold with a feather-fine brush, were the words, *An artist must see beyond the shadows to the colors hiding there.* When I opened it, when I traced the script on the back, I felt something strange. For the first time in years, I felt hope.

I wrapped the statuette and went through

the gate. The courtyard, with the crooked tree and basin of rainwater, was quiet.

The studio wasn't as bustling as my first visit. Two women, dressed sensibly alike in crisp white blouses, dark skirts, and neckties, smoothed clay over cast molds. One woman, in a gray smock, with a paintbrush tucked behind one ear, stood near the window and squinted at a mask in her hand. It was the older woman, who I'd met at the gate with the basket of pears. I couldn't see the mask, but it glowed with enamel, the colors of flesh stretched across bone, of shadows and ridges. I began to see why the waiting *mutilés* looked so hopeful.

Madame Ladd, I spotted right away, in careful consultation with a small bearded man who looked so French and provincial and artistic. Papa would've felt at home in this studio, with its airy sunlight and the sounds of Paris through the windows. If he ever traded the tranquility of the country- side for a studio, it would be one like this.

Under the flags, soldiers were grouped in a cluster of horizon blue, smoking and laughing. Tumblers of wine and dishes of chocolates were scattered between checker- boards and playing cards. One young man, in an apron and narrow spectacles, refilled glasses almost overeagerly, wiping down tables after each pour. One half of the room a studio, smelling of clay and turpentine and the sharp tang of galvanized copper, and the other half practically a café.

I didn't even realize I was looking for her, searching every face in the room, until a pert woman stepped up. "You are Monsieur Crépet? Monsieur Luc Crépet?" She tucked bobbed hair behind her ears.

It still felt odd to hear my name, as though I were the same person I was in the past. The same Luc. "Yes. I have an appointment."

"I'm Pascalle Bernard." She tightened the sash on her apron. "Today, I will be taking a cast of your face."

"Mademoiselle, you?" I glanced around. "I'm sorry, I don't mean to be rude."

"You're not," she said, though with an edge to her voice. "Is there something the matter?"

"No, but the artist who sketched me the other day . . ." I stepped farther into the room, wondering if she was tucked into a corner. "She . . ."

"Mademoiselle Ross?" She drew her lips into a bow. "She is not in today. I will be beginning your mask."

I took a step backwards. "I don't know."

"Please, monsieur." She waved to the

young man with the apron and bottle of wine. "Évrard! Come, bring a glass."

The man filled one and bounded across the room, sloshing wine as he went. He wiped the edge of the glass with his towel and then offered it to me.

"I might not —"

"Just a glass of wine."

I took it. The glass shook in my hand.

"Don't be nervous," Mademoiselle Bernard said.

"I'm not nervous." I straightened. "There should be nothing to be nervous about, correct?"

"Nothing." She nodded to the young man. "You know, Évrard here came to the studio thirteen times before he stayed long enough for a mask."

Évrard hung his head, but the smile didn't leave his face.

"And see what it's done for him." She gestured.

Tucking the towel into his waistband, Évrard reached behind his ears and unhooked the temples of his glasses. But when the glasses pulled away from his face, they brought a mask away with them, a mask I hadn't noticed until now.

The smile that didn't leave his face, it was painted on. The eye, the nose, the cheek, all replaced what was missing below. He had lost so much more than I had, yet, when he slid the mask back on, I realized what he had gained.

The paint was smooth, and the pale color of his skin, even down to the shades of dark stubble on his cheek. So thin that, when it was on, I saw no seam. It must have been a glass eye, but it sparkled the same pale blue as his other, surrounded even by curls of eyelashes. He raised his hand in a salute. Without thinking, I saluted back.

"Do you see, monsieur?"

Hands still shaking, I drained the glass. "Where do I sit?"

Mademoiselle Bernard led me to a chair in the corner. "We will make many casts of your face. We need both positive and negative casts . . . positive means that —"

"If you please," I said softly. "I grew up surrounded by artists. I understand positive and negative."

She looked delighted. "Then you have nothing to worry about. You are safe in my hands."

"I'm not nervous," I said for the second time that day. This time, though, it wasn't said to convince her. I was trying to convince myself.

"As I said, we'll need to have positive and

negative casts of your face as it is now, and then, from these, we'll build up your face as it was then. We'll cast it in copper and then an electric deposit of silver."

Despite myself, I was interested. "Why in silver?"

"It will add to the mask's durability." She smiled. "We'll paint it, fit it with the attachments that will secure it to your face, and *voilà!* You, monsieur, will have a new face."

Although I tried to avoid it, my fingers flew to my cheek, to the rough pits and gouges. "And the old face?"

"It's still yours, monsieur," she said quietly. "A memory of a time when you were stronger than what you were fighting. A reminder that you came home."

I exhaled. "I think I'm ready to begin."

With a quick smile and a nod, she led me over to a low chair, backed against a table. "If you'll sit, please, I'll make you comfortable." She brought a stack of bed pillows to the table and covered them with a spotted sheet. "Lean back against these."

I settled back as she draped me with another sheet, from the neck down. "I feel like I'm at the barber for a shave."

She picked up a bowl of something pale and creamy. "Nearly." She scooped up a fingerful. "It's Vaseline. I'll rub it on your face

395

and —"

"Please . . ." Suddenly my jokes didn't feel so funny. Just nervous conversation, as they often were. "May I?"

"What, rub on the Vaseline?"

I held out my hand for the bowl.

Instead she set it down and leaned against the table. "Monsieur, I know you are sensitive to your condition, but, to help you, we must touch your face at times. Please let us."

"No one does."

Of course, the doctors in the hospital had touched my face, when it was still raw and oozing. Surgeons had cut it and stitched it up again. Mabel had washed it and changed the dressings. But since leaving the hospital, since it had begun healing, pink and tight and itchy, that all stopped. Even I avoided touching what had become of me.

Until the first day I came in the studio, and Clare so unexpectedly put her fingers to each side of my face, feeling the scars of the last four years, feeling everything she'd missed, no one had touched me with such gentleness. I didn't trust that anyone else could.

"I'll do it." I took the bowl and, closing my eyes, began smearing the Vaseline onto my face.

"Be sure you get plenty in your mustache and brows. And along your hairline, if you please." I kept rubbing until I heard her say, "That's enough."

I opened my eyes to lashes stuck together.

"You can keep them closed if you'd like. I'll prepare the rest of your face for the plaster." She pulled a wad of cotton wool to stuff each ear. "We don't want any plaster to drip in there." And a soft, thin piece of fabric twisted into a rope, snaked along my hairline and was tucked behind each ear.

"Is this how it feels to be packaged in a crate, I wonder?"

"I see your humor has returned."

"At least until you start." Through my gummy eyelashes, I saw a bowl on the table, filled with a thick white soup of plaster. "That's what you'll put on my face?"

"Yes, but quickly, before it begins hardening." She gave it a few more stirs as I settled back deeper into the stack of pillows. "There. That should be ready. The quills and then you can close your eyes."

"Quills?"

She held up two hollow sections of quill, cut short. "Now this will only be uncomfortable for a moment."

The two quills went in my nostrils, so it was more than a little uncomfortable, and it definitely was longer than a moment.

"Close your eyes now."

The first few drops of plaster hit me as heavy and cold as mud. She dripped it across my face, then up over my forehead. I felt it spatter on my eyelids, and squeezed them shut even further. "Relax," she said firmly, and I tried to oblige. Wet plaster slid along each side of my nose and I inhaled sharply through the quills. "Relax."

"Easy for you to say," I mumbled, but she pressed a damp finger to my lips. I flinched.

"Still, now. Please."

Plaster covered my mouth. If I tried to scream, it would fill my mouth, roll down my throat. I dug my fingernails into my legs.

I wasn't getting air. Those two quills in my nose, I knew they weren't enough. I breathed so fast I could feel them quivering. I need . . . I need . . . I couldn't even tell her.

"You're fine, monsieur," she said calmly. With the cotton in my ears, her voice was wavy, like I was underwater. Or maybe I was faint. I was blacking out, hurtling into the void, going to die. All of those stones in the old well were falling down on me. The ceiling of the quarry was closing in. I'd be buried alive.

And still she wasn't stopping. I could feel

the layers on my face getting heavier and heavier. Surely the weight would crack right through my skin and seep into my blood. I wanted to tell her to stop, to tell her that was enough, that surely she could make a mask with what she had right now, but when I tried, my lips tasted like plaster.

So heavy, and hot. How long did she say it needed to stay on? It had been at least a few minutes, more than a few, many agonizing minutes. So hot; was I burning?

"You're fine," she said again, and I tried to shake my head. "No!" I said. Or maybe it was her, because she was pinning me down, holding my head still. "You mustn't move. Monsieur Crépet, no!"

But I had to move, I had to escape, I had to find a place to breathe. How could they do this to a man and say it was for his own good? My throat tightened. Oh, God, it was closing up. I was dying. I reached up, to touch the mask, to tear it away. I had to.

Then through the fog, a voice broke through, "Pascalle, no!" Commanding. "You can't hold him down like that." The weight on my chest eased, let go. "He's terrified of small spaces. Oh, Luc."

Like an angel, Clare was there. "Louise, open the window." Light fingers unbuttoned the top of my shirt. Cool air reached my chest. "Pascalle, that wet cloth." She was speaking English, in a tumbled rush. "Luc," she said in a low voice, "I have you." Quickly, quietly, she repeated that over and over until my breathing slowed. She took my hands, sticky with plaster, in hers. "I have you."

A chair squeaked and she sat next to me, still holding my hands. "Do you remember, Luc, all of the wood violets that grew around the chestnut tree? We'd step right over them and the air always smelled sweeter. I was so silly, but I used to take a handful up to my room and pretend that you picked them for me."

I squeezed her hand.

"And all of the cicadas! Their song was our symphony that summer." Her hands were warm. "Remember the fable of the cicada who spent all summer singing rather than storing food? La Fontaine, wasn't it? You told me that's why you never hear cicadas singing in the city. Parisian cicadas would never forget their larder." She laughed. I'd forgotten her little peal of a laugh, so rare. "I understand that now.

"And do you remember the time Bede went missing? Marthe packed us a bag with oranges and brown bread and cheese, and we hiked all day through the pines looking for his footprints. And when I fell and bumped my head, you ran to the stream and carried back the water in your two hands for me to drink. Hardly a few drops by the time you found me again. Did I ever tell you how vile that water was? Muddy and dank. But I drank those palmfuls of water because you brought them."

My lips moved against the inside of the cast. I wanted to tell her that, yes, I remembered. That I would've gone to the Amazon and back for water if it would've made her feel better.

"Here we go," she said, and I felt other hands on the side of my face, easing the plaster cast off. When it lifted, my eyes found Clare's. "Do you remember what you said to me the day we met?" she asked.

I remembered her standing in the front hall of Mille Mots like a lost fairy queen. She looked so sad and scared and defiant, all at the same time. I'd offered my hand and ended up giving up my heart.

"You are safe with me," she said.

■ ■ ■ ■

PART 5
THE MASK

1919

■ ■ ■ ■

CHAPTER 27
CLARE

1919

Mrs. Ladd had urged a morning off. "You are tireless, Miss Ross."

"These men have given so much," I told her. "My time is the least I can give."

"Miss Bernard did express some concern." She folded her hands. "She said there was a guest the other day who . . . affected you."

Mrs. Ladd had the ability to make suggestions sound like privileges, *mays* instead of *shoulds.* While Pascalle nodded and made shooing motions behind Mrs. Ladd's back, I said, "Thank you," and stayed home the next day.

I'd taken to watching for the post anyway. I kept hoping that the Crépets would write to me, tell me they were wrong, tell me that they wanted to help. I sat by the window of the apartment, letting my artist's imagination conjure up scenes of happy family reunions. In all of them, I hovered along the edges of the embraces.

I kept myself busy that morning off. After a slow breakfast of tea and a newspaper I wasn't really reading, I bundled up in my coat and cherry-red scarf. I walked to Les Halles through a hesitant snow. I'd make Grandfather a *flamiche,* if I could find leeks.

The market in Les Halles wasn't as bright as any in Africa or Spain. No woven rugs or baskets of couscous or cones of ground spices. The produce wasn't as shiny, the fish not as fresh, the flowers not as plentiful as the other markets I knew. Pascalle promised that it once was and that it would return to that as soon as France recovered. In the meantime, the market was crowded with housewives and cooks doing their shopping quickly with downcast eyes and half-empty bags. American soldiers, ruddy and clean, brushed past the old poilus, faded after four years of war. Those refugees who had nothing to return to, they crouched on corners, waiting patiently for the charity of strangers. My heart ached for them, always, but I couldn't buy enough bread to feed every lost one in the city.

The flower seller, in her spotted head scarf and layers of bright-dyed skirts, waited on her usual corner. "Flowers, *ma chère*?" She held out a small, fragrant bunch of violets. "Ask your sweetheart to buy you flowers?"

I gave her a few coins, like I always did, but left the flowers for the next customer. "No sweetheart yet, mademoiselle."

And there hadn't been. I had my easy friendship with Finlay, but both of us knew it could never be more than that. There'd been a boy in Lagos who tried to kiss me, and one in Seville whom I'd let. There'd been one in Marrakesh, an American artist, who sketched me nude when Grandfather was gone. But none that I'd call "sweetheart."

I told myself it was because I didn't want to compromise. What good was gaining a sweetheart if it meant losing everything else? *What are you waiting for?* Finlay had asked me once. *Who are you waiting for?* I always answered, *No one,* because I wanted that to be the answer. And because any other admission would break my heart. I didn't want to confess that, even then, even not knowing, I was always waiting for Luc.

I went back to the apartment with my shopping, unpacked my groceries, arranged and rearranged the few stores on my shelves. While I was out, Grandfather had come back from his morning coffee at Café Aleppo, and he'd fallen asleep on the sofa still in his shoes. I paced. I washed my hair. I tried out my new marcel iron. I paced.

Who are you waiting for?

I wished I'd brought Luc's old letters with me from Perthshire, so that I could spread them all out on the bed the way I used to, so I could try to remember a time when he would meet my eyes instead of looking away. But the letters were tucked in my dresser drawer at Fairbridge, wrapped in a silk scarf. Memories, however, weren't so easy to tuck away.

I had a letter that morning, from Finlay. His letters lately had been infused with regret. They'd been doing life drawing, which always made him think of his sister. His letters were filled with lines like, *Stubbornness is no excuse for loss,* and *I'd give up my other leg to go back in time,* and *Why do you still write to a miserable soul like me?* But this last letter was all about the new life model, Evelyn, an aspiring art student with, from the sound of it, the longest legs in Scotland. It held an uncharacteristic note of hope.

I thought to write him back. Tell him about Luc. If I went to post a letter, it surely wouldn't hurt anything if I stopped by the studio for a moment. A quick moment. I'd be passing by and, anyway, I needed to give Pascalle her scarf back. I could even bring her a spot of supper. She'd appreciate it, to be sure. Bread was hard to come by, but I had half a loaf and cut her off an end. As I buttered bread, sliced cheese, scrubbed a pear, and packed it all in a basket with a half bottle of wine, I managed to convince myself that this had been the plan all along. If it so happened that a letter had come to the studio from Monsieur Luc Crépet, so much the better. I brewed mint tea for Grandfather to have when he woke from his nap. I forgot all about Finlay's letter. I caught up my basket, spread a blanket over Grandfather, and headed to the studio.

I heard Pascalle's shout when I was half-way up the stairs. I dropped the basket of food and ran the rest of the way up.

Inside the studio, Luc leaned back on a stack of pillows, his face covered in a thick layer of wet, white plaster. But he was kick-ing and twisting between strangled cries. Pascalle held him firmly. Across the room the waiting *mutilés* craned their necks over their checkerboards.

I didn't even pause to take off my coat. I hurried across the room and took his hand. "Luc," I said, "I have you."

He quieted at my voice, so I knew I had to keep talking. I pulled out memories and long-forgotten adventures. "Do you remem-ber when" and "there was that time" until the sentences ran together. But at each word, the tension left his hand a little bit more. I hoped he wouldn't hear the quaver in my voice, the hitch of worry that made me breathless. When the mask was lifted, he stared straight up at me, not a hint of that guardedness. "You are safe with me," I said. I hoped he believed me.

Luc's eyes stayed on me as I took the cast to the drying table, as I helped him sit up, as I carefully sponged the plaster and Vaseline from the edges of his face with warm water. I didn't rush, though it was the end of the day and the sun slanted low through the windows. I let those precious still seconds with Luc last.

"Clare," he said. The first time he'd said my name in years. "Clare, will you?"

The question hung in the air. Behind me, the room quieted as artists and *mutilés* gradually filtered out, headed to suppers and homes and dreams still to come. Mine was right here.

"Luc." I felt his name against the roof of my mouth. It tasted like summer. "I'll help. Of course I'll help." I combed down his damp hair with my fingers. "But not only for the mask." I hated the words as they came out of my mouth. "You have to do more than walk the streets again; you have to walk through life."

He broke my gaze at last and put his face to a towel. "You make it sound so easy." His voice muffled through the thick fabric.

"I know it won't be." I thought of Finlay, of his ups and downs, of his estrangement from his family, of those days when he had to fight with himself just to leave his flat. But also of his classes, Evelyn the model, and his newly hopeful letter. "But the mask is a bandage. To heal, there must be more."

"Is there more?"

There had to be. Luc walked through the door of that studio, and suddenly the future stretched out, past the battlefields and shells. If he couldn't step beyond all that, then what use was seeing the future at all?

I squeezed the wet sponge, leaving drops of water on my skirt. "Have you found employment?"

He shook his head. "Who would hire someone like me?"

"A hero of France?" My voice echoed in the room. Even Mrs. Ladd had gone down to the courtyard, to rinse the bowls and plaster brushes. "Plenty."

That old guarded look was coming up again. "Wounds and medals don't make a hero."

"I'm sure you could take up your old

place at the university. Finish your studies. War interrupted that."

"But then what? I studied to be a teacher." He wiped the corners of his eyes with a thumb. "I wouldn't inflict myself on a roomful of students now."

"You'll have your mask."

He stayed quiet. I didn't know if he was considering or ignoring.

"Tennis?"

He reached to his shoulder in response. I wondered what old wound hid there. "Those days are past."

"You could coach, I'd think. Couldn't you?"

"Clare." He sighed. "Don't."

"Maybe you need something new." Water dripped into the basin. "I have a pamphlet I'll send with you. There's an institute now, you know."

"To teach *invalides* and *mutilés* a trade. I know."

I tried to push a brightness into my voice. "You can learn just about anything. Tailoring, shoemaking, tinsmithing. Clockmaking, I think. Typesetting, binding . . . oh, all sorts of things." I blotted along the curve of his cheek. "I had one fellow who trained to be a bookkeeper. He thought of industrial design — that's a choice, too — but decided —"

"Please stop."

"Close your eyes again." I moved the sponge to the skin beneath his brow. "Why not art, then?" I said quietly.

"Art?" Behind his lids his eyes moved. "I was never that good."

"At teaching, you were." Like at that lesson under the chestnut tree, my fingers were on his face. "I don't know how you would have been at history or philosophy or whatever you were studying to teach, but as an art tutor, you were —" My voice caught. "You were very good."

He exhaled against my wrist. I knew he was remembering the same scene. "And did it work?" he asked.

"Did what?"

"The lesson."

"I ended up at the School of Art, after all." I couldn't keep the pride from my voice.

He smiled, the first one I'd seen in eight years. "See, you were too busy to miss me."

"But I did," I said without thinking. "Miss you."

I expected more of that smile, but his face tensed. "Still so teasing, are you?"

"You once said you were always at my

413

service." The sponge reached the edges of his scar. "There were days I wished for a knight."

"That night you spent in Paris," he said. "You could have used one then."

He had to be guessing. He didn't know about the taxi ride to that house, about Stefan in the mirror, about the night huddled in the cemetery of a little white-stoned church. My fingers tightened on the sponge. "What do you mean?"

"What happened that evening."

How could it be more than guessing? I didn't tell him. I'd never told a soul. "I'm sure I don't know what you're talking about." Water dribbled between my fingers.

"You didn't travel with —"

"No," I said, too quickly. The taste of Suze rose on my tongue, and it made me flush. I'd gone with Stefan. I'd taken the drink from him. I hadn't locked the door. "I told you, nothing happened." I dropped the sponge in the bucket with a splash.

He opened his eyes. "Please don't. I'm . . . sorry." He was saying it for now and for all those years ago. "Clare, I'm sorry." Maybe even for Stefan and the night in Paris. "Don't go." He reached up and touched the knob of my wrist, just once.

Everyone else had left, but I had stayed by

his side. And I would, as long as he'd let me.

I turned my hand. Our palms brushed. "I promise."

The mask took me a month to complete. It wasn't because I wasn't diligent. No, it took me so much longer because I wanted it to be perfect. It was Luc. I couldn't give him any less.

I cleaned the negative cast we took of his face. With fresh plaster of Paris, I made a positive and smoothed out any little lumps and divots left behind by the casting process.

"It was a good cast," Pascalle complained. "I didn't do anything wrong."

"No, you followed the procedure," I said quietly, scraping my knife across the dried plaster. "But this is one I need to do myself."

She stirred a bowl of wet plaster of Paris. "This will start hardening in a moment. You need to take the next cast."

"It's not ready yet."

I fiddled with smoothing until I'd ruined that bowl of plaster and had to mix another. Pascalle sighed, but she helped me make the second negative. We then filled it with plasticine clay to make a positive "squeeze." An inelegant name for a piece of sculpture.

I lifted the plaster cast off the gray plasticine. Luc's ruined face looked up at me from the table and I swallowed back tears.

"Miss Ross." Mrs. Ladd was suddenly at my elbow. "Miss Bernard told me you've been crying."

"No, I haven't." I shot Pascalle a look across the room, but she was studiously involved with a brush and some turpentine. "I've been tired."

She settled into a chair across from me. "You understand why we cannot cry in the studio."

"The soldiers are sensitive to their appearances," I said automatically. "They have a difficult enough time with reactions outside of the studio. I know. But . . ."

"But you're only crying over a squeeze. Is that what you were going to say?"

"Yes."

"Miss Ross," she said, "look at those soldiers sitting over there."

Though they sat with wine and hearty conversation, there was an alertness about them. A tense watchfulness. They were like deer ready to bolt, waiting for the first sneer or startled look.

"They don't care that you are only crying down onto a squeeze. In that squeeze, in that other ruined face, they see their own."

I swallowed, and I nodded.

"Is this the same soldier as the other day?" She reached across and pulled the plasticine closer. "It is a clean cast. He doesn't appear too bad. You should do well on this one."

"I hope I can."

"You always do. Why are you doubting now?"

I ran a finger along the edge of the plasticine face and didn't answer. I couldn't tell her how seeing all of the details, being able to touch each and every scar in the clay, made it seem so much more real to me. That, even though I helped soldiers worse off than Luc all the time, helping *him* meant so much more.

"Would it be better for someone else to work on this one? It doesn't have to be Miss Bernard." Everyone had seen my frantic run into the studio the other day, when Luc was panicking beneath the wet plaster. I'd dropped the basket of Pascalle's supper. The stairs still bore a dark streak of wine.

"No, please. I can do it." I looked up. "I'll hold it together."

She sat quiet for a moment, her hands crossed on the table. Finally she sighed. "Do you think me heartless? Unaffected by what I see in here every day?"

"Of course not, Madame."

"When I first came to France, before I

opened the studio, I went out and toured the hospitals. I needed to see the state of the French soldiers. I even went out closer to the lines — guided, of course — and saw these injuries when they were fresh."

I held my breath. I couldn't imagine; when their faces were contorted with more than emotional pain.

"I'd come back here, to the Rue Notre-Dame-des-Champs, which wasn't yet a studio. It was an empty room. I'd sit here alone and sometimes I was overcome." Her eyes misted in a quick instant, but she blinked and forced a sunny smile. "We are like the masks. We need to be. Strong metal covering vulnerability. They both exist, mademoiselle."

"But even the strongest copper can crack."

She smiled gently. "We don't let it."

I went back to my squeeze, feeling too fragile to be made of metal but knowing I had to, for Luc's sake. For the sake of all the men in the room. So I ignored the scars, the pits, the ridges, and I concentrated on his eyes.

While taking that first cast, a soldier sat with eyes closed, covered over with thin slips of tissue paper. The plasticine squeeze gave us the chance to open those eyes with a burin and a steady hand. It was a necessary step for those soldiers who needed an eye on their mask to replace one lost. Luc didn't, but I still etched them in. I wanted it to be the Luc I remembered.

I sat, with burin in hand, my own eyes closed against the reality of the room, and tried to remember his. It wasn't hard. They were the one thing I recognized when he came back to the studio. Brown like almonds, narrow, ringed with thick, dark lashes. Those eyes that startled wide that first morning when I ducked his tennis swing in the front hall, the eyes so intense and watchful as I tasted my first mouthful of ginger preserve, those eyes that shone in the dark the night that Grandfather took me away from Mille Mots. I knew them well.

It was short work to etch them in, but I wasn't satisfied. Turn up a little more at the corner. No, too much. A few more flecks here, where, in my memory, it was darker brown. A gleam, a strength, a surety. I could do my best, but those last, I couldn't etch in.

When Mrs. Ladd was ready to lock the studio, I still sat, curls of clay littering the table. She took the burin from my hand. "Miss Ross. Clare. He's waited this long for a mask. Another day won't matter much."

But it wasn't just "another day." I spent

419

three days alone working on the squeeze, until Pascalle was glaring and even Mrs. Ladd looked drawn. Then I cast again with plaster of Paris, one negative and one positive. On this last positive, I built Luc's face.

I worked slowly, carefully, scraping away the plaster grain by grain. I had my sketch right beside me, the sketch that first revealed the battered soldier as my lost childhood love. I worried over every line in the sketch. I doubted my memory.

But I also doubted my doubt. Maybe there was something, some chink in his armor. An honest something to hope for. With each scrape of my knife, with each shower of plaster dust falling onto the table, *maybe, maybe,* said my heart.

At the end of each day, I caught up the dust into my palm. I went to the Square du Vert-Galant and stood with my feet on the point of land. It was the place Luc had mentioned in his letter, the place where he said he always felt the breath of Paris on his face. Now, it was my quiet spot in the city. I let the wind carry away the palmful of dust into the river and I hoped.

That first week, after Luc touched my wrist and asked me to stay, he didn't come to the studio at all. Then one day he appeared in the doorway, shy, hat in hand like a suitor. I blushed to see it.

But he didn't talk to me. He just nodded and went to sit with the other *mutilés* and their checkerboards. Another patient. I bent my head and tried to forget he was right there, watching.

I smoothed out his left cheek, his jaw, the corner of his eye. With my knife, I gave him that angled cheekbone I remembered. That straight jaw that always tightened when he was nervous. That left eye that crinkled at the corner in one of his unexpected laughs. Luc, always so serious. Even as a boy — studying, working, wishing he could do more for the château — he always looked like he carried the world on his shoulders.

That's why his letters surprised me. They weren't at all serious. Hiding behind pen and paper, Luc bantered, joked, teased, in a way that he didn't often do in person. That was the Luc I thought I'd meet again someday. In all of those sunshine daydreams I had of coming back to Paris, of climbing the paths in the Parc des Buttes Chaumont and painting by the Seine, that lighthearted Luc was there by my side. None of the adolescent awkwardness we'd known before. Instead, the comfortableness, the humor, the friendship we'd built through our letters.

But here I was, in Paris at last, with Luc at last, and there were no smiles. His face was drawn and weary. He had no laughter left.

With my knife, I sculpted the Luc of my letters, the Luc of my daydreams. I curved the left side of his mouth upwards in a smile. I quirked an eyebrow in a moment of suppressed mirth. It didn't matter. Mrs. Ladd would make me change it in the end.

To my surprise, she didn't. She paused once at my table, nodded down at the plaster, and said, "That's the face of a man healed."

Each morning, he'd arrive at nine-thirty in his wrinkled gray suit and secondhand fedora to sit with the *mutilés* and a glass of wine that he'd nurse for hours. Though he always held a book in front of him, I pretended he was watching me over the top of the spine. And then hated myself for wishing. He was waiting for a mask, to allow him to move on, and here I was sighing like a schoolgirl and stretching out my work so he wouldn't have to leave. He'd stay until three o'clock and then, with a quick glance my way, would slip out the door.

One day when he arrived, it was to a sketchbook and pencil waiting at his usual seat. He blinked, and I smiled to see him so

startled. He looked up, questioningly. I nodded. That whole morning, as I pressed the
sheet of copper against my plaster sculpture,
as I traced each line and curve until it held
the imprint of Luc's face, he warily regarded
the sketchbook. I trimmed away the extra
copper and the right half of the face; he had
no need to cover that. As I smoothed down
the raw edges, Luc finally picked up the
pencil. Arm held stiff, he began to draw.

After he left, when I was cleaning up, I
opened the book. He'd roughed in a soldier,
a poilu in a dented helmet and greatcoat.
Though the soldier's shape was blurred, his
face was full of careful detail. Weary lines, a
grim line of a mouth, yet eyes boyish wide.
It wasn't anyone I recognized, but it was
someone Luc knew well.

The next day, when I put the copper into
the electroplating bath, he wasn't alone. A
few other *mutilés* had pulled chairs nearby
and were watching Luc work. He didn't say
a word, but they kept his wine refilled. He'd
added two other soldiers to the sketch, both
facing away. One leaned on a rifle, the other
was praying. By midday there was a fourth
soldier, sitting with his head hanging between his knees.

On the third day, Luc tore sheets from the
back of his book. There was now a tableful

423

of *mutilés* with paper and pencil, sketching away at trees and houses and airplanes. Every once in a while he'd look up from his own drawing to offer a quiet suggestion or two. Meanwhile he added a parapet and row of sandbags behind his penciled poilus.

The next morning, when I took the gleaming half mask from its bath, Luc finally approached. He didn't even glance down at the drying mask, waiting to be painted. He only looked at me.

"Thank you," was all he said. "You knew what I needed."

When I looked at his sketch later, the young soldier in the middle held a sword, a great sword with a twisted pommel. In the midst of war, he looked invulnerable.

You knew what I needed.

CHAPTER 28
LUC
1919

The day the mask was ready, I was as nervous as Christmas morning.

I'd spent months hiding — behind my scarf, behind my guilt, behind my excuses. At Mabel's insistence, I went reluctantly that first time to Mrs. Ladd's studio. I knew I was going to another mask, albeit one more tangible than the regret I'd been wearing. I didn't expect more than a more polite way to hide my memories. I didn't expect to be fixed.

Then I met Clare. There'd never been façades between us, even when we had nothing but letters. She'd put on a falsely cheerful front for her grandfather, as I had with Maman, but we didn't with each other. Our words, our pictures, our ink-smudged fingerprints in the margins, all were honest. With Clare in the studio, my defenses slowly began crumbling. They wouldn't have mattered to her anyway.

I'd held her hand while she sponged plaster off my cheeks. I'd watched her across the room while she spent far too long making the mask. These past weeks, my heart made me more vulnerable than my ruined face ever had.

But here she was, as nervous as I was, fingers tapping the underside of the table, waiting to pull the cloth from yet another mask. She'd seen me bare, and yet was handing me something to cover all that again.

"I did the best I could," she said right away. "Well, are you ready?"

I was freezing cold all of a sudden, and no, I wasn't ready, but I swallowed and I nodded. She pulled up the cloth.

Despite her doubts, Clare had done it. That curve of my brow, the shape of my lips, the angle of my cheek. She'd taken half of a ruined face, a handful of memories, and she'd made me. No one else could have done it.

"*Magnifique.*" I reached for it, almost. "Of course it is." What was I imagining? Something as stiff and distant as the plaster casts lining the walls? Something that wasn't me? "Mademoiselle . . . Clare . . . can I have a moment, please?"

She opened her mouth as though to

protest, she bit her lip, she nodded. After a moment of withheld breath and withheld words, she retreated to the other side of the room.

I was left alone with my own face.

As perfect as it was, it was unsettling. To see half of my own face, too shiny, a single gaping hole for my eye, staring up from the table. Half of a carefully stubbled cheek, a half a mouth caught up in an almost-smile, a look I hadn't worn in far too long. Too perfect. It could have been a painting, a sculpture, something hanging from the wall of a gallery. It was vivid and lifelike, but it wasn't real.

Was this my choice, then? To be a gargoyle or, instead, to be a work of art? I touched the metal with my index finger. Perhaps these days I was as cold to the touch.

"Luc." Clare was suddenly at my elbow.

She stood by me, so shining and hopeful. I thought of all her patience and persistence, when I'd given her nothing but bitterness in return. She didn't demand, just said, "Please."

I picked up the mask. Clare was right. She did make a thing of beauty. I put it on.

For a moment everything went dim. She fussed and adjusted, her fingers light as pearls. I blinked and, through the narrow

427

left eyehole, I saw her stop and press a hand to her mouth. So quickly, I wondered if I was wrong. I wondered what she saw.

It rubbed at the edges, the way a new pair of shoes did. The weight of the metal pushed against my scars and made me feel every ridge. It was cold and smooth as ice, but Clare had done well. The mask skimmed my face like a second skin.

She finished fiddling with it and asked, "Would you like to see the mirror?"

"Take me outside," I said, drawing a deep breath. "That's all the mirror I need."

She waited a moment, but nodded. "Good," she said. Again that quick hand to her mouth. "I can see how the colors hold in the sunlight."

I let Clare lead me down the stairs and out into the light of Rue Notre-Dame-des-Champs.

Between the sun and the opening for my left eye, I couldn't see much. It was like a single horse blinder. My cheek sweated beneath the metal, then itched. I reached up to scratch underneath, but she pulled my hand down. I stumbled on the cobbles.

"Stop worrying," she whispered. "You're counting your steps."

"It's like being in a cave. I can't see the sky on that side." My arm tensed beneath her fingers.

"Then tip your head up."

And so I did. I stopped, and turned my face up to the sky. Cool air dipped beneath the mask. Above me, clear blue.

"Luc," she said softly, "look."

The narrow streets of the Left Bank were busy with people coming home from work or the day's shopping. Smartly dressed shopgirls, women in long striped aprons and wooden sabots, students in faded black jackets, vendors in dark smocks. Women in flowered straw hats, some with books or music cases tucked under their arms, brushed past shabbily dressed men with ink on their fingertips. Everyone was so brisk and sure. But, most important, they didn't give me a second glance.

What would they see if they did? Smooth metal and a false smile hiding a man with shaking knees, who clung desperately to the woman next to him. A perfect face on an imperfect man.

I scrabbled at the edges of the mask. The metal bit into the pads of my fingers.

"No, no, Luc!"

"I can't see," I said, though my mind was still filled with blue sky. "I can't breathe anymore."

"You can." She took my hands, took my

whole weight as I sagged. "Remember . . . remember when we'd pick grapes down near the pasture? We found a beehive and you were stung twice." She was trying to do what she'd done that day in the studio, when she held my hands and brought me back to Mille Mots with her. When she tried to make me forget my fears. "And remember when you'd bring me bread and jam from the kitchen when Marthe wasn't looking?" My breathing had slowed. It almost matched the rhythm in hers. "You'd spread your jacket out on the lawn and arrange the treats just so, like a little picnic only for me."

It was only for her. Always.

"And remember when I followed you to the caves? We ate so many oranges the air smelled like happiness. I ducked into the cave and you waited right outside for me, worrying the whole time. You know, that day was the first time I wished you'd kiss me."

I let go of her hands. "Stop trying to make me remember." I stumbled backwards into the street. "Stop trying to make me hope."

"Hope?" She straightened. "If nothing else, I wished to give you hope."

I ran a finger beneath the edge of the mask to wipe away sweat. "I thought you wanted to give me a future."

"Exactly," she said, her eyes too bright.

430

"With a mask, think of what you could do." She pushed a strand of hair behind her ear. "Remember the pamphlet I mentioned? The Institut National?"

"You think I can just pick a new future from a pamphlet?"

"See it as a new beginning." Through the narrow eyehole, I could see her, standing straight and cold on the pavement. She'd forgotten her jacket. "Whatever skill you want, whatever job you're hoping for, you can have it."

"Men like me, we take what we're offered. We can't afford to expect anything more." I touched my metal cheek. "A man like me can't hope."

Arms wrapped around myself, I left her standing on the pavement in her sweater.

When I got back to the apartment, I needed to wash away Clare.

Demetrius whistled "Mademoiselle from Armentières," so I shushed him. Lysander, ever the fretter, took up my shushing. I poured out a pitcher of water and splashed a handful their way, until they bristled with outraged squawks. Lysander smoothed down his feathers; Demetrius swore in English.

I took off my new mask and scrubbed with

431

icy water until my arms and face were red. I stripped off all my clothes — the outfit I'd picked out with such care that morning for the studio. The pressed suit, the shirt the color of cornflowers, all neat and all new, like I was setting off for a wedding. I changed into a soft pair of old pants. Dripping, shirtless, I stared down at the enameled face on the washstand. I wondered what Clare saw.

But when a knock sounded on the door, my heart gave a funny leap. I threw a towel over the parrots' cage. I fastened my mask over my wet face and pulled a clean shirt from the hook.

It was her.

"What are you doing here?" I nudged open the door, enough to see the pale curve of Clare's face beneath the brim of her red hat. "How did you find me?" Behind the door I buttoned my shirt one-handed.

"Mrs. Ladd gave me your address." She hesitated. "Are you angry?"

I ran a hand through my damp hair. "No." A cold drop slid down the back of my neck. "But I've been home for an hour at least."

"And I've been standing across the street for an hour at least."

I leaned against the door, waiting, ignoring those funny little leaps in my chest.

"I just . . ." She twisted the cuff of her jacket. "Luc, you said back there that a man like you can't hope." She barely breathed the next words. "But you can."

I hadn't heard her right. "Do you —"

"May I come in?"

I glanced back over my shoulder, at the stained and threadbare rug, the unmade bed, the foul-mouthed parrots, the cracked, dirt-streaked window I kept open because the latch was busted. "No," I began, but she pushed through anyway. And stopped.

Though my single room was gray and narrow, pale frames hung from each wall, each containing a single pencil drawing. The reasons I lived in this dingy room, why I never had money for the streetcar, why I bought day-old bread. Clare stood in the middle of my room, her open hands straight down at her sides, and spun to see her own drawings.

"I saw them and —" I started, but she cut me off with a chop and a shake of her head.

She'd seen me lying back on that table in the studio, plaster in my eyebrows, my face under the light. Now I was seeing her just as naked.

All of those memories, jumbled up, came back, all of those rare instances of Clare's face as open and unguarded as it was right now. How her eyes shone at the first sight of the Brindeau caves, how they laughed when she saw my childhood portraits, how they stared into mine that moment when she touched my face and I wanted to kiss her. I wanted to again right now.

"I never thought I'd see these again," she breathed. She stepped to one framed drawing of a man, craggy-faced and harsh, yet holding to him a small boy with such tenderness that you almost didn't notice his withered arm. "He was born the day the war began. The bluest eyes, like his father."

I cleared my throat. "Your cross-hatching . . . I thought they were blue."

"As cobalt." She turned to a picture of a young soldier balancing a harmonica on two stubbed wrists. "He brightened the hospital with his music." A woman, pale hair tied beneath a head scarf, sat with elbows on her knees, bared forearms puckered and scarred. Her chin rested on open palms with seven fingers between them. "She's from Belgium, a nurse who I met at the Princess Louise Hospital. Lost everything but her grandmother's knitting needles. She made me this scarf, you know."

Eyes still on the framed pictures, she unwound the scarf from her neck and passed it to me. It was as soft as new grass.

"So you were the one who bought all of my drawings," she finally said. "Monsieur Santi said I had a secret admirer."

"Secret . . ." I handed back the scarf. "I didn't think you'd want to know it was me." I wrapped my arms around my chest, suddenly aware that I didn't have a jacket on.

She stopped her perusal of the drawings. Those bright eyes were turned on me. "I don't hear from you for years — not a word — and when I find you, it's to see every drawing I ever sold hanging on your walls." Her voice lowered, brittle at the edges. "You never even asked what I've been doing these past years."

"I don't have to. I can see." I waved a hand around the room at the frames. "You were off capturing life. Like you told me all those years ago, telling a story through art."

The last framed drawing was of a man seated shirtless on a bed, one trouser leg rolled up. A wooden leg rested lengthwise across his lap. He held it loosely, watchfully, reverently, but he looked out through a thick tangle of hair with eyes warm and appreciative.

"I don't know your subjects, but I know how it feels to be on the other side of your sketch pad." I dipped my head. "For a moment, you made them feel whole."

She touched her cheek, as though holding in a blush. "Is that how you felt sitting across from me in the studio?"

That's how I'd felt that very first time she sketched me, under the chestnut tree. I nodded.

"It's my job," she said, and twisted the scarf in her hands.

"These days, I frighten small children." I tried for a smile. "It was nice to sit and not frighten anyone for an afternoon."

She took a step forward. "Do you think your face bothers me?"

"It should."

"It doesn't." She reached out, her hand smelling warm like clay, and unhooked my mask.

I tried to catch it, to put it back on, but it slid off. "Please, no," I said, and closed my eyes. I heard a soft clink as she set it down.

And then I felt her lips on mine.

I allowed myself half a second. Half a second when the world was all right, and then I pulled back. "No. No, no, no." I opened my eyes. She was right there, so close her exhales brushed across my neck. So close she couldn't help but see the wreck of my face. "Please."

She moved forward, half a step, and dropped an index finger on my lips. "You didn't ask what I was doing all of these years." Through her glove, her finger was warm. "So I'll tell you."

From outside the window, the bell at Bonne-Nouvelle rang out three, but I stayed still in the middle of the room.

"Once upon a time, there was a boy who taught me to see the world through the eyes of an artist." She drew her finger straight down to my chin. "A face is circles and angles, shadows and light, bones and muscle, tension and desire." She traced up the right side of my face. "The line of a jaw?" And down the left. "Beauty."

"I don't —"

She stopped my words again with that soft finger. "I'm not done telling you my story." She gave a little smile and her hand trailed down to my shirt, damp from my bath. "Even after that boy left my life and, far away, grew into a soldier, I remembered what he taught me. I searched for beauty, through Morocco, through Algeria, through Mauritania, through Glasgow, through Paris. I haunted the halls of Fairbridge and the School of Art, I wandered the winding streets of the Latin Quarter, seeking those truths in lines and shapes that the artist-boy taught me to look for all those years before."

As she talked, she slowly drew out the buttons of my shirt until it hung loose and open. I shrank back into my shirt, but she slipped her hand, so warm in that glove, onto my chest. I swallowed.

"I've thought about that boy. I've wondered what he looked like, grown up. I've tried to picture those brown eyes I remember watching me under the chestnut tree. The sound of his voice, the one time he accidently asked if I'd stay forever, that sound was just beyond my imagination. I knew, if I ever met him again, that he'd be taller. Stronger. More comfortable in his own skin." With both hands under my shirt, she slid it from my shoulders. "I found that."

I caught the shirt before it fell from my left shoulder. "But I'm not." And suddenly felt barer for the admission.

"Luc, you are." She eased my hand and the shirt away. "The first time you walked through that studio door, you met my eye. You dared me to think of you any less."

I followed her gaze to my shoulder, that knotted, crooked mess that, thankfully, kept me from the army. The shoulder that still ached when it rained and when I tried to hold up a brush for more than a few minutes. The shoulder that Mabel had tried her best to massage into usability. Clare covered it with her palm.

I flinched, but she didn't move her hand.

"How did it happen?" was all she asked.

I sucked in a breath. "Trying to prove something that doesn't seem to matter anymore. Trying to win." I closed my eyes. "Could you . . . could you take your glove off?"

She did. "Luc, what are you afraid of?"

"This."

And she kissed me again. This time I didn't stop her.

I forgot that my bed was unmade, that my carpet was threadbare, that my window was cracked and streaked with grime. I forgot Paris, Bauer, the letters unsent to Maman. I forgot Chaffre and every soldier I ever shot. I forgot that I was a man broken. In her kiss, I remembered. Every sweating dream of her, every restless sketch of her fifteen-year-old face, every crossed-fingered wish.

"You have to see." She took my shirt the rest of the way off.

I let her. "See what?"

She put her lips to my shoulder, then my cheek, then my mouth. "How beautiful you are to me."

She showed me. She pushed me back onto the unmade bed, dropped her own clothes on the threadbare carpet, and, with sunlight streaking through the cracked window, we made love. Later, as I fell asleep with her warm in my arms, she murmured, "I always did like summer."

CHAPTER 29
CLARE
1919

Even in lovemaking, Luc was shy, tentative, apologetic. As I slipped off his clothing, as I kissed him down into the bed, he kept murmuring excuses and warnings. "You don't really want to do this," and "Clare, I'm too broken," and "I'm sorry, I should've made the bed." Nonsense that I ignored.

I just kept touching his hair, his face, his body, his everything, until he stopped protesting and a kind of wonder crept into his eyes. "My Luc," I whispered into the side of his neck, into his knotted shoulder. His arms tightened around me and held me safe against the world. I'd found him again.

The light slanted lower through the windows, but he didn't talk, didn't let go until the room grew dark. We dipped in and out of contented sleep. In the corner, something rustled within a covered birdcage. He stood to find a light, and as he did, said, "Don't leave?" I wasn't sure if he meant at the moment or forever.

I shook my head. "I won't."

He lit candles, fat candles stuck in cracked holders all over the room.

"No electric light?" I asked.

He shook his head, but I saw the bulb on the ceiling. He pulled a linen towel from the washstand and over his shoulders.

I thought I understood. "You don't have to light them, if you don't want."

Wrapped in his thin towel, he sat on a wooden chair, his knees tight together. "It's fine." He swallowed. "I don't mind."

"You do. You're as nervous as a duck."

He cracked a smile. "Ducks aren't nervous."

"Have you been in a brasserie lately? French ducks are." I propped myself up on my elbows, the sheet sliding down to my waist

"So are French rabbits."

"Luc, come back over here."

And he did.

It wasn't until after the second time that he let me uncover his shoulders and look at him, really look at him, in the candlelight. I couldn't see him blush in the dim.

"I suppose my dreams of the Championnat de France are well and truly past now," he said ruefully. "I can barely hold up a paintbrush, much less a tennis racket."

"How did it happen?" I asked, running a finger up the side of his arm. He tensed, then curled the arm around me. At least he could still do that.

He sucked in a breath. He seemed to be considering. "Do you remember me talking about Stefan Bauer?"

I felt icy cold. "You played tennis with him." I let my hair swing loose over my face. "You used to write to me who was winning."

"In the end, he did." He closed his eyes. "Bauer was in a group of German prisoners being held near our camp."

"Good," I couldn't help but say.

He passed a hand over his eyelids. "You were right about him, you know." I took his hand, but he didn't open his eyes. "I let myself get too close," he said. "Even though you warned me, I still trusted him." A shudder ran the length of his body.

"You couldn't —"

"I deserved to be attacked."

"Look at me." His eyes were dark in the candlelight. I spoke to him and to myself eight years ago. "You didn't deserve anything."

He shook his head. I'd had eight years to convince myself. He'd had a fraction of that.

"He was a prisoner," he repeated. "Bauer manipulated me, like he always did on the court. I had a weapon with me and I just . . . let myself get too close."

I touched the line of scar along his shoulder. "Knife?"

"Bayonet. And across my face." He hesitated and put a finger to his jaw. "And a hobnailed boot."

I pulled the blanket up, over us both. "Luc," I asked softly. "Who is Michel?"

Beneath me, he tensed. "Why do you ask?"

"While you were sleeping, you said his name."

He rolled from under me. "I never called him Michel."

I followed him across the little room, to where he fussed with a gas ring and a coffeepot, to where he gave up and filled two mugs with cognac instead, to where he fell against the table and tipped one over before even taking a sip.

I pressed myself against his back and wrapped my arms around him. "Tell me." He leaned back into me. "Tell me about Michel."

Cognac pooled at the edge of the table. "Clare, I . . ."

I kissed the hollow between his shoulder blades.

He shivered.

"Here." I brought the blanket from the bed.

He drank a whole mug of cognac before he coughed and cleared his throat. "Michel Chaffre. Bastard was the best friend I've ever had. Never had a bad word to say about anyone. Never thought of himself."

I remembered the boy who'd given over his weekends to cheer a friendless Scottish girl. "A good man."

"The best. But he . . ." He leaned heavily against the table. "Damn him."

I moved the empty mugs to the washstand and refilled them. The cognac was cheap and smelled like paint thinner.

"Clare, he killed Chaffre."

I took a sip from my mug. It burned. "Who did?"

"Stefan Bauer."

He spat the name. I lit another candle.

"Chaffre was guarding the cellar where the prisoners were. He let me in — he shouldn't have, but he trusted me." He turned to face me, eyes dark and deep. "Bauer took my bayonet, attacked me, left me for dead on that cellar floor and . . ." He swallowed, reached for the cognac, swallowed again. "And he killed Chaffre."

I knew this wasn't the only night he'd

spent drinking in the half-dark. All these months, he'd been punishing himself for someone else's crime. He was punishing himself for trusting Stefan Bauer.

I'd spent too many years doing the same. Telling myself that I'd been stupid and weak and that I'd let myself be led into that brothel bedroom, into a situation I might not have gotten out of. I spent more time blaming myself than the one really at fault. I understood. So I said, "It's not your fault." I said, "Bauer betrayed you." I knew something about that.

"No." He slid down the wall to the floor. "I betrayed Chaffre." Beneath the blanket, he shuddered. "Clare, he killed Chaffre with my own bayonet."

"Bauer betrayed you," I said again, because I didn't know what else to say. I knelt and took his hands. "You didn't give that bayonet to him. You didn't tell him to kill your friend."

"But he did." He stared at the floor, that haunted look again in his eyes. "And all because I was weak enough to think that an enemy might . . . might still be my friend."

This was it. Not his cheek, not his shoulder, not his lack of a job. This right here was the reason he kept his distance, why he refused to be close to anyone. Why he'd take

446

temporary comfort when he could, but shy away from anything that could make him feel.

"But you understand all of that, don't you?" he said. He pulled his hands back and crumpled them in his lap. "You understand . . . him." His gaze was penetrating. "That night, in the cellar . . . he told me what he did to you."

I bit my lip. I didn't know how to answer.

He spoke in a rush. "Believe me, Clare, if I'd known then that he'd hurt you, I —"

"He didn't hurt me." I said it quickly, to wipe the anguish from his face. "Though he . . . tried, he didn't touch me."

His eyes went to my hand, where I still had a thin pink scar from that hat pin. "Ah." He caught it in his and turned it over. "And to think I once thought you were the one who needed protecting." He brushed a kiss onto the scar. "Clare Ross, you're stronger than I could ever be."

CHAPTER 30
LUC
1919

I woke to a room smelling warm and light, something like summer. Next to me, wearing nothing but my old brown sweater, Clare curled against my side, asleep. In a rush I remembered last night, in little snatches like photographs. The candlelight on her bare shoulders, that smile that tipped up to her eyes, her curls spread out on my chest, the way I could feel her breathing, watching, waiting while I fell asleep. She'd kicked the blanket down in the night and my gaze traced the curve of her hip and leg beneath the sweater. I tried not to breathe. Her feet were tucked up against my knee. I didn't want them to leave.

I edged out from under the blankets. Twenty-four hours ago I'd woken up alone, the apartment feeling too dark and too close. I'd dressed thinking of her, of those few hours in the studio where I could steal glances she'd never miss and tuck away the lilts of her voice like forgotten bread crumbs.

But this morning it was as though I'd let the sun straight into my room. It glowed, and it was all because of Clare.

Clare.

On the floor was a bundle of cloth. A pale brown coat, bright red scarf, striped dress, layers of white that could only be what had been under the dress. I didn't even remember sliding them off. Had I done that?

On the bed, she sighed and toed the blankets.

Yesterday I thought I had nothing in my life but settling. A replacement face. A pamphlet full of replacement careers. Now, I had Clare, at least for a night. For longer? She had come to me.

On the bed, she settled into a rhythm of breathing.

I lifted the edge of the cloth covering the bird cage. Lysander regarded me curiously and I tipped in a flat handful of nuts. "I'll be back with breakfast," I promised. I tugged the cover back over the cage and hoped they'd stay quiet.

I pulled on my trousers, stiff and wrinkled from a night on the floor next to her clothes. I found a clean shirt in the drawer. My jacket was on the back of the door, where I'd left it yesterday. The water in the basin was tepid. It was the same I'd washed in after coming back from the studio. I slipped my hands quietly in the water.

From the drawer in my desk, I took out a sheet of paper and my gold fountain pen, that too-ornate pen Papa gave me for my thirteenth birthday. I brought that ridiculous pen with me to the trenches. Because, as absurd as it was out there in the middle of war, it was the thing that made me feel like an adult. It made me feel somehow above the muck and playing soldier.

I think often of that summer, of *our* summer. Last night we were there again. I woke this morning and it was the shade of the trees and the roses and the river below. With your touch, you erased my nightmares. Don't leave, Clare, not now and not tomorrow. You're my happily ever after.

In the drawer was also Chaffre's little lead Madonna in her case. I'd always before hidden her away, hoping to hide my memories of that night. Today, though, I tucked her in my pocket.

I leaned toward Clare, smelling warm and loved, and kissed her ear. "Don't leave," I whispered into it, though she didn't wake. I slipped on my mask and caught up her red scarf. Tossing it around my neck, I left the apartment.

Madame Girard was in the hallway buttoning up her coat. "I'll be out when you return. Bringing my sister fish, though I don't know why," she grumbled. "If she had the gout I do, she wouldn't ask me to come out." She eyed the mask. "What's that? Did that woman bring it yesterday?"

"This?" I touched the metal. Today it didn't feel so cold. "It's a fresh start."

I went to Les Halles to find the things I remembered her eating, things that I could find at the end of winter, in a city still caught in food shortages. Grapes, dates, a basket of late brown medlars. A loaf of crusty *ficelle* bought at an exorbitant price. I tucked it into my coat. Chestnuts, of course, a pocketful. It took a while longer to find oranges in the middle of winter, but I found a vendor with small, bruised Spanish oranges.

The old flower seller was waiting on her corner. "Flowers for your sweetheart?"

I dug into my pocket for my usual change and my usual line. In her basket were small bunches of wood violets, just like the ones that grew beneath the chestnut tree. So I smiled, the one half of my mouth matching the other on my mask. I smiled and said,

"Yes, I think I will."

She laughed, toothlessly. "I knew you'd find one."

"She found me." I took the flowers, the fragile stems damp.

The last thing I bought, from a narrow shop on the other side of the market, was a dozen soft Conté pencils. Eight years before, I'd bought pencils for Clare. I'd wanted her to know then that someone believed in her.

I'd spent weeks watching her head bent in concentration as she made my mask. Her face had been serene, satisfied. And, when she looked at her drawings hanging on my wall, exultant. I didn't want her to lose that the way my own *maman* had.

Last time, I hadn't given Clare the pencils. It was that young girl's dress and that hopeful expression she wore when she ran up to me at Mille Mots. Then, I was afraid of letting her get too close. The shopkeeper wrapped the pencils in paper and I tucked them carefully at the bottom of my haversack. This time, I wouldn't be afraid.

I wondered if Clare would still be in bed when I returned, wearing nothing but that brown sweater. I pictured her tangled in the blankets, smiling when she opened her eyes. I'd give her flowers. I'd kiss her one more time.

But I turned onto the Rue de Louvre. And I didn't go home.

CHAPTER 31
CLARE
1919

I thought I'd wake to a sleepy repetition of the night before, or at least to awkward yawns and blushes. I was already blushing before my eyes were open. I didn't expect to wake to an empty apartment.

Maybe he was down the hall at the toilet or talking to the concierge. Maybe he'd stepped out so that he wouldn't disturb me with his pipe. Maybe he'd gone in search of breakfast.

I stretched and waited. And waited. From the street below came the sounds of Paris waking up. Carts rattled, horses snorted, the rare engine from an automobile growled.

I stood and straightened the sweater. The window was cracked and the room chilly. My arms wrapped around my chest, I walked the length of it. I hadn't even heard him get up. I tried to picture him soundlessly moving around the room, quietly pulling on his clothes. His blue shirt and tie were kicked to the corner, but his jacket and trousers were gone. I picked up the shirt, shook it out, folded it, found his drawer with a few others.

The room looked smaller, dingier than I'd thought yesterday. Was this really where Luc lived? On the desk he'd left a small stack of paper and a fancy gold pen. That one little reminder of his château life.

But that wasn't all on the desk. He'd left a note, written in a morning-after haze. *You're my happily ever after.* I let the note fall back down to the desk and leaned against the chair. Happily ever after.

The night I'd gone with Finlay, I'd stopped myself before anything had happened that I'd regret. I'd remembered my plans. I didn't need anything beyond a good friend. I didn't need anyone to take care of, anyone to disappoint, anyone to make me disappoint myself. But last night, when I stepped into Luc's apartment and remembered that long-ago kiss, I'd stopped thinking. Plans, worries, expectations; I thought of nothing but how perfect it felt to be near him.

His note hinted at a promise I hadn't made. My words, my kisses, my stepping into his apartment, his bed, his heart — maybe I had made one without realizing it.

Maybe I wanted to.

"No," I said aloud. I pushed through the romantic haze of the night before. I could be pregnant right now, I realized. In that moment of impulse, I might have changed everything.

I lowered the basin of water to the floor and washed, squatting over it. My teeth chattered. No one had ever told me what to do the morning after. I hoped it was enough. I hoped it wasn't too late. I scrubbed and worried and thought about how quickly plans could change. I poured the water out of the window onto the roof. The morning suddenly seemed too glaring bright.

I didn't want that. Did I? With a house, a husband, a child, I couldn't have anything else. The women at the School of Art left when they married. They left or they convinced themselves that art as a hobby, in between planning meals and arranging vases, was enough. I wanted more. I wanted everything I had now.

But I also wanted Luc.

The whole walk home, I tried to pretend that I was simply another Parisian taking the morning air. That I hadn't just spent the night, alone, with a man. That I didn't stand on the edge of my future, not knowing how many steps to take before I fell.

When I walked in, Grandfather was sitting hunched at his desk in his shirtsleeves, surrounded by balls of paper and empty teacups. The curtains were shut tight and the kerosene lamp was smoking. The way he turned, blinking, when I opened the door — he hadn't even realized it was morning.

I waited for him to say something about me appearing well after breakfast, about my skirt wrinkled from a night on the floor, about my hair knotted and pinned without benefit of either mirror or brush.

He didn't look me up and down, didn't do more than scratch his nose and say, "Is it suppertime already?" and "Where's your scarf?"

I went across the room, slipping off my coat, and kissed him on the forehead. "It's morning, Grandfather. When did you last eat?"

"Noon." He yawned. "Is that right?"

"That was yesterday." He'd been using his left cuff as a pen wiper again. "Change your shirt, dear, and I'll make you a cheese sandwich."

Though bread was still hard to come by, his baker friend kept us supplied. When he wandered out of the bedroom, it was in a sweater that the laundress had shrunk. The knobs of his wrists poked from the sleeves.

He picked up a sandwich, looking faintly puzzled.

"Were you just arriving?" he asked around a mouthful of cheese.

"No, leaving. I have to be to work."

He nodded and chewed, but wasn't satisfied. "But then why are you humming? You haven't hummed in years."

"I wasn't humming." I gathered up the empty cups. "Tea?"

"I'll make it." He set down his sandwich. "You think I can't take care of myself?"

I slipped into my room to change into a fresh blouse and skirt. "Why else are you in Paris?" I called through the door.

"Patricia Clare, you give yourself too much credit."

I pulled open the door. "Clare." I brought my comb and hairpins out into the large room while he made tea. "I was only teasing."

"And see, that's why I came to Paris." Between haphazard measuring of tea and water, he ate the rest of his sandwich. "Because I enjoy your company."

"And my sandwiches."

He grinned. "Mostly your company. Marie makes better sandwiches."

"Marie?"

"The baker. You've *met* her."

I shrugged and attacked the knots in my hair.

"You take care of me, it's true, but you let me take care of you in between. Alice, she taught me that."

"Grandmother did?"

"We didn't have much time together, but in the time we did have, it was a privilege to take care of her." He set down the spoon, scattering tea on the table. "I loved her so."

I set aside the comb. "Grandfather, did she plan to give up her art? When Mother was born?"

He swept up the spilled tea leaves onto his palm. "She was painting up until the day the baby came. She wouldn't have stopped even if I'd asked her. And I never would have. Her passion for art, it awed me." He brushed his hands over the wastebasket. "It's like yours. You glow with it, Patricia Clare."

"I still don't feel I've accomplished it all."

He poured out the water. "You have the years your grandmother didn't. You have the talent and the stubbornness and the compassion to accomplish even more. I'm honored to have been part of your journey."

I left the pile of hairpins on the end table and crossed to where he stood by the kitchen table. "I'm happy I didn't have to do it alone."

"You never have to, you know." He wiped out a mug. "Be alone."

I inhaled. *Those who love us don't ask us to mask our true selves.*

Chapter 32
Luc
1919

I almost walked straight past him.

His hair was longer than he'd ever worn it and he had a mustache now, like a Frenchman. He slouched at a café table, nursing a cup, collar turned up against the morning chill. In his short jacket, soft scarf, felt cap, and indifferent expression, he looked like any Parisian.

But, despite his almost casual pose, I noticed an alertness to his spine. The watchfulness of a soldier. I slowed and, as I drew close, I knew him.

It's the little things that give us away sometimes. The way Papa always pulled on his beard when he was worried. The way Maman pinched inside my wrist when she wanted me to pay attention. The way Clare touched my face. For the man sitting at the café table, it was the way he tossed his roll back and forth between each hand.

It was a small movement, one that only

confidence could bring. He always did it with bread rolls. Tossed it once, twice, three times, before he broke it open to eat. It looked almost like he was palming a tennis ball.

I stood out on the pavement I don't know how long before he noticed my stare. He started, ducked his head, dropped a handful of change and stood. I didn't think he recognized me, but I pushed against a shop window, out of the way.

He slipped past with a battered brown suitcase in hand. Not his usual stride, but an almost furtive skulk. He shouldn't be in Paris; I wondered why he was. The peace talks might have begun, but Europe was far from peaceful. Germany hadn't been invited. Bauer had no reason to be here. If the Parisians on the Rue du Louvre knew a German walked in their midst, someone who could've held a gun on their husbands and sons during the war, they wouldn't let him pass. Cries of "Boche" would echo to the Seine and back.

But I didn't tell them. Call it curiosity, call it fear, call it the desire to look him in the eye before spitting in his face. Pressed against the window, I held my breath until he passed. I'd dropped the violets, and Bauer trod straight over them.

He continued down the Rue du Louvre, but still I stood, motionless. Sweat pooled at the back of my neck. I could follow. I could confront him like in the scene that always played in my mind, the one where I didn't trust him as I had last time. The one where Chaffre lived. Or I could let him slip away and I could go back to Clare and wait for the nightmares to pass. Across the street an automobile started with a growl that made me jump and cover my head. Everything was suddenly louder. The glass behind my back rattled. It was only after a woman stopped with a "Monsieur, are you well?" that I lifted my head.

"Monsieur?" she asked again.

I waved away her hand and shook my head in reply. The street was bright, too bright, too crowded. Where had he gone? My memories of him were in moonlight. Then I spotted his light hair, high above the crowd, and I knew I couldn't go home.

I followed him. I walked close to the buildings, head down. The stealthy march came back to me. That advance against an enemy. My hands itched to be holding a rifle, so I pushed them into my pockets. Still, they twitched on an imaginary trigger.

I don't know how far he walked, but I recognized the building when he stopped. It was Lili's, a whore he used to visit. He'd sometimes bring girls there, when he had no place else to go with them. Very likely, I thought, girls who were alone in the city. *Though he tried,* Clare had said.

I waited there, watching the building, as the shadows lengthened. I took the *ficelle* from inside my jacket and ate it in the doorway across the street. Through the upstairs window, I caught movement. I brushed crumbs off my hands and settled in. He shouldn't be long.

At the end of the day, that was when we'd prepare for an attack. We'd be checking our weapons, tightening our laces, saying one last prayer. Then we'd head out, creeping from shadow to shadow, tracking an enemy we couldn't yet see. This time I had mine right in my sights. I felt more at home in this dimming dusk than I had in the bright light of morning. Evening was when I was used to prowling.

But Lili came out of the building by herself, dressed in pearls and silk. Though I waited until I heard another clock chime, Bauer didn't reappear. He was staying the night.

I paced to the end of the street. I counted the hours. The night deepened and the streetlamps flickered. Lili returned with a gentleman, then the building went tight and dark. At one point I slumped in the doorway across the street in that soldier's half doze. I thought of the nightmares I used to have, half expecting them to return. But the source of all my nightmares, he was right across the street.

I wasn't prepared for an ambush, yet I was afraid to leave my post for supplies. In this battle, there was no reserve. I'd tracked him all day, but I didn't have anything beyond the fruit and cheese in my bag. I'd almost forgotten it in my relentless advance. I took out an orange, peeled it, and, suddenly, in the scent of the peel, remembered. Fruit, cheese, bread, chestnuts. The little breakfast I'd meant to surprise Clare with.

And now it was nearly a day later and I'd left her alone in the apartment, waiting for me. Probably, now, thinking I wasn't coming back.

I almost turned around right then and there. Walked back to the apartment. Walked to the studio on the Rue Notre-Dame-des-Champs. Found her and promised to never leave again. But down the street, the front door of Lili's opened and Stefan Bauer stood silhouetted in the doorway with his suitcase.

It wasn't only me who had been hurt. It

wasn't only — I felt for the little lead Madonna — Chaffre. Even before someone handed Bauer a gun, he threatened. *He tried,* Clare had said. I shouldered my bag. *He tried.* Her words in my head, I followed.

Just before dawn, the streets were empty. It wasn't as easy to hide the fact that I was tailing him, and as my footsteps echoed, his quickened. He was too smart to turn and look over his shoulder, but he ducked through alleys and around buildings. I didn't lose him. I knew Paris as well as he did.

When his footsteps slowed, near the Gare du Nord, I should have, too. He lunged from a corner shadow, the flash of a knife in his fist. I dodged, catching myself on the side of a building. My mask clattered to the ground.

"Why are you following me?" he said in French.

I picked up the mask and stepped into the light. "Retribution."

"How did you —" he began, before correcting to: "You are mistaken."

"I know you." I held it up to my face. I watched his drain of color. "And you know me."

"Crépet," he said, and I knew I hadn't mistaken him. He cleared his throat. "Didn't think I'd see you again."

"Didn't think I was alive, did you?"

"It was war. I didn't know what to think." He shifted his suitcase from one hand to the other. "Didn't know if I'd be alive one moment to the next, did I?"

"Neither did Michel Chaffre."

"Who?" he asked, and then, "Oh."

I had years of vitriol, of blame and censure. I wanted to ask him why. Why me, why Chaffre, why anything that took him from a life in France to a life against France. But I lowered my mask again. "This is what you gave me." I bared my face and I said, "This was my souvenir."

His eyes traveled up along my scar, along the pits and grooves, along the puckered skin. Finally he said, "Crépet, I didn't mean . . ." Exposed in that moment of honesty, in that almost-apology, he turned away. When he turned back, it was with his cocky smile. "You mean to make a battle out of everything?"

"What?" I had to ask.

"The war is over now. And yet you can't move on. You are still looking for a *grand adversaire.*"

"You're wrong. I did." And, if it wasn't true before that moment, it was now. "You left me for dead, but I came back to life."

He shrugged, but took a step backwards.

"And do you know who else moved on?" I slipped the mask in my bag. "Clare."

He squinted. Either he didn't remember her or wanted me to think so. "Oh, the fräulein?" he asked dismissively. "She had nothing to move on from."

"Betrayal doesn't only exist in war." I slipped my bag from my shoulder. "Sometimes it comes from a trusted companion on a train or in a whore's house."

He flinched and I knew I'd guessed right.

"You haven't said, Bauer. What are you doing here, in Paris?"

He didn't even pause before throwing out a lie. "I never told you, but I had a girlfriend here." He rubbed his nose. He didn't know I'd followed him from Lili's. "And . . . and a little daughter. I came for them." He lifted the brown suitcase. "See? They're meeting me at the station. We're returning to Berlin."

But I was finished believing his lies. His carefully set up drop shots.

"A girlfriend?" I took a step towards him. "You mean one you don't have to pay for?"

At my advance, he stepped back. "Why is that so hard to believe?"

I moved closer.

He hesitated just for a second, and I swung my shopping bag. It wasn't full and

468

it wasn't heavy, but enough to throw him off balance so that I could get a fist in his stomach. Like with Martel, it was a lucky shot. His knife clattered to the ground and his suitcase sprang open. A camera and bundles of photos tumbled out. Gasping for breath, he lunged at the suitcase, not the knife. I grabbed the latter.

"Keep back or I cry 'Boche.' "

He glanced back over his shoulder. The street was quiet, but he kept his distance.

I pulled up a handful of photos, wondering why they kept him here on the street. He could have turned to run the moment I took the knife. Instead he waited.

As I sifted through the handful, I saw. Each one showed Paris in shambles. A city as shattered by war as I was. They were photos of tumbled buildings, of boarded windows, of craters in the street where bombs had fallen. They showed trees, splintered and leafless. They showed *mutilés* on the corners in ragged uniforms, begging. The photos, they were specific. They were intended to show Paris vulnerable.

"You once loved France." I flipped through the photos. The buildings destroyed, the citizens depleted, the shops still shuttered. "You betray more than the people in your life."

He hovered just out of reach. "The war is over, Crépet." He tried to put a sneer into it.

I'd only seen the city's wounds here and there as I passed down the streets, but to see them put together in photos, to see Paris looking so crippled and broken still, now, months after the armistice. To see it looking so exposed, it made me furious.

I snapped the suitcase shut. "But the battle's not." Though I had the knife in my hand, I swung a fist, the way I should have that night in the cellar. The way I should have years before that, when I stood in the dormitory as he promised that he didn't know what had happened to Clare. One punch and then another and another and he was doubled over on the street.

But he didn't stay down long. Bauer had always been faster than me, and he hadn't spent the last year of the war recovering in a Paris garret. He drove up with his shoulder. I stumbled back, but kept my grip on the knife. He brought up his arms, trying to shake my grip. For a moment I thought he would. He was always more vicious.

But when he struck me, something kicked in. The same instinct that had led me to track him through the dark streets. I knocked his arms away and shifted the knife to my other hand. Bauer lunged again, but I did, too. The blade caught him on the back of the wrist. He didn't flinch.

"You think you'll even the score?" He bared his teeth in a grin. "You?"

All of my training came back. My movements were automatic. A year away from the lines didn't erase the three years in them. He used his fists. I used the knife and my hatred. I drove him back towards the wall along the pavement. This close fighting, the smell of sweat and blood, it was familiar. I swung and my muscles remembered.

On the battlefield, we fought over an uneven landscape. And yet it was a loose cobble that brought Stefan Bauer down on that Paris street. He lifted an arm crisscrossed with cuts.

"My mistake was always trusting the world." I leaned down over him, knife in hand. "Yours was underestimating it."

CHAPTER 33
CLARE
1919

That night I dreamt of redemption.

Luc had found it, it seemed, in his mask, in my arms. He'd gone to fetch me breakfast that morning and, while he was gone, I read his note, worried, and then left. But later I dreamt that he forgave me, that we talked, that he told me we'd cross the world and back hand in hand. I dreamt that we walked to Mille Mots and he kissed me under the poplar. I wondered if things could work.

I went to his apartment, to apologize. But Luc, he wasn't there.

At his building, the suspicious fish-eyed woman frowned, but let me into his apartment when I mentioned that I was with the Red Cross. "Apologies. When you came the other afternoon, I didn't realize you were a nurse."

I didn't correct her. "There are many people looking after his recovery."

She turned the key with a grunt.

Nothing had changed from the last time I'd been there. The parrots rattled the cage beneath their cover. The sweater I'd left was still folded on the bed. A flash of relief that he hadn't just avoided me was quickly replaced by the realization that he'd been gone all day and night. "When did you last see him, Madame Girard?"

"The morning after you brought that mask." She jiggled the door handle. "I was leaving to take my ungrateful sister a parcel of fish. He left at the same time."

Something had happened, before he left or before he returned. Something that kept him from his apartment. I paced the room, but nothing was out of place. "Did he say where he was going?"

She shrugged. "Why would he tell me, mademoiselle?"

That night, he'd been nervous and reluctant to talk about what had happened during the war. I'd been worried about all those tomorrows, but Luc, he still worried about yesterday.

"Madame, please. When Monsieur Crépet left, how did he look?"

"He said something about a fresh start. I've never seen it before," she said, "but for the first time, he was smiling."

I turned from her so she wouldn't see the

473

sweep of fear on my face. The smile meant he didn't abandon me or our night together. He must have left with the intention of coming back to me. Whatever kept him from the apartment these past twenty-four hours, it wasn't himself.

I went to the birdcage and pulled off the cover. The larger parrot cocked his head. "Summer," he said, then in English, "Fuck it."

I pushed grapes through the bars and pieces of crumbled cheese. "Would you feed the birds until I return?"

She gaped at the parrots. "These brutes?"

"And call the *policier.*"

She straightened.

"I am going to find Luc."

This time, I didn't knock on the front door of Mille Mots.

I walked around to the back, to the kitchen, where I knew the Crépets were staying. But I didn't go in. In the kitchen yard, with my hand on the door, I spotted them down by the river.

Monsieur, I'd recognize anywhere. He perched on a stool in front of an easel. His beard, shot through with new gray, bristled over the front of his smock. When he was melancholy, it was nothing but blues and purples. I couldn't tell what he was painting today, but saw oranges and yellows and bright melon greens.

But he wasn't alone by the riverside. Madame, her battered picnicking table covered over with a canvas cloth, sat. Her smock spattered, her face content, Madame was sculpting. The clay was the rich red found all over in Picardy. Her arms streaked in it, she was reborn.

Both looked so utterly content, I hated to intrude. Indeed they scarcely noticed me walk up. Not until I came right up to the table and cleared my throat did Madame start and Monsieur set down his palette.

"Bonjour," I said, then: "Has he been here?"

Madame blinked and Monsieur tugged on his beard. He left a smear of viridian. "He?" he asked, but she sat up straighter. I knew then that she'd been the one to change her mind. She had been behind his re-appearance in the studio.

"Luc. He . . ." I inhaled. "I can't find him."

"You two, you have a habit of losing one another." He laughed and wiped his hands on his smock.

"Claude, hush," she said. I'd never heard Madame speak with anything less than

475

adoration to her husband. She set down her knife. "Clare, he came to the studio?"

"Yes. Didn't he write to you?"

"He doesn't."

"He came and I made him a mask." I pressed my fingers together. "I thought he was happy."

"Ma chère." Monsieur stood from his stool and brought it to me. "He's gone far since that summer you knew him. So have you." I let him take my arm and lead me to the stool. "All that you've given him, but what he needs most of all is time."

"But if he's in danger . . ."

"Do you not think Luc is used to danger?"

Madame's breath caught and she put a hand to the wet clay in front of her. I saw then that she sculpted a young boy.

"So what do I do?" I asked.

"What we've been doing all these years," she said. She ran a finger down the clay boy's cheek. "Wait."

CHAPTER 34
LUC
1919

I sat in the Gare du Nord with my head in my hands. I'd stood over Bauer with the knife in my hands. If that milk cart hadn't come by when it did, I would have killed him. I would have. But he scrambled up and away, and I was left with the battered suitcase and blood on my hands.

I brought it into the train station. I cleaned up as best I could in the lavatory and dropped the knife through the tracks. And then, not knowing what else to do, I sat on a bench in the departure court, sitting on my shaking hands.

Bauer was bleeding and bruised. He was without his camera and suitcase. Did that mean he wouldn't finish his mission? I knew him too well. He'd lay low until he could get another camera. He was probably at Lili's, licking his wounds. Wondering what had given him away on the streets of Paris.

I sat all day, watching trains come and go,

watching people pass, not quite knowing what to do. I walked from the departure court into the station, pacing the edge of the tracks. Would he come here? Would he try to leave Paris? I leaned against the wall, tired and watchful, and bought strong black coffee. With all of the refugees crowded in the station, one more itinerant didn't matter.

Gare du Nord was crowded and buzzing. Suitcases and trunks were piled higgledy-piggledy on the platforms, overflowing from the baggage rooms. People clustered, holding tight to cloth bags and parcels and the odd treasure saved when they fled. Clutching wedding tickings, Bibles, or gilt-framed paintings, they complained to each other in county patois. Most were refugees who had come into Paris years ago; only now were they looking to leave.

Their nightmares were over. I thought that mine were gone, too. That other night, that night Clare kept watch, I'd slept soundly, for the first time in a long while. Maybe it was her lingering perfume, maybe the pad of her bare feet, maybe the way she couldn't help but touch the side of my face when she thought I was asleep. But I'd dozed, for once at peace.

Now, crouched in the station, slipping in

and out of that half sleep, the nightmares returned. Nothing specific; not the kind of dreams Chaffre's Austrian doctor could find anything in. Sharp, shapeless shadows, screams that burrowed into my brain, aching pain in each limb. I woke sweating and buried my face so no one could see it. Through my haversack the mask dug into my hip.

It was exhausting, this remembering. My shoulder throbbed, and again and again I heard that thump as Chaffre fell next to me. I closed my eyes, to summon up memories of the other night, of Clare in the candlelight, of Clare touching my face, but all I could think of was Bauer, taunting, telling me nothing had changed. He had said "battle," and, like an infection, the word had brought up every blood-slick battle there'd been, until I was afraid to close my eyes.

I could end it all. I could take the suitcase to one of the *policier* on the platform. It's what I should have done the moment I entered the station. Passed on the suitcase and said there was a spy in Paris. He'd probably slunk back to Lili's or else was lurking around the station the way I was, watching for a train to Berlin. They could find him.

But he was right. The war was over. The only one left was my own. My battle was with the past and what it left me with. I wasn't alone. I saw it in the shattered, spent faces of the refugees in the station. All we wanted to do was sleep, not because our bones were weary, but because our hearts were.

"Monsieur, are you hurt?" It was a young girl, a refugee, with red-brown curls falling from beneath a knit cap. "You look tired." Though she looked too old for it, she had a faded rag doll tucked into the front strap of her knapsack.

"Tired." I rubbed the corner of my eye, remembering I wore no mask. But she didn't flinch. "But why, of everyone in the station, are you speaking to me?"

She shrugged. "I thought you were lonely."

"Where's your family?" No one came to shoo her away from the monster. No one came to shake a finger at me for talking to this girl who looked so like Clare. "Mademoiselle, I could be a bad man."

A sadness crept into her eyes and she touched the doll at her shoulder. "I don't think there are really bad men anymore." Behind her, a train whistled. "Only scared ones."

Once I'd been scared and my best friend

had died. I stood. I couldn't look the other way while Stefan Bauer hurt someone else again.

A *policier* strode the platform in his dark uniform. I approached with the battered suitcase. "Monsieur."

His hand went to his belt as he turned. I ducked my head.

"What is it?" He tapped his heels impatiently.

I wondered if I was making too much of it. In my hands, the suitcase looked innocuous. And maybe it was. The Paris I saw every day, shedding its mourning, wasn't the defeated city of Bauer's photos. Maybe he had nothing in the suitcase.

The refugee girl stood by the bench with her knapsack. Though she'd lost her home, she still refused to see the bad in the world. She didn't know that it stalked the streets of this very city.

I lifted my chin. "Monsieur, I've seen a spy." I opened the suitcase. "And I think I know where he is."

CHAPTER 35
CLARE
1919

The soldier stood on the threshold of the caves beneath Brindeau. The caves were dark, but he kept to the splash of sunlight outside, holding a stick like a rapier.

He came alone, lurking in the entrance, not quite stepping in. Once fearless in the face of a trench wall, he was afraid of a cave. Inside, it still smelled of an army, of horses and wood smoke and drying wool. Debris littered the caverns — rotting hay, scraps of torn cloth, tins, bottles, forgotten letters. Memories strewn underfoot. The soldier who hesitated outside, he was afraid of that more than anything.

I moved from the shadows. "Luc."

I was nervous, too. Taut from my journey from Paris, terrified that I wouldn't find him, that, once again, he'd disappear from my life, I left Mille Mots for the place I'd once felt safe. I went to the familiar darkness of the caves.

And then here he was. Amazingly, beautifully here. I remembered an afternoon in the hallway of Mille Mots where he told me the story of his mother leaving and of his seven-year-old self wishing for her so hard that she felt it across the Channel and came to him. I'd come from Paris, sending wishes into the sky with every mile. And he came. I held on to the end of my coat sleeves and stepped towards him.

At the sight of me, the stick clattered to the ground. And suddenly he was there, so close I could have taken him in my arms. And I should've. Instead I said, "You were gone."

He wore my red scarf, loose around his neck. "I'm not now."

"But you were. I didn't know where you'd gone, only that you left in the morning and you didn't come home." I pressed a hand, wet from limestone, to my forehead. "I wondered if you ever would."

"I didn't mean for you to worry." He swallowed. "I just had to be sure the war really was over."

"And is it?" I moved closer. I could feel the warmth from his coat.

He put a hand to the wall of the cave. "I think so." He ran fingers down the wall. In the dim light from outside, I could see a roll of honor carved into the stone. "This is where it all happened, you know."

"Where what . . . it is?" And I took a step back to look around. I'd known that the war came close to here. I'd seen the ground churned up outside, smelled the lingering memory of horses and men, saw tatters of cloth and discarded shoes. In one corner, I'd overturned an empty pot with my toe. Soldiers had stayed here, but to think that Luc had been one, so near to home, yet a world away. "This is where Michel . . . and Stefan . . ."

He inhaled and nodded. "I never thought I'd come back to this cave."

"Do you wish you hadn't?"

The question echoed, hung in the still air a moment. Water dripped deep within the cave. "If I hadn't, it would be like pretending it never happened." He hitched his haversack further up his shoulder. "It would be wearing a mask to forget the scars beneath."

"I made that mask." I straightened. "I meant it to help."

"Doesn't it?"

"You're not wearing it."

"Clare, all those days you spent sketching me, shaping the mask, painting it, all those days matter." Shadows caught in the scars on his face. "You believed in me when I didn't believe in myself."

"And do you now?" I wrapped my arms around my chest.

He touched his face, craggy without his mask. "I'm starting to." He reached into his haversack and took out a slim parcel, wrapped in paper. He seemed almost nervous, turning the package back and forth in his hands. "I should have given this to you ages ago . . ." he said.

He peeled back the wrapping and held it out. It was a bundle of soft Conté pencils, bunched tight.

It was an odd gift, for someone who was once an art student, for someone who worked in a studio. "For me?"

He must have seen the question on my face, even in the dim of the cave mouth. He twisted the paper. "You don't know this, but once before I bought you pencils. It was the summer you were at Mille Mots."

"I remember you brought your father pencils."

"They were meant for you."

I stood silent for a moment. "Why?"

"Because I believed in you. I knew I'd see your drawings someday in a gallery." He took a step closer. "Even then, you knew what you loved."

You, I wanted to say.

"Did I?" I asked instead.

"You did. You do. Your Something Important."

"Something," I repeated. "It's a singular word, isn't it?"

"Clare," he said, holding out the pencils, so much more on offer. "You're not your mother."

Though I never thought I'd make a promise, I said, "I won't leave." And I meant it.

"If you do, take me with you?" In the dimness, I swore he held his breath.

I smiled. "I always have."

From his bag he took a stub of a candle and lit it. The flame jumped. "So did I." He held out his hand. "Let me show you something."

I took it.

We walked into the dark, his hand warm and safe around mine. I closed my eyes and let him lead me. Softly, under his breath, he counted. Steps in from the entrance, steps to where he'd eaten, rested, prayed, dreaded, hoped. "Where did it happen?" I asked.

He slowed and his hand tightened. "Outside, up by where the old farmhouse was. There was a cellar near the line of trees."

"Did you . . ."

"It looks different in the daylight," he said. "I buried the past."

"I'm glad."

He drew me closer. He didn't say a word.

"Remember that summer when we'd walk here?" I said, as though he would have forgotten. "It's silly, but when I would come back here into the caves, I used to scratch our initials on the wall with my fingernail. A little deeper, each time, so that it didn't fade."

He handed me the candle. "It didn't."

Right there, on the soot-streaked walls, was scratched a pale C.R. and L.C.

"So many years." I reached out with a finger to trace the initials. "I wonder what the soldiers here thought of it."

He put his hand over mine, the one that held the candle. "I can't speak for all the soldiers, but those four letters helped one soldier get through it all." He moved my hand and the candle along the wall. "So much that he carved right beside them."

It was me. My face, charcoaled and half carved into the limestone. Me, wild-haired, with eyes wide. Through sudden tears, the candle blurred.

"It's how I first saw you, in the front hallway, and how I've always remembered you. Fascinating and frustrating, determined

487

and impulsive, fragile and strong as stone."
He lowered the candle. "A face I couldn't
forget, even in the middle of war."

In his face, I could see the boy I'd lost
and the man I'd found again. I loved them
both.

EPILOGUE

Tangier, Morocco
21 June 1922

Dear Grandfather,
We've found the old monastery, where you once stayed. Grandmother was right: the stones sing. The building, though, is maybe not as quiet as you might have known it. Now it houses a school for colonial children. It rings with laughter and French. It's the perfect setting to capture life on canvas.

One of Grandmother's paintings hangs here. Did you know? In the room where Luc teaches, in the old refectory, is a self-portrait. She's swathed in white from head to toe, but her eyes peering from the cloth, they are familiar. Even though Grandmother returned to Scotland, she left a piece of herself in Morocco.

She's wrapped all in white, but her hands are bare, and they cradle her belly. When she painted it, she must have known. Known that soon the pair of you wouldn't be alone. Known that she might have to give up all of the heady days of painting her way across Africa. Known that things would change more for her than for you. Maybe it was all those thoughts that brought her back to Fairbridge. Maybe it was less fear and more a fierce resolve.

I'm not the only artist who came to Tangier in search of memories. The old gardener said that a dozen or so years ago a lady artist with hair as red as mine came seeking refuge. Of course it wasn't a monastery anymore — it was already a school — but the headmaster gave her a bed in exchange for work. She told him she'd been home, only to find her husband dead and her little girl gone. She had nobody left to ask for forgiveness. She was also dying of consumption. He couldn't turn her away, so he set her to restoring a crumbling mural in the old chapel.

But the restoration wasn't the only thing that she did for the chapel. She designed a new altar, and the gardener built it under her direction. You should see it, with legs twining from the ground like rose vines. It looks as though it's springing, living, from the chapel floor. Grandfather, they said she died here in the old monastery, that artist with her regrets and her red hair. But she left something beautiful behind. You would be proud.

There's a new painting hanging now in the old refectory, one that hangs above the rows of curly-headed girls, swinging their legs and doggedly sketching apricots for young Maître Crépet. It's another self-portrait of a woman swathed in robes. She, too, is cradling her stomach for the secret inside. But only with one hand. In the other she holds a wet paintbrush. The woman won't stop for the baby in her stomach. No. But she also won't leave her baby behind. She'll put the paintbrush in her child's hand and, together, they'll paint the world.

Love,
Patricia Clare

AUTHOR'S NOTE

The core of this novel — artist and soldier meeting over a copper mask in a Paris studio — was inspired by very real history. In researching *Letters from Skye* and the prostheses available during World War I, I came across a footnote mentioning advances in craniofacial prostheses. Intrigued, I dug deeper. While doctors were making strides in plastic surgery and engineers were improving artificial limbs, artists were helping soldiers with facial scars and disfigurements. British sculptor Francis Derwent Wood, while volunteering at the Third London General Hospital during the war, pioneered techniques to create lightweight copper masks. Under the administration of the American Red Cross, Boston sculptor Anna Coleman Ladd opened a studio in Paris offering the same for French soldiers.

The Smithsonian's Archives of American Art holds Anna Coleman Ladd's papers and photos from her time at the Studio for Portrait Masks and I was fortunate to have access to these in researching *At the Edge of Summer*. Most of the archived documents were used as wartime publicity for the studio — contemporary articles meant to encourage donations, photos of French soldiers both with and without their masks. From the photos alone, the studio's work was impressive. Before their masks, many of the soldiers had disfigurements and scarring so extensive that they hadn't been home in years. They didn't want their families and friends to see them like that. As impressive as the photos of the masks were, more impressive were the personal letters to Anna Coleman Ladd from women writing to thank her for giving their husbands and sons the courage to stop hiding and return to them.

Thank you to the Archives of American Art for accommodating my research, despite an ice storm that closed much of the city. Thanks also go to my mother, Beth Turza, for joining me on a road trip to Washington D.C. and for patiently listening to all of my research-fueled ramblings on the drive home. That's what you get for raising a history nerd!

A research trip to France allowed me to

not only walk the Parisian streets near where the Studio for Portrait Masks once was, but to take an illuminating guided tour of WWI battlefields and memorials. Many thanks to Olivier Dirson of Chemins D'Histoire tours for showing me the France that my characters would have known. His expertise was boundless and his enthusiasm for the history of the area was infectious.

One of our stops was at the medieval quarries beneath Confrécourt, near to the village of Nouvron-Vingré. Used as a hospital and, later, as a shelter for French troops and their horses, the caves at Confrécourt became a place for artistic soldiers to record and react to the war on the fields above their heads. Like my fictional caves, these are full of carvings, from formal rolls of honor to quick initials scratched into the limestone, from crude pictures of women or wine to studied scenes carved in relief. One of the most poignant is a woman's face, sketched in on the wall, but the carving itself only half-finished. A reminder of how, even in the relative peace away from the lines, war could disrupt. Thank you to the tourism office in Soissons for arranging a private tour of the caves at Confrécourt. To see the artwork, to soak in the history, to just *be* to feel and hear and sense, all was invaluable.

Thank you to my mother-in-law, Candace Brockmole, for tirelessly accompanying me through Paris's art museums and across snowy battlefields. Somebody had to come with me to France, if only to help me eat all those macarons and chocolate crepes.

I would be amiss if I did not offer a few other thank-yous.

To my editor at Ballantine, Jennifer E. Smith, for giving me the space and encouragement to find my story. To Hannah Elnan and Nina Arazoza for pushing me in the right direction. And to Anne Speyer, for a seamless transition. I look forward to what comes next!

To my agent, Courtney Miller-Callihan, for cheering me on and up. She is smart, sharp as knives, and fearless enough for the both of us. This road continues to be much less scary with her by my side.

So many friends keep me writing, even on the days when I want to do anything but. To Kate Langton, for so many ideas and glasses of wine. To Ardea Russo, for executive tables, cheese dips, and coffee-fueled brainstorming. To Danielle Lewerenz, for those Skype talks all the way from Morocco just when I need them. To Pamela Schoenewaldt, for thoughtful reads and insightful suggestions. To Sarah Lyn Acevedo, for being not only the brilliance behind the camera, but for being my one-woman street team. To Rebecca Burrell, for loving me even in Buffalo.

To Owen for offering tea and to Ellen for offering story suggestions. (Sorry, dear, no tragic ends on the Eiffel Tower.) To Jim for knowing when I need a weekend away from the laptop . . . and for knowing when I then need to find a quiet corner and a cocktail napkin.

In order to carve a place for her story, the historical novelist must chip away at history. Please pardon the dust.

ABOUT THE AUTHOR

Jessica Brockmole is the author of the internationally bestselling *Letters from Skye,* which was named one of the best books of 2013 by *Publishers Weekly,* and a novella in *Fall of Poppies: Stories of Love and the Great War.* She lives in northern Indiana with her husband, two children, and far too many books.

jessicabrockmole.com
Facebook.com/jessicabrockmoleauthor
@jabrockmole

The employees of Thorndike Press hope you have enjoyed this Large Print book. All our Thorndike, Wheeler, and Kennebec Large Print titles are designed for easy reading, and all our books are made to last. Other Thorndike Press Large Print books are available at your library, through selected bookstores, or directly from us.

For information about titles, please call:
(800) 223-1244

or visit our Web site at:
http://gale.cengage.com/thorndike

To share your comments, please write:
Publisher
Thorndike Press
10 Water St., Suite 310
Waterville, ME 04901